UA   99

Belva Plain

Legacy of Silence

Doubleday Direct Large Print Edition

Delacorte ▬ Press

Published by
Delacorte Press
Bantam Doubleday Dell Publishing Group, Inc.
1540 Broadway
New York, New York 10036

ISBN 1-56865-792-7

Manufactured in the United States of America

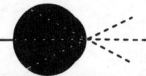

**This Large Print Book carries the
Seal of Approval of N.A.V.H.**

LEGACY OF SILENCE

PROLOGUE

My mother's lover said, "How beautiful you are! You look like Rebecca at the well."

Did I dream that, she asked herself. My mother, Caroline, died before I was old enough to know her. And Eve almost never talked about Caroline's lover. More likely, as I think back, it was Lore who told it to me.

She told me how alike they were, Eve and Caroline, with their black exotic eyes, and only twenty years between them, so that although they were mother and daughter, they were often thought to be sisters.

The worlds in which they began their lives could not have been farther apart. One was a stolid, dependable town near the shores of Lake Erie, while the other was Europe, bleeding its way toward war. In the end, these worlds with their secrets came together, woven into a coat of many colors, as my mother's lover might also have said.

PART ONE
1938
CAROLINE

ONE

The house, built of creamy stone, was square and substantial, made, as in all of Berlin's prosperous suburbs, to endure forever. Its tall, narrow windows overlooked in various directions a sloping park across the avenue, elms, horse chestnuts, houses, hedges, and gardens; in its own garden, at the center, a rose bed had a sundial on a marble pedestal.

Here Caroline, while her poodle, Peter, lay under her chair, had often used to read or do her lessons. Now though, in 1938, there were to be no more lessons and no more examinations, for the university was closed to her, and her sole present problem was simply to decide what skill would be most practical for an emigrant. She was eighteen, but she felt much older, and she was much older because people age in times of fear and danger.

"For you, it's easy," said her father, who was a doctor. "You can tutor, in English or French. There's always a demand. But for me, all those licensing examinations in another language! And at my age."

The vision of their radical departure from everything they had known, everything that had been normal, house, friends, and their very language, was sometimes too hard to bear, especially on a shimmering, mild afternoon. She stood up, closed her book, fastened Peter's leash onto his collar, and crossed the avenue to the park.

Dry leaves, amber and faded red, lay on the walk. A windstorm earlier in the week had piled heaps of them beneath the trees, and into these Peter leaped and scrabbled with great yelps of joy. She stood and watched the scene: a girl and a dog in sunlight; change the girl's costume and she could be a subject for Vermeer, who had painted in the seventeenth century, or for any painter in any century. It was all so *natural,* she thought again. And it was just this naturalness that made the heart ache. How was it possible, while so many terrible, unbelievable things were happening every day, perhaps at this moment, somewhere in this city? Somewhere.

"That's a fine poodle you have."

She had not heard anyone approach. He was a young man holding a German pointer on a leash.

"Don't worry. Siggy's gentle. He doesn't fight with other dogs."

"Peter doesn't, either."

Indeed, the two dogs had begun to sniff at each other, entangling the leashes.

"Funny creatures," the young man said. "And yet some of us can't do without them."

"That's true. We've had Peter for three years. He's Peter the Second. We got him after the first one died."

"I like his natural haircut. I always think there's something pathetic about poodles who are decked out like clowns."

"Oh, I agree."

People said that the best way to start a flirtation—although she had never experienced anything like a flirtation—was to go walking with a charming child or a dog. In ordinary circumstances, this would have been a delightful little adventure. He was a very attractive person, well built, well spoken, with fine features, and only a few years older than she. But the circumstances were not ordinary. All this went through Caroline's mind.

"Were you planning to walk farther?" he asked.

Yes, she had been. Usually, she went as far as the pond, circled it, and started home. Sometimes she even went twice around the pond.

"Well then, do you mind if we go together?"

"Not at all."

She had poise. She was known to have it. So no one could have guessed at her sudden excitement. He had such a beautiful face! His light eyes, under dark brows, were friendly, while his mouth was serious, as a man's mouth ought to be. Yet she was at the same time aware that she was being foolish, schoolgirlish and absurd.

"Walter Litzhauser," he said with a bow and extended hand.

"Caroline Hartzinger," she answered, shaking the hand. And they walked on with the dogs on either side.

"This dog-walking is a new experience for me. My parents are away and I've been made responsible to take Siggy out for his exercise. I usually don't have much time at home. I'm at the university."

"I take Peter every day. He's my own dog. He lives in my room."

There seemed, then, nothing to say. She was thinking how odd it was that human beings, no matter how casually met, have to keep talking in order not to appear rude or indifferent.

"May I ask," he inquired, "are you studying for the university, or are you perhaps already there? I am not very good at judging how old people are, so forgive me if I—"

So he, too, was self-conscious. And she answered quietly, "I have not yet decided whether I want to go or not."

There was, after all, no reason why she should tell the truth to this stranger. *We are going to leave the country.*

He nodded. "Yes, it is hard to know what to do with one's life. I have only a few more months before I'll be finished with my courses. Then I'll be at a crossroads. What I want is to go on further in art history and eventually become a curator, but my father wants me to enter his firm." He made a small grimace. "They manufacture ball bearings."

"You have quite a problem," she said ruefully.

"I do." He picked up a pinecone and threw it for the dog to retrieve. "Well, on a more pleasant note, do you go to the opera? The Ring Cycle starts again soon."

"Yes, it's wonderful, isn't it?" She could have explained, *We are not allowed to go. That is, my mother is not allowed because she is Jewish, and of course my father would never go anywhere without her.*

But she did not say so. What use would it be?

So they walked, managing all the while to produce more desultory conversation until they had made the circuit back to the starting point.

"I live here," Caroline said, indicating the house across the avenue.

"Oh, not far from me. I'm down that way, left, only five minutes' walk. Shall we meet again tomorrow? My parents will not relieve me of Siggy until next week."

"Perhaps. I'm not sure," she answered.

Her mood had reverted to the somber gray that had enveloped her before their walk. Unready just yet to enter the house and its inevitable daily anxieties, she sat down again in the garden. And those same anxieties came flooding. . . . She had been twelve years old in 1933, when the Party took power with its red banners flying, its thousands cheering and thousands marching. Always the endless marching. Suddenly everything was organized: children's groups, student groups, veterans' groups, everyone, even the physicians—except her father.

Because of Mama, he had been removed from the state medical plan and had lost his post as lecturer in the medical college. Uncomplaining, he continued to serve whoever among his old patients still wanted to consult him. Often he took payment in kind: a carpenter replaced a door, or a plumber repaired the pipes. Often he took no payment at all, so that they were rapidly using up their savings.

Mama said that his profession was one of the two things that kept him from leaving the country. The other was his conviction, with which she did not agree at all, that this regime could not last. Only after Crystal Night, two weeks ago, had he lost that hope. Mass arrests of the innocent, thugs rampaging through the streets while the police stood watching, fires, broken glass and broken heads, weeping women and children, all had finally put an end to his now admittedly foolish hope.

So they were leaving. Or, to be exact, trying to leave. It was not such a simple matter. It was, in fact, a very complicated matter of quotas and transit visas, of affidavits and money.

"What are you doing out there with your daydreams?" called Lore, coming down the rear steps.

"You're off early today."

"I switched with someone. I had to go to the dentist. My aching teeth, as usual."

She was still in hospital white with the Red Cross insignia. Her walk looked confident. Her homely, wide face was strong. She knew what she was about. And Caroline had a sudden thought: If I were sick, I would want Lore to take care of me.

"I saw you from the kitchen window. Since you're doing nothing else, anyway, you might as well help me peel these leftover vegetables for soup. It's a shame to waste."

This was an oblique reference to Mama, of whom Lore was otherwise fond. But Mama was a poor cook. Mama played the piano most beautifully and read good books. Ever since the servants had been dismissed, she had, with Caroline's help, been preparing the meals and doing her best. Nevertheless, it was always a relief when Lore was home taking charge.

"Cut the carrots finer, Caroline."

The sun was almost as warm as in spring, a freakish comfort with Christmas only a month away. Basking in it, they sat silently, with a sense of being talked out. The talk, the subjects, were always the same, either the anxious unknowable future or the wistful past.

Lore spoke suddenly. "I remember every single detail of my first day in this house. You were three months old, asleep in the perambulator right here in this garden. I even remember the pink coverlet with the ribbon bow in the center. Like a rosette, it was."

Caroline could hardly count the times she had heard this story and all the stories: how one of Father's patients had told him about an orphaned twelve-year-old niece—such a bright, good child—how the patient could no longer afford to keep her, having eight children of her own and an unemployed husband, and how Father, having himself met the child Lore and been touched by pity, had taken her into their home.

From her parents, Caroline had heard their side of the story. Lore, at twelve, had been such a cheerful, obedient little girl! She had been so grateful for everything, for good food and clothes, a pretty room of her own, and kind attention. She had been a hardworking student. At nursing school she had done very well. Indeed, she did everything very well.

More than that, she was the elder daughter of the family; midway in age between Caroline and her mother, she was the confidante of both.

"My teeth," Lore said now. "Look at them crumbling away. I was six years old when the war began in 1914, just in time for scarcity. We never had proper nourishment. No wonder my bones are soft. And then all the men were killed, my father and my two older brothers." She looked around the yard, and seeing no one there, leaned toward Caroline, whispering, "That's why I have to get out now before the next war comes." Then she laughed. "And before all the young men die and I'll never be able to find a husband."

Caroline felt sad for her. Poor Lore! She never went out anywhere except with other women. Nature was very uneven when it handed out eyes or noses or human skeletons, she reflected. Lore was short and large boned; she had scanty dull-brown hair and a large, flat nose with large nostrils. Unfair. Men would not bother to find out how smart and competent and good she was.

"There. The peas are shelled. I've already done the beans, and you have the carrots. Now, with yesterday's leftover meat, we'll have a fine soup. There's nothing like a thick soup and some fresh bread."

They went back into the house. Already, though no furniture had been moved, it had begun to feel deserted and temporary. Many of the rooms were never used anymore; the English governess had gone home the year before, and the French one, being Jewish, had left long ago for France. Five-course dinners in the long, formal dining room had given way to simple meals in the breakfast niche. In the glass-walled sunroom one felt too exposed to the bands of roving toughs who sometimes came through the neighborhood. The little library at the back of the house felt safest, and there they all huddled in the evening to read or listen to concerts over the radio, or to Mama playing softly on the piano.

Now, especially since Crystal Night, in their very own house they were afraid.

"EXCELLENT soup, Lore," Father said.

"On Sunday, I'll be free and I'll make apple charlotte for you."

"There's nothing like your cherry strudel," Mama said, sighing. "I remember last summer on Caroline's birthday, it was good enough for a king's banquet."

So they talked for a while about food, recalling dinners that none of their friends—of those who were left—ever gave anymore. And restaurants to which they never went anymore. They talked about a book that Mama had finished and recommended, or about a surgical case that Lore was tend-ing. Quite obviously, they were trying to skirt the one question that was on all their minds.

Lore, whenever she did private duty nursing, was sure to bring back a few tidbits of interesting gossip, most of it harmless stuff about forbidden romances. Sometimes she had more than gossip to relate. And then, inevitably, they would return to what was foremost in their minds.

"Yes," she said now, addressing Father. "They really are building that airport you heard about. A man who was visiting my patient this afternoon is working on it. But I only heard a bit because someone shut him up."

"What difference?" Father said glumly. "We all know what's coming."

"You had better hurry," Lore warned, as always.

"What are you talking about? Visas for England are impossible. And as for America, it's wait your turn on the quota. Hurry up and wait. Wait, especially for poor Eva, who was born in Poland and has a filled-up quota. Please don't tell me we should have applied a long time ago because I already know it."

"The world is closed," Mama murmured.

Our ancestors, Caroline thought in the silence. God alone knows how long Father's people have been in what is now Germany; from prehistoric times, most likely. And Mama's have been in Europe for how many centuries? Before 1492 they were in Spain, perhaps since the destruction of the temple in 70.

"Maybe you should leave now, Lore," Father said thoughtfully. "Why should you be stuck here with us if we can't get out?"

"No, you're my family and I go where you do. Right now, I'm going to bed. I'm on duty early tomorrow."

"God bless her," said Mama, when Lore went upstairs. "She's a princess, a saint."

It was true. Lore was Caroline's older sister and her best friend.

"Poor soul," said Father. "That nose of hers is her main enemy. Well, other things besides. If she ever stops living with us, I'm afraid she will live alone for the rest of her days. Men are such fools. . . . Play something, Eva. Play some Bach. He is hopeful and filled with faith."

Long after Caroline had gone to her room, the piano sounded faintly from below. Because it was routine, it was reassuring. Peter's warm little body pressed against her feet was also reassuring.

Then her thoughts traveled back to the meeting in the park. She felt vaguely troubled. Had she been curt when he asked her whether they would meet again tomorrow? Or if not curt, exactly, perhaps just dismissive? Or cool? A teacher had once remarked, kindly enough, that she should stop analyzing herself. Perhaps, he said, she had been very strictly brought up, with heavy emphasis upon manners, and so she had a fear of giving offense.

Yes, carried too far, that business could become ridiculous. You spent a few minutes with a total stranger, and now you are worried that you hurt his feelings. You will probably never see him again. And if you do, what difference would it make? He walks his dog, you walk yours, and that's the end of it.

Yet she knew she would see him again.

He was standing across the avenue from her house the next afternoon, and it was obvious that he had been waiting for her. Indeed, he told her that he had.

"I would like to know you," he said.

"Well, I walk here every day, unless it should be raining too hard."

"That's not what I meant. I would like to go somewhere with you, to a concert or to the opera, since you said you like music."

Had she said so? She did not recall. Although they had begun to walk side by side and she was not looking at him, she felt that he had turned toward her with expectation.

"Your neighbors, the Cassells at the end of your street, are friends of my family. You can ask them about me."

"Oh, no, I don't need to. I can tell for myself, I—"

"Can you?" There was a slight amusement in his tone, and as she looked up at him, a slight, appealing twinkle in his eyes. "From the first minute yesterday, I was sure we would get along. That happens sometimes, you know, not only in fairy tales."

"Yes, I know." She hesitated, and then, diving into cold, unfriendly waters, said directly, "You shouldn't even be talking to me. I'm half Jewish."

For a moment as she watched, he stood still, regarding her. Then he said quietly, "It doesn't matter."

Even though she had not known what to expect from him, the stillness, as though he was disappointed, and also the words, were startling.

"I don't understand," she said. "How can it not matter, the way things are?"

"It is only a complication. One finds one's way around complications. That's all there is to it."

Their eyes were looking into each other. In his, she saw a sympathy that would have made her cry if she had given way to it. There was so little kindness these days.

And she said gently, "I wouldn't want you to have any trouble because of me."

For an answer, he took her hand, saying only, "Let's walk."

Already, they were behaving as if there was going to be a *connection*. Neither spoke. They arrived at a place where the path sloped toward a small lake on a wide sward, where in fine weather people walked and children played ballgames. There were benches. To one of these he drew her, and they sat while the dogs lay down willingly at their feet, as if they, too, sensed the mood of the day.

Unlike the day before, there was no sun, and it was very cold. Bitter November had finally settled itself upon the world. All was quiet. In the windless air, the topmost elm twigs made a delicate black pattern against the pale gray sky.

"Look. Like a Japanese print, or calligraphy," Walter said, pointing upward.

He was still holding her hand, and she was still holding back tears. Why? What was happening?

From the lowest branches of the trees, there sounded a sweet twittering of birds, little winter creatures with dark heads.

"Hunting berries, going their cheerful way as usual, in spite of everything," he said. "Yes, nature. Nature and art. Nothing else lasts, so in the long run, nothing else matters."

"Nothing matters? How can you say that?"

"In the long run, I said." Letting go of her hand, he faced her to ask abruptly, "What are you going to do in the short run?"

"My family, you mean?" She had not needed to be warned against putting trust in strangers. Yet this time, she did just that. "We are trying to emigrate to America. But we are very late, and you need to have people over there who will support you so you will not be a public charge. My mother has gotten hold of some New York City and Chicago telephone books. People are all passing them around. She writes to people with names like those in her family, although we have no relatives abroad. Perhaps generations ago they were relatives. Who knows? But perhaps they will have a heart anyway."

He shook his head. "It's all insane. Insane and evil. This whole country—"

"It's dangerous to talk that way."

"I know that. I don't usually talk that way."

"Except at home? One has to talk some-place."

Again he shook his head. "Never at home."

For a few moments he was silent. Three lines were drawn across his forehead. She wondered, and had never noticed, whether other people as young as he was ever had such marked lines. When he spoke again, it was with sadness.

"We don't argue. I respect my father. Be-sides, he is a man with whom people never argue. This has troubled our relationship because I can't speak openly. Still, he must know how I feel about affairs here. It is often what one does not say that expresses things as clearly as what one does say."

Then, brightening as if with an effort, he changed the subject. "Well, Caroline, since we find ourselves in rather special circum-stances, where are we going to meet from now on? It can't be always in the middle of the park, especially because"—and he held out his hand—"it has started to rain."

"We will go back to my house," she said.

AND so, Caroline's life reached a divide: There was before Walter and then there was after Walter.

Lore, who had been at home that first afternoon, was intensely curious. "You go for a walk in the park and look what you bring back! His manners, his looks. Real elegance. But tell me, does he know—know about—"

"About Mama? Of course. He doesn't care. He's a cultured, intelligent man. What do you think, that he's some kind of Brownshirt thug?"

Lore teased, "Look at you, defending him already. Have you fallen in love so fast?"

"What's wrong with you? I have not fallen in love, Lore."

"Maybe not yet, but I'm sure you will. It's only natural. And they say it's wonderful," she added wistfully. "Still, in these times, you have to wonder."

There was great confusion within Caroline, a dread of appearing foolish, as if her thoughts could be visible to other people.

She embarrassed herself with the thoughts that were taking shape in her head.

When the week passed and there were no more daily walks in the park, Walter began the evening visits that introduced him to the family.

"A fine young man," her father said cordially. But after the first two or three times, he expressed his doubts. "I don't have to tell you that we are living on the thin edge. Walter should be more careful, too. I'm surprised that he comes here at all."

Mama says nothing, thought Caroline, because she feels such a weight upon her. A heritage that she had always been proud to hand on had now, in this mad time, become a danger to her daughter. Her husband had lost his career and was leaving his country for her sake.

"What do you know about his family?" Father asked, meaning: What is their work and do they belong to the Party? "No, of course they can't, or else he wouldn't—" he said, thinking aloud, and then stopped, resuming a moment later. "Anyway, we shall be leaving soon. And you are so—"

So young, he meant. Father's little girl. He had developed this new habit of spilling half a thought into a broken sentence. And Caroline remembered how he had used to be, positive and sanguine, a doctor, a father who knew all the answers to whatever you needed to know.

One day she took Peter for his walk in the direction of Christina's house. As little girls up to the age of twelve, they had gone to school together. After that, when Caroline changed to a school run by Jewish teachers, they had, in memory of that first childhood intimacy, kept hold of a tenuous friendship. Nostalgia now drove her simply to walk past the house without having any intention of going in.

It happened that Christina was coming along the street from the opposite direction, and glad to see each other they rushed to meet. Yet after the first few greetings, each felt some constraint. Christina was a university student. She was going to Italy over the holidays. There was little else to say, and they were about to part when a long black official-seeming car with a chauffeur stopped at the next house.

Christina grimaced. "Litzhauser. Ball bearings. With a swastika on his lapel. Big Party man," she said contemptuously. "My parents detest him, although I don't have to tell you, he'll never know it."

Caroline understood: Christina's people had always been religious Christians. Also, she understood that Christina would not have dared to talk like that to any of her current friends. Caroline had an impulsive wish to trust and confide, to ask about Walter, to ask anything. But, almost instantly thinking better of it, she did not, and watched with a hidden shudder as Walter's father, bulky, important, and with his close-shaven head a caricature of his kind, walked into his house.

So she embraced Christina and went home with foreboding like a chill all through her body.

To tell or not to tell. This was too crucially important to keep secret. On the other hand, once her parents knew, it would be the end of Walter. And there was no other place for them to meet besides her house, which in itself wasn't wonderful; her parents sat and sat, as if he had come to visit them. When finally they did go upstairs, it was almost time for him to leave, anyway.

At dinner that night, very casually, her father inquired, "Is Walter coming again this evening?"

Her reply was equally casual.

"I don't know. He might just drop in."

"He has been here five times in the last two weeks," Mama said.

Lore winked at Caroline. *Take it easy,* her wink meant.

"We only mean," Father said, "that you shouldn't be getting any ideas. I certainly don't have to give you reasons why."

"Goodness, he's only a friend. We talk, and it's fun. And I don't have—"

Father interrupted. "You don't have any fun, and young people should have it. We know that all too well. That's why the sooner we get away, the better. God knows we're trying," he finished wearily.

There had been no replies from the United States to any of the appeals that they had been sending, the so-careful let-ters that, because of censorship, dared not reveal the fear, the terrible urgency, and the terrible truth.

"It's almost like putting a message in a bottle and floating it out to sea," Mama said.

But Father, true to his nature, reminded them that other people had received an-swers and had even been taken into Ameri-can homes by total strangers.

"It happens, although I admit it's asking an awful lot and there can't be too many people in the world who will do it. Still, I have a feeling we'll be lucky."

"What shall we do for money?" asked Mama. "They've frozen everything. Frozen. Stolen is more like it."

"We can raise some when we sell the fur-nishings, and buy some jewelry to hide. We'll see. We'll work it out somehow."

But Mama had no faith. Sometimes, whenever she was not doing some chore around the house, and constant reader that she was, she would sit with a book; but it was only to put it down on her lap and stare into space. After a while she would rise abruptly and go to the piano, filling the rooms with waves, a tumbling ocean of music.

"Poor Eva. She drowns her sorrows in it," said Lore, who saw through everyone.

Walter arrived one evening while Eva was still playing. "I stood at the front door until you finished the sonata before I rang the bell," he explained. "It was too beautiful to be interrupted."

"You shouldn't have done that, standing in the cold," Eva said. But she was pleased.

"Am I interrupting anything else?" he asked. For the little group looked as if it had gathered for a purpose.

"Not at all," Mama assured him. "We were only having our usual discussion about emigration, and as always, since we were getting nowhere, I decided to make some music. Come, Arthur, we've some things to look at upstairs."

At last they are taking some pity on me, thought Caroline. For once I can talk to him without them.

Yet suddenly now, alone with Walter, she

could not think how to begin. She was too aware of him and of the way he examined her, making her wonder whether her hair and her dress were right, making her awkward.

"There's a beautiful feeling in this house," he said, "with the pictures and the books lying around, books that people actually read. It's almost a religious atmosphere."

"Religious? No. My parents have never declared themselves one way or the other."

"I meant it in a different sense, in a truer sense that belongs to all religions. The way your father talks about his work, his calling. And your mother's music. She plays with her whole soul. I think she must be a very gentle woman. Am I right?"

"Yes. But she can be lively, too, and very funny. Not lately, though. Not for a long time."

"Affidavits and visas. A frustrating business. I understand."

"We don't know what's going to happen."

"They mustn't wait if they can help it."

Walter spoke soberly. "People are talking, not too loud, of course, about war by next summer. After Austria and the Sudetenland, anything's possible."

"I know."

"I shall miss you," he said.

There was an ache in her throat. An ache and a yearning for things lost, as if the future had already happened, as if she had already lived through the coming together, the joining, and the parting. Then she said a thing that she had not intended to say.

"I saw your father going into your house."

An instant later she had no idea why she had told him. To what purpose had it been? Perhaps because all things must be truthful and clean between them?

She saw that he was startled, even alarmed. "When was that?"

"A while ago. He came home in a car."

"A government car?"

"I thought it was."

"So now you know."

She was looking at the lines on his forehead, the three painful lines above the level brows and the kind, beautiful, translucent eyes.

"Have you told your parents?"

"No."

"It hurts you to keep secrets from them?"

"Yes, but they would be terrified if they knew. And you? What would your father do?"

"To you, do you mean?"

"And to you."

"God only knows, Caroline."

"Have you always been afraid of him?"

"Mostly because of my mother, to keep peace in the house for her sake. It's not pleasant to be there when he's angry. And now, with this powerful national cause . . ."

The space, the warm room that contained them, seemed very small; the night, so full of unknown danger, peered through the windows and pressed the very walls.

"Come here," Walter said. "Sit with me."

On the small sofa between the windows he took her hand. "I haven't held your hand since the day we sat on the bench in the park."

"Because we are never alone."

"I understand. Your parents are afraid for you. I would be, too, if I were your father."

She smiled. "But you are not my father."

For a long minute he stared at her. "My God," he said.

When they kissed, she felt the strong, racing beat of his heart, and was struck by awe. His living heart. So they stayed unmoving for long minutes, unable to draw away.

"It's like coming home," she murmured, "as if I have always been like this with you, all my life."

Smoothing her long hair away from her forehead, he gazed at her face. "How beautiful you are. Rebecca at the well. So tender and so young."

"No, Walter. I'm not tender. I'm very strong. And I'm very old, too. Old enough to know what I want."

"Six weeks, and I have thought of nothing else but you. I love you so, Caroline."

There were footsteps on the stairs, and Mama called her name. "Is that you, Caroline? I saw the light and I wondered."

Walter stood up. "I'm sorry, Mrs. Hartzinger. It's my fault. We have been talking and I had no idea it was so late."

"That's all right, Walter. I was just wondering about the light."

Mama was still partway down the stairs when he left. As soon as the door closed upon him, she came the rest of the way.

"What are you thinking of, Caroline?" she reproved.

"I don't know what you mean. We simply didn't look at the time."

"You must consider appearances. A young man and you alone, so late . . ."

It wasn't really appearances or the lateness that Mama minded. It was her suspicion that they were in love.

"Lore thinks you are in love with him."

"Lore doesn't know anything about it."

"But she cares about you so much, and she knows you. She doesn't want you to be hurt."

"I won't be hurt."

Her mother was looking at her with pity. "Even if there were nothing else to hinder you, you're too young to experience love," she said.

"I'm eighteen, and you were nineteen and of a different religion, too. But you fell in love. That was twenty-two years ago, and you're still here together."

"The times were different, Caroline. There was no terror."

"Mama, this is ridiculous. I hardly know him."

"That's true enough. What do you know about his family? He never mentions them. I have a feeling that he doesn't want them to know he comes to this house."

She thought with dread, If her parents knew about his father . . . To look at her, you wouldn't think Mama was so sharp.

"It could be dangerous for all of us. We don't want to attract attention."

"Mama, don't worry. I tell you, there's nothing to it. He'll soon get tired of coming, anyway. In fact, I think he's beginning to already."

But no one was fooled. In the kitchen, not thinking they could be overheard, Mama and Lore were talking.

"Caroline is an innocent," Lore said. "He should leave her alone and find somebody a few years older, nearer his own age, more experienced. Still, in the end, I don't think anything will come of it. We mustn't worry too much."

Mama sighed. "I hope you're right. What can I do? The more you talk against these things to a young girl, the more you are apt to make matters worse."

THE New Year came, winter turned toward spring, and Walter had become an unacknowledged member of the house and of the establishment, although not of the family. He appeared routinely on most evenings after dinner; occasionally he accepted an invitation to dinner, to which he always brought a small, proper gift, some chocolates or flowers, and once, a history of the opera for Caroline's mother.

Conversation roamed all over the globe and touched on every subject from architecture to zoos, on anything except politics.

There was a tacit agreement to leave politics alone.

Plainly the two men enjoyed each other, which Caroline thought would have been a very good thing if so many other things had been different.

One morning before going to work, Father took her aside in the hall to ask rather delicately whether Walter was serious. "It's obvious that I like him very much, but that's not the point. I'm not comfortable. I hope you have no crazy thoughts about marriage. You must be open with me, Caroline. Have you?"

"We've never even mentioned it," she said, feeling as though her back were against the wall.

"You must see that it would be impossible."

"What shall I do? What do you want me to do? Shall I tell him to stay away?"

She saw in her father's sorrowful gaze that her heart, where the pain lay, was transparent.

For a moment, he did not answer. "No,"

he said tiredly. "No. Just don't do anything foolish."

"What does he want with a baby like you?" said Lore, mixing teasing with love. "He's a man, an exceptional man, and you're just a pretty baby. Don't tie yourself down. You have the whole world to explore. You'll have a dozen men before you finally choose one."

"Lore's a smart woman," Walter said when Caroline reported this comment. "But she's wrong this time." He had driven Lore to the hospital on several evenings when he was going into the city, and had remarked that she could talk like a professor. "Yes, she's very smart, but not this time."

On the sofa under the soft lights, they kissed and listened to music and talked about everything except reality. Once, while his arms were around her, Caroline had a vivid recollection of the day he had said, *I shall miss you,* and she would have cried out to him, *What are we going to do?* if she had dared. But perhaps it was better not to know.

Soon, though, they would have to speak

out. How carefully they were walking around in a fog of denial, as if the fearful future were not looming, as if they could keep on as they were! And all the time, they were only longing to be completely alone. They were longing for each other. . . .

THEN one day there came a letter from America. It was a simple note written on lined paper that had been torn off a pad. Mama read it aloud.

"My name is Sandler, like yours, Mrs. Hartzinger. I don't believe we can be related by blood unless your people also came from Lithuania. But in times like these, we are all related. My wife and I cried when we read your letter. I am not a rich man, just a worker, but our children are grown. We have food and beds for you in our apartment. It's small, not grand, but it is yours for as long as you need it. We have been talking it over every day all week. I will sign papers for you that will satisfy the authorities."

The letter was signed "Jacob Sandler,"

and there was a postscript: "We are religious people."

"In the best sense," said Father, who was plainly much moved. "Imagine, inviting us, willing to share with strangers. I told you that somewhere, somebody would."

They had sent a snapshot labeled "Jacob and Annie." There was nothing to distinguish them from millions of men and women who were neither old nor young, thin nor fat, handsome nor ugly, merely ordinary.

"You wonder," Father said, "what makes them different enough to do what they're doing."

In the dusk, sunk in a corner chair, Caroline observed the scene. Her father, true to his nature, was shaking his head over the miracle. Her mother was looking around the room at the Dresden figurines of shepherds and shepherdesses, caressing with her eyes the photographs, the books, and the piano—always the piano—as if she were already seeing them for the last time.

And then she remarked, "I suppose they will be surprised to meet you, Arthur. And you, Lore, with your mother's gold cross around your neck."

"Nonsense, Eva," Father said. "More than a few Christians are also departing from this insane asylum, or trying to."

His father, Caroline thought. His father, with the swastika in his lapel. We should have talked about it. We should have met the truth head on.

Her own father seemed abruptly transformed, taking swift charge, as in the old days that she remembered: the cheerful doctor, hurrying off in the morning, sure of himself and sure of his answers.

"God bless these people, whoever they are. I'll tell you one thing," he said. "We won't cost them any more than a few days' lodging, if that. I'll find a job in a hospital. I'll clean the floors and do anything until I can get a license to be a doctor again. Eva will give piano lessons. Caroline, you can tutor in French or teach English to other refugees."

"Yes, and she'd better help me with English," Lore said, "so I can get back into nursing."

"Only one thing remains." Father was listing everything on his fingers. "Our American visas. I'm going to ask again on Monday, the first thing in the morning. They must be sick of seeing me. And Eva, you'll take your jewelry and get what you can for it. Don't take the first offer. Try as many places as possible, although I don't imagine there'll be too much difference among them. They all know Jews are desperate."

Timidly, Mama asked, "You mentioned something, didn't you, about some doctor who wanted the piano?"

"Yes. Braun. He's a decent sort, nothing Nazi about him. He told me he'll pay the true price, doesn't want to take advantage."

"Maybe there are some more like him."

"I will try, Eva. And when we have raised enough money, we'll buy jewelry."

"Then what's the sense in selling mine now?"

"My darling wife, I'm sorry to say that nothing you've ever owned is valuable enough for our purposes. We need to have a few small, superb gems, rings that can easily be concealed."

Lore spoke. "Let me be the first to leave. I can quickly get things into Switzerland. They won't bother me, a working girl carrying my shabby suitcase."

Mama burst out crying. "Who could have thought? Who could have dreamed? Lore, you, too, to be driven out of your country."

"I'm not being driven out, I'm departing of my own free will." Lore laughed. "I don't feel like starving my way through one more war."

Her laughter lifted the mood. Mama wiped her eyes. Father was busy with his list. And nobody, immersed as they all were in this sudden activity, had looked toward—perhaps had not even thought of—Caroline.

IN the rear garden, the first snowdrops had poked through the hard earth, and it was warm enough, when wrapped in heavy clothes, to sit in the sun. The Sunday morning quiet was so profound that they spoke almost in whispers.

"Did you really think that when the time came, I would let you go without me?" asked Walter.

"I didn't want to think about it. I only remembered that once you had said, 'I shall miss you.'"

"That was a thousand years ago. No, I shall never miss you because I shall be with you."

"What about your family? Are you going to slip away one day without saying anything, or what?"

"Slip away, and the sooner the better, because a real crisis is coming. I shall be finished with my examinations by May, and then there'll be not only a showdown about entering the firm, but worse yet, about taking some sort of position in the Party. My mother's in a women's group, my brother has an army career, my sisters are in Hitler Youth, and I am the only one who's kept apart from all that. I guess you can have some idea," he said grimly, "about the pressure that's put on me. I hate being home even for an hour at dinner. My life is lived at the university."

He got up, walked to the wall, and looked out over the avenue into the park. When he came back and stood before Caroline, she saw that he was extremely agitated.

"The strange thing is that in spite of all I've told you about him, I still cannot really hate my father. In all decency, how can a person forget the years of nurture, the labor that made life comfortable for me? When I was ill, when I wanted or needed something, he was there for me. No, I can't hate him, but only what he stands for and what he is trying to make me stand for, too. Oh, Caroline, when can we get away?"

"Father and I are promised our visas for America by May. Mama's number will not be reached for months. She wants us to leave without her. She says it's wrong for us to be delayed because of her. They almost had an argument about it last night." And feeling her lips quiver, she stopped for a moment before resuming. "One of the doctors who used to be a friend of Father's, and certainly isn't one now, has divorced his Jewish wife. Can you imagine, Walter?"

"Swine."

"Father says if it comes to that, he'll die with Mother. But he doesn't believe it will come to that. Or at least, he says he doesn't believe it."

"Of course, then, you didn't have a chance to talk to them about us," Walter said gently. "Not that they don't already know."

"It wasn't the proper time. And you're right, of course they know. It's pretty obvious, isn't it?"

"They haven't wanted to hear it. But now they have to. May we go inside so we can tell them officially?"

The parents were still at the breakfast table, where they had been sitting since earliest morning, thrashing through their predicament. Caroline's father looked up in surprise when Walter appeared with her.

"I wouldn't disturb you at this hour," Walter said, "if we didn't have something important to tell you. Or, I should say, to ask you. Caroline, shall I do it, or will you?"

They looked so tired, she thought. This isn't the way it should be. There should be laughter, congratulations and a bottle of champagne, as it's described in all the books. Walter's family would come for a gala dinner to get acquainted. . . .

"I think we can guess," her father said.

"I hope you have no objection to me," replied Walter.

"To you? No. In these last few months you've become a friend. It's all the unknowns in this situation that trouble me and my wife."

"Then the thing to do is to clear up the unknowns."

"Sit down, please, and begin, if you can."

And so Walter, deliberate and decisive, laid out the facts as carefully as though he were writing a chart for a study. Caroline, holding Peter close on her lap, watched their faces; Walter's with the earnest lines on his forehead, Mama's dismayed, as without words she observed her husband's reaction, and Father's, whose lack of any expression at all actually showed how stunned he was.

"That's how it is," Walter concluded. "The whole story."

There was a moment during which no one said anything. Then Father asked slowly, "And what place does our daughter have in such a family? Surely you see that—"

"No place. She will have no place in it, nor will I. I will be a part of your family instead, if you will have me. I want to go with you to America and wait to marry Caroline there, so as not to complicate the visa that is being prepared for her."

The two men regarded each other, measuring each other more astutely than either probably had until this moment.

"It is predictable, Walter, that you will be called to the army soon."

"Quite right. My father is a decorated veteran of the last war, and with his connections has already made plans to place me in an officers' corps."

"In that case, how do you expect to get out of the country?"

"I'm told by people who ought to know that we have some months' leeway. I'll find an errand in Switzerland and go there very soon. I have money inherited from my

49

grandfather, and I plan to bank it there temporarily."

"You can't get currency out now."

"*You* can't, that's true. But I can. There are ways."

"So you have it all thought out. What do you think, Eva?"

"Well, you know what I have been thinking, that Caroline is too young. Yet now all of a sudden I'm remembering how, when we wanted to marry, people found all those obstacles that really weren't there."

"There was no war coming, Eva. We had just gotten over one."

"All the more reason to act quickly now," Walter said. "And if there should be no war, and possibly better minds will prevent it, who knows, why then—"

"Then we shall be in America, anyway," Caroline shouted. Jumping up, she kissed her parents, and there, right before them, kissed Walter, too, and laughed and cried.

By late afternoon, everything had been talked over and decided. Caroline was to leave for Switzerland as soon as her visa was received. There she would wait for her parents at the home of a Swiss doctor, a friend from Father's days in medical school. Lore, as a "normal" citizen, would make one or two trips back and forth with jewelry, as already planned. And Walter, another "normal" citizen, would take a few weeks' vacation in Switzerland.

"My friends have a house on the edge of a lake, not far from Geneva," Father said in conclusion. "It's a beautiful part of the world, a fine start for a long, happy life."

TWO

It was dark, after a long day's travel, when Caroline and Lore arrived at the Schmidts' house and Caroline laid her head down in the strange bed. For a long time, she was aware of a hurried heartbeat. The future, in spite of all that had been said and all the measured, careful plans that had been made, was only an enormous, shapeless vacancy, a stepping off from a precipice into empty air.

Minutes passed. Then, gradually, the thought that Lore was in the next bedroom began to have a quieting effect. In a way, Caroline had resented her parents' insistence, and also Walter's, that Lore and she leave together. To have need of Lore had seemed to be a reflection upon her own abilities. Yet, remembering now the emotional scene at the railway station in Berlin, she saw how much more emotional it would have been if she had ridden away alone, if alone she had strained for the last look at Father and Walter waving their hats and Mama waving a yellow handkerchief.

Walter, who had analyzed Lore surprisingly well, had named her "the stabilizer," which indeed she had been. She had quieted Mama's fearful premonition that this parting might be a permanent one, and so had turned the packing of trunks from tragedy into adventure.

The white spring night outside shone now on the enormous bulk of the new trunk. They had bought probably the largest one that was manufactured and had crammed it full.

"Take everything you own that's wearable and useful," Father said. "Don't waste space on party clothes. Maybe a few nice summer dresses for your stay at the Schmidts' and for Walter's Switzerland visit," he had added with his most knowing smile.

Clothing and a few photographs were to be the only remnants of the old home and the old life.

"Books you can buy, if all goes well," said Mama, and most astonishingly for her of all people, had added, "books are not a necessity. Clothes are."

So her precious books, from childhood fairy tales to the histories and the classics, were left behind. More painful by far was the parting from Peter. Lore had found a home for him.

"One of my patients has a poodle she adores, but he's quite old. Peter will be a new companion for him and for the family."

Tonight was the first night in three years that he had not slept next to Caroline's feet, and she wondered now how he was sleeping. Walter had understood.

"As soon as we set up our house, we will buy a poodle and call him Peter," he said.

He understood everything. He was rare. She knew that to many older people her admiration of him would be dismissed affectionately as "infatuation." But practical as she was—although her family didn't see her that way—she had recently made a list of the qualities she needed in a husband. Measuring Walter against the list, she had quite honestly discerned only one slight flaw. Perhaps he did not have any sense of humor? But then, she was herself neither amusing nor witty. And then again, was there any reason for anyone to find humor in the world right now?

Yes, they were perfect for each other. They were very young, and life was long. And he would be with her in a few weeks. . . . Thinking so, she fell asleep.

THE clang of ancient church bells woke her, so that for an instant there woke, too, a memory of the holidays they used to spend in mountain villages long ago when it was still possible to have such holidays. From the hall came voices, Lore's and Mrs.

Schmidt's; they were saying something about the weather, which was apparently marvelous, and something about Caroline, who had slept late. Lore's brisk, familiar tone was encouraging, and determined to be equally spirited, she got up to dress, fastened her hair back with a bow, and went downstairs.

Dr. Schmidt was at the table having, as he explained, his second breakfast, a Sunday luxury before church. He must be about Father's age, she thought. Although with his ruddy face and mustache he did not resemble Father, there was an undeniable "doctor" quality about him. Asked to explain what that meant, she would have been unable to describe the quality; it was simply there.

"You slept well, young lady. I can tell by your eyes," he said cheerfully.

Mrs. Schmidt, who definitely did not remind Caroline of Mama, unfastened the apron she had worn when she had, as she said, baked the hot coffee cake that lay wrapped in a napkin.

"Doctor and I are going to church. I didn't know whether you or—"

"Lore does," Caroline said. "Do go, Lore."

"No, I can skip a Sunday for once. It won't hurt me. I'll have coffee with you, Caroline. You just go ahead, Amalia, we'll be fine."

"First names already! That's nice. Friendly," Caroline remarked when they were alone.

"Yes, very. They showed me around the house while you were asleep. I was really feeling funny about our being here, but they kept telling me that it was no inconvenience, even a pleasure, to have Arthur Hartzinger's daughter as a guest. It's a reminder of his student days, Doctor says."

In little more than an hour, Lore had typically found out all about the family and the neighborhood.

"Doctor works in a rehabilitation hospital for crippled children. Amalia works in a government office in the town. They have no children. Travel is their hobby. Doctor said he's glad they've been almost all over the world because the war is coming, and there won't be any more traveling for a long while."

"The war again! If people would only stop predicting one. It seems impossible when you look out at this May morning with the apple blossoms and the calm blue lake."

Lore, not replying whether she believed in the coming war or not, spoke instead about the lake, which lay directly at the bottom of the sloping lawn.

"There's a walk you can take for quite a long way, I think. I woke up early and did a little exploring. Or maybe we'll wait for the Schmidts to take us later. There's a tiny village up the hill. The church looks interesting. Seventeenth century, by my guess. Finish your breakfast and let's go out."

The air was filled with birdsong. The glint of light on the water was so strong that one had to shade one's eyes. To right and left, houses in long gardens half hidden by trees rimmed the lake. The Schmidts had placed outdoor chairs around a table in the shade, and there now they sat, Caroline with a travel magazine from their parlor and Lore, never idle, with her knitting.

"I found this pink wool on a top shelf in your mother's closet when we were cleaning up. Goodness knows what she was planning to do with it. I never saw her knit anything. There's enough for a blanket, so that's what I'm doing. There's no sense wasting it."

Caroline was looking at a color photograph of Angkor Wat in its dense green jungle and thinking that one day, she and Walter might see such things, this and the Taj Mahal, and—

Lore interrupted her thoughts. "France is just across the lake. We could take a tour boat one day if you'd like, and have a French lunch over there."

"We can't afford to, can we?"

"Oh, I have a few pennies of my own." Lore laughed. "Or we could sell the rings."

She had brought them with her, sewed into the lining of her handbag. One was Mama's own ruby, and the others diamonds, blue-white, and almost flawless, according to Mama. They were lovely indeed, but it was shocking to know that these minerals, for that is all they were, had cost the entire proceeds from the sale of all the furnishings in the beloved house. The paintings and the grand piano, with Father's insurance policy besides, had gone to buy these small pieces of mineral dug out of the earth.

"It does seem incredible," Lore acknowledged when Caroline said that it was. "Wait till we see what the house will fetch. There's sure, I hope, to be enough left for another couple of rings after putting something aside for steamship tickets and cash." She sighed, then frowned as if she were counting. "I'll stay here with you for the next two or three weeks, leave these rings here, and go back. If any questions are asked, you can say that I have a sister in Switzerland, and that's why I've gone back and forth a couple of times. You don't remember her name."

"The Schmidts would never ask that."

"I wasn't thinking of the Schmidts," Lore answered.

So even in this place, there were people

to be feared. And saying no more, they returned to knitting needles and travel fantasies.

"Well, you two look as if you've recovered from yesterday's ordeal," observed Dr. Schmidt as he and Amalia joined them. "Sitting in a train for hours on end is more exhausting than a hike uphill."

"I hope everyone likes roast duck because that's what we're having for dinner," Amalia said. "I make it with black cherries. We like that better than orange sauce."

They were affable, kind people. It must be hard to welcome strangers into your home, Caroline thought, and make comfortable conversation with them, especially since the Schmidts know our circumstances. They don't want to show any pity, although surely they pity us.

"Sing for your supper," Mama always taught, meaning that a guest must bring pleasure to the host's house in return for hospitality.

"Duck is one of my favorites," she said brightly. "But it's so lovely here that I could just sit and enjoy it without any dinner at all."

"Yes, it's nice to relax and enjoy the spring. My husband doesn't get a chance to do much of that, busy as he is at the hospital."

"My father told me about your work with children and about when you were both students, too."

"I will guarantee that he never told you about some of our practical jokes, Caroline," the doctor said. "Your father was a terror when he was a student." He laughed. "Oh, I could tell you—but I won't."

It was hard to imagine Father as a "terror." But the conversation, just as Mama had said, was now off to a good start. It ran happily through the midday dinner and a long walk, and was still flourishing when at four o'clock they returned to the garden chairs and afternoon coffee. By that time they had exchanged information about Lore's pastry, Caroline's languages, her parents' wedding—at which Dr. Schmidt had been present—and the Schmidts' respective careers. Among other things, it had been agreed that Caroline, for the following weeks, would spend her time between giving intensive English lessons to Lore and volunteering at the children's hospital. At that point, everyone being contentedly talked out, they all resorted to the still unread newspapers.

Except for the crackle of turning pages, there was for a while no sound until Amalia's outraged cry.

"Listen to this! Complaints about refugees. 'If we keep admitting them, we won't have enough food for ourselves.' As if we were admitting all that many to begin with! What an ugly attitude. Can you believe it, Willie?"

"I can believe it very well," her husband answered her. "I'm surprised that you're surprised." And to Lore and Caroline, he explained, "We have a new chief of the alien police—that in itself is a new division of the federal police—and he is a first-class rabble-rouser, I'm sorry to say."

The familiar old alarm ran up and down Caroline's spine, and it must have shown on her face because he said quickly, "Don't worry, you're all right. You're here as guests, tourists with visas to continue on. So you're really all right. Don't worry."

She knew she must make every effort not to. In the mornings she went to the hospital with Dr. Schmidt and there forgot herself in her pity for children born without a hand, injured in a car crash, or sometimes abused by unimaginable cruelties. In the afternoons she struggled with Lore's English or helped her in the kitchen, where Lore, wanting in some fashion to "pay their way," was busy at the stove.

By the end of the second week, they had established a routine for themselves, fitting into this household almost as if they belonged there. It was remarkable what native optimism—in Caroline's case, almost surely inherited from Father—and sheer willpower could do. Besides, at the end of the month, Walter was coming.

MUCH later in Caroline's life, she was to have many varied memories about that time, from the most significant to the trivial:

sounds, moods, and colors. She was to remark on the curious fact that even as some of these were occurring, she was saying to herself: I shall always remember this.

There was the boat trip around the lake, not with Lore after all, but with Walter. It was the first time they had been out in the world together.

There was music—with him there was always music, *Swan Lake* or jazz according to mood—from the radio in the rented car.

There were the dresses of summer, lilac and yellow and pink, the last of her wonderful dresses, in which she felt lovely and loved.

Both Schmidts remarked upon the "very fine young man." Yet, holding themselves no doubt responsible for their friend's young daughter, they did not invite him to stay overnight in the house, but at an inn a few minutes away. He was invited to dinner, to which he brought, as he had done at home, a correct, small gift.

After dinner, the Schmidts kept tactfully to themselves. Still, Caroline and Walter were never left securely alone.

"I am waiting to be in a room with you behind a locked door," Walter said.

Then one day the Schmidts lost a relative, Amalia's aunt, who was to be buried near the Italian border. They would be gone all day until late that night. Left to themselves at last, Walter and Caroline drove to Geneva, a city that he knew well. They ate lunch, wandered about, cooled off in a church where they listened to an organist rehearse for a recital, and wandered out again into the sun. They bought pistachio ice cream cones; this was one of the facts that stayed in Caroline's mind, though goodness only knew why pistachio should have marked the day, along with the fact that they were both so strangely silent with each other.

Dusk had fallen, dark blue and warm, when they returned.

"We don't have to go into the house," he said, and they lay down on the grass. "You can feel the sunlight still on it."

It grew dark. They were still lying as they had used to lie at home, with their arms around each other and her head on his shoulder, when she opened her eyes and saw the moon.

"Look! The moon is green."

He murmured something that she was barely able to hear: It was her name. Then he said, "We should go inside. I should leave you. Make me leave you."

She understood his meaning and knew that she should rise now and let him go. But she could not do it, and neither could he. She felt his long, deep sigh.

When she opened her eyes again, the moon was still there. A night bird twittered once and was still. The whole world was still. The world beyond this hidden grove did not even exist. Closer and closer they pressed.

"Make me leave you," he said again, while his hands moved her dress, loosening sash and buttons. She heard him saying something about not tearing it, and then she heard her own voice, hurrying, whispering, "It doesn't matter."

Long afterward, with the wistfulness that time brings, Caroline would think how inevitable it was that after the first time, the rest must follow. The remaining days were merely hours to be lived through until nightfall. Some distance farther down the shore, Walter had found a cove that apparently, he said, had no purpose except to accommodate lovers, and there they went.

Once he took hold of her left hand, saying gently, "I know you must be wishing for a ring on this finger. I know you have thought it because I have. But these are the worst of times. Listen, Caroline. I feel married already. We are married. In America we shall make it official."

Suddenly there was only one day left. "I dread going," he said.

"Must you?"

"There are things to attend to, preparations and stupid things, like money." She watched him as he spoke. The lines on his forehead had deepened. She saw and felt his nervous tension.

"After all, I am leaving there for good. Besides," he went on, "I may be of some use to your parents and Lore. I'm glad she's been there for them. While you were here, I took her out to a restaurant a couple of times and once to a show. She's told me how desperate they are about your mother's visa. So, darling, I have to go. When I come here again, by midsummer surely, I won't leave you, ever."

LORE returned to report that everyone was well and the house had been sold.

"Some Party member bought it, or it would be more accurate to say that he stole it. But at least we've gotten two more rings out of it, not as precious as the first ones, but better than nothing. I've brought the steamship tickets, too, yours and mine."

"Only yours and mine?"

"Yes, Walter's taking care of his on the same ship, sailing from Le Havre. Your parents can't commit themselves to a date until your mother has a visa."

Weakly, Caroline asked when that might be.

"They don't know any more now than they did in May, God help us."

"It's already almost July."

"That's true."

"Why don't they at least write to me?" cried Caroline. "Why don't we hear from anyone? There's been no mail since we arrived."

"Censorship, of course. The mail's not safe for anyone, especially for your mother. She doesn't dare call attention to herself. They're sending Polish-born citizens back to Poland, and since Poland won't take them, these poor souls are stranded outdoors in camps on the border. No-man's-land."

"My heart's pounding. My mouth is dry and my hands are wet. I think I'll go lie down."

"No," said Lore, the nurse. "It will be better to take a walk in the fresh air. Walk until you're tired out. Then you'll sleep soundly."

The days passed. They were both grateful for having work, Caroline's at the hospital and Lore's in the house, where she had by now almost taken over the kitchen.

"We can't stay as permanent guests while they wait on us," Lore said again. "I feel very uncomfortable as it is."

"How much longer can it possibly be?" asked Caroline, expecting no answer.

At last, when she had almost stopped expecting anything, there came a note from Walter. It was ambiguous, alarming, and without a signature.

"There's nothing new to tell you except that my business may possibly delay me longer than I expected."

"Now what can that possibly mean, Lore?" And again came that hammering in the chest. "What kind of a letter is this?"

"Something to do with getting money out, I should guess. What else can it be?"

"If only we could telephone! Oh, between my parents and Walter, it's unbearable. If I could only do something instead of waiting and waiting. It's doing nothing that's the worst."

One night at dinner she burst forth, "I can't stand it here any longer without knowing what's happening at home. I'm taking the train to Berlin tomorrow to see for myself."

The other three at the table stared at her.

"You what?" cried Lore. "Are you out of your mind?"

"Lore, it's the first of August tomorrow. What are we doing here? We can't just stay forever."

Dr. Schmidt seemed about to say something, stopped, and finally said it. "Caroline, you're right, unfortunately, right about staying here. You can't. Your visas will expire, and—as a Swiss citizen I'm ashamed to tell you that you won't be allowed to stay in this country. They are sending people, political refugees, back across the border if they don't move on. That starts this month."

From across the table, Caroline met the doctor's compassionate eyes. No one spoke.

Lore stood up. "I'm going upstairs to throw some clothes in a suitcase. I'm not a refugee. I can come and go as I please, and I intend to find out what's going on. No, sit where you are, Caroline, I only need a few things. It'll be a turnaround trip. One day, or maybe two, and I'll be back."

"I think," said Caroline, "I'd better start

putting my things in my trunk so I'll be ready in case . . ."

There being no need to say more, she went to her room. The plain little room, really not much more than a clean white cubicle, with a linden tree close to the window, had become a refuge and was now no more. Where would the next room be? The next bed? All was uncertain again. A delay, Walter had said . . .

She was folding dresses when Lore came in. "Here are the other two rings. Put them with the first ones. They're our savings. What are these stains on your pink linen?"

"Oh, that. Those are grass stains. I wasn't able to wash them out. Not very expert at laundry, I'm afraid."

"My goodness, whatever were you doing?"

Sometimes, not often, Lore made her feel as if she were ten years old, being scolded by M'amselle.

"Obviously, I was on the grass, Lore! We went up the hill one day to the pastry shop in the village, and coming back down, I fell on the wet grass."

Was she imagining that Lore's look was queer? Well, no matter. There was too much else to worry about beside whatever Lore might be thinking.

IT was very late on the fourth evening when Lore and Dr. Schmidt, who had gone to call for her at the train, returned. Caroline, coming down from her room, was stopped on the stairs by their voices.

"A great deal can happen in a couple of months." That was Dr. Schmidt.

"No doubt his father got hold of him. And there's such great, patriotic fervor now, spreading like a forest fire or a disease. 'Germans are being mistreated in Poland and we have to stop it'—oh, you've read it all. You know." That was Lore.

"His peers must have gotten hold of him, too," said Dr. Schmidt. "At that age, just out of the university . . . The schools are hotbeds for this stuff . . . Some of the best minds can be turned. Have been turned."

Caroline, grasping the banister, descended fearfully.

"She was too young, anyway, to get herself involved. I said so from the start. Now I hardly know how to tell her."

"Oh, the poor girl," cried Amalia.

Caroline rushed into the room. "What is it? What's happened?"

"No one's dead, no one's hurt. Come here. Please, Caroline."

"What is it? For God's sake, tell me. Has anything happened to Walter?"

"No, he's not hurt or anything. He—oh, Caroline, I don't know how to tell you, but he's not coming back here. It's impossible to believe, but it's true. He's gone over to the other side. I checked, and it's true."

"Other side? What are you talking about?"

In sorrow and concern, they had all drawn their chairs close, as if to protect her.

"What a pity," Amalia murmured. "What a pity."

Lore drew a long breath. "It's his father. It must be. I went to the house. There was no other way to find him. At the university, there were some fellows. They didn't want to talk, but I said I was his cousin, and they said he'd gone away to the country. That's all they would, or could, tell me. So then I knew there was more to it, and I went to the house. There were only servants home. No family. I said my sister was his girlfriend and hadn't heard from him. The chauffeur was there, washing the car. He said Walter was away someplace, and when I asked where, he said, well, Walter was a member of the S.S., and you didn't question where they went. He was a Party man now. My sister should stay away. I said innocently, "A Party man? That's wonderful." I said I hadn't known Walter was so active in the Party. One of the maids said yes, it was quite a change for him, very recent. He had been seeing a Jewish girl and the family found out. But the boss, his father, had finally opened his son's eyes. They all seemed very pleased, very proud."

Caroline stared at the three faces, at her own numb hands, and at the slowly spinning walls.

"He has gone insane," she said, very

low. "Either that, or I have." Then she jumped, seizing Lore's shoulder. "Tell me this crazy story again. Do you know what you're saying? Do you?" It was as if the full force of the news had suddenly, really, struck her. And she screamed again, "It's not possible! No, no, you don't understand what you're saying!"

Softly, Lore reminded her that she herself had told them about Walter's family, and he had told her, too.

"More than once, Caroline, heaven help him."

"No, Lore. You can't have understood. This is Walter you're talking about. You don't know what you're saying," she sobbed.

"What can I do? What else can I say?" And Lore threw up her hands.

Dr. Schmidt, in his quiet way, reasoned, "Caroline, my dear, it makes no sense that anyone would have invented such a tale. Everything tallies, what is known about the father's family ties, and, above all, more than anything, the fact that Walter has not returned."

"He seemed such a fine young man," lamented Amalia. "An intellectual, still so full of youthful spirits. An idealist, too, I thought. How can he have become a Nazi? It seems such a contradiction."

"Contradictions and deceptions are common to humanity," Dr. Schmidt replied. "You have only to look around you. It's perhaps best that Caroline has to find out now, so she won't be hurt even more cruelly later in life."

Words went buzzing past her head. She had risen to stand in the center of the room, looking around for the door, the hall, the outer door, and the night outside. To flee, to run! To find an explanation, to find Walter, to cry to him: *Why? Why? You love me. You can't do this. You don't mean what you're doing.*

Her stomach heaved, and she ran upstairs to vomit in the bathroom. Afterward, she sank down on the cold floor.

"So he's left me," she said aloud. "Everything that happened means nothing. Nothing." And she lay there.

"Open the door," Lore called. "You've

been in there too long. Caroline, let us help you. Please open the door. Must we break it down?"

Amalia had brought hot herb tea. "It will soothe your stomach."

Dr. Schmidt came into the bedroom to offer a sedative. "If you think it will help you, I have a pill here. My best advice, though, is to fight things through with all your faculties intact." He held her hand. "You're a strong young woman, Caroline. I can tell."

But she did not feel strong, merely strong enough and prideful enough to hold back her tears until the door had closed and she could be alone in darkness. There she wept, her body shaking with long sobs, muffled lest Lore hear and come back again.

She raked over the past, the months, weeks, days, and hours, from that first meeting in the park. Had she missed a clue, some remark or gesture that should have warned her? No, she had simply trusted her own belief in love. But perhaps, as Father often said, nothing is really "simple," not even love. . . .

There came now a jumbled recollection, fragments of random speech: *peace, sometimes at any price . . . my gentle mother . . . I dread going home . . . the pressure . . . the survival of the family . . . people don't argue with my father . . .*

They must have been tearing him to pieces, those people. Pity moved in her throat, and she longed for him, to hold him, to speak to him.

But he wears their insignia! He has renounced me and what I am! Then bitter rage fought the pity, and she thought of her parents and of their suffering because of those madmen, so that a dreadful panic overran both pity and rage.

The sailing date from France was only twelve days away. How could they leave without knowing about Mama and Father? She beat the pillow and implored the air. There was no answer. There was no answer to anything.

On the ninth day, a note arrived in the mail. Unsigned, it was in her father's hand: Will see you shortly. The Schmidts and Lore puzzled over it. Obviously it meant that they were on their way to Switzerland.

"Without a visa? I don't understand," Caroline said.

Dr. Schmidt stared down at his breakfast plate. When he looked up, he spoke somberly. "I don't want to tell you this, but I must. There's a new order this month, August: Refugees without a transit visa will not be admitted. They will be turned back at the border no matter what their circumstances."

Horrified, Caroline repeated, "Turned back? What will happen to them?"

She need not have asked the question. No one spoke. She was sick. She had been stabbed. Against all reason she had thought, and hoped, that the note might be from Walter. Now this note, mysterious and alarming, had come instead. And she read the future exactly as the others at the silent table were reading it. No, not exactly as they were reading it, for those two fugitives

—the bright, brisk, hopeful man and the soft, skeptical, dreamy woman—were *her father and mother.*

She saw them standing before some uniformed official, he indifferent and hasty, they desperate and supplicating, perhaps dusty and worn out . . . She was sick again. And excusing herself, she ran toward the stairs.

From behind came Dr. Schmidt's voice. "It's a horror. Those poor people. That poor girl."

"She's been sick for the last two weeks, ever since the Walter affair," Lore said. "And now this. She vomits every morning."

"Her nerves," said Amalia. "I'm glad you're with her, Lore, glad she doesn't have to go the rest of the way alone, with all that's happening to her."

THE little house, during the days remaining, took on an atmosphere of gentle concern as houses do in which someone is ill or has died. On the last day the husband and wife took Lore and Caroline to the train.

"I will keep in touch with people I know," the doctor promised, "and if there is any news of your parents, Caroline, you will get it at once. Meanwhile, look forward, and God bless you both."

She would remember the Schmidts to her own last day.

THE ship was crammed. Not only was it almost the end of the tourist season, but there was also the looming war; permanent residents were racing back to safety, and refugees were racing out of danger. This was farewell to Europe, the end of the past.

Although it made no sense to do so, Caroline immediately read the passenger list. By some miracle, could her parents have managed to board? Or could Walter? And, as the shores of France slipped away and the ship moved through the Channel, she strained for the last look, as if somehow she might glimpse them standing on the shore. Then she braced herself, left the railing, and went below.

At home they had had their separate

rooms, so being cooped up here with Lore was a new experience. It was uncomfortable for her to be sick in the cramped bathroom within hearing distance of another person. The North Atlantic was rough; nevertheless, she spent hours on deck. Tossed against the ship's rail, she groped her way to a chair, there to lie wrapped in blankets and gaze at the cold, tumultuous clouds, the heave and swell of the dull-green ocean.

"You look miserable," Lore said. "Wouldn't you be better off in the room?"

"Father told me once that fresh air is good for seasickness. Also, that one should look steadily at the horizon."

"Yes, and eat a chicken sandwich. I've heard that, too. But I still think you should see the ship's doctor."

"Do you have to wonder what's wrong with me besides being seasick, Lore? Maybe I have a few things on my mind, on my heart?"

"I'm only trying to help you, Caroline."

"I know. I didn't mean to be impatient."

Lore sighed. "I understand."

They kept to themselves. On this crossing there was none of the gaiety that they had always read about. Faces were thoughtful, and conversation in the lounges and the dining room was subdued. People crowded around the ship's officers, asking for news.

"Do you feel as if you're at the theater?" Caroline asked one day. "None of this seems possible. Where are we going, Lore? We don't even know where we're going."

"Well, we know we're going to bump into land. Wherever the ocean ends, the ship has to stop."

The empty response was purposeful. Lore was worried about her and did not want to show it. A moment later, though, she did speak very earnestly.

"I talked to the ship's doctor about you this morning. He can see you right after lunch."

"Me, and all the rest of the seasick passengers. He must be bored with the sameness of it. Anyway, you treat me as if I were a child again, and I wish you wouldn't."

"I'm very well aware that you're not a

child. You're a woman who needs help. And I am a nurse, remember? I'm not entirely ignorant. You forget that."

"All right, I'll go."

"Good. He's a nice young man—French, but he speaks English or German, whichever you want."

He was a pleasant young man, who began by telling her that he understood she was going through a very hard time. "Your sister has explained it all."

She hoped he wasn't going to be too sympathetic. People meant well, but often they did not understand that sympathy can make a person cry.

"So we won't have to go into all that," he said.

"No, since the main cause is seasickness."

"I'll be blunt. Your sister thinks you may be pregnant."

"That's ridiculous, Doctor."

"Well, if it is . . . If you're sure it is completely impossible, there'll be no sense in going further."

Completely impossible . . . If you're a virgin, he meant.

She put her hand on her hot cheek, murmuring, "It's not impossible. But I don't think—"

"Let me ask a few questions."

Aware that he sensed her dismay, she was grateful. The ensuing dialogue, which was very short, proceeded in cut-off clauses whose meaning was, nevertheless, quite clear to both of them.

"—not always regular, so that I was not concerned—"

"—but nausea, generally in the morning, I believe?—"

"—true, but nerves, all the trouble, not sleeping much—"

"—might undo your blouse, if you don't mind—"

She minded terribly, but minded more that the wrong answer might send her into another fit of weeping. But to be pregnant! And she had asked Lore whether she felt as if she were watching the theater . . .

"I'm not a gynecologist," the young man said, carefully not looking at Caroline, "but by the appearance of your breasts, I think it's safe to conclude that you are well into the second month."

"My God," she whispered.

"You must have a proper examination when you get where you're going." Now he looked at her. "Above all, keep it a secret. You might have a lot of trouble at immigration if you don't. I believe they have something in the States called 'moral turpitude.'"

Her fingers fumbled at the buttons on her blouse. Her heart hammered. Yes, it was like a small hammer held by a frantic hand. She stood up, thanked the man, and stumbled out of the office. Then she went to her suitcase—in which, for some stupid reason, she had packed a little photo of Walter—walked to the deck, and threw it overboard.

She had expected a display of some sort from Lore; shock, or dismay, or wringing of hands, but there was none. Instead, she was calm and tried to console.

"I'm not going to ask you any questions. There's nothing to ask, anyway. It happened, and it has to be faced, that's all.

You're not the first, Caroline, nor will you be the last. We'll think of something. First, let's get our feet on land."

They spent half the night talking while the ship creaked and sped westward.

"I'm stunned, Lore. I hate him. How quickly love can turn to hatred!"

Lore put a hand over hers. "Listen to me. He was no good. Your parents were right. Not that I want to make you feel guilty, but they only went along with it for your sake. They didn't want to deny you any joy, but they had their doubts. And if you recall, so did I."

Caroline tried to imagine herself walking into the library at home and telling her parents, who would be reading in the chairs beside the big window, that she was pregnant with Walter's child. It was unimaginable. She cried softly.

"I loved him so, Lore."

"Of course you did. But you'll get through. Remember. You're not alone."

She looked into the good, homely face. "Thank God for you, Lore," she said.

LEGACY OF SILENCE

THEY were two days away from the Statue of Liberty when the news came. It was September 1, 1939. Germany had invaded Poland, and the Second World War had begun. If ever there had been a chance for Father and Mama, there was none now. If ever it had been possible for Caroline to speak of "the end of the past," it was not possible anymore. Her past was to stay with her for the next seven months, and for the rest of her life.

THREE

"**O**nly two of you?" With a shy smile, eyebrows raised in surprise and a large paper square marked "Jacob Sandler" pinned to his chest, he was there waiting when they emerged from Immigration.

Through several long formalities, the retrieval of the luggage, the clamor and shouts in the new language so hard to understand when too quickly spoken, panic had almost overpowered Caroline. What if there had been some misunderstanding and no one was there to meet them? Where would they go?

But here he was with his friendly, outstretched hand, saying friendly words. "You must be Caroline. And this is Lore. You see, I know all about you. Your father wrote everything. Is he—" He stopped, looking from one to the other; his smile died, for Caroline's eyes had filled.

"My English," Lore said quickly, "it's not fast. I try—"

"My parents—I hope they will come later. We don't know whether . . ."

"Well," Mr. Sandler said briskly, "let's load up the car. I've brought my friend Lew to help, and borrowed his delivery truck, too. For myself, I don't own a truck or a car. You don't need a car in New York. You walk, or you take the subway. I myself take the subway to work every day."

He was chattering, Caroline knew, to fill empty space. These facts, our coming here and the probable reasons for my parents' absence, are painful for him, too. Yet it seemed unnatural to ignore the facts. Wet eyes or not, she needed to express herself.

"I wish I knew some words that could thank you enough, Mr. Sandler."

"Jake," he interrupted. "And my wife is Annie. She's home making a good dinner for you. I hope you'll be hungry. You don't need to thank us again. Your father did it many times, wrote beautiful letters."

Lore, understanding much of all this, tried English again. "The ship was seasick. We don't eat much there."

"Is that so? Me, I never was on a boat, but my mother was. Came from the old country long before I was born. Must have come on a tub, the way she tells it. Not like this one."

Behind them the grand liner towered, with its flags and pennants stretched in the wind. The Old Country, Caroline thought. This ship was her last link with it. She stood for a moment, taking a final look, and then turned to watch the two men hoist the trunk and suitcases into the small truck. RIGHT AND READY DRY CLEANING it said on the side.

"Okay? All aboard!" They climbed in, the two women sitting in back with the luggage.

So they entered the stone alleys of the

city, a place unimagined in spite of all the photographs that had gone around the world. The sky-high towers were narrow as needles; it seemed miraculous that they did not fall. The sidewalks were clogged with people, pushing and rushing. They looked poor and sweaty in the heat. Then suddenly came wide avenues with glittering shops and fashionable people going in and out. Then came narrow streets again, this time with shady trees and baby carriages. Caroline and Lore were silent, gathering it all in.

Jake turned around. "Capital of the world. What do you think of it so far?"

"I don't know enough to think anything yet. It's bewildering," Caroline replied.

"Say, you have an English accent, don't you? How's that?"

"I had an English governess for many years." She felt self-conscious. This man would not be familiar with governesses. He might get the wrong idea about her. And yet she knew that being completely open was the only way.

He was equally open. "We're plain people. I only recognize the accent from the movies. I'll tell you, I never thought I'd live to see another war."

"It will be far away from you, I'm sure."

"Are you kidding? We'll be in it soon enough. Not me, I'm forty-five, but the young guys will."

Walter, she thought, and was stabbed. He deserves to die, she thought, and was stabbed again.

There was no help, no escape from her thoughts. From every angle, they pierced. And she leaned toward the window to concentrate on the scene instead, to fill her head.

The city went on and on. They went over a bridge, there were more bridges that seemed to connect with each other, there were bays and inlets with boats, and still it was New York.

"Enormous," Lore murmured, speaking German, "but I wouldn't want to stay here."

"Why? Do you like a smaller place better?" asked Jake. And seeing Lore's discomfiture, he explained. "I can understand some German. I grew up hearing Yiddish, and it's a relative, you know."

"I didn't mean—" began Lore.

"It's okay. You two have to decide where you want to go. This is a big country, and there are committees that can help you find a place in it. Don't worry."

For the first time, Lew spoke. "You ladies listen to Jake. He'll steer you right. He knows his way around."

Here they were in a car with these two strange men, driving through strange streets. It was like reading Kafka, or seeing a Dali landscape, where time was a warped clock seen in a dream. The streets rolled past; gas stations, groceries, shoe stores, and lines of identical houses repeated themselves without end. And suddenly they stopped.

"Home," Jake said. "This is it. And not too much later than I expected, either."

There was a row of stores, and above them curtained windows, some with flower-pots on the sills. Jake pointed upward.

"See the red geraniums there over the Right and Ready Dry Cleaners sign? That's our flat. Annie's crazy about flowers. Come on up. She's all excited about you."

They climbed the stairs, which were narrow, dark, and clean. Cooking smells from roasting meat and onions drifted down. No doubt that was Annie waiting at the top; in the dimness, Caroline saw a flowered apron and outspread arms.

"Oh, my God, you're here!" First Caroline, then Lore, were taken into a hot embrace. Annie was crying and laughing. "I don't believe it. Really you. How are you? I thought you would never get here. Where are the rest of you? The Hartzingers?"

"Not now, that's a long story. Later, Annie," Jake said. "Let them get in first and catch their breath."

Surely there was no precedent anywhere for a meeting like this one. You could fall on your knees and thank these rescuers. You could burst into tears or you could be stricken dumb. Caroline and Lore were, for the moment, stricken dumb.

"Go in, go in," Jake commanded. "You'll have to excuse Annie. She gets emotional." For Annie had started to cry. "Annie, don't burn the roast. I'll show them their room. Now there's the bathroom at the end of the hall. This here is for you, twin beds and a nice lamp between. I've put in a bright bulb in case you like to read in bed, though maybe you'll be too tired tonight. You want to change clothes? If you do, Lew and I'll bring your things right now, but I think Annie's got the food ready, so maybe—"

"We'll wash quickly. We won't keep her waiting."

"Great." Jake rubbed his hands. "Smells good. Annie's a great cook."

He left them standing in the middle of the room. Between the two beds and the large dresser, there was scarcely space to do more than stand. The summer evening beyond the window sent a weak shaft of light across the brown and tan interior, the tan walls and rug, the varnished brown furniture. Caroline walked to the window and saw the rear of a building similar to this one; a boy stared silently at her across a fire escape. Behind him hung a torn curtain. When she turned back to Lore, there was a weight of sadness in her chest.

"I could cry," she said.

"Does it seems as awful as all that to you?"

"No. Because of their goodness, I meant."

They went in to dinner. Four places had been set on a small table covered with a smooth white cloth. At the center were some red geraniums in a jelly jar.

"Jake and I, being alone now, usually eat in the kitchen," Annie explained. "This table that folds we keep for company. First I had it set for six, but I took the plates off just now when I saw—"

"Annie, please, I asked you—" began Jake.

Caroline stopped him. "It's all right. We have to face the truth. My parents haven't been able to get out. I don't know where they are."

"I'm sorry," Annie said. "Sorry about it and sorry that I brought up the subject. We know all about it. So many people in this neighborhood have relatives or friends over there. The world has gone crazy. And you are sisters? You don't look alike at all."

"Annie!" Jake protested with such desperation that Caroline had to smile.

"It's all right," Caroline said for the second time, and after giving them a brief family history, went on to tell them that Lore was a beginner in English, but that if they would speak Yiddish, she might understand some of it. "Speak slowly," she added.

The result was some fairly successful conversation over a hearty dinner. By the end of it, Lore and Caroline knew a good deal about the Sandlers. He was a house painter. She worked downtown in a basement housewares department. They had two sons, who had gone to California colleges on part scholarship and had decided afterward to stay there.

"Annie has five more years to get her twenty-five-year bonus, and then maybe we'll join them. Me, I can be a painter anyplace," Jake said. "Now let's talk about you folks. Seems to me the first thing you need to do is cable your friends in Switzerland and tell them you arrived safely. But that's in the morning. Right now you must be knocked out. Lew and I will bring your stuff upstairs here, you can unpack what you need and get to bed. Tomorrow we'll talk more."

So ended the first day.

LORE had made a list. "Number one," she announced, "we need a doctor for you. Number two, sell the rings. Then go to one of the aid committees Jake told about and get some advice about where to go. A small town will be cheaper."

"I won't get much tutoring work in a small town."

"In a couple of months, you won't get much work of any kind anywhere, Caroline."

"Then what are we going to do?"

"I'll get work. I can get a job without having a nursing license. I can take care of some old sick person at home. And we ought to get good money out of the rings. We'll sell only one of the four to start. Save the rest in case we hear from . . ." Lore did not finish.

In case Mama got her visa, she meant.

Instead, she said, "Here, read this. It's the doctor's address. Annie said we'll need a taxi."

"You told her about me?"

"I told her nothing except that you haven't been feeling right. She called the doctor before she went to work this morning."

Caroline looked around the little parlor, to which the Sandlers referred as the "front room." The table had been folded up, and for the last two days, ever since their first dinner, they had all been eating in the kitchen as "part of the family," Jake said. The meagerness of the parlor, with its maroon three-piece set of sofa and matching chairs, its tired-looking rug and ugly, bulky radio, saddened her now and she said so.

She touched her heart. "I feel so sad for them."

"Sad? Why should you?"

"Because they're so wonderful and kind, and it's not fair for them to be poor."

"Poor!" cried Lore. "You don't know what you're talking about. You haven't the slightest idea what poverty is."

She spoke so sharply that Caroline was taken aback. But then, she reminded herself, Lore is apt to do that sometimes, though only to me, never of course to Father and Mama.

"Being poor, Caroline, is having no job, no roof over your head, and nothing to eat."

Rebuked, she said nothing. Clearly, she still had a great deal more to learn about the world. And, heavy with all her anxieties, she rode in the taxi beside Lore, whose silence must have been as anxious as her own.

Suddenly, Lore spoke. "You look terrified. But it may all be a false alarm. That often happens. By the way, the doctor's a woman. That should make it easier for you."

Yes, it would. But she was certain that the alarm was real. Her morning nausea, though it was lessening, had not left her. It was with her now as the cab lurched through traffic and bucked to a final stop before a building as unhappy-looking as a courthouse or an unemployment office.

The doctor was gray-haired, plain, and shrewd. She saw at once that Caroline was trembling, and Caroline knew she had seen it.

"Sit down," she said easily. "I'm told you don't have any trouble with English. That's a big help for me. I don't know any languages, although my grandparents did come from Europe. You've just come from there, too, I understand."

Annie Sandler had reported everything. You couldn't blame people for having, along with charity, some curiosity, some sense of the great drama that was playing in Europe. They had no way of knowing what anguish it brought to keep describing it, again and again. And she hoped that this doctor would not ask a hundred questions.

The doctor said, "I read the papers and all the reports every day, so I have a fair idea of what you're going through. And I'm not going to bring up the subject, especially since there's nothing you can do about it right now, anyway. Tell me instead why you are here. Something about your nausea, is it?"

Caroline nodded. She saw the woman glance at her left hand. There was no sense in playing games. Come out with the truth. Get it over with.

"I think I might be pregnant," she said, and blurted then, "oh God, I hope not."

"Well, we'll simply have to have a look, won't we."

An inner door was partly open, revealing a cold whiteness: chrome, shining objects behind glass doors, sheets on a high, narrow table. The doctor, still observing Caroline, caught the glance; she caught everything.

"Have you ever had an examination?" she asked. "No? Well, don't be afraid of it. There's no pain. It's only a little bit uncomfortable. So we'll start with that."

And here it was. "Next spring, around the middle of March, you'll be a mother, Caroline."

A mother. On the way to the shops, you passed the maternity hospital. "It was a lovely summer morning," Mama said. "You came at eight o'clock, in time for breakfast. We took you home in a yellow dress and cap. Not pink. I wanted to be different. So many friends came to see you. The house was full of people and presents wrapped in tissue paper.''

A mother has a home and friends and time to care about the color of the baby clothes. A mother has a ring. She has the man who put it on her finger.

"Are you all right?" asked the doctor.

"I'll have to be." She wiped her eyes angrily, roughly, with the back of her hand. "I'm so ashamed. What a clumsy thing to do with one's life. I'm so ashamed."

The doctor, handing her a tissue, spoke mildly. "I know. In your milieu it's not supposed to happen. But it happens."

Your milieu. She sees my dress, Caroline thought, the proper, dark summer dress that one wears in the city. No doubt things are the same here as at home. People recognize each other's differences the way Jake recognized my accent.

"Your parents, if things go well for them, and I pray that they will, will not cast you away, my dear. It will be hard for you all, but it will work out. In the meantime, take very good care of yourself. If you move away from here, find a doctor and do what you're told. You're a beautiful young woman, and beauty always helps."

"So?" asked Lore when they were out on the sidewalk.

"So, you were right."

"I thought so."

Caroline lowered her head. In a few months' time, she would most likely not even be able to see her feet.

"I've made a mess of things," she said.

"Well, it happened, and there's no sense mourning over it."

On the return ride they were quiet again. A hot wind, bearing grit and smelling of chemicals, blew in at the windows. The streets were doleful. This was not the other New York of the photographs, the leafy avenues and grand vistas through which they had passed a few days ago.

"We need to think about money," Lore said. "That's number two on the list."

"I should think we have to see the refugee committee about where to go."

They couldn't possibly stay here. The poorest little town, a log cabin—did they still have log cabins in America?—with trees and grass and sky, would make it easier to bear whatever would have to be borne.

"First we need money. No matter what they say about it, we owe the Sandlers a little something. Then, no matter where we go, we'll need to pay rent. I wonder whether Jake has any idea how we can best sell the rings. I wouldn't be surprised if he has. He's a practical man."

"Practical like you, Lore. What would I do here without you? I'm a useless dependent, a fool, a burden even to myself." And there in the taxicab, Caroline broke into soundless weeping.

On a pillow, gathering all the room's meager light, lay the four rings. There was a sapphire, two diamonds—one of them glorious even to an amateur's eyes, the other less so—and a ruby. Lore caressed them one by one.

"Your mama said she had always loved rubies. She called them lovers' gems. Heart's blood, she said. I think it hurt your father that he couldn't let her keep this."

When Lore put it on her own finger, it went only as far as the knuckle. "My hands are too big. You try it. Hold your hand up, so I can see."

It meant nothing to Caroline. A sparkle, that was all. It was hard to believe that this small object could be worth more than a decent house.

"Which do you like better, Caroline, this or the round diamond? It's almost flawless, worth a fortune."

"To tell you the truth, I can easily do without either. I can name a few things I need much more. Things like a peaceful mind."

Lore put the rings away and sighed. "Well, some lucky women are going to be wearing them. I asked Jake for advice about selling them. He's got a friend who'll come over this week and price them for us. He works for one of the best jewelry stores in the city. Then we'll know enough not to be cheated."

"I'll leave it to you, Lore. It's not that I'm lazy. I just can't seem to think. My brain's sick." She flung herself down on the bed. "Oh, Lore, I don't want this baby. I don't want any baby now, but especially not this one. What shall I do with it? Will I hate it? I'm afraid I will, because I hate it now. I hate the way it was—was made."

The little grove. Crickets and stars and sweet grass. Made for lovers, he said, lying to me, using me.

"With each minute that goes by, my hatred grows. Do you understand? I shall never, never trust a man again as long as I live."

"No, no, you don't mean that. Think about your father. And Dr. Schmidt. And Jake Sandler. You can tell by looking at Annie what a good man Jake is."

Caroline gave a bitter laugh. "What are you trying to do, persuade me to find a husband?"

"You're laughing. Actually, that's what Annie said you need."

"What? You've told Annie?" She sprang up off the bed, screaming at Lore. "You had no right! This trouble is my business, not Annie's or anybody's. You had no right to shame me so—" Anger cut off her words.

"Now look here," Lore said calmly. "It's

also my business. Don't forget that. Can you imagine yourself here alone? Your parents wanted me to be a protection for you, and they didn't even know the half of it, did they? We're going to need a lot of help before we're through, Caroline. Let's not be so independent. This is a big country, and we're lost in it the minute we step out of this front door."

Chastened, Caroline said only, "It's that —what can she think of me?"

"That you're in trouble. That's all she thinks. You've seen for yourself what kind of people these are."

"I don't believe there's anything more they can do for us than they are already doing."

"We don't know that yet. Now go fix your eyes, if you can, so they won't see you've been crying. Act natural. Nobody's going to say a word. I'm going in to make the dinner. After a woman works all day, it's nice not to have to make dinner. That's the least I can do."

"That's what you said in Switzerland."

"Well, it's the truth. Also, I'm going to ask

Jake how soon his jeweler friend can come over."

The next evening, after the table was cleared, the rings were brought out and displayed there on a napkin.

Annie was awestruck. "Can you imagine wearing a diamond like this? I've never seen anything like it that wasn't fake."

"If you'll be satisfied with a fake, I'll buy you one tomorrow," Jake said. He liked to give his wife a little teasing. "Who'd know the difference except my friend Vinnie here?"

"Who?" said Vinnie, who was squinting into the loupe. "Plenty of people. On Fifth Avenue they know the difference."

To Caroline, Lore whispered anxiously, "What is he saying? I can't understand him."

"Nothing yet. I'll tell you when he does."

Caroline's thoughts, unlike Lore's, were not wholly involved with the rings. There had been no response to their cabled message to the Schmidts, which meant that there was no news of Mama and Father. This chilled her body from head to feet. A moment later, as she remembered that the Sandlers now knew all about her, she felt waves of heat. Standing there so close within their view, she might just as well be naked before them.

"Stop biting your lips," Lore whispered.

Vinnie removed the loupe. "What did you pay for these, if I may ask?"

Lore handed him a slip of paper. "I have it here. Mrs. Hartzinger wrote it all out."

Mama's handwriting was said to be distinctive. "Artistic," people remarked of its flourishes and shadings. It occurred to Caroline that she possessed no sample of this writing. The books with their loving inscriptions had been left behind, and there were no letters. Perhaps there would never be any letters. . . . But she must take hold of herself. It was wrong even to have such a thought, let alone to dwell on it. Father and Mama would survive. A combination of his hopeful courage and her caution would see them safely through anything. It could. It would.

Vinnie examined the figures. "What is this, marks or dollars?"

"Marks," Lore told him. "Where would they get dollars?"

Vinnie frowned. "To tell the truth, it doesn't make any difference. You've paid top prices, ladies, for nothing."

"You mean that Mama paid too much?"

"I mean that your mother was robbed. The diamonds aren't worth a lot more than top-quality costume jewelry. The only thing that has any real value is the ruby, although it's not first class, by any means."

"It's not possible," Caroline murmured. "Not possible for people to be so cruel."

The others just stood there stunned, and Lore, reading their expressions and needing no further explanation, put her face in her hands.

"Oh, it's possible," Vinnie answered. "You of all people should know by now about cruelty. They lied and stole, whoever they were. When people are desperate—" He shook his head. "It stinks. They knew what she needed it for."

Jake ventured a suggestion. "Don't misunderstand, but shouldn't they maybe get a second opinion? Not that I doubt—"

"No offense taken, Jake. And it would be a good idea to get an appraisal on the ruby. That at least is genuine. I'll give them the name of a guy in the market who's pretty straight. He's a friend of mine. Not that he'll do you any favors. Business is business."

The future loomed near and dark and complicated. Lore and Caroline were given a list of instructions in duplicate: how to telephone Annie at work or at home, how to take the subway, and how to reach the jewelers' street. It was like setting out into a desert or a jungle.

The sun blazed. Never had they felt such wet, suffocating, airless heat. Everyone hurried. Never had they seen so many people crowded on the sidewalks, jostling each other, pouring across the streets the moment the light changed, and sometimes before, so that brakes shrieked inches away and barely in time.

"A madhouse," said Lore.

On the first day, they went to six places, where Vinnie's report was each time confirmed. The ruby was really not bad, not bad at all, but flawed. Of course, it was a rare treasure that did not have some flaws; everyone knew that. But this one, where you had an expert eye—and so on, and so on.

"The best offer came from Vinnie's friend," Caroline told the Sandlers, concealing her discouragement as Father would do. "He offered four hundred dollars more than the others. I think he did it because Vinnie told him our story, and he felt sorry for us," she finished, wondering whether "our story" included her own very personal part of it.

"So what's the total?" asked Jake.

"Twelve hundred."

The ring lay on the table among the coffee cups. It means very little to me, Caroline thought again. But Mama had called it *heart's blood, a lover's gem.* And slipping it onto her finger, she held her hand up toward the light.

"They all said this one was not bad. If they admitted that much, then it must be pretty good, but I don't really know."

Jake smiled. "You know plenty. There's a shrewd brain in that little head of yours. Personally, I think you should keep it.

Someday we'll be out of this depression and values will rise again."

"Lore can tell you I never cared about jewelry."

"What can I tell?" asked Lore.

"That I'm not interested in jewelry."

She didn't care much about anything anymore. Every morning now she woke up with an immediate, vague sense of dread, of something hovering and fearful; it took only two seconds to recognize reality.

"All the more reason why you should sell it. We need the money," Lore said.

"Better to keep something back for a rainy day," Jake argued. "Then if a rainy day never comes, please God you'll have it."

"He's right," agreed Annie. "Don't rush into things. Especially now." She stroked Caroline's bent head. "It looks so beautiful on your hand. Hide it away. Keep it. That's my advice."

The glare from the overhead bulb, the bickering voices, and the stifling heat in the apartment were exhausting. No fortune-teller, no prophet of doom, Caroline thought, could have predicted anything more bizarre than this scene tonight. How long ago it seemed that she had slept in the white bed overlooking the rose garden with Peter lying on her feet! How long ago the Swiss lake, the last embrace and kiss and promise!

"Look," Annie said, "she's worn out. Go to bed, Caroline. It's been too long a day for you."

She got up and said good night. Already she was being treated like a pregnant woman who needs to be considered.

IT was still early enough in the morning for Lore to have the lamp lit while she wrote. For a few minutes, Caroline watched her, as, half crouched on her bed, she raced her pen across the notebook.

Father had said, "Lore, that autobiography is going to be a classic someday. When are you going to give us a look at it?"

"When I'm dead," was the answer. "Or maybe I'll burn it up before I die so you'll never see it."

120

Whereupon Father would tell her that she was "a funny female, but we all love you, anyway."

"Lore, how did it all end after I went to bed?" Caroline asked now.

"We're to buy a strong chain and you'll wear the ruby around your neck under your clothes until, when we're settled, we can put it away in a bank."

"Are you angry about keeping it?"

"No, they may be right. But listen, Caroline, this is our second week here. We're bound to be a nuisance to these strangers. If we aren't already, we soon will be. So right after seeing the jeweler today, we're seeing the refugee committee. Jake gave me the address. They'll be glad to settle us somewhere, especially since we'll have a little money of our own."

The city was still hot, it was still crowded, and the waiting room at the refugee committee was more crowded than the streets outside. It was, nevertheless, very quiet. And Caroline felt the tension. All these people had retreated into themselves with their anxieties. They were a varied group: Americans, some obviously well-to-do, inquiring, probably, about relatives; foreigners from every European country inquiring about families left behind.

Were there any who had her problem? That serious girl about her own age, sitting there with her relatives? Certainly not that young woman, far into pregnancy, sitting there with her husband? He had his arm around her shoulder. Caroline tried not to stare at that arm.

"Lore, don't tell them about me, will you?"

"No, why would I?"

"You told Annie."

"That was different. Annie's like a friend."

Friend or not, the disgrace was the same. *Moral turpitude,* that doctor, that one on the ship, had said. Disgrace.

After a long wait, they were called into an office, a cubicle with a desk and a tired woman behind a partially obscured sign that read: Hilda ——.

"Do you speak English?" she inquired.

"I do," Caroline replied. "Lore knows a little. I'm teaching her." It seemed strange to be sounding so authoritative, when she was actually so dependent upon Lore.

"We'll speak German," said Hilda.

She was efficient and compassionate, which was quite wonderful, thought Caroline, when you considered how many times she must have listened to the same sad story.

As the first half hour moved on to the second half, a plan took shape; an entirely new life emerged out of nowhere and settled onto a geographical dot. The dot was a Great Lakes town with the attractive name of "Ivy," the small center of a stretch of farming country. A few immigrant families had settled there and established a community shortly after Hitler took power.

The smart ones, Caroline thought ruefully, and then reminded herself of Mama's visa. Another thought came.

"My father isn't Jewish," she said.

"That doesn't matter. We're not concerned with how anyone wants to worship God, or whether he wants to at all. Where are your parents now?"

The question was a shock. It was Lore who replied quickly, "We don't know."

"Oh." The tone was very gentle. "I asked because there is a sizable hospital in the county seat, about half an hour's drive away. I was thinking of some possible opportunity for a doctor. And for a nurse, too," she added.

Caroline, still unsure, had a question before they left. "Do you think our money will see us through? We don't know what money is worth here, and we'd really like to be independent."

"Well, as everywhere, some people would say it's a substantial sum, and others would think it's small. So it depends on your wants and your needs. I would say in your case that you should live very frugally and spend as little of it as possible. Try to live on what you can earn. You're both young and healthy. Between the two of you, you should do all right."

Two, Caroline thought as they left. No, not two. There are three of us.

They were to wait two weeks before their departure. The little community was preparing an apartment for them, and it had not yet been vacated by the previous tenants.

"Well, we're glad about the delay," Annie told Caroline.

They were alone on a Saturday morning. Lore had gone out to buy a pair of shoes, and Jake had gone to the synagogue.

"You've given us so much, Annie. We can never repay you or thank you enough."

"It's far, far from one-sided. You've given us an experience we'll never forget. We've learned so much." Annie studied the red geraniums, which were bending under a downpour. Then she said slowly, "Maybe I shouldn't bring up the subject, or again, maybe I should. I know you're ashamed that I know about what's happened to you. But you shouldn't be. Jake and I have talked about it—no, please, you shouldn't be upset that Jake knows. He's a good, religious man, he doesn't condemn people and especially, for heaven's sake, especially a girl who's been raped."

The lie, although it was not hers, made Caroline feel unclean. Lore should not have told it, but she said nothing.

"Raped by a Nazi. My blood boils to think of it. I've been thinking about it all week."

When she still said nothing, Annie continued. "I was wondering whether you'd like to come with us tomorrow to Jake's aunt's house. You and Lore haven't been anywhere at all. We're invited to have dinner there, and you're invited, too. Aunt Tessie would love to meet you."

Caroline would have preferred to eat a sandwich, read a magazine, and go to bed early. Although she understood that her tiredness was mostly psychological, it was also real. But it was clear that Annie wanted her to accept, and so she did.

Later that day, she scolded Lore. "Why ever did you make up a story like that?"

"Because it arouses sympathy."

"Pity is what you mean, and I don't want to be pitied."

"Life is very, very hard and cold, Caroline. You don't even understand that much yet? We're going to have a struggle. We're going to need all the sympathy we can get. We're two women and a baby in a new world, without a man to defend us."

Neither slept more than a few restless hours that night. In the humid air, the sheets were damp; shrill voices carried from the building in the rear; desperate thoughts sped through a maze.

"Dress nicely," Lore said in the morning. "It's too bad you got grass stains on the pink linen."

"I wouldn't have worn that anyway. It's not a dinner dress."

"To these people it is. Besides, we're not going for what you and I call dinner. It's at one o'clock, lunchtime. What about this black and white print? It's quiet enough, and still very pretty."

Here was Lore turning the clock back again, treating her like a child. Why on earth should she look "quiet enough"? But it wasn't important, and Caroline wasn't going to argue about it, so she put on the dress and was ready on time.

They were to walk the short distance. Jake, walking alongside Caroline, described the points of interest along the way.

"There's the ballpark where I pitched. My high school is just down the street, that redbrick building at the end. I've lived in this neighborhood all my life. We've got everything here. I seldom need to cross the river. Most of my relatives still live around here. You'll meet a few at my aunt's. She's a character. Know what I mean? Speaks out whatever's on her mind. Some people don't understand her. But her heart's gold. She'll do anything to help somebody. That's the way she is."

Except for the red geraniums, the building was a replica of the Sandlers'. They climbed the narrow stairs and entered a front room, just like the Sandlers'. The radio had been moved to accommodate a large table set for ten people.

Caroline counted. From the way they had spoken, she had expected a fair-sized gathering. But in addition to the newcomers, there were only six more: the widowed, elderly Aunt Tessie, two married couples, also old, and a young man who looked uncomfortable. Introductions were made. The couples were cousins. The young man, Joel Hirsch, was a distant relative of Aunt Tessie's late husband. In stiff European fashion, he bowed.

"Joel's a newcomer here like you, Caroline. Arrived two months ago. Do you understand what I'm saying, Joel?"

"A little. I learn, Uncle Jake."

Almost immediately, they sat down to dinner. The women waited on the men, as well as on Lore and Caroline, bringing a succession of bowls, platters, and pitchers of hot coffee, iced coffee, and iced tea. The food was appetizing, although there was too much of it.

The poor old woman must have labored for the last two days to prepare such a feast, thought Caroline, and was for some reason made uneasy by the thought.

Jake opened the conversation. "What about it? Can Aunt Tessie cook, or can't she?"

"Everything is delicious," Caroline said.

One of the cousins remarked that Caroline's English was perfect and asked about Lore. "But your sister doesn't speak it at all?"

"A little. I am teaching her."

"She's a good teacher," Lore said, smiling.

Caroline was thinking: They have been discussing us. How else would this woman know that Lore is my sister? Nobody, on seeing us together, would assume that we were sisters.

"I wish we could find a good teacher for Joel," Aunt Tessie remarked. "He's so smart and ambitious. Once he learns the language, he'll get somewhere."

Automatically, everyone looked toward Joel, who now seemed more uncomfortable than ever. He had very fair skin, so that, in contrast, his blush looked raw. Although he was not fat, his cheeks were puffy, and he kept blinking as though his eyes hurt. His thick sandy hair was curly; having tried unsuccessfully to slick it down with water, he kept pushing it back. He was—what was the word?—pathetic, like a lost, bewildered dog.

Her mind jumped erratically from "dog" to Peter, then to the garden, the house, and her parents . . .

Where were they, now that the war had

sealed them off from the world? Where was her brave resolve to "think positively"? What was she doing here in this place?

When she brought herself back to the moment, they were talking about Joel. There was an expression of horror on Lore's face. Aunt Tessie was speaking.

"Yes, even before the invasion, the right-wing fanatics were running wild in Poland. They stood a whole line of Jews in the village square and shot them."

"You should ask Joel whether he minds your talking about it," Jake said.

"He doesn't mind. He wants people to know the truth. He saw them kill his parents before he escaped."

One of the cousins expressed an opinion. "There'll be millions more killed before Hitler is through. Jews, Catholics, Englishmen—every kind."

"We'll be in it, too, before it's over," said another.

"Do you really think so?"

The conversation was now leaping back and forth across the table, skipping only Joel, who was silent, and Caroline. No one as yet had asked about her family. It was because they already knew; she was more than ever sure of it. First Lore, and after that Annie, had covered the whole subject of Caroline, including the rape. She wondered whether they had perhaps even mentioned Walter's name, not that it mattered. He was on the other side now, the side of the killers; he had begun by killing Caroline. And feeling that her eyes might fill, she blew her nose.

"You three, Joel and Lore and Caroline, have a lot in common," said one of the women, meaning to encourage. "Europe is behind you, Europe and sorrow. Now surely you have some good things ahead."

These kind words, at that moment, went flat. Yet Tessie pursued the subject.

"Why don't you people get acquainted? Go on out, walk in the park, practice your English. Or speak German, if you want to make it easier."

"Not I. Let the others go," Lore said promptly. "No walking for me today. I have new shoes on, and they hurt my feet."

"Then Joel and Caroline do it. Go ahead,

Joel. Buy Caroline a real American ice cream soda."

This was absurd. They wanted to throw her together with that poor young man, who was probably as unwilling as she was. And surely there was no point in starting a social life when she was going to depart in two weeks. She was about to make a polite excuse, when he stood up.

"That would be nice," he said.

This time it was her cheeks that flushed. She was being forced to do something against her will. Lore could certainly come along and make things easier. Her feet don't hurt any more than mine do, she thought.

Joel walked ahead down the stairs, as a man should. At the bottom, he opened the door to let her go ahead of him. At least he had good manners. This judging of him was snobbish, she knew it was, and was sorry about it. But she was just so angry!

They went along the street together. Speaking in German, he asked her whether she would like some ice cream. Actually, she did not, but to sit and pass the time eating was better than this aimless walk, so she told him that she would.

He led her through several turns and corners to an ice cream parlor with a marble-topped counter and small, intimate tables. The wiry little chairs were like the ones she had seen long ago in Paris parks.

By way of conversation she asked him how he knew his way around so well. He told her that he had spent almost every day since his arrival exploring the city. He had gone to the top of the Empire State Building, had visited the Statue of Liberty and the Metropolitan Museum of Art.

"I always wanted to see a museum," he said. "I come from a small city where we don't have such things, statues and cups and coffins a thousand years old. No, two thousand, I think, from ancient Greece. Am I right?"

"Yes, from ancient Greece and Egypt." His naivete was touching.

"Good. I thought so, but I wasn't sure. You must have great museums in Berlin. I suppose you go there often."

"I used to. But things have changed—for us, I mean."

"Yes, I know. It is terrible everywhere for us."

They stopped speaking. Both laid down their spoons and sat still, staring into the vacant air. Then suddenly Joel broke the silence.

"In a way, it is easier for me than for you. When people are dead, you don't have to worry any longer about what may be happening to them."

As always, it was compassion that weakened her. She looked at him with wet eyes.

"I'm sorry," he said. "Perhaps it's better if we don't speak about it at all. Just pray. I go to daily prayers, and it helps me. What about you?"

"I shall probably shock you, but I don't go."

"You don't believe? You don't pray?"

An innocent question, she thought. He has an innocent, good face, perhaps a bit stupid, and then again, perhaps not.

"I believe in nature," she answered quietly. And since he looked blank, she went on, "In the beauty of the world, I mean, with everything related to everything else, the trees, and us, too, all living things, all related."

"That's not enough for me," he said, "but each of us must do what's best for himself."

She liked him for saying that. And she went on as if compelled for her own benefit to express herself.

"I mean something like the American Indians that I read about. 'My mother, the earth, my father, the sky,' they say. I can understand that. The sky, the unknown, that's where God is. I need only to look up."

"I don't know anything about Indians, but then I have never read very much."

He puzzled her. What a narrow life! And yet he had gone to a museum and been awed by what he saw.

"But you learned German. How is that?"

He shrugged. "We lived near the border. You hear it every day, so you pick it up. And you? How is it that you know English? And French, too, I hear."

I hear. Again she felt as if her privacy had

been invaded. And her anger returned. Heaven only knew whether they had told him, too, what they knew about her.

Still, it wouldn't be his fault if they had. She explained simply, "At school we had to study languages." There would be no sense telling about the governess. He would not know what she was talking about.

"You've had a very different life from mine. Your father was a doctor, an educated man. My father had a bakery. A large bakery," he said with some pride. "We had six bakers working for us. In one morning we could bake enough bread for half the city. Well, not quite half, but it was a good business, anyway. And I was learning to run it, keeping the accounts and all that, so my father wouldn't have to work so hard. And now—" He threw up his hands.

Gloom came down again over the table. The ice cream had melted on the plates. Neither of them had really wanted it.

"Shall we walk back?" she suggested.

"I suppose they will be expecting us."

He took out an old-fashioned coin purse,

counted money, paid, and counted the change as Caroline watched him.

"You already understand American money," she said. "You're not confused?"

"No, I told you, I'm a man of business."

He phrased the words importantly: "A man of business." He could not be more than twenty-two or twenty-three, she estimated, and yet, in spite of his youthful body, in spite of both his innocence and his ignorance, there was an air of lonely old age about him. She glanced at him sideways as they walked and he kept talking, being sociable, with an account of the view from the top of the Statue of Liberty.

And with a sudden insight, she saw that he could not possibly be as innocent as he seemed. Once you had watched your parents and all your people being gunned to death, you could no longer be innocent.

Before they started up the stairs, Joel stopped at the foot to ask a timid question. "I was wondering whether you would help me with English. I bought a grammar book, but it's not enough by itself. Aunt Tessie tried to help me, but she's not a very good teacher. Am I asking too much? If I am, please say so."

It was unthinkable to refuse, especially since she was already helping Lore every day. "I'll be glad to," she said. "But we're only here two more weeks, you remember."

"That's all right. I can learn a lot in two weeks."

That night, Caroline scolded Lore. "You knew he was going to be there today, don't deny it, Lore."

"I do deny it. But what's so terrible? I don't know what you're fussing about."

"I'm fussing because it's not a nice feeling to know that strangers have been discussing all your affairs. I suppose even he has heard that I'm pregnant," she said bitterly.

In her agitation, she walked back and forth through the sliver of space between the two beds.

"Annie's a bighearted woman, God knows, but she has a big mouth, too. You should especially never have told her that lie."

"We've been over that. I've explained

why I did it. And I still think it made sense in our circumstances to do it," Lore said seriously. "But I apologize again if I've hurt you."

Her nostrils quivered, signaling distress, and Caroline at once felt contrite. For who now cared more about her than Lore did?

"I'm sorry," she said. "I know you meant well; you always do. It's just that half the time I'm not thinking straight. For a few minutes I can think of something else, something in the newspaper, for instance, and forget where I am or what I am, and then all at once it flashes back and I know who I am." Panic, like a huge cold hand, clutched her chest. She wanted to cry out, *Oh, Lore, what am I going to do?* but did not.

"He's coming tomorrow for our English lesson," she said.

JOEL arrived every afternoon all that week. He and Lore were both desperate to learn the language.

"I cannot understand a person who lives

here all his life without learning the language," he said.

And Lore explained how quickly she must qualify for the nursing license.

"Well, I don't have a profession," Joel said, "unless you can call business a profession. But I also have a trade. I'm a baker. Nobody ever taught me, but I grew up in the business, and I watched everything. I can make you any kind of bread you want: rolls, twists, wheat, rye, anything. Until I can speak the language really well, that's probably what I'll have to do. To earn my bread," he finished and smiled, pleased with his own wit.

"A nice young man," Lore observed when he had gone. "He has strong nerves. To have seen what he's seen, the whole community put to death and not a friend left, and still be sane! Still be able to think of the future. That's quite something, don't you think so?"

Caroline agreed that it was indeed "quite something."

One evening Annie invited Joel to stay to dinner. As on the night of Caroline and

Lore's arrival, she set the table in the front room, spread a white cloth, and put geraniums in the jelly jar at the center.

She was creating a festive atmosphere. It's for Joel's benefit, thought Caroline, and felt again the uneasiness that had moved her on that Sunday in Tessie's house.

Jake, as he came in, remarked that one could smell Annie's fancy apple pudding in the outer hall. "Fragrant," he said. "The neighbors will know that we're having a banquet."

"Hardly a banquet," responded Annie, "just a family dinner." She looked around the table. "Yes, in this short time, you feel like family to us. I've told you how we're going to miss you girls. And you, too, Joel."

Lore inquired where he was going.

"I don't know, but somewhere. I can't stay with my second cousin's widow much longer. I wouldn't want to even if she wanted me to, which I know she can't. She's done more than enough by signing for me and taking me in."

"Wherever you go," Jake said, "you'll do fine, Joel. Tessie feels she's gotten to know you pretty well, and Tessie's a sharp old lady. You have to get up early in the morning to fool Tessie. In her book you rate A number one."

This praise, given in a mixture of English and Yiddish-German, was, although probably just half understood, still sufficient to bring another flush, this time of pleasure, to Joel's cheeks. It seemed to Caroline that he had changed. In these few days, he had become more sure of himself.

He leaped now into the conversation, addressing her and Lore. "You two are lucky to have each other. To be alone in the world, to have nobody, is a terrible thing. It's a sickness." He said this not as if he were asking for sympathy, but making a declaration with which anyone must agree.

"Joel, tell me," Jake asked, "what are your thoughts about the war? Do you think Hitler can win?"

Joel shrugged. "I come from a little place, and I don't know much. Yes, I think he could win, but he can also be beaten if the whole world will go after him."

Jake assenting, the two men took over

the conversation and kept it up between them until finally Annie made a suggestion.

"Why don't you people take in a movie? There's a good one playing over on the avenue."

"I'm too sleepy," Caroline said quickly.

"There's a catch for some smart young girl," Jake said when Joel left. "Yes, yes, the girl who gets him will be in luck, mark my words."

Annie nodded. "No doubt about it."

Lore said nothing. And Caroline had some thoughts that, during the past hour, had taken a definite shape: These people were trying to push Joel Hirsch and Caroline together. But for what purpose? It was ridiculous.

In their room later, she confronted Lore. "Do you realize what they're doing? Why did she invite him to dinner tonight? And those remarks about the 'smart girl who catches him.' Do they really think I would want Joel? That's the craziest notion I have ever heard. It makes me furious."

"They mean well. And perhaps it's not as crazy as all that."

"What, Lore? You're really saying that to me, or didn't I hear you right?"

"I'm not saying anything." Lore laughed. "Don't get excited. He hasn't declared his love, has he? Wait till he gets down on his knees to you and pleads for your hand."

"Ha ha. Funny. Very funny."

As usual now, she slept badly. Toward morning, she became aware that Lore was tossing in the other bed.

"Is anything wrong?" she whispered.

"My teeth. My rotten teeth again. I think I have an abscess."

"Can I get you anything?"

"No. As soon as they're up, I'll ask for the name of their dentist."

"I'll get dressed quickly and take you there."

Later Jake said, "I've got a job to do right near the dentist's place. You can ride with me, Lore, and I'll talk to him for you."

The front room, where Caroline sat alone, faced west and was dark in the morning. She drank a cup of coffee and listened to a news reporter on the radio. There was nothing unusual: The French, behind the Maginot Line, were still doing nothing, and the Germans, because they were doing nothing, must surely be plotting something dreadful. Therefore, the news was still ominous.

Where were her parents? And where was Walter, the stranger in his uniform under the swastika flag? Shutting off the radio, she sat with the unread newspaper on her lap.

The doorbell startled her. "Who is it?" she called.

"It's Joel."

"But your lesson's this afternoon," she began as she opened the door. "And Lore—"

"I know. Lore's gone to the dentist. Tessie told me."

Did these people run an information service? If she wanted to be sarcastic, she might ask him whether he knew what kind of cereal she had just had for breakfast.

"Do sit down," she said, for he was standing in the center of the room, holding his hat. And she thought again that he really did have manners.

When he sat down, he still held the hat,

twirling it on his knees. He seemed about to say something, hesitated, and said, "I hope Lore will be all right."

"She always has trouble with her teeth."

He nodded knowingly, said, "Ah," in sympathy, and then nothing more.

She wished he had not come. This was not the time for an English lesson, and as it seemed apparent that he had no other business, he ought to leave. The awkward silence was exasperating, and she broke it.

"It's because of the war, the last one, I mean. They had no nourishment for their bones."

"Ah," he murmured again, and blinked hard.

He needs glasses, she thought.

"It was a fine thing for her when your parents took her in, a poor, twelve-year-old orphan. A very fine thing."

"You seem to know all about us," Caroline said, trying to conceal annoyance.

Apparently she had succeeded, or else he did not care either way, because he answered plainly, "Yes, they told Tessie, and Tessie told me."

BELVA PLAIN

For a few moments she said nothing, but sat there feeling her resentment grow along with her awareness of his gaze. It went from her feet to the hand that lay on the arm of the chair, to the narrow gold chain around her neck, and stopped at her face.

"Well," she said abruptly, "shall we begin the lesson? It's the third chapter, past tenses."

"I have to tell you I didn't come for the afternoon lesson. I came this morning because I knew you were alone, and I wanted to talk to you."

"Yes? What about?"

"I'll get to that. First—well, you just said I seem to know all about you, but—please excuse me—you see, I really do. I know about your trouble. Such a terrible thing. This Nazi, this animal, even to touch you . . . a terrible thing."

"Who told you? Who dared?" she demanded.

"The Sandlers told Tessie. Don't be angry. They only want to help you."

As so often now, Caroline had the sense that this was all theater. And she did not

148

know what answer to give, although he was evidently waiting for one.

"I was thinking," he said, "that your child should have a name." His brilliant flush covered his face up to the uneven fringe of his curls. "A name and a decent man's protection. So I am willing to marry you."

She was stunned. *Willing to marry you.* What? Doing me a favor? She could have cried with the shame of it. She could have thrown something at him or shown him the door.

But he was sitting there almost humbly, still twirling the hat, with a look of gentle concern in his blinking eyes. The man was an imbecile.

"Well," she replied, "this is rather unusual, wouldn't you say?" The words came snapping out of her mouth. "People usually know each other a bit longer than ten days, and there is usually some talk of love, I think. Don't you think so, too?"

He considered the words as if they had been spoken in full sincerity. "This is not a usual situation, though," he said earnestly. "It would be wonderful if it were; if, for instance, I could say, 'I am in love with you.' If I say it now, you will say, as you just have, that people don't fall in love so fast, and you'll be right. Or perhaps you won't be right. If I say that you're so beautiful that I— but you surely know that already. So what is there left for me to tell you? Only that you have a need, and I have a need, too. I want to have somebody to belong to." His flush had receded, but he was sweating, overcome with emotion. "It would not have to be marriage in the usual sense," he said delicately, "only familial, a companionship. I think it would work out very well."

The door opened, and Lore, having been given a key, came in. Her cheek was painfully swollen.

"So you're here, Joel. Have you started the lesson?"

He stood up. "Not today. I have to leave. I hope you'll feel better, Lore." At the door he turned back toward Caroline, saying, "Please think it over," and went out.

She stared after him. "Can you imagine?" she cried to Lore. "He's asked me to marry him. He must be out of his mind. If he isn't out of his mind, he has more gall than any man alive. Who and what does he think I am?"

"I wouldn't take it as an insult," Lore said.

From the window, Caroline watched him go down the street. He was not much taller than she. He looks bulky, she thought with distaste. Then abruptly, amusement followed. It was really silly of her to be angry because the thing was—it was ludicrous! *Someone to belong to.* And he actually thinks that I, that I—

"Is that what he wants you to think over?" asked Lore.

"Yes, of course. But what's more important is you. Was it an abscess?"

"Two of them. He had to extract both teeth. Too far gone. I'll have to go back again tomorrow. Then I'll need crowns. He promised to have them ready in time for us to leave." Lore sighed. "And I have other teeth in terrible shape. My whole mouth is wrecked. Money. Nothing but money. You see how far it doesn't go? Already there'll a nice hole in our great wealth." She sighed again. "I'll go get some ice and a towel."

"I'll do it. Sit down."

When she came back, Lore said anxiously, "Tell me everything he said."

"It's too fantastic, too stupid."

"No, tell me."

So she told. And at the end Lore made a comment. "It's fantastic, all right, but I wouldn't say it's stupid of him."

"What? You can't be serious. You can't think I would—"

"No, no, I'm not saying anything about you. I'm talking about him. He's not a fool. His idea is not so far-fetched. These marriages of convenience are being made all the time—"

Caroline interrupted her. "Lore, I don't believe you. Is that what you want for me? Is it?"

"You aren't listening to me. Did I say I wanted it for you? I only said that they happen. Why, Annie was just telling me about a young woman, a doctor, who was in this country on a visitor's visa last year when Austria was invaded. She would have been killed if she had gone home, so she married a doctor here and was able to stay."

"That doesn't apply to me. I'm not here on a visitor's visa."

"Good Lord, I know that, Caroline. I'm only talking. Forget it."

She would have liked to forget it, and had intended to, when in the evening after Lore had gone to bed with her aching jaw, the Sandlers brought up the subject.

"I hear Joel came today," Annie said.

"Yes, for a few minutes."

And Caroline waited for what was bound to come next, for surely Joel had gone back and reported to Tessie. Some men were like that; Father called them "old women."

In the evening, the Sandlers' routine often went this way: Jake, who stood on his feet all day, might go to bed early, while Annie would have another cup of coffee and a cigarette at the kitchen table. Now, with a cup in one hand, she exhaled a thin stream of smoke and said hesitantly, "I always believe in being open. What is the use of hiding things? He likes you. In fact, he's in awe of you, Caroline. Let's admit, you're a beautiful young woman."

"Thank you, but I don't feel beautiful."

"Of course. You're worried to death, and with good reason."

"You said you believe in being open. He made a proposal that shocked me. Marriage! You'd think, the way he put it, that it was like buying something you see in a shop."

"And you don't like Joel."

"Annie, I don't even know him."

"Stay with us here a few more weeks and get to know him better."

"It's so wonderful of you to have us here as long as this. Now we have to get out on our own. Anyway, Annie, I don't want to know him better."

"There are plenty of girls who would be happy to give him a chance. He's a really decent young man."

"I believe you, but I'm not interested in men. Not at all."

It was true. Why should she trust any man again?

"Let's drop the subject for now," Annie

said gently. "You're very tired, and I am, too. And it's ten o'clock."

Caroline was wrought up. For too long had her worries been milling around in her head, and now this pointless conversation with Annie Sandler, the generous, well-meaning, meddlesome stranger, had aggravated them beyond endurance. She lay down with another long night of troubled sleep before her.

Now, in late September, the heat still held on to the city and filled the stuffy room. Lore, not wanting to trouble her, was only pretending to sleep; she moved gingerly and was in pain. They were both waiting for morning.

This time, Caroline went along to the dentist's office, where she listened and translated for Lore.

"The doctor will take care of this problem. The X rays, however, show that there is another problem on the other side of your jaw. For this you will need oral surgery, and he is not an oral surgeon. It is nothing to be frightened of, he says, but you must not neglect it. As soon as we move—I explained to him that we are leaving the city—you must have it taken care of."

Once more, the bills were drawn out of the wallet and an appointment made for two days hence. Once more, in the taxicab, Lore groaned.

"Money. You see how fast it disappears?"

Yes, she saw. And the thought of going back to that dismal flat only to repeat the same theme was just too much on this bright morning. She suggested a little walk in the park instead.

"You go. I need ice on my face. I have the key and I'll let myself in," Lore said.

The park, not much more than a sizable playground, was not far from the apartment. It was crowded with mothers and baby carriages. Children played in the sandboxes or rode their small three-wheelers. Sitting there watching them, it seemed unreal that in a few months—so few and so rapidly passing—a child like these would belong to her. Anger and fear beset her.

She thought again: What if she were to hate it when it came? She wasn't ready for it, she had no place for it, no father for it that she would ever want it or anyone else to know about. Or about her disgrace.

A little boy dragging a pull toy stopped in front of her and stared. He evidently had some thoughts about her, or some curiosity. But what?

"Hello," he said, and she answered, "Hello." At his smile and his tiny white teeth, pity lumped in her throat. He knew nothing, nothing at all of why he was here in the sun, wearing his little blue jacket and cap. How could he know whether he had been wanted or not? Every child should be wanted.

What have I done? she thought.

Her mind went blank. The sun poured, and she sat there on the bench in the strange city, feeling the wind as it moved through the trees and over her face.

After a while, someone asked her the time, and she had to look at her watch. It was half past two, the hour for the English lesson. She got up, hoping against hope that Joel would not have come.

But he had. They were both waiting for

her, Lore holding an ice bag to her cheek, and Joel neat as always in shirt and tie.

"Lore is running a fever," he reported. "You can feel it with your bare hand. Now that you're here, I'll go to the store for some medicine."

"We should phone the doctor," Caroline said.

"I know what to take. We don't need a prescription."

"Go in and lie down, anyway."

"I guess I will."

Lore had never been ill. She was always the strong one, a machine that didn't break down, so the sight of her giving in to sickness was especially alarming. Caroline stood at the foot of the bed until Joel brought the medicine and Lore swallowed it, declaring that "Joel is as good a nurse as I am." Then they went out and closed the door so that no noise would disturb her.

Yesterday's resentments faded now in comparison with this new trouble. "I wish we were in a place of our own," Caroline said. "If Lore has to get up at night, I'll feel we're disturbing these people. They're doing so much for us as it is. They must be tired of us. It's so uncomfortable, being in somebody else's house."

"I know what you mean. I feel the same way. That's part of the reason I roam around the city, not to be underfoot in Tessie's house. I've even done baby-sitting. Besides, I can earn a few dollars that way."

"How can you when you can't speak to the children?"

He grinned. "Infants only." Then, taking his hat, he prepared to leave. "I'll come back in the morning and see how she is. If you need anything, you can ask me. That way you won't have to feel you're imposing on your hosts."

"I'll do that," she said, almost humbly. "And thank you, thank you so much."

He understood her fears. They were both refugees, after all, on an equal footing, both insecure. And she stood in a kind of daze. In no consecutive order, her thoughts crisscrossed. Surgery. Equipment for the baby. You were admitted to this country on condition that you were not to become a public charge. So if you couldn't earn enough to support yourself, you would have to ask for private charity. But that was no disgrace, no, not at all. It would kill me all the same, she thought. Rightly or wrongly, it would, and I can't help it.

LORE was very sick. Annie, before she went to work, telephoned their doctor and asked him to come. You could see that Annie was disturbed for Lore's sake, while at the same time you could understand that she was thinking of the disturbance to her household. One sick woman and one pregnant one were a lot more than she had bargained for.

Joel and the doctor arrived almost simultaneously. The doctor wrote out a prescription for the latest medication, called an antibiotic, and Joel was to get it at the drugstore. The cost astounded Caroline as she drew the green bills out of what she and Lore called their "bank." The account was dwindling. . . .

"It doesn't look as if you'll be able to

catch your train as you planned," Joel remarked when the new week began.

"No, we'll have to postpone it. This was a
serious infection, and the doctor says she'll
need another week's rest before we can
travel."

Lore was sitting up in bed by this time,
and Joel had come by every day. He had
run errands and sat with her while Caroline
went out occasionally for air. Not once had
there been any more personal talk between
them, for which she was grateful.

But now he resumed it. "Annie thinks you
should accept my offer, Caroline."

She frowned, beginning to say, "What
Annie thinks is really not—"

"I know you don't care about me, but—"

"What do you mean? I do care about
you. You've been a real friend, and even if
you hadn't done anything for us, I would
still see what a good person you are."

"Then why not take me for what I am?
Can't you see the advantage for all of us? I
like a small town, which is where you're going. I'll find work. Lore won't be able to do
much after her operation and won't earn

much afterward for a while until she gets her license. As for you—"

"I know."

"Well then, if we pool what we have, we'll all be better off."

"Joel, I'm sorry, I'm sorry. You make it sound just too easy to be possible."

"I'm not giving up, you know. I'll try again."

This business was a nuisance. Yet she could not very well show anger toward him. He had a right to try. She could not afford to be angry, either, at others who really had no right to try. Here in the Sandlers' house, receiving their incredible charity, she had to listen with courtesy to their advice.

In the evening Jake said, "I haven't spoken because Annie hasn't wanted me to interfere. But I'm going to speak now. Listen, Caroline, your father isn't here. I hope he will be soon, but in the meantime, you need to listen to a man. If I had a daughter and Joel Hirsch was interested in her, I would be glad. Glad. He's the salt of the earth. And in your position, how many men would —well, I guess I don't have to spell it out."

"I know what you're saying is true, but I don't love him," she said stoutly.

"All well and good, but love is a thing that grows. It's like a plant. Romance is a luxury from the movies. You, especially, have to be practical, Caroline. I can picture your family. Can you picture how they'll suffer, as if they haven't already suffered enough, to see you, an unmarried mother whose child was the product of a Nazi's rape? What will it do to them?"

If only they would let her alone with these dreadful predictions that, unfortunately, God help us, rang so true!

"You need protection right now, and your child will need it."

"Lore will see me through that."

Jake lowered his voice. "Now let's be sensible. Lore can't earn what a man can until she gets her license, and that's a couple of years away. And Lore can't be a father to your child. You need, and the child needs, the respect that comes with a ring on your finger."

Imprisoned here, sitting across the room from this responsible man as old as her father, she was unable to contradict what he had said. She was beside herself.

Annie put in quietly, "A marriage of convenience means 'in name only,' and it's done every day, as I've told you."

"You were talking in there a long time tonight," said Lore, who had been reading in bed.

"They really want me to marry Joel. Why are they so eager? It makes you wonder."

"I'm sure they have no ulterior motives, if that's what you're thinking. They're good people, and they believe they're giving sound advice. Besides, it's only human to play God. It makes people feel important. Useful. Wise."

"Well, I'm not going to do it."

"So be it," Lore said.

A few days passed. Joel did not come back. Lore got out of bed, went for a walk, returned, and began to repack the clothes. "We have six days and then we're off again."

Once more they were rushing against the

calendar. Last time, it was six days to the sailing. This time, it was six days to the train. And another bedroom in another strange house would be left behind.

"By the way, I ran into Joel's Tessie on the street. I have an idea from something she let drop that you might be hearing from her, although I may be wrong."

"Good Lord, I hope you are. I've heard more than enough. Much more."

They were folding clothes when the bell rang. "If it's that woman, don't leave me alone with her," Caroline said before opening the door.

They sat down in the front room, Tessie upright and stiff in the middle of the sofa, clasping her big black handbag.

"I'm going to come right to the point," she began. "There's no sense wasting time in talking about the weather. It's about Joel. He's in love with you, as you probably know."

Caroline sighed. "I'm sorry to hear it, because I am not in love with him."

"But you like him. You respect him."

"That's true."

"I should hope so. He's an honest, hard-working man from a respectable family, my husband's family. No criminals, no beggars, no scandal, no disgrace."

Disgrace. Some unnamed organ in Caroline's body seemed to wince. She straightened her back and said very low, "I, too, come from a good family."

"All the more reason that you should do the right thing for the baby you're carrying."

Caroline looked toward Lore, who was examining her fingernails. So she, too, was feeling the humiliation. She looked at the old woman, of whom Jake had said, "You have to get up early in the morning to fool her." You could believe that, when you looked carefully at the sharp, weathered face and the sharp, bright eyes. Jake had also said that she had a heart of gold.

"You've both suffered because of those maniacs in Europe. Joel understands the horror of what was done to you. Many men, perhaps even most men, would not."

Tessie looked toward Lore. "You tell her. You're older than she is, and in your work you've certainly seen much more of the world. Tell her."

"She's my sister. I'm too involved with her to think straight. I can only feel. And what I feel is that she must make her own decisions here."

Caroline would have expected Lore to come down hard on her side. But instead, she had left the question hanging in the air, which only admitted the possibility of another answer.

"Well?" asked Tessie, turning back to Caroline.

"An arranged marriage—"

Tessie interrupted. "It's been done for years, all over the world, from the royal families of Europe down to my own parents. They hardly knew each other. But they lived together afterward for forty-seven years, and let me tell you it was a good marriage, a lot better than many that you see around you today."

The woman was pounding and pounding. Where has my strength gone, Caroline asked herself, that I do not stand up to her?

"You don't have to sleep with him unless

you want to. He's ready to take you with that understanding. Oh, don't be embarrassed. We're all women here, old enough to know what we're talking about, old enough to be pregnant."

At this point, Lore did stand up. "Caroline's heard enough, I think. All this—everything she's gone through these past months has been very hard for her. Do you mind if we end this now?"

"Of course not." The old woman, wrinkled, gnarled, and worldly, spoke with dignity. "Whatever you decide, I hope you will be happy, my dear. Only remember, Joel Hirsch is a good man and he loves you."

The door closed. And to Caroline's astonishment, Lore burst into tears.

"Lore! Don't take this so hard. What's the matter?"

"It's not just this. Or rather, it is, because things are all tied up together, twisted, so that I don't know what to think anymore. Twisted!" she cried, demonstrating with her fingers.

"I don't understand."

"It's me. I'm sick. I didn't want to tell you

how sick. The dentist's nurse spoke German, and she told me first. My jaw, where I need the surgery, it's cancerous, and—and I'm not as afraid for myself, Caroline, as I am for you. What are you going to do if it's true? We're all alone, you and I."

"My God, are you sure?"

"The doctor said so. 'A textbook case,' he said."

"Then why in heaven's name are you waiting? I won't let you wait. It must be taken care of right now!"

"No. I'm not having surgery until you're settled someplace."

"That's crazy, Lore!"

"No, it's sensible."

"What have we done to be punished like this?"

"Don't be silly." Lore spoke sternly. "You're too intelligent to talk such nonsense."

Caroline had been struck in the chest, on her heart. And she stood there, shaking.

"I want you to go out and take a walk," Lore said. "You need oxygen, fresh air. I can't have you falling apart, Caroline."

"Have you told Annie and Jake?"

"Yes. I had to tell somebody. I suppose I shouldn't have, but I couldn't keep it all in."

So that was the reason for the urgency . . .

"Go. I'll do some ironing and finish the trunks."

It was cool under a fair sky, a day for everything alive to be glad of life. Birds flew southward toward summer, dogs strained at their leashes, and big boys chased balls. She passed the park, where the mothers still sat beside the carriages, passed the ice cream parlor where she had gone with Joel, and passed the house where Tessie might even now be telling him about her visit.

It seemed impossible that in a matter of days, so much had happened. Impossible, too, that so much had happened in just one year. No, it was not even a year since she had met Walter in that other park so many thousands of miles away.

Now here she was with a baby growing inside her and Lore perhaps about to die. Poor, good Lore, who longs for a man to love her, and very likely, if she lives, will never have one, while I, who do not want one, I—

Three thousand miles wide, this country was. To set out in it and walk with all the time in the world, just walk in a straight line across the plains, through the cities, over the mountains to that other sea, leaving everything and everyone behind, just freely going, without thoughts, memories, just free.

Never to love again with that whole, that perfect trust that ends in grief.

She turned around, arrived at the house, climbed the dark stairs, went to Lore, who was at the ironing board, and kissed her cheek.

"I want you to be well," she said. "And whatever happens, I will take care of you. Tonight I will tell everyone that I am going to marry Joel Hirsch. I will be satisfied with whatever plans are made. Now I am going inside to lie down. I am very tired."

Behind the closed door, she sobbed and sobbed. After a while, she had no more strength, and lay still.

ANNIE and Lore arranged everything. Annie obtained a rabbi who would perform the ceremony in his study. She planned the dinner that she would cook. Lore chose Caroline's dress and shoes from the store of clothing in the trunk. Through the refugee committee she arranged for larger living space in Ivy. Caroline was carried along as in a moving vehicle, riding with her eyes closed, conscious only that it was moving fast.

Suddenly she found herself standing next to Joel Hirsch in a musty brown room filled with old books, traffic sounds, and unctuous language about God and love. Under wine-colored silk, her skin tingled with heat. Was it the heat of terror, of despair, or of shame? Which?

Then she found herself at the Sandlers' table staring at geraniums in the silver bowl that she had bought over Lore's objections.

"It's too expensive. It's out of place in their house, anyway."

"No. It's a bread-and-butter present.

Mama would be shocked to know that we took so much and gave nothing."

"Mama was never in our circumstances. We can't afford it."

"We'll do without something else."

"We'll do without a lot of things, the way money is evaporating. Unless you want to sell the ruby."

"Never. It's our only security in an emergency."

Besides, Mama loved it. I'm keeping it for her.

The dinner was brief. As if everyone realized the strangeness of the occasion, talk was subdued. Only Joel was ebullient; his eyes, which he kept on Caroline, were shining. But she scarcely saw him. She was far away in her fantasy of a house where a sundial stood in the center of a rose garden and piano music floated through the tall, grand windows. Far away and long ago, she thought, and looking up, beheld the particles of food that were lodged in Joel's teeth. And then she was ashamed of herself for noticing or caring.

When the dinner ended, Joel returned to

sleep in Tessie's apartment. Then, in the morning, Caroline, Joel, and Lore, with all their baggage, crossed the city again to Grand Central Station and boarded a north-bound train.

FOUR

"Adelbert," said Dr. Schulman, "is too German for America, so I changed it to *Alfred,* and that's what I'm called. That, or *Al.* Only my wife, Emmy, calls me *Bert.*"

He had met their train in Buffalo, and obviously trying to put everyone including himself at ease, had been chatting all the way since.

"I try to take as much time from my practice as I can to help settle refugees. Emmy and I came here in 1932, when it seemed inevitable that Hitler was going to come to power."

"Inevitable? You knew it?" asked Joel.

"Yes, it was quite clear to both of us. So we came. It's a nice place, Ivy. You might say it's a big small town. You'll like it. Look at the colors. Splendid, aren't they? The leaves change early this far north."

Caroline was feeling sick from the flicker of sun and shade, from the swerve of the car as it sped through red curves and down gold-colored slopes, or perhaps it was simply the panic that sickened her, the terrifying thought that she was losing her mind —or to put it more politely, having a nervous breakdown.

Her hands were clasped tight in her lap. Every aching muscle in her shoulders was tense. She stared at the back of Joel's head. He was looking out at the scenery, a blurred field skimming past, a wooden farmhouse and mild cows waiting at a gate, as if this ride and his place on the front seat were quite normal, as if this were a normal outing with family or friends who had a common past and a common destination.

And she had a crazy wish to flee, to open the door of the car and leap out.

"It may seem immodest, though I hope you will take it as I mean it," said the doctor, "to tell you that we people have brought new life to this town in more ways than one. The high school now has a teacher who was once a professor of ancient civilization in Heidelberg. We have a thriving little chamber music group. We have a cancer specialist from Vienna who commutes between our county hospital and the city, also a dermatologist, the first one Ivy has ever had, and then, if I may speak of myself, I, once a cardiologist abroad, am now an internist as well. I understand you're a nurse, Miss Lore? I may call you that, may I? If you will call me Alfred, or even Al, in the informal American way. We all want to be as American as possible."

"I have a first-class degree, Alfred. What I need is a license."

"Ah, well, that will come. There will certainly be room for you in the county hospital. Meanwhile, we won't let you starve, I promise."

In the rearview mirror, Caroline saw again the man's reassuring smile. You could see the kindness in him. Maybe she should speak to him of her despair. He was different from those good people in Brooklyn; that, too, was plain to see. The environment that had made her what she was would be familiar to him; he would understand her.

He said now, "To me, it's always a happy thing to see a young couple in love and already starting a baby, a new life. It's nature's way." And then, no doubt having seen Caroline's face in the mirror, he added quickly, "I'm sorry. Is it a secret? Was I not supposed to know?"

Just as quickly, Joel turned to face her. "I told Alfred when I asked him not to drive too fast. It's my fault."

Why did he have to be so—so possessive? Clumsy fool, playing the loving husband!

"It's all right," she said very calmly. "Sooner or later everyone will know, anyway."

Lore put her hand on Caroline's. The hand was warm and strong. Lore alone was familiar and steady. But if Lore should die . . .

Silently, attached by their hands, each watched the scene run past; now farms and vineyards were interspersed with roadside stands; then came a canning factory and a small farm machinery outlet. Finally, they were in the scattered outskirts of a town.

Joel read the sign aloud: "Welcome to Ivy." And the doctor, with hearty emphasis, repeated it, adding descriptions as they progressed: "Main Street. Practically everything you'd ever need is on this one street. There's Berman's Department Store. It has clothes and housewares, even some furniture. Fred's father had a place like that in Austria, so he grew up knowing the business. He's doing nicely, considering that we're only now starting to come out of the Depression, and there still are a lot of men without jobs. Here's the Great War memorial. It's strange to think that my father fought on the other side. There's the library. Wonderful that the smallest towns in this country can have a public library. Really wonderful."

To Caroline, the scene was monotonous and drab. These wooden structures were insubstantial, as if it were a cardboard village for children's play. Yet a cardboard village would have a backdrop of mountains, snowcapped or green. It would have a duck pond and window boxes with bright flowers—

"So! Here we are. Sycamore Street, number seventeen. Home! They're all waiting for you."

Several cars were parked in front of a narrow gray house that needed new paint. It had a rickety front porch and a scrap of unkempt lawn, both in contrast to the fresh lace curtains in the upstairs windows.

"I see that Emmy finished the curtains," said the doctor. "She swore she'd have them ready and hung by the time you arrived." He swung about in the seat to face Lore and Caroline. "The house belongs to Gertrude Fredericks. Used to be Friedrichs, but she anglicized the name. She's a widow. Emmy says she seems like a pleasant woman and keeps a clean house. The second floor's been made into a nice apartment. Plenty of room, and you will have use of the yard, which will be good when the baby comes. You'll get along fine with Gertrude and Vicky. Victorine, she's twelve, Gertrude's niece. Well, you'll set everything straight for yourselves in no time, I'm sure."

Joel, obviously impatient, had already gotten out of the car and was lifting the luggage from the trunk.

"He takes charge, doesn't he?" Lore whispered to Caroline. "He always does. Haven't you noticed?" She approved.

Of course Caroline had noticed that about him. But it was of no importance. She followed the short procession into the house and up yet another flight of narrow stairs. And climbing, as her hand slid up along the banister, she watched the pale gleam of the ring, that sliver of gold that legitimized the growing life below her ribs. She was trapped.

In the front room waiting for them were four women and a girl, although, when she recalled it later, it had seemed as if there were many more. There had been all those voices, talking at once in German, in English, then back again, babbling with Lore. There had been much noisy, cheerful laughter, embraces, tears, and questions. The women showed them through the rooms, revealing their labor: the curtains, the new carpet, the kitchen wallpaper in red and white with matching red teakettle, the radio, the three easy chairs, the cupboard with shelves for books, and even some books already provided. Everything was either new, or carefully, lovingly refurbished. The little bedroom with its single bed, flowered spread, and carefully painted blue-framed mirror was for Lore. Then they entered the "big bedroom," which, not much larger than the first, was chiefly filled by a huge, carved walnut bed.

"We brought it with us when we came here," Alfred Schulman explained. "It was in Emmy's family, and we didn't want to leave it behind, although we had our own bed. So now it will have good use again." His smile beamed. "A real European marriage bed, feather quilt and all. New feathers, of course."

Flushed with a humiliation that must be hidden, Caroline looked at him. No, he would never do as a confidant or adviser. Doctor or not, he was merely a good-hearted man who would have foolish platitudes to offer.

He resumed, talking to the air. "They have been married only a few months, so this is practically their honeymoon. Their honeymoon house."

Joel, with his back to them all, stood looking out onto the yard. The women smiled nervously at Caroline, meaning to say that they sympathized with her modest embarrassment.

They were so warmhearted, so extraordinary, these good women who had made this home for strangers, and Caroline was grateful. Yet she was beginning to feel tired of having to be grateful. How right was that old saying about how much better it is to give than to receive!

Emmy, who was obviously the leader of the group, said now, "Well, we'll be leaving you. You've all had a long ride on the train and a long day. If there's anything you need, I'm sure Gertrude will come right up and help."

Gertrude was a heavy woman with dull-blond hair drawn back into a strict bun. The girl, Vicky, would be heavy, too, someday, when she had passed first through a voluptuous youth. Both of them had prominent, glassy gray eyes and wet, pursed lips. They looked like fish. The other women, Emmy and Fanny and Mae, were cows, benign and solid. It was queer that you could have such weird, awful thoughts while in the very same moment you knew how weird and awful they were. Perhaps she really was going to lose her mind.

She stood bewildered in the center of the room when they had left. "I don't feel that anything is real," she said.

Joel, turning from the window, answered quietly, "It's because you're tired and afraid. You're not losing your mind, if that's what you're worried about."

How could he have guessed that?

Lore agreed. "Of course. You're simply tired. Why don't you go to bed? I'll fix some soup and bring it to you. They've stocked the pantry very well, I see."

"I'll sleep here on the sofa," Joel said. "Then Lore can have the room intended for her, and you can have yours to yourself, Caroline."

To this, although the idea of sharing a bed with Lore was not very welcome, she protested. "It's not fair to you. It's wrong."

"It's fair and it's right," he said cheerfully. "I've slept on far worse than this new sofa."

THE room, when Caroline awoke, was dark except for a thin slice of light that struck through the space where the door had been left ajar. The sheets were slippery smooth and smelled of potpourri. There was a little bowl of pompon chrysanthemums on the bedside table. Somewhere a dog gave the complaining bark of one that has been let out and forgotten. She must get up and let Peter in. From nearby, Father and Mama were talking in their room. They must not have heard him.

But no, these voices were only Lore's and Joel's. Ah, God, only Lore's and Joel's. Close your eyes again. Turn back the calendar, Caroline. You are in your old room. You have lain in Walter's arms. You are going to go away together, and you are both so happy. Remember the feeling, the warmth and the start of laughter. . . .

In the front room the voices stopped. The floor creaked. That was Lore going to bed. Then the light vanished. Joel had gone to bed. So now they were three. Why do things that come in threes seem to stick in your head? Three little maids from school, or three men in a tub? Miss Fawcett, the English governess, had a little rhyme: "The rule of three doth puzzle me." So here we are, this curious company: an unemployed man, a desperate pregnant woman, and another woman with cancer of the jaw.

Oh, Caroline, whatever has happened to your life?

"PAIN?" Lore's cheek was very slightly swollen. "Oh, quite some, but it's not unbearable," she said.

Of course, it was like her not to complain. Unconquerable as always, she sat at the breakfast table, checking yet another list out loud.

"*Unpacking.* Finished. There's nice closet space. It's a joke, considering that all we own fills two trunks. *Location of market.* It's two streets over, across Main Street, Gertrude says. But we don't need to go yet. Those women bought perishables enough, milk and eggs, to last out the week. *Letters to the Sandlers and Schmidts.* I woke up before six this morning and took care of those."

"I hope you didn't write to the Schmidts about—about Joel, did you?"

"About your marriage, you mean?"

The word "marriage" made Caroline wince. It sounded like a taunt, although it certainly had not been intended that way. But she wished Lore wouldn't use it so often.

"If, by some turn of good luck, they

should find Father and Mama," Caroline said, "I wouldn't want them to learn about what's happened from anyone but me."

"I haven't said, and I won't say, a word."

"I need to explain it myself." As if the whole grotesque affair could ever be properly explained to people like Father and Mama!

And yet, if she could only be sure of seeing them again, what would that matter?

"Well, that covers everything I can think of right now," Lore said. She looked at her watch and stood up. "Ten past eight. I'd better get a move on. Dr. Schulman—Alfred —I can't get used to this intimacy—Alfred has really gone out of his way for me, hasn't he? Taking the day away from his office and driving me all the way to Buffalo. And the specialist has squeezed an appointment in for me, with no charge, besides. These people are wonderful."

Caroline, almost afraid to touch the subject, could not help but ask how soon they would know.

"The biopsy? It can be rushed through.

When I get back tonight, I'm sure we'll know."

Bravely, Lore was going about the fateful visit, adjusting her hat and pulling on her gloves. Her clothes, provided by Mama, were stylish enough, and yet she was dowdy, her lipstick too bright and her stockings the wrong color. She was awkward. And as always, Caroline thought: Lore doesn't deserve what life has given, or failed to give her. And surely she doesn't deserve what's happening to her now.

Her eyes were starting to fill, so she turned away, murmuring, "I wish you would let me go with you."

"No reason to. You stay here and relax, if you can. By the way, Joel went out early to see that Italian baker about a job. If he should come back, there's stuff for a sandwich in the meat drawer. Well, I'll go down and wait in front of the house."

A sandwich. She makes it sound like a wifely responsibility for me. But I am not a wife. This is not a family. This is an insane dream.

Now there was the whole long day to be

gotten through with nothing to do and nothing to think of except negatives. She stood at the window until Lore had driven away. Then she went to the shelf and chose a book that seemed interesting, but finding no interest in it, put it back. Clearly she was in no mood for books. She was a clock that has run down. No, she was a clock whose gears have gone berserk, so that it keeps striking the hour long after the hour has passed.

She took a hat from the closet. Then, remembering that it was autumn and one didn't wear a straw hat whatever the weather, she replaced it. With a brown felt hat on her head—not the dark blue because in the autumn one never wore navy blue— she went downstairs and out into the street.

There was no one in sight except a horse-drawn milk wagon at the corner. Children were in school, women were doing their housework, and men were at their jobs. She ought to think about finding a job, although she had no idea what she was fitted for or what the town offered. The best way to find out, then, was to look for herself.

It did not take very long, merely a tour of Main Street, both sides, to see that Ivy was not bustling. In the drugstore, where she bought a pocket comb and toothpaste, she got into conversation with the man behind the counter. No, there were very few jobs for a woman in Ivy, just now and then in a shop for ladies. And women who had such jobs held on to them. Jobs in the farm machinery factory or the fertilizer plant outside town were, naturally, for men.

Caroline walked on through the uninspiring streets, past the bank, the three churches and two schools. At the war memorial, she stopped, read all the names, and was sad. She felt empathy. These were farm boys, small-town boys, who had possibly not even traveled as far as Buffalo, but had been sent across the ocean to places they had never seen, to die there. And she lingered, senselessly reading their names again and again.

After a while, she turned back toward the place where she now lived. Yesterday's awful panic, that awful sense of unreality, swept over her once more. She was terrified that she might faint or cry out some crazy plea for help here on the public street.

On a bench outside of a hardware store, she sat down to take control of herself until the feeling should ebb. People passed, average people, hardly distinguishable from each other. Then a large, pregnant woman lumbered by, carrying a new life, a new citizen for Ivy, U.S.A. The new life that I am bringing to this place, she thought, was conceived in Switzerland by the son of an arrogant, crop-headed bully in Berlin. A bitter little smile broke out on her lips at the thought of that man's outrage if he could know where his seed was to take root.

When she returned to Sycamore Street, Gertrude hailed her from the front porch. "Come join me. I'm going to bring out some cake and a pot of coffee to wash it down. I can't keep away from fattening sweets, and I don't even try anymore. What's the use? I have no man to admire me." She laughed. "Come on. Take the rocker. You'd better enjoy these last warm days because you won't have a chance to sit outdoors again until next May, if then. Anyway, I want to hear all about you."

No doubt she did want to hear. It was only natural. Besides, she looked like a woman who would love a "good gossip." And Caroline prepared herself.

"Oh, I have something to tell you first. While you were gone, your husband came back to change out of his suit and put on working clothes. He got the job at Ricci's. I had a hunch he might. Anthony's getting older, his son's gone into the army. He didn't like helping in the bakery, anyway. So your husband's come along at just the right time."

"That's nice," Caroline said.

Greater enthusiasm had been expected.

"Nice! I should say so. In hard times like these, with not much English and just off the boat, he's very lucky."

"Oh, yes. But his English is improving fast. I have been teaching him and Lore."

"Where did you learn to speak it so well? You sound like an Englishwoman, like Churchill on the radio."

It had not been too difficult to tell the un-adulterated truth to the Sandlers, but the sudden purposeful curiosity on this face that otherwise reminded her of a fish warned Caroline against telling too much.

"In school. We had a British teacher."

"But Joel—you don't mind if I call your husband Joel?—must have gone to a different school."

"In different cities. Your cake is delicious."

"Glad you like it. Help yourself. So you met while you were in Europe?"

"No, we met here." The refugee committee must have told them so. But what about the date of the marriage? Either Lore or Joel might have said something quite different. They must work out a consistent story together, and do it tonight. Meanwhile, cornered as she was, the best thing for her to do was to finish the cup of coffee and go upstairs.

"He left Europe a little earlier than I did. We met here, and that's the whole story," she said, hoping to put an end to it.

"So it was love at first sight."

Caroline returned a modest smile.

"And you're going to have an American baby. Funny, the last tenants I had were also expecting. That is, their daughter was. An unmarried girl, a runaround. I felt so sorry for the parents. They were decent people. Some people around here blamed them, but that's ridiculous. It was the girl's own fault and nobody else's. Don't you agree?"

"Oh, yes," Caroline said.

Gertrude's rocker creaked back and forth to the singsong rhythm of her remarks. "Yes, it's nice to see a respectable couple with their lives still ahead of them, and a new job coming right in time."

"Yes, right in time."

"Joel said Anthony showed him how to bake an Italian bread, and he copied it perfectly. People around here have taken a liking to Italian food. It's a change."

Caroline agreed that it was a very nice change.

Now it was Gertrude who switched the subject. "Emmy told us that your parents are still over there. I have some distant relatives over there, too. I don't close my eyes any night without thinking of them. But I don't feel too defeated. I'm confident that they will get out, and you must keep confidence, too."

"I try." And Caroline, avoiding those penetrating eyes, turned her head toward the weedy grass where two squirrels chased each other.

"Your father's a doctor, they tell me?"

Why are you asking me, when you already know the answer?

"Yes, he is."

"It'll be wonderful for you when your parents arrive and find you with a new, steady husband, a good, young, working man like Joel."

Why don't you come right out and ask me what I'm doing married to a baker? As if I don't know what you mean, as if we don't all know that social classes do exist.

"Lore and I are both trying not to worry too much, but it's very hard."

"Lore's a nice person. She's not your real sister, I hear."

"To me, she's real."

"Oh, of course. She's adopted, I meant. What's nice is that even though she's not Jewish, she's not at all anti-Semitic. In these times especially, I mean."

Caroline's head began to throb, and she did not answer.

"Well, as you say, she's your sister. But adoptions don't always work out that well. Take my Victorine. I've had her since she was three. I took her in when there was nobody else to take her. I had never had children—had a hysterectomy when I was in my thirties. It wasn't easy, I can tell you. She's a moody girl, a real handful. Doesn't know the meaning of the word gratitude. And she's not doing as well as she should in school, either." Gertrude sighed, and the rocker gave a shrill creak, as though it were breaking apart. "Listen, I have a thought. Do you happen to know any French?"

"Why yes, I speak French."

"Maybe you could help her so she won't fail it this year. I would deduct the charge from the rent."

Poor Victorine! Moody, was she, living with this substitute for a mother? It was in

Caroline's head to say at once that she would do it for nothing. But then the thought came that this could be a small contribution to expenses.

"I'll be glad to teach Vicky."

Gertrude nodded. Then something else came to her mind. "Is there anything wrong with Lore? Vicky heard Emmy Schulman say she was going to see a doctor in Buffalo."

"We hope there is nothing wrong with her," Caroline said, hearing the veiled rebuke in her own voice.

It was fortunate that a few loud spatters of rain came down just then, giving her an excuse to go inside. "Oh, I think I kept the windows open. I'd better run. Thanks for the coffee."

Once alone, she tried a book again, but still unable to fix her mind on anything impersonal, lay down instead. It's not my body that's tired, she thought, only my mind. Yet one could hardly separate the two.

The monotonous rush of increasing rain was restful. Closing her eyes, she tried to transport herself out of the present, forcing her mind to wander back through pleasant years before trouble had come: to a mountain village where horse-drawn sleighs jingled through the white streets, or to an Italian garden on the side of a cliff above the sea, or—

She was jarred awake by the sound of footsteps on the wooden stairs. Her heart jumped. It was already dark, late evening. In a moment the bedroom door would open and Lore would come in to tell her whether the news was bad, very bad, or too bad even to talk about. Her heart hammered.

But no, it was only Joel, treading heavily into the kitchen. Really, she ought to get up and say something to him about his new job. It would be only decent. She had not been alone with him for a single minute since that monstrous, dishonest ceremony that had "united" them. Inevitably, they would have to face each other. Lore couldn't be present every single second, after all. The odd thing was that she had been able to talk to him quite naturally before that ceremony, and was now hardly able to look at him.

Could it perhaps be the same for him? He conversed so well with Lore. On the train coming here they had sat together for a while and talked with animation, as if they two were the newly wedded couple. One could almost laugh about it if it weren't so awful and so tragic.

All of a sudden there were more steps, and then loud voices, Lore's and a man's, no doubt the doctor's. He had come to explain the diagnosis, to soften the blow with generalities, as doctors do, as Dr. Schmidt had done on that evil night in Switzerland a thousand years ago.

She leaped from the bed and opened the door just as they came in from the outer hall.

"Idiots!" Schulman bellowed. "The idiot in New York who made that diagnosis ought to be shot. Cancer, my foot. We waited for the biopsy, that's why we're late, and the whole thing comes down to a viral infection of the parotid, the salivary glands."

"That's not dangerous?" asked Caroline.

"No, no. It just swells up. It's nothing. Dr. Wolf was just about flabbergasted. He knew right away without the biopsy. A first-year student would know better, he said."

Relief like a warm shower poured from Caroline's head down to her feet. She stared at Lore, whose whole face had crinkled into a smile.

"And you're really all right? There's nothing wrong with you at all?"

"Nothing at all. Can you believe it?"

"Oh, God, I'm so glad for you. So glad! You can't know."

The two women hugged each other, laughing and crying, while the two men grumbled together over the strain and dread that the women had so needlessly been suffering.

"How could anyone have made such a careless diagnosis?"

The doctor shrugged. "Thank God it doesn't happen more often. Anyway, Miss Lore, you're out of the woods. So settle down, you people, and rest. If anybody needed rest, you do."

IN the larger room there was a tiny desk at which Lore wrote in her interminable diary while Caroline lay against the pillows. She was full of thoughts. The peaceful rain had turned into a downpour, and the sound was curiously gloomy. Anyway, the evening's first rejoicing had begun to dwindle.

Lore is heartier than I am by far, she said to herself. Now, in her third month, her waist was just starting to thicken. No one could see it, but she could feel it. And as she lay there, moving her hand over her changing body, a peculiar anger began to take shape.

It was fear and pity for Lore that had brought her to this miserable place and this miserable hour. Now in her line of sight stood the narrow closet where hung the dress that she had worn at her so-called wedding. It must be given or thrown away in the morning, out of sight and mind. What insanity had possessed her? It had all been unnecessary, the result of a dentist's stupid mistake. And without planning them, words fell from her mouth.

"Why did you make me do this, Lore?"

Lore laid down the pen and turned in the chair. "*I* made you?" she repeated.

Caroline held up her left hand. "You know I didn't want this damn fool ring."

"Don't blame it on me." Lore spoke calmly. "It had nothing to do with me."

"It most certainly did. Now that we're here, and you're well, we could manage without—without him. After the baby comes, I would go to work somewhere. I'd find something. And the two of us would manage. It all hinged upon your being well."

"Oh, yes? Do you really think we would be welcome here without Joel? Miss Caroline Hartzinger, unmarried mother. Imagine what it would be like. Imagine."

Then Caroline was struck into silence. She had only to think of Gertrude this very afternoon.

"Be fair to me. I wasn't exactly happy about this make-believe marriage. Believe me, I wasn't. But it did—does—seem to be a solution, and not too crazy at that."

Caroline burst into tears, her brief anger defeated. "It's only that I don't know how long I'll hold up. I try, but I'm sick inside. Don't you see that I'm sick?" She sobbed. "I don't know whether I'll ever see Father and Mama again. Oh, could you have dreamed when we lived at home that we could ever be in a place like this?"

Lore laid her hands on Caroline's head. Her strong hands soothed the tension in her neck and stroked her back. Her voice soothed, as always.

"You've done the right thing, Caroline, for yourself and for the baby. It didn't ask to come here, darling. And who can ever foretell what will happen? Exactly as we didn't foretell anything, including Hitler, or Walter, or anything at all. Let's just get on our feet. Let the rest of the future unfold itself. And I'm here. I'll take care of you. I'll take care of everything."

AN early fall brought a foretaste of winter. One day a fine snow blew in on the north wind, coated the last brown brittle leaves, then blew away, leaving a promise of prompt return. Great waves surged across the arctic expanse of the lake, as Caroline, a lonely figure in the early morning, stood unmoving, feeling the loneliness. She had extended her morning walks to the lakefront, where across the road stood the residences of people prominent in the town. Her doctor was one of them.

"I thought I recognized you walking on the lakefront the other morning," he said. "Was it you wearing a red coat?"

It had been she wearing the coat that was bought in Switzerland to wear in America with Walter. He had liked red.

"So you're getting your exercise. That's good. Do you always walk by yourself?"

"I like being alone."

He looked at her. Having listened often to Father's observations, Caroline understood that he had recognized her melancholy. Or, might you not say instead, her *despair*?

He said then, "I know you have things on

your mind, your family abroad. I'm sure it's very hard for you right now, especially when you should be purely happy about your baby."

He would be shocked, this respectable gentleman, if he knew how much I do not want this baby, how I dread the day.

"The best antidote for worry, as you probably know, is to keep busy and to be with people."

"I do that. I give French lessons in the afternoons."

Vicky had found two friends who also needed a tutor. Caroline was grateful for those hours that could take her briefly away from Ivy and back to a France that in her imagination now seemed to have been eternally filled with flowers.

"You make it sound so beautiful," Vicky had cried, who was not "difficult" at all, just terribly unhappy.

The doctor approved. "Good. Keep busy. And before you know it, you'll have something else to keep you busier. Are you hoping for a boy or a girl?"

He was trying to cajole her into a smile.

You can't cajole me any more than I can do it to little Vicky. But he meant well.

"It doesn't matter, as long as it's healthy." That was what you were expected to say.

"Good," the doctor repeated.

Life was so simple for some people. He lived in his own country in a fine house. On his desk stood a photograph of his children and his pretty wife. Most probably, they loved each other.

She turned back toward home. The Schulmans' house was the last in a row that faced the lake. They were good, charitable people. Emmy and the others in the little group who had busied themselves with the apartment had taken Caroline in, had invited the new young couple, always including Lore, to dinners and lunches. They are probably disappointed in us because we don't always accept, she thought now, although Joel and Lore had valid excuses. Lore, through Alfred Schulman, worked five afternoons a week caring for an invalid man, while Joel had long hours at the bakery, starting at five in the morning. Her own afternoons were busy with the lessons, but she was free at lunchtime, and Emmy knew it.

"If you keep making excuses," Lore had said, "after a while you won't be asked anymore."

"Oh, I go sometimes."

"But people can feel your reluctance. They'll start thinking that you don't appreciate all they've done."

Lore was right. When the women at Emmy's lavish luncheon table were talking, she kept mostly silent and only half heard them. She knew that somebody once had assumed she was hard of hearing, and so had raised her voice. She tried to be sociable, but it was difficult to act like a normal, newly married woman when she was not. One of Emmy's friends had brought her daughter, a cheerful girl not much older than Caroline, with the obvious intent to create a friendship between them. They were both married; one had a baby, and the other was expecting a baby. So they had much in common, didn't they?

All this went through Caroline's head as

she walked toward her daily three-mile goal. She might not want the child, but she had no right to deprive it of health, and so her body must be kept strong. What went on in her mind was another matter.

People were taking numbers at the counter in Ricci's bakery as she passed. Mrs. Ricci, Angela, was waiting on customers. Fat and lively, she looked "motherly." And she really was so. Last week she had brought them a real Italian dinner, hot out of the oven. She liked Joel. Anthony did, too. So did Alfred Schulman. It seemed as if everyone always did like Joel. . . .

He and Lore were becoming fast friends. Often it seemed as if they had long known each other, or were even related, distant cousins in some far-flung family met after long absence and trying now to make a home together. It was ridiculous.

Yet, on occasion, as Caroline observed them in the evenings, Lore knitting yet another sweater while listening to the classical station on the radio, swinging a little to the emotional music, the Chopin waltzes or Liszt rhapsodies that she loved, and Joel in the minute kitchen putting up another shelf —absurd as it all was, she had to feel a certain respect. At least they were trying to make the best of the situation. The odd trio was maintaining itself without any other aid.

Nevertheless, it was barely self-supporting, and Lore was right about that, too; without Joel, they would have needed charity. Lore kept telling her that she should be grateful to him.

"Especially in these circumstances," she would say. "And he's not bothering you. He hardly ever speaks to you. He hardly notices you."

"I know that. But it's like having a stranger, a boarder, in this little place. I hate the intimacy, going in and out of the bathroom in my robe."

"He doesn't think a thing of it, I'm sure."

"Well, I do. And how do you know he doesn't think a thing of it?"

Often, while the hammer tapped, she could hear him humming a phrase of repetitious, melancholy song. Yes, truly she ought to show a little friendliness toward him. It was odd that you could be sorry for a person and yet find it so hard to stand up and cross a room to say a few words.

Ostensibly to get a glass of water, she did just that.

"It's very nice of you to do all this work," she said.

"That's all right. We need the shelves," he replied.

He was awkward and self-conscious. But so was she. With glass in hand she went back to the other room, feeling guilty and exasperated with everything, including herself.

She had now and then caught him looking at her, then quickly looking away. She wondered where he went to satisfy himself. There weren't many men who lived virginal lives. A horrid thought came to her: Would he, after the baby came, demand something of her? They were, after all, married. There in the top drawer of the chest lay the certificate in plain, legal English. Coming in now out of the cold, she went to look at it, and was standing there holding it when Lore entered.

"I did some marketing before I have to go

take care of my old patient. Why are you reading that thing?"

"I don't know. Maybe to make myself more miserable than I already am."

"You may be miserable, but you certainly don't look it. You look blooming. Many pregnant women do."

"My cheeks are pink because I've been out in the wind, Lore, and I am not blooming. I am dying inside, but you don't want to hear about it."

"That's not true. We both know it, Joel and I, and we both want to help you. We will help you."

"Oh, so you discuss me with him?"

"He's a very good man, Caroline, and he understands more than you may think he does."

Turning her back on Lore, she gazed down into the yard. A few months from now she would be sitting there minding Walter's baby. And, unbidden, a cry came from her: "I hate it! I hate everything!"

Lore said softly, "I know. It's Walter you hate. But don't take it out on the baby, or on Joel, either."

"Don't you think I try not to?"

"Listen to me. Will you come sit in the front room again after we eat tonight? All this week you've been alone, marking your lessons in your bedroom. It's not good for you to remove yourself this way."

Caroline looked at her, thinking: How devoted she is! I owe her so much. I am making things harder for her.

"All right, I will," she said.

THE fragrance of baking chocolate came into the front room. Lore sniffed.

"Delicious. I gave Joel some recipes, Caroline, some of your favorites, the chocolate torte and the plum strudel. He's never baked anything except bread before, but he followed the directions perfectly, and Mr. Ricci was really impressed. They sold everything he made today. Isn't that wonderful?"

In the lamplight, a flicker of pleasure passed across Joel's round pink face, but weariness was more deeply marked there.

As if Joel were not present to speak for himself, Lore went on speaking for him.

"Joel suggested to Mr. Ricci that it might be a good thing to have some variety instead of only Italian. He'd like to try French pastry, although that can be very difficult, more complicated. But the business could be tremendously expanded, he thinks. Don't you, Joel?"

He nodded. It seemed to Caroline that he was either on the verge of sleep, or else deeply thoughtful, off in some distant place or time. No doubt he had plenty to remember.

So did they all, gathered here in this cramped space. Against one wall where in another house had stood a floor-to-ceiling bookcase of African mahogany, there stood the bulky sofa on which Joel slept. It was new and clean, but tasteless. In the corner nearest the window where in that other house had stood a grand piano, there was a boxy chest bearing a pair of photographs in silver frames: Father faintly smiling, Mama serene in unadorned black velvet. Caroline sighed.

Perhaps Joel had heard the sigh because he looked over at her and spoke. "You need to stop thinking so much about what's past and gone."

She was astonished. It was the first time in weeks that he had addressed any remarks specifically to her.

"I'm sorry I'm hard to be with," she answered him quietly. "I don't know whether you can understand what I mean, but—everything is gray to me. If you have never felt like this, you probably won't understand."

When he failed to reply, she continued, still very quietly, "You are the only one who is earning a living wage here. It is a pity for you to be burdened this way. You would be far better off by yourself."

"I have not complained," he told her, "and I am not complaining now. But if you don't mind, I have to get up very early, and I am very tired."

The two women rose at once and left the room.

HER charm, he thought, if only there were some way to bring back her charm. She had seized him the very first moment he had seen her. Her voice, and the words that had come from her lips. He remembered every word. And the whiteness of her, like marble, or milk, or white lilacs. Then her eyes, those enormous, mysterious eyes. But they held no message for him other than indifference, or even distaste. He had been a fool to think that he, Joel Hirsch, could have anything to offer to a woman like her other than rescue from shame and the respectability of his name. Well, she had not pretended otherwise, had not lied to him, had she? So it was his own fault, and he had no right to be angry at her now.

One day he had asked Lore what she was really like, what she had been in that other life before her trouble. "Delightful," Lore had told him, she had been delightful: lively, affectionate, eager to see and learn and do. She had been a treasure.

Very fine, but what had that to do with him? It was all the worse for him to know it, since she was now a different person in the depth of her black despair. She was ruined, beyond restoration, like a damaged painting, a book with torn-out pages, or a battered violin that could not be played.

I have made a mistake and I must face it, he said to himself, lying there on the uncomfortable sofa in the grim night. I wanted her, and I still want her, but it is only mockery, a fool's stubborn fantasy, and hopeless.

I'll see her through until the child is born, God help the unwanted little thing, and until the two women can support themselves. That should not take an unreasonable time. Then we can end it.

BEYOND the hospital's second-floor windows, a wild, springtime wind tore through the bare treetops.

"It's a splendid day for homecoming," Lore said, "but awfully cold. I've brought your heavy red coat and three blankets to wrap the baby."

Caroline was smiling vaguely; she was in a strange trance, as if she were not yet fully awake. Her body, now emptied of its prominent burden—for as Lore had predicted, she had "carried" large and heavily—was relieved, and she had at last been able to sleep in comfort.

"Youth," the doctor had observed. "The younger, the easier."

"Well, not always." Lore liked to contradict doctors. "I'm a prime example of medical mistakes, if anyone is."

No matter. It was over, and the collapse of spirit that Caroline had so much dreaded had not happened, at least not yet. . . .

"You look half asleep," Lore said.

"I've been so lazy here."

"Well, you won't be anymore, starting now. Look at her. She's waking up."

On the bed, ready to be dressed for her first venture out of doors, the baby lay with wide eyes and dancing fists.

"The nurse wanted to show me how to get her clothes on, but I said you would save her the trouble."

"Nothing to it. The main thing is not to let the head wobble backward when you pick her up. Joel should be here in a minute. The

Riccis lent their car to take you home. Oh, here he is."

He was standing in the doorway, hesitating. "They gave me the whole day off," he said awkwardly.

Of course. It was only right to give a new father a day off, along with the jokes and congratulations. No wonder he was flustered and awkward.

"Come have a look," Caroline said, holding the baby with her head resting properly on Caroline's shoulder.

Joel made a surprised comment. "She has blond hair."

He means, that man must be blond.

"My father had light hair."

"Yes," said Lore, "Father was a handsome man. Maybe she will look like her grandpa."

"See, she's staring at me!" cried Caroline.

"Not really. Their eyes aren't focused yet at this age," Joel said.

Lore nodded. "You're right. Most people don't know that."

"Well, I'm the oldest in a large family. There was always a baby in the house."

Caroline had never held a baby. This one was only seven pounds, but unexpectedly heavy and warm. The wet mouth was kissing her neck.

"She's hungry," Lore said, noticing.

There was a hard lump in Caroline's throat, and she needed to cry, but would not. Her thoughts raced: I thought I would hate it—her; her fingers are pulling at my collar; if Father could see her he would have tears; he teared so easily. And Mama would have a velvet coat ready, size two. Mama and velvet. Oh, my God, and I was so sure I would hate it—her.

She is mine, entirely mine. I made her myself. All her blood comes down from Father and Mama, from my people, through me. She belongs to me and to no one else.

"I want to tell you both something," she said passionately. "You have to promise me that as long as you live you will never let her know anything about who—about how she came. She must never know. Do you promise?"

The two others looked at each other in astonishment. "Of course not. That's understood," Lore said. And Joel exclaimed, "Who in heaven's name would hurt a child that way?"

It was bizarre. Here she was, this baby, just seven days old, going home with this odd, patched-up family to start out in the world. Yes, it was bizarre.

"What is her name?" asked Joel.

"Eve."

Lore corrected her. "Eva. Your mother's name is Eva."

"In America, people say Eve, and this is America. Her name is Eve."

FIVE

She remembered how, from the first, people remarked upon the child's beauty. The first pale fuzz had soon turned into black silk, and the black eyes were brilliant in the tiny face. They were Mama's eyes.

"An Italian bambina," exclaimed Mrs. Ricci, who kept bringing feasts, along with wine and kisses.

Emmy Schulman came with her ladies, piling glossy boxes tied in pink ribbon on the table.

The Sandlers sent a snowsuit and a loving card, which unlike other people's cards said nothing about "Happy Parents."

Gertrude, always chary of praise, observed that the baby looked healthy. It was still early in the morning, and of all days, today Joel had forgotten to put the sofa back in order. "Eve had a wakeful night," Caroline quickly said, for she had followed Gertrude's gaze, "so Joel moved out here to get some sleep."

Lore had knitted a yellow blanket. Often, when Caroline laid her book down for the late night feeding, she took a final look at the round lump under that blanket. An awful fear made her heart beat faster: What harm might life do to this child? This child had a legacy. . . . She reached down and gently rocked the cradle.

Joel had built it for Eve. It was made of fine wood, well joined and polished to a gleam. When Caroline, thanking him, expressed surprise at his skill, he answered simply, "What a person doesn't know, he can learn." And he explained, "Cradles are best for newborns. The motion reminds them of rocking in the womb, or so I have heard."

"He's full of surprises," Lore said later, "and the soul of kindness." She said it too often, for surely Caroline needed no reminder. "A father couldn't be more attentive to that baby."

In the pet store one day he bought a puppy, an unidentifiable gray mongrel with a rough coat and a pleading expression.

"A child should grow up with a dog," he said earnestly. "Besides, he looked so sad in his cage. He talked to me."

Joel had really taken too much upon himself, Caroline thought, bringing back a dog without asking whether it would be welcome. Nevertheless, she let it sleep on her bed at her feet, and she named it Peter.

Life in the little flat was undergoing a definite change. Drying diapers, midnight bottles, and the general fussing that a baby collects around its presence—to say nothing of the dog's possessions underfoot, its bowls and rubber bones—had diminished privacy and space. In these narrow quarters, they were living as someday people would live in college dormitories in brotherly or sisterly indifference, without emotion. Or so Caroline thought . . .

No longer could she feel uncomfortable about the shared bathroom, or about walking past the front room where Joel was sleeping. Nor did he seem to notice her. If he still cast quick glances at her when she passed, she did not see them.

Lore rebuked her. "You don't pay any attention to Joel."

"Why? What am I supposed to do? I'm too busy for small talk."

"You're never too busy to talk to me."

"Well, you are a slightly different person from Joel," she answered, somewhat impatiently.

"You could make a little effort. Aren't you ever sorry for him?"

"I'm perfectly nice to him. I'm comfortable with him, but I'm indifferent. And that's progress, Lore, counting from where I started."

Indeed, as the months passed, she began to feel that she was making progress. One morning when she woke up, she realized that the feeling of hopeless dread with which she had so long been waking up was gone. It was as though a fog had suddenly lifted. She looked in the mirror and whispered to herself.

"I always used to think that I was a strong woman. Dr. Schmidt told me I was that day when my life fell apart, but I didn't believe him. I knew I was not strong, not at all. Now I feel again that maybe I can be. And I must be, for Eve."

Now they were all making progress. To begin with, Mr. Ricci gave Joel a substantial raise. With Al Schulman's help, Lore was studying for the licensing examination. And because Vicky was willing and eager to baby-sit, Caroline was able to put a notice on a bulletin board outside the post office offering lessons in both French and German at two dollars an hour. The response surprised her. It was a good feeling, now, to pay her fair share of expenses. They were all beginning to see daylight. Everything seemed to have changed since Eve arrived.

It was as if the baby had given a sense of authentic purpose to those three who had boarded the train together in New York.

What was to come next, they could not know, and for the time being at least, Caroline tried not to think about it. Perhaps it was just enough for each of them to have this period of calm relief in which to pause and breathe and let the future wait. . . .

"A lot has happened since we came here two years ago," Joel said one evening.

Long afterward, Caroline recalled the moment in precise detail. He had been reading the evening paper. Lore was hemming diapers, it being too expensive to rent them from a diaper service. She herself was correcting a French test.

He put the paper away. "Yes, a lot has happened," he repeated.

Into the casual ordinariness of the time and place, his remark fell, heavy with importance. "A lot of things have changed, and a lot of things have stayed the same.

Perhaps it is too complicated for me to explain."

Both women stopped their work and looked expectantly toward him. But avoiding them, he spoke to the air.

"The fact is, I'm going to leave you. The time has come." When he paused, it was plain that this speech was going to be hard labor for him. "I am a businessman. My English is good, thanks to you, Caroline, and I am ready to do more with my life than spend it in a small-town bakery. Although," he added quickly, "I mean no offense to anyone. Anthony Ricci is content with it, so it's fine for him. But I am not content." He took a breath and continued. "I am not the person I was when you first knew me. You must have thought, Caroline, that I was some sort of idiot, a good-hearted fool who could expect by putting a ring on your hand that I could somehow make you love me. And I'll tell you, you were right. I was a fool. I myself look back now and wonder how I could have failed to see how much you disliked me. And you dislike me now. The marriages they call 'marriages of convenience' are more truly named 'fraud.' No, don't go, Lore"—for Lore had laid the diapers on the floor and was about to stand up—"I have no secrets from you. You are a part of all this."

Caroline was trembling. His words were hard to refute, and still she tried. "But I do not dislike you at all, Joel. How could I? The most loving brother could not have cared or done more than you have. Why, when I think of Eve and how you—"

He put up his hand to stop her, and interrupted. "I had a sister, you see, the baby of my family. Her name was Anya. She was three years old when they shot her there in the courtyard. She was holding a rag doll."

The women were silenced. Awful tragedy had silenced them.

"We have both been through terrible times, Caroline, and your parents still weigh on your heart. I asked too much of you. You cannot force yourself. I understand. Believe me, I do. And so that's why I'm leaving. I'll be going fairly soon. It will be better." His tone grew harsh as his voice rose. There was anger beneath his sorrow. "Yet something at least has come out of this mistake. Eve has a name."

Lore coughed and turned to Caroline, who was expected to make some response, and was too shocked to make one.

"Joel, we shall miss you!" Lore cried. "It will seem so strange—"

"We'll be friends. Everyone will know where he stands." Joel looked toward Caroline. "We'll be friends, with no further expectations. I'm sorry. I don't express myself well."

On the contrary, he expresses himself all too well, she thought. And he says correctly that he is not the person he was two years ago. He has been working hard, he is thinner and older and somehow stronger. The overgrown boy with the flushed cheeks is gone. Now that he has spoken, he sits in a weary thoughtfulness; perhaps he is wondering how he ever arrived here with people who have no relationship to anything he has ever known or can have anticipated.

Deeply moved, Caroline stood up, went to him, and took his hand.

"I will never forget you," she said. "If we

should come to live as far apart as Australia and the North Pole, I will never—"

"You don't have to do this," he told her, gently withdrawing his hand. "I'll be all right. And so will you."

ON Sunday she pushed the stroller as far as the lakefront. Eve, well wrapped against the arctic weather, sat up and watched the scene with interest: A man shoveled snow, gulls in raucous cry swooped overhead, and Peter in his plaid coat trotted alongside on his short legs.

It is too cold to have been out so long, she thought. But the little rooms at home were so oppressive, filled with a subtle anger, although possibly she was only imagining the anger. Joel seemed to stay away as much as he could; she had an idea that he lingered late at the Riccis' house. He was unusually silent.

Certainly she had never expected, let alone wanted, their singular arrangement to be permanent. Yet Joel's choice of this time did seem to be very strange and sudden.

"It's no mystery to me," declared Lore. "It tortures him to be near you. He's a man, after all." She hesitated. "Do you think you could ever—" And she stopped, blushing.

She meant: *Would you ever sleep with him?* Lore, however, being Lore, so prim and repressed, would never actually say those words.

As if I didn't know, thought Caroline. He's a man, after all. And I am a woman with needs of my own, one of them being that I want to love. I want to *want* again.

She paused, gazing out over the gray lake, huge as an inland sea, and she thought, as she often did, how small they were, she and her baby girl, with their little needs and heartbreaks, in the face of these rocks and the waves that shape them, and the wind that shapes the waves.

Ah, well, so it is! Shaking the mood, she turned around toward home. On the corner, the Schulmans' car passed; they waved, and she thought ironically about the astonishment they would feel when they learned that Joel was leaving his "little bride."

Lore and Joel were listening to the radio.

They motioned for quiet when she and Eve came in. A voice almost hysterical was speaking.

"Over three hundred Japanese planes have attacked so far. The loss is incalculable. Our ships, battleships, destroyers, and cruisers, were at anchor in the harbor . . . The *Nevada, California, Arizona,* completely destroyed . . . Thousands dead, thousands wounded . . . Disaster . . . The United States crippled in the Pacific . . ."

The three stood solemnly looking at each other. "This means war," Joel said. "We'll be in it by tomorrow."

So the last hope for Father and Mama was gone. Silently, Caroline took Eve into the bedroom and laid her in the crib for a nap. She went to the window and stared down at the trodden snow in the dreary yard. She felt nothing. Then she remembered having read that wounded people have a few moments without any feeling at all before the agony begins.

THE hours pass in a dream. The Riccis' son Tom is lost on the *Arizona*. In the little brown house behind the bakery, the broken parents are left to bear the unbearable. Al Schulman has brought medication for Angela and sends her to bed. Anthony refuses help; he sits in a frozen trance and stares at the wall. People crowd the room to approach him on tiptoe and murmur words that he does not heed. Only when Joel comes does he respond at all. Joel kneels beside him on the floor, taking his hand, saying nothing. Anthony grasps Joel's hand in both of his and is able to weep. . . .

Afterward, the Schulmans walked a short distance with Caroline and Joel, the two men ahead of the women.

"Joel has a remarkable way with people," Emmy remarked. "A natural sympathy. It's a very healthy trait."

"Yes," said Caroline.

"I suppose you can't be aware that you've made a great change in him. He seems so much older. But those poor Riccis now! Whoever thought we'd be in another war? This is supposed to be an enlightened century."

Meaning well, she talked and talked until they reached the corner and went their separate ways, leaving Caroline with a fresh headache and fresh thoughts.

Her footsteps, matching Joel's, were loud on the sidewalk. Everybody was indoors listening to the news on the radio. They walked rapidly and in silence until Joel said abruptly, "I'm not going to wait till I'm called. I'm going to enlist tomorrow. I want, I really want to fight them. Yes," he said, " 'a date that will live in infamy.' There've been more than a few of those days these last years."

She did not answer. What was there to say?

Lore was in the front room, walking up and down with Eve. "I don't think there's anything really wrong with her," she reported, "but I just don't seem able to quiet her. She must have had a bad dream."

A bad dream? What fears could possibly trouble this new little untried life?

"They have them, you know," said Lore, seeing doubt.

Caroline took Eve and laid her in the crib, but the child protested and struggled so desperately that there was nothing to do but pick her up and walk with her. Lore, who had had a long, hard day, gave up and went to bed. But Joel stayed and watched. After a while he stretched his arms out for Eve.

"Let me have her," he said, and carried her back to the crib.

For the first time since her child's birth, Caroline was more than willing to hand her over to someone else. She was feeling overwhelmed. The sorrow that is drowning the world is drowning me, too, she thought: Dunkirk, Pearl Harbor, Nazis marching in uniform, Eve's father among them, Father and Mama . . . Everything.

And why? Why, when the world is so beautiful, with it all! The summer has sails on the lake, the winter has Eve's red cheeks in the frost, and there is music somewhere all the time—

Very quietly, someone is singing now. It is

Joel in the bedroom. She gets up to look, and there is Eve with her head on his shoulder. After a while, he moves to the crib and puts her in it. He covers her and strokes her back, faintly humming. The man and the sleeping baby make a picture, captioned *Father and Child.*

And Caroline, bowing her head, stands there fighting all the accumulated sorrows in her heart, the world's and her own.

"What is it?" whispers Joel. "Is it poor Tom Ricci?"

"That and more."

She turns around and sees the pity in his eyes. Then, although she doesn't know why she does it, she says, "You ought to know it wasn't a rape. I loved him."

"Ahhhh." The sound comes painfully, as if something has choked him. "I've wondered about that. There was too much sadness in your anger. Yes, I always wondered."

"The sadness is not for myself anymore. It's for Eve."

"I understand."

"Yes, I believe you do."

"But it will never touch her. Lore and I are the only people who know about it, and surely you trust us."

Light from the street lamp falls upon his face, which is bent toward hers with a look that seems to be probing her mind. They are standing so close that she can breathe the pungent fragrance of his shaving soap. In brutal shock, she thinks: He, too, will die in the war. This strong body, this decent man, will die. And as her child has done, she lays her head on his shoulder.

Gently he asks her, "What has happened to you?"

She does not answer because she cannot bring herself to say, and perhaps is not really certain that she ought to say: I have been starved, and I need love. I am ready now if you still want me.

In the half dark his eyes are filled with tears, though as he strokes her head, he whispers, "Don't cry, don't cry."

After a moment or two, he lifts her, carries her to the bed, and takes her into his arms.

LORE was aghast. Living as they did in these close rooms, it did not take long before she became aware that Joel no longer slept on the sofa. Her bright eyes glistened with avid curiosity. She stammered and filled the void with long, tense pauses, as if she were waiting for Caroline to answer her unspoken questions. Ladies did not ask personal questions, nor did they offer information about their sex lives, even to someone as intimate as Lore. Therefore, very little was said about the unbelievable change that had occurred, or at least very little of substance was said. Besides, even if she had been willing to confide, Caroline would have had only confusion to disclose. The thing had simply happened in an indescribable, chaotic swirl of emotion. And now that it had happened, there must be a quiet acceptance of it. He was, after all, a clean man, clean in body and mind. And he adored her.

SIX

In Ivy, as everywhere, life that had ambled, or even perhaps stood still, now began to race. To his chagrin, for Joel had had visions of hand-to-hand combat and personal vengeance, the army rejected him. He was diabetic. His case was a moderate one; he was given instructions to keep his weight down, watch his diet, stay in touch with a doctor in regard to insulin, and help the war effort at a defense job. This he did promptly, not half an hour after a call went out from a local machine tool plant that had just received another huge government order.

One day, only a few months after Pearl Harbor, the Riccis came with a proposal. The two of them, sitting side by side on the edge of the sofa, seemed very small. They had shrunk and aged ten years. Two furrows made parentheses in Angela's smooth cheeks. She was tired, and she wasted no words.

"We want you to buy the business and the house at the back of the lot."

"You can't be serious," Joel said.

"Why? Because you can't afford to? We don't need the money right away. We're going to live with our daughter in Denver. Get away from this place. It was home once, a good home. But now it's nothing. You understand?"

"I do," Joel said, "but still, it's out of the question for us."

"We'd gear the payments to your wages at the factory. In the end, it wouldn't come to much more than you're paying for these few rooms here."

"And who would run the business?"

"Your wife would run it."

Anthony looked over at Caroline.

"She could run a bakery, Anthony?"

"The two women who've been working there will stay. They need the wages, and you've taught them a great deal, Joel. They can turn out bread as well as you or I can. Maybe some of the fancy stuff, too, but there won't be much need for that with sugar being rationed. Caroline can run the business end."

Joel shook his head. And Anthony, interrupting him before he could speak again, went on. "Don't shake your head. Think about it. It's a future. It did well enough for us."

Joel was impatient. "What are you saying? You want to hand it to us for nothing, out of charity?"

"No, we'll take a mortgage on the whole thing. You'll pay out of what you earn. Take your time."

Joel laughed. "You want to wait seventy-five years?"

"I said we're in no hurry. Anyhow, it won't take any seventy-five years."

Crazy, thought Caroline, catching both Lore's eye and the tightening of her lips. She almost read Lore's thoughts: How far you have come from where you began, Dr. Hartzinger's daughter! Look at this room. Look out at the cold, wet night on this dingy Sycamore Street. And now they want you to run a little bakery in this dingy town of Ivy.

"It would be wonderful for the bambina. Our yard is two times the size of this one. No, three times, with plenty of sun and shade. There's the vegetable garden, and Tony's grapes. It's nice to have supper in the arbor."

Angela was urging. Yes, it would be wonderful for the bambina, not like this place here. That much was true. Not like this place.

"The house is sound," Anthony said. "I put in a new furnace two years ago. We've got plaster walls, a tight roof, and a good cellar. No leaks, no matter how high the snow gets."

Joel asked, "Why don't you sell it to somebody who can pay you for it now?"

"Because we want you to have it. You're our kind of people."

"We'll think about it," Joel said, clearly wanting to end the subject. "Ridiculous," he said as the Riccis went downstairs.

But Caroline, lying long awake that night and the next, began to think that maybe it might not be so ridiculous after all.

So began the years that Caroline was to recall as "our times in the small brown house." Time is long or it is short, depending upon what one cares to remember, or what, even if one does not care, will not allow itself to be forgotten.

Is it possible to forget Edward R. Murrow's stern voice broadcasting from London under bombardment? Or the long lines of blood donors during the Battle of the Bulge? The magnificence of Churchill? Or even to forget a popular song about "love and laughter and peace ever after"? Or the unbelievable rumors of the death camps?

From the moment of her last good-bye to Father and Mama, there had lingered in some hidden part of her mind, against her will, the knowledge that she would never see them again. It was this knowledge that startled her, stopping her in the midst of some simple activity, perhaps just walking down the street on an ordinary errand; it struck like a blow to the heart and stopped her breath.

Yet there is a personal life that keeps its own momentum from day to day. Everyone in the house had to pursue his own path. Lore, whose English was by now almost perfect, passed her licensing examination with no trouble and was accepted at the hospital with no trouble, either. She learned to drive. If only, Caroline thought, that ten-year-old Nash holds up long enough to get her to work every day! The roof leaked in a heavy rain, but still you couldn't expect much from a ten-year-old car that cost thirty-five dollars.

Joel worked hard at labor to which he was not accustomed. But he did his best, and he was helping the war effort.

As for Caroline, having conceived an idea and undertaken to finance it, in large part with Joel's wage, she was now under heavy obligation to make it work. She began with a few tables in the shop, an embryonic café. Eventually there would be a full-grown addition to the building. Brown would be painted over in buff, with burnt-orange trim and awnings; there would be good music, and on the sunny side in a bow window there would be an orange tree. The whole would be called the "Orangerie." The Riccis' little enterprise was to be expanded in a way that would astonish them. Hour after hour, the idea took shape as her enthusiasm grew.

Joel was dubious. "You want to put a piece of Europe in Ivy? They won't accept it. They've never seen anything like it."

"All the more reason why they will accept it."

"Ivy is much too small to support anything like it."

"Ivy is growing right before your eyes, can't you see? Actually, we should be in a better neighborhood, though. On Main Street near the town hall."

Joel remained skeptical, even a little

amused, but since the place was already paying its way and even profiting, there was no reason for him to protest too much.

"I don't know where you get your energy," he said.

She did not know, either. It had been hard work from the start. She had not even realized how much there was to learn and do, how much lifting and scrubbing that, in spite of all the help she had, would be left to her. Yet it seemed as if she was never tired.

Who was it who first said, *If you build it, they will come?* And they were coming. On winter nights after the movies they came for warm muffins and fresh-roasted coffee. In the summer, they took their iced drinks in the shade, looking out upon Angela's vegetable garden. And as the modest undertaking grew, so grew Caroline's ambition. Someday they would have a chain of places like this. The orange awnings would bloom throughout the growing town and on the highways. She kept these thoughts to herself, because they were grandiose and might make her sound like a fool. Yet, as the Chinese proverb goes, every journey begins with one step.

Each of them worked hard in his own way. Lore was well regarded at the hospital. Joel learned fast and was promoted; his extra wages went into the Orangerie, where the profits mounted and the quarters, fifty-cent pieces, and dollar bills were turned into war bonds.

The war was the stimulus behind Caroline's labor, the war and Eve as well; yet truly these were one and the same. For the sooner the war was won, the greater the chance that Father and Mama might survive to see her.

Sometimes it seemed as if Eve had been born just yesterday, and as if Pearl Harbor, which for her would be only history in a book, had happened yesterday. Yet in half a year she would be in kindergarten. Already she spoke French, and to Lore, German. She was tender and often mischievous. Joel spoiled her and denied that he did.

Almost shyly one night, he began to say, "I wonder whether we'll ever—" and then changed to, "Would you like to have another child?"

They were reading in bed, he with the newspaper and she with a book. A kind of mental chill—that being the closest she was able to come to a definition of the feeling—ran through her. She did not want another child, a *disruption.* Eve was all to her. Perhaps if other things were different, that would be different, too. *Other things.* Passionate need, for instance, something very much bigger than her sporadic moments. Then would one not *need to have* the man's child, the lasting symbol of the union? And she wondered how many women could answer honestly that they had such a passionate need.

It was sad that she did not have it, and yet, in the scale of things, this did not rank first. What ranked first was the fact that each of them, Joel and she, had once hung on a cliff by their fingernails and were now on solid ground.

And sensing that he wanted to make love, she put the book away and turned to

him in the bed, saying gently, "If it happens—"

She would be careful, though, if she
could, not to let it happen. . . .

THEN suddenly the war was over. Then suddenly the world resumed its ways. New cars
came rolling into the dealers' lots. Trousers
and sleeves had cuffs again. Dior brought
the "New Look"; after the skimpy years,
skirts were full and feminine. New houses
were planned to go up along the lakefront.
And with accounts of the Nuremberg Trials,
newspapers printed the ugly faces of
Streicher, Kaltenbrunner, von Ribbentrop,
and many more, condemned to death by
hanging for their crimes against humanity.

Caroline and Lore spread the paper out
on the kitchen table. Neither spoke until
Caroline wondered aloud why there had
been no word from the Schmidts.

"I suppose they stopped writing because
there was nothing more to report," Lore
said.

"Look at these pictures. Is it possible to explain such evil?"

"I don't think it is, especially for people like me who work at saving lives." Lore paused, and then almost as if she were afraid to do so, asked gently, "Tell me, do you still ever find yourself thinking of—him?"

"How shall I answer?" The question stung. "Yes, all the time. Whenever I look at Eve, I must, mustn't I? And she is the joy of my life."

"A pity. A tragedy," murmured Lore. "And Father and Mama. You've had too much. Still, maybe there is some hope for them."

"There isn't any. You know that, Lore."

And of course, there was none. It was Joel who eventually found, through the Red Cross, where and how they had died. Caroline was at the desk in the back of the Orangerie, going over the bills, when he came in.

He spoke softly. "I have something to tell you."

When she looked at his face, she knew what it was.

"I want to hear everything," she said. "Where and when?"

So he told her. There was not very much to tell, just bare facts, a date and a place—two places, for they had been separated in death.

"Not even allowed to die together," she said.

"No. Not even that."

"It's strange. You know what they say about drowning? How your whole life flashes before you? When you came into the room and I saw what you were going to tell me, I saw Father in his new car, my mother's piano, the ship coming into New York harbor—everything. All a jumble. Everything."

"You need to cry," Joel said, looking into her eyes.

"No. I've been expecting it so long."

"But you need to cry," he repeated.

And taking her arm, he led her outside. They walked together as far as the lakefront, where he sat down with her on a rock and held her close. When she had wept enough, they got up and turned toward home.

BELVA PLAIN

SEVEN

Joel liked to take the Sunday newspaper outdoors into the shade. There, in his comfortable chair, he read, sometimes drowsed in the heat, and woke to see Eve doing her science or history homework at the picnic table. There was something about her, at twelve still a child biting her pencil, and yet so soon to be a woman, that was painful to watch. She was so vulnerable, so ignorant of anything beyond this place where she was cherished and protected! Yet, should it be otherwise? Could it be otherwise? He

255

was reminded of a poem, one of the few he had ever read, and only because it had been required at school. Caroline had read it aloud again in German only the other day. How did it go? *You are like a flower, so lovely, pure and clean; when I look at you, it hurts—*

Yes, she was lovely with those cheekbones and marvelous eyes, almost a replica of Caroline. Always he wished that she were his own, and wished he could drive a certain arithmetic out of his brain: Add nine months to the few years of her age, and you knew how long it was since Caroline had lain with that other man, that "other," who would probably never cease disturbing his soul.

So she had indeed loved him! The rape, hideous as it was, would have produced less conflict in Joel's mind—indeed, no conflict at all.

The man had been handsome, graceful, very tall and fair, a blue-eyed aristocrat, full of charm and laughter. He had been a university scholar who could talk to Caroline about art and music. Also, he was a scoundrel, a criminal, a Nazi . . . But she had not known that when they made this child together. And he tried not to imagine the scene—the act.

But then she had accepted him, Joel, into her bed. Should he not be thankful and satisfied? More than satisfied? Yet, knowing as he knew that she did not feel for him the passion he still felt for her, he had to wonder how different she might have been with that other. He wished now that Lore had not told him so much, in such detail. It was, of course, his own fault for asking the questions; he should not have asked them. But he had needed, really needed to know. And he would certainly never want to ask Caroline. It would be, yes, it would be obscene.

I know very little about you, Caroline, he thought, except that you are honorable and that ever since Eve came you have been calm and good to live with. At night you come into my arms when I ask you to, although you are never the one who asks me. And still, it sometimes seems to me that I can tell what you are feeling. Maybe it's because of the remarks you make now and then, or your voice when you read to Eve, or the way you listen to the summer-night sounds of crickets and cicadas with such pleasure on your face.

I'm a simple man. I didn't grow up with poetry, you know that. And the music that you and Lore love so much, I never heard. Oh, never in my life could I have expected to meet a woman like you!

Lore sees it all. She understands. A remarkable woman, Lore is. When we moved here and she offered to get a little place of her own, to "give us our privacy" as she explained, I wouldn't hear of it. At home my parents always had room for another old maid cousin or aunt. It doesn't flatter a woman to be called an "old maid," but Lore is forty-two, after all, and looks older. There's no hope for a woman at that age, anyway. But at least she has us. She has a family.

There they are in the kitchen now, Lore and Caroline, fussing over tonight's company dinner. It's pleasant to hear their bustle, calling back and forth from kitchen to dining room, where Caroline is no doubt fixing flowers for the table. Now I hear Vicky's voice. She must have come in with a message from the restaurant. It's a good thing she's smart and competent enough to take charge when it's necessary. Business school really made a change in her, that and getting away from sour Gertrude. Still, maybe there was a little to be said for Gertrude. Vicky was some handful as a teenager, with her tough swagger and her tight, Lana Turner sweaters. She still swaggers some, and the sweaters could be less revealing, but she attracts people and we're lucky to have her, especially now that we have two places.

There's another thing. Two busy cafés grown out of Ricci's little bakery! Who could have dreamed that Caroline had such ambitions, or the ability to carry them out? She had never had the smallest connection with any kind of business at all. That day she came to me with the news that we could buy the Main Street property—

"Yes," she says, "here it is on paper. The asking price, the mortgage offer—" And I interrupt, "Where are we going to get the down payment?" And she tells me, "From the ruby. I sold it yesterday to some cousins of the Schulmans' who live in New York. Six thousand dollars. It's a fair price. I had it appraised. It's more than fair."

I feel a shock when I look at her finger and see that this treasured remnant of beauty, prosperity, and peace is gone. I feel regret, almost as though it had belonged, not to her mother, but to mine. "You wanted to save it for Eve," I protest.

"No. This business will be worth many rubies someday."

Of course, that's what the ambition is all about. I've always known that. It's for Eve's sake, which is natural. When you've gone through hell you can never feel secure enough. I should know . . .

Eve was still biting the pencil. "You'll ruin your teeth," Joel said.

"This is the worst history assignment. We're studying immigration and we're supposed to tell about our families."

"That shouldn't be hard. You know how we got here, how Mom and I met in Brooklyn. The Sandlers, the people who are coming tonight, are the ones who took in Mom and Lore. You remember how they had to promise to support them? No welfare in those days. You remember how Dr. and Mrs. Schulman helped us get started here, how we went to work—"

"I know that. The teacher wants history, Daddy. Something about the countries people came from, what it was like there and why they left."

Joel laid the paper aside and sat up, saying soberly, "We've told you about that, too, about the concentration camps and the death camps."

"Yes, but it's very hard to describe it all, to explain it."

"Very hard. In fact, it's unexplainable."

Across the yard, two butterflies danced in a fantastic orange swirl of chase and avoidance. When they had gone out of sight around the corner of the house, Eve said softly, "I remember something that a child over there wrote about never seeing another butterfly. I suppose they killed the child."

"They did."

BELVA PLAIN

"And we take Peter to the animal hospital when he has only hurt his paw a little."

Peter, hearing his name, came out from under the table, where he had been asleep. "He's as old as you are, which is fairly old in dog years," Joel said, wanting to change the direction that Eve was pursuing.

She was not to be diverted. "How could they have treated people like that?"

"Well, that's your history project, isn't it? That's what you must try to find out if you can. Have you taken any books from the library?"

"I have two upstairs, but they're awfully hard to understand. It would be easier if I were an Indian, a Mohawk, or an Algonquin. There wouldn't be so much political stuff to learn."

At the childish wish, Joel smiled. Yes, it would be a great deal easier. The complexities of European politics, he supposed, were difficult enough for even an educated adult to understand.

"When is this paper due?" he asked.

"Not for two weeks."

"All right Tomorrow evening we'll start to help you."

"I think sometimes I'm so lucky that I got born here, to you and Mom, Daddy."

"You certainly are."

"Maybe I don't need so much history, dates and that stuff. Maybe it'll be more interesting if you and Mom just give me more details of what it was like when Hitler came and how you escaped."

"That makes sense."

"You know what I'm thinking? If they had killed you, then I wouldn't be alive."

He was filled with tenderness. She was so earnest, with her forehead creased into a frown of dismay and her eyes wide with indignation.

"You know what, Daddy? If I ever meet any of those Nazis, I will kill them."

"The war is over. They're all gone."

"Well, even so. If I ever meet anybody who's been one, I'll kill him."

"Then you'll be acting like a Nazi yourself," Joel said gravely.

"I don't care. I will."

"Didn't Mom say you should change your

dress for dinner? These are special guests whom we haven't seen since we came to America. Mr. and Mrs. Sandler have retired. They're moving to California, and they're making a long detour just to visit us."

EIGHT

"We had no idea," Jake Sandler said, "that Ivy was this big. I guess we expected to see cows on the streets."

"You should have seen it twelve years ago. There were cows not two miles away when we came here. Now you'd have to go six miles or more to find farmers. The change came on account of the war," explained Joel. "New factories, stores, houses, and the highway, most of all. It used to be a two-lane blacktop road."

Jake nodded wisely. "Same thing in the

twenties after the first war. Let's hope all the prosperity doesn't end in a crash this time."

"There's no sign of it yet."

Joel, tipped backward in his chair, was feeling a pleasant satisfaction in the occasion. The house, while hardly a mansion, must still be impressive to the Sandlers. The table was set with red-and-white china and real crystal goblets, with a bowl of red zinnias from their own garden; "the girls"— he often thought of Caroline and Eve that way—were lovely as always; Lore, ready for her shift at the hospital, was her usual dignified presence in starched white. The whole scene spoke of prosperity and peace.

There was a great deal of gratitude and a little pride in his satisfaction. Well, maybe there was more than a little pride, he thought, and thinking so, could not resist a piece of news.

"We're expanding again. This will be our number three Orangerie, much larger than the two you've seen. It'll be mostly daytime business near two office buildings that are going up along the highway. But there may be nighttime business, too. You never know. Anyway, it's a great location. Location is everything.''

Joel was being expansive, Caroline saw. It was surely not his usual way, but it was understandable. These people had only known him at his lowest point. And she, sitting at the opposite curve of the round table, could only imagine their surprise at the sight of this confident man who had once been a pudgy, emotional, stammering boy.

It was, however, time to change the subject. ''Tell us about yourselves, Annie,'' she said.

''There's not much to tell. We're out of Brooklyn for the first time in our lives. We sold everything we owned except your silver bowl. I couldn't part with that. It's the most beautiful thing we ever had. So now we're on our way, a little older, a little fatter, but otherwise the same.''

And both of them really were the same, Jake still blunt and positive, Annie unable to sit still and stop talking, but forever the two kindest people in the world.

Annie got up now and went to the window. "Oh, my, all those pink geraniums. Remember my red ones? Look, Jake, they have corn and lettuce, all kinds of stuff. This place is a regular farm."

"It's only an acre," Joel protested.

"Well, it's gorgeous, really gorgeous. What a beautiful home!"

Caroline suggested that they have their coffee and dessert at the picnic table before it got dark. The September sun was markedly lower in the sky than it had been only a few weeks before; a soft haze lay over the little harvest. The birds were going south, and it was very quiet. Lore brought out the coffee, while Eve carried the cake, seven rich layers of chocolate.

"Don't tell me that's one of Lore's marvelous cakes!" cried Annie.

"Yes, and in your honor," Joel said. "We don't get them very often because Lore's too busy. She has no time for us. They say at the hospital that she's the best surgical nurse on the staff."

Lore waved him away. "Foolishness. Get away with your foolishness."

"I will not. Al Schulman's told me so more than once, and I've heard it from other people, too. We have a fine hospital here since the county took it over. Remember, Lore, the old car we bought so you could get to work? Ten years old with holes in the roof? Now," Joel said, "she's bought her own spiffy Chrysler, and she's a speed demon, a menace on the roads."

"Lord, when I remember that business about your jaw." Annie sighed. "All that needless worry. But thank God it turned out all right. Lore, you look great. You haven't changed a bit."

Lore laughed. "Yes, I'm still homely."

"You look pretty darn good to me," Jake said stoutly.

"Did we tell you that our daughter-in-law expects twins? No? I thought surely I did. Well, she's only in her fourth month. I'll send you a picture when they arrive. But I'm awfully slow at writing." Annie apologized, "I mean well, but I always postpone it."

"I haven't been very good about it, either," Caroline said.

"Oh, we understand. You've had a lot to

bear, with what happened to your parents and all. But we have to look at the bright side. Life goes on, doesn't it?"

If there is a cliché that fits, Annie or Jake will use it, Caroline thought, although not unkindly. She had actually not expected to be as moved as she was now by the sight of these two in their simple goodness. And she was on the verge of saying something that would convey her feelings to them when Joel spoke first.

"When you first saw me, I was sure I could never be happy again, that there was nothing left for me on this earth. But you two, Jake and Annie—you two have a lot to do in so many ways with what's happened. Me sitting here with Caroline and Eve—" He wiped his eyes. "Excuse the emotion. I get sentimental. Maybe the wine helps. You understand how it is."

Annie touched Joel's hand. "It's okay. It's okay, Joel."

Eve's eyes were on them all, moving from one to the other, observing everything. No longer are they the eyes of a child, thought Caroline, although what does that expression mean? That children of her age are innocent? Ignorant? Not so. Let her not be too innocent, this joy of my life, lest someone harm her. Let her not be ignorant, either, except of one thing. There was only one thing in all the world she must never know. Never.

Annie had turned to Eve. "I knew you before you were born."

Another cliché, well meant. Many times before, on every appropriate occasion, Eve had heard it spoken by people who had met them on their arrival in Ivy. Being well mannered, she smiled.

"You have your mother's eyes. I suppose everybody tells you that you look like her. Two peas in a pod."

"Yes." And Eve, turning away from the scrutiny, bent down to feed a scrap to Peter.

Annie was curious, of course. Caroline could tell she would have liked to get her alone, woman to woman, the older woman in motherly fashion asking the younger what on earth had happened between her and Joel. How had it ever come about? Or has it come about? I passed the bedroom when I used the bathroom upstairs, and it looked as if . . .

I suppose I would be curious, too, Caroline admitted.

The conversation was winding down. It had been a long afternoon, and there was after all a limit to what people can say to each other after so many years' absence and with nothing much more in common to start with beyond an enormous act of charity.

Joel was apologizing for the size of the house. "If only we had another bedroom here, we'd surely never let you go to a motel. You'd stay and get a good breakfast in the morning."

"Think nothing of it," Jake said. "We plan to start at the crack of dawn tomorrow, anyway. Take breakfast on the road. All we need are directions to the motel."

"It's not far, but there's a detour where the street's being torn up. Let's see. You know how to get back to Main Street from here? Okay. Go past the war monument, that'll be on your left. Make a right turn at the next light after the monument, go about a mile and a half, then when you see the detour sign, go past it to Remington Street—'' Joel frowned. "No. It'll be too easy for you to get lost. You'll be going in circles. And my car's in the shop till tomorrow afternoon, or I'd lead you. And Lore goes in the opposite direction, and she can't be late. Tell you what. Let Eve ride with you as far as Remington. You can bring her home, drop her off, and go right back. It'll cost you another fifteen minutes, that's all, and Eve would love to do it. You'll pass her new school on the way.''

Eve did not exactly "love to do it," but on the other hand, it meant that she would not have to help with the dishes. Because of the company, there were an awful lot of extra-fancy ones tonight. That's probably why Daddy was going to help instead of her. Mom was probably afraid she would break something, especially those crystal things. Anyway, Daddy often helped. He said it was only right, since Mom worked in the café offices all day.

"We came in by the lake," Mrs. Sandler

BELVA PLAIN

said when they were in the car. "Some lake!
You can't even see the other side."

"Oh, it goes for miles and miles till it joins
up with more lakes. We like to hike around
our side here. When I was a little girl, Mom
and I used to have a picnic there sometimes during school lunch hour. Not many
kids did that, but Mom loves the lake, and I
do, too."

"Well, you're a lucky girl to live here,"
Mrs. Sandler said.

Eve was in the front seat with Mr. Sandler. He had made the suggestion himself.
"Kids always like the front seat. I remember
how our boys used to fight over it."

He was a nice man. She was a nice person, too, or would be if she didn't talk so
much or ask so many questions. It was
funny when you thought about it, how many
ways there were for people to be different
from each other, and how, in the first few
minutes, you could like a new person very,
very much or not like him at all. Daddy said
it was wrong to be so quick to judge; you
had to give a person a chance. Daddy was
really, really fair.

"Now if I lived here," Mrs. Sandler said, "I'd choose one of those houses facing the lake. They were gorgeous, weren't they, Jake?"

He laughed. "Nothing but the best, eh?"

"We have friends who live in one of them. He's our doctor, Dr. Schulman, and we visit them. Mom says that's what she wants someday, a house like theirs with a view of the lake."

"The way you folks are going, she'll have it, too," Mr. Sandler said. "Your father tells me how smart your mother is, and I can see that myself. She's one smart woman."

"Well, you've got a fine home, you really have," Mrs. Sandler said. Her voice, blown forward across the back of the seat, was loud in Eve's ears. "Lore's in a class by herself, an angel. When I think of those two, Caroline and Joel, those young people fresh off the boat, I could still cry."

"Well, that's all past, so don't. My wife's got a heart as soft as mush, bless her," said Mr. Sandler.

"Oh, you, Jake! I'm not crying, I'm only saying how wonderful they are. And what a wonderful day it's been to see them here together, Caroline as beautiful as ever—after all she's been through. And Joel's turned out to be such a wonderful father after all that happened, such a wonderful father, as if he were Eve's real father instead of only—"

"Dammit all, Annie, you're talking so much that I can't concentrate on my driving. Will you keep still for even half a second? Do you think you can? I almost hit the curb, dammit! Are we near—what was that road, Eve, Remington? Are we near it?"

"It's the next one. Now you know the way, so you can take me home."

In the light of the street lamp, she saw his face. He had turned to look at her, but she was staring straight ahead, being *impassive.* It meant "having no expression, showing no emotion." Mom was always telling her to use the dictionary. Mom said she had a gift for languages, so she would be *impassive,* while her heart was beginning to run so fast that maybe it would stop and she would drop dead here in their car.

As if he were Eve's real father, Annie had

said. And he stopped her. He's furious with her, and she knows it because she hasn't opened her mouth since. He hasn't, either. He just keeps trying to get a look at me every time we pass a lighted spot. *Eve's real father. Instead of.* Instead of what? Then who? I feel carsick, and I haven't been carsick since I was four years old.

It seemed to take twice as long to go back as it had to get this far. No one spoke until, when they were almost home, Mr. Sandler said, "You were a big help, Eve. I never would have found the way by myself, but now I'll be okay. So thanks a lot."

"You're welcome," she answered properly.

Be calm. Be impassive. And hope you don't vomit until you get to the bathroom.

They drove away. Mrs. Sandler had changed to the front seat. Before they reached the corner, he would be giving her what-for. Giving her hell. Say it: hell. But had she been telling the truth? Of course she had been. Why would anybody make up a story like that? That somebody's father wasn't her father? And then they had acted so queerly right afterward.

Mom, still in the kitchen, heard her running upstairs. "Where are you going?" she called. "Will they find their way all right?"

Instead of going to the bathroom, Eve had run to her bedroom and lain down on the bed. Nausea had turned into dizziness, and the walls were slowly circling. *Real father.* She closed her eyes. If Daddy isn't my father, then is Mom not mine, either? And am I not Eve but somebody else? Who?

"Where are you?" Mom called from the foot of the stairs. "Come on down."

She wasn't able and didn't want to go down. She just wanted to lie still.

"Why, you've locked the door!" Mom cried, rattling the knob. "What's wrong, Eve?"

"Nothing."

Mom said quietly, "Eve, we don't play games with each other, do we? Please open the door. Are you sick?"

"Please let me alone. I'm not sick. I just need to be alone."

"But I need to know what's happened.

Have you hurt yourself? You have to tell me."

"I haven't hurt myself."

"Honestly?"

"Honestly. Mom. Mom, go away."

"What's going on?" That was Daddy's voice.

"She won't let me in. She's locked the door."

"Leave her alone, Caroline. She's entitled to privacy. She's collecting her thoughts, and she'll come out when she's ready."

Eve whispered into the pile of stuffed animals, a polar bear, a kangaroo, and a monkey, on the pillow. She whispered, and without a sound, cried.

"People need privacy. . . . She's collecting her thoughts," Daddy said. He always understands better than anyone else does, even better than Mom and Lore. Is it really possible, what Mrs. Sandler said about my "real father"? No, it couldn't be. It's too stupid, a stupid mistake. Yes, it can be. Even stupid people don't make a mistake like that.

After a while, another thought came to

her, and she sat up. Maybe I am adopted. So many people are, and there's nothing bad about being adopted. You can be perfectly happy. There's that boy Edgar in school. He knows he's adopted. Everybody knows he is, and it doesn't make any difference. But if I am, they should have told me.

Mom and Daddy were sitting at the kitchen table drinking coffee when, having wiped her face, Eve came downstairs. Plainly, they had been discussing her; she could see the worry in their faces, even in Daddy's, and he was never a worrier like Mom.

"Come sit down," Mom said. "Would you like a hot chocolate?"

Eve shook her head. She didn't want to be babied and soothed with hot chocolate or anything else. She wanted the truth, the truth that would say Mrs. Sandler didn't know what she was talking about. Still, if they were to tell her that, she wasn't sure she would quite believe them. It was very complicated.

Daddy said gently, "Sit down with us, anyway. If there's something you want to tell us, something that's bothering you, we're ready to listen. But you don't have to say anything at all unless you're ready to."

She sat down opposite him and studied his face while he stirred milk into his coffee. He wasn't allowed to have sugar because of his diabetes. She hoped so much that he would never be really sick; some people died of diabetes. At the thought of that, she felt her eyes sting again, and she wiped them angrily. It really made no difference, though, because they could certainly see that she had been crying. Her eyes were small and ugly under their puffed, shiny lids. In the movies, women looked so lovely when they cried. Their eyes got bright, while the tears slid down their perfect cheeks.

Her parents were pretending not to see her tears, which was nice of them. They were really nice people, not like some people's parents, like Vicky's cranky mother, who really wasn't her mother. But maybe these were not her parents. The thought kept fighting itself in her head. She didn't look in the least like Daddy. He had a long nose and light-brown curly hair. His cheeks went pink when he laughed, and—

"Are you looking at a fly on my forehead, or what?" he asked.

He wanted to be funny, to make her fears go away, but it wasn't going to work.

"Mrs. Sandler said you aren't my father," she said.

Two coffee cups clinked on their saucers. Mom's cup overturned, and she cried out, "What? What is this? Has she gone out of her mind?"

"Wait. Wait, Caroline." For a few seconds, no one said anything. Daddy gave a long sigh. Then he spoke slowly. "What exactly did she tell you, Eve?"

"She said you were a wonderful father, as if you were my real father, 'instead of,' she said, but she didn't finish because Mr. Sandler didn't let her."

"I see."

He wasn't smiling anymore. She looked from him to Mom, whose face had gone red, as if she had smeared it all over with rouge. Why did neither of them say right out that Mrs. Sandler was an idiot or a liar?

And then Mom did say it, or almost. "Annie Sandler often doesn't know what she's talking about. She can say the most ridiculous things."

Eve got out of her chair. It felt awful, sitting there between them. It felt like stretching a rubber band, knowing that it's bound to snap if you keep on, but keeping on anyway until it does snap and stab you. She stood up, clenching her fists at her sides.

"You're not answering me. You're not telling me anything. I think I'm adopted, and you don't want to hurt my feelings."

Now they were looking at each other as if they were asking: What shall we do? So that's it, Eve thought. They adopted me because they weren't able to have a baby of their own. Some women can't. Yes.

But then, why do strangers always exclaim when we're introduced: *My! Anybody can see that you two are mother and daughter!* And what about the times we stand together at a mirror and laugh at how alike we are? Lore's known Mom since Mom was a baby, and she says—No. Not adopted. I've got to be Mom's child.

"If you won't tell me what Mrs. Sandler meant, I'm going to phone her at the motel right now and ask her."

"Don't do that!" Mom screamed. "You can't do that."

"But you won't answer me. Daddy, are you my father?"

He seemed so sad, the way he looked at her. And he sounded sad, too, even though what he answered wasn't sad at all.

"I've been your father since you were born, Eve. I built your cradle for you."

Oh, there is something they don't want to say. They can't fool me. And Mom is trying not to cry. The red has gone from her face. It looks terrible.

And Eve persisted, "What did she mean when she said, 'instead of'?"

She waited. Daddy was looking toward Mom. And suddenly, in that same low, sad voice, he said, "Caroline, the truth has to be told. If we don't do it, Eve will never again believe anything we say."

Mom stared at him. She was really crying now, sobbing. "For God's sake, what are you doing, Joel?"

284

"Do you think I want to do it? But it has to be done."

Eve's legs were shaking. Her heart was running again as it had run before when she thought it might stop.

"Take hold of yourself, Caroline. It's our fault. We should have brought the whole thing into the light from the very start."

"You don't know what you're doing! Why? Why?"

They were talking over her head, as if she wasn't there. The clock was ticking, the cat was sleeping on the window ledge, and her heart was going to stop and kill her.

"I do know, Caroline. This was bound to come out."

"From across the ocean? How?"

"Well, you see that it has."

"You'll destroy everything."

"No. We'll destroy everything if we don't do it."

"I beg you, Joel."

Daddy took his handkerchief and wiped Mom's wet face. She was scared, and he was almost crying himself.

"Go upstairs," he told Mom. "Let me talk

to Eve alone. It'll be easier for you that way."

"No," Mom said. "I'll stay. Get it over with. Go ahead. You've gone this far, too far already, so get it over with."

"Listen to me, Eve," Daddy began. "You can make a long, long story out of almost anything if you want to, or you can just tell the simple truth, which is all that matters. There was a man in Europe whom your mother thought she loved. They were going to be married. She was very young, and she made a mistake. She didn't know then that he was not a good man. He went away. So she came here to America without him, knowing that a baby—you—were going to be born. Do you understand so far?"

"Yes."

Of course. Don't you think I know anything? I think about things like that a lot. It's really sort of nasty when you do think about it, the way they make babies when they're in bed. Still, it's the only way to make a baby, and only married people are supposed to do it. I suppose Daddy and Mom do it, although they haven't had another baby. But now I see. She did it with somebody else, not with him, so that's why he's really not my father.

"Then Mrs. Sandler was right, and you're not my father?"

"Well, in a way not, but in the only way that counts, I am. Because I love you, Eve. That's what it is to be a father, to love and care."

Mom had turned around with her face hidden in her arms. I don't feel sorry for her. She did this to me. It's her fault, Eve thought, and whispered,

"Who was he? What was his name? Why did he go away?"

"You might as well tell her," Mom whispered without looking up. "Since she knows this much, she might as well know it all."

Daddy began to cough. It was a make-believe cough. He was forcing it. Then he drank some cold coffee, made a bitter face, and said, "His name was Walter. That's all I know or want to know. Perhaps sometime Mom will give you more information if she wants to."

"You said he wasn't a good man. What did he do?"

"He was a Nazi."

"A Nazi who killed people in the camps?"

"How can I say whether he personally killed anyone, Eve? It's best not to think about it. He was one of them, and that's enough."

It seemed to Eve that she had never been as angry. The walls were going slowly around and around. She stood up, stood over her mother, and shouted, "You gave me a bad man for a father. How could you do that to me?"

Mom's face was still terrible, and she didn't answer.

"Don't say that, Eve," Daddy said. "That's not fair. It's cruel."

"She wasn't even married, and she did that. She always says it's wrong, everybody says so, and she did it herself."

"People make mistakes. You'll make plenty in your life, too, although I hope not that one. So don't blame your mother. There's no better mother in the world."

"But a Nazi . . . Maybe he even killed

her own father and mother, or yours, Daddy."

"Not likely."

"You said she loved him." The anger, the terror in Eve were making her want to smash the dishes and tear down the curtains. "Did she love you, too, when you got married?"

"Yes, of course she did. People are supposed to love each other when they get married."

"So why didn't she marry him?"

"I told you, he went away. It was all a mistake from the start. Mom can tell you more when she's ready, but she isn't ready now. Wait, Eve. Please give her a chance."

"I don't care. I need to know everything right now, this minute."

"Listen, Eve. This is terrible for her, too. She's exhausted."

Daddy was frightened. Perhaps this was very hard for him, too.

"I'll tell you what, Eve. Let's let your mother rest. Look at her. I'll go up to your room with you, we'll sit and we'll talk some more. Let Mom alone now."

He took her elbow, propelling her to the door. At the top of the stairs he bent to kiss her cheek, but she didn't want him to. He wasn't her father. He had lied to her, pretending to be her father. And suddenly she hated him. She hated the man named Walter, who went around killing people and was supposed to be her father. Most of all, she hated Mom, who had done those things with a strange man, a horrible, evil, Nazi monster. And now because of Mom, this monster was her father. Somewhere, he was alive. What if he should ever come looking for her? She would kill him. Yes, she thought, I would. She would spend her life wanting to kill him. Mom had spoiled her life. Yes, it was spoiled. She wasn't herself. She had turned into somebody else, not Joel's daughter. She didn't even belong in this house anymore. If only there were some other place she could go. But there was nobody to go to, except maybe Vicky, and that mean old Gertrude wouldn't want her, anyway.

Hating the world, Eve went to her room

and slammed the door shut in Daddy's face.

It was after midnight when Lore arrived home to find Joel and Caroline still awake downstairs.

"You look as if you've been struck by lightning," she cried when she had heard the tale of events.

"We were struck," Joel said. "I don't think either of us could pick up a kitten right now."

Caroline lay back on the sofa. From the open door to the dining room, she was seeing what was left of the day, the flowers and the cherished crystal still on the table, waiting to be replaced in the cupboard. A few hours ago the crystal, her first extravagance since they had been in this place, had been important to her. Foolish, foolish!

Now her child lay upstairs with God only knows what terrible lonely thoughts in her poor, frenzied little head. The steady progress of time and friendly habit, working and doing together with Joel, had built a strong affection; the past had almost faded; they never spoke of it; there was no need. Now here it was, alive and back again, sorrowful and ugly.

Lore observed, "Poor Annie never had any tact. Big heart, big mouth, and not too bright. Remember?"

"To tell the truth, I don't," Caroline replied, "but I'm not thinking very clearly."

"No wonder they scurried away when they brought Eve back," Joel said. "They didn't even wait to see her in at the front door. They realized what they had done."

"I'll talk to her tomorrow," Lore said. "I'm sure I can help some. She's had a terrible shock, and it will take a lot of explaining, that's all."

Through the years, Lore had always been an encouragement to fortitude and optimism. When your spirits fell, it was Lore who lifted them. Had she not done so again and again for Mama all during those darkest hours before the war? But this was different.

Disconsolate, Joel stood at the window. People in trouble always seemed unconsciously to go to a window, as if a solution somehow lay out there in the world beyond. This window, though, being open, admitted only the aroma and the sibilant rustle of warm leafage. He stood unmoving, with his hands behind his back.

People are supposed to love each other when they get married.

Suddenly, he turned around. "I'm going to write and let those people know what they've done, what Annie did, with her meddling in other folks' business. She's not going to get away with a clear conscience. Dammit, she's not."

"I wouldn't do that," advised Lore. "You'll upset yourself for nothing. She'll probably answer that she assumed Eve knew. Best let it rest and take care of Eve."

"Yes, Joel, she's right. And you were right, too," Caroline murmured. "We should have told Eve from the start. I can't explain why we didn't."

"Certainly you can. You've forgotten the reason. You didn't want the neighbors to know. We were ashamed."

He had spoken the bitter truth. But it

hadn't been only on account of the neighbors. Why should a child be given an unnecessary burden? Life was hard enough without one. That, too, was the bitter truth.

"After all the good years, now, at twelve, she has turned her rage against me. Didn't you see that, Joel? Against me, instead of —of *him*."

"She doesn't know him to rage at," Joel said.

"The longer she thinks about this, the more she will hate me."

"I will not let her," Joel said firmly. "Lore, when you talk to Eve tomorrow, don't let her blame her mother. You'll know what to say. Now let's go upstairs. It's one o'clock. Come, darling. This thing can't be allowed to destroy us."

Lore agreed. "Absolutely not. Get some sleep. We've had some big trouble here, that's sure. But the sky hasn't fallen."

THE next day, however, it seemed that the sky had not only fallen, but crashed. By eight o'clock Eve was still in her room with the door locked. Gentle knocks and calls and persuasions had no result but defiance.

"I'm not coming out. I'm not going to school anymore. You can't make me."

"Eve, don't do this to yourself," Joel said. "Please listen to us."

"Why should I listen to you? You're not my father."

"Oh, God," Caroline groaned, meeting Joel's sad eyes. He, the innocent, should not have to suffer these wounds.

"He is your father if anyone is. You know better than that. Don't hurt him like this, Eve. Come out. Let me talk to you."

"No. You're not my mother, either. I don't want you, not after what you did."

These last words ended in a sob. And, helplessly, the pair stood in the hall at the locked door.

"What's going on?" asked Lore.

"She won't come out or let us in. Will you try? Maybe she'll speak to you."

"All right. You two go down first. Eve, don't be a baby. We need to talk sense. We always do, you and I, don't we? Let me in."

In the kitchen, in the same places where

they had sat the night before when peace had exploded, they took their seats. All was quiet upstairs, so Lore had evidently been admitted and was at work with Eve.

By its appearance, it was an ordinary morning in early fall. Amber light fell over the linoleum, a few early dropping leaves swirled past the window, and the cat, having jumped down from the ledge where she often passed the night, lapped at her bowl of milk in the corner. All was as usual except for the sore lump in Caroline's throat, strained by the effort to control herself.

"You didn't expect anything like this when you wanted to marry me," she said abruptly.

"You didn't expect, either, when you met that—that man—what resulted." Joel got up and stroked her bowed head. "I wish I could stay home with you today. But I have to go to work. Wholesale orders for the three places go out this morning."

She nodded. She was still sitting there when Lore reported that Eve was getting dressed.

"She refuses to go to school. She says

she's ashamed. It seems, poor little soul, that she phoned her best friend, Jill, early this morning to give her the news. And Jill laughed. She thought it was funny."

"It's a truism, isn't it? Children are cruel."

"Adults are, too. You'll find that out, I'm afraid, when the news spreads, which it will. I wish to heaven she hadn't told her friend."

"I'll find it out, you say? I never knew it before, Lore?"

"Yes, you knew it. But when it touches your child, or so I'm told by people who have a child, the cruelty is far worse."

That was true. She would never forget the look on Eve's face last night. Never.

"It's bad enough to have a skeleton pop out of the closet, but in a way it's worse having to worry all your life about when it's going to pop out." And Lore gave her sad smile.

You saw it seldom, that sad little smile, which made it the more impressive when you did see it. Father used to insist that Lore was fundamentally a very sad person.

"Well, it's out. We'll simply have to contend with it, and we all will. Joel's very patient, and he'll be a support. I wish I could stay home all day with you, Caroline. I'd be a buffer between you, but I can't. But maybe it's just as well for you both to face it by yourselves."

At noon, Eve emerged briefly to eat the lunch that Caroline prepared. She cast off Caroline's arm, stuck her fingers in her ears, wiped away Caroline's kiss, and went back upstairs. When she had gone, the stillness became unbearable. The house was forsaken and shiveringly cold. Alarming thoughts ran wild through Caroline's head.

There was so much to be undone, to be explained away. Think of the thousand questions that a girl will ask her mother and recall the thousand fabrications with which you replied. Girls are fascinated by weddings: *What did you wear when you and Daddy were married?* So you stumbled over the response: *Oh, the usual. It was a very simple wedding.* You always tried not to contradict yourself and tried, for your own sake, too, not to dwell on the truth of that day. . . .

Late that afternoon when school was out,

Caroline opened the door on a small delegation of girls from Eve's class.

"We've come to talk to Eve," announced Jill, the best friend. "We want her to go to school tomorrow. We want her to know that nobody's going to say anything or do any teasing. After all, it isn't *her* fault."

The teacher had had a hand in this. The words were fairly spoken: It was certainly not any fault of Eve's, but purely the fault of Eve's mother, at whom these girls were casting their curious glances.

"Go up, girls," she said calmly. "Eve's in her room."

So now Walter was back in her life. He was up now in that room where a bunch of little girls, echoing their mothers, no doubt, were reviving him, giggling and speculating as they understandably did over a cheap romance at the movies. Ah, but never mind them! Never mind, if you can help it, the furtive glances and the excessive politeness that will be given you as you go about your customary life. Never mind, although you do indeed mind, the sly male jokes about Joel that will be told behind his back, and that he will know men are telling behind his back. Oh, the only thing that counts is Eve. How great is the damage to Eve?

That evening it was very great. Apparently the visit of her friends had done nothing for her but increase her resolve to stay out of school. When she failed to come down to dinner, Lore went to her room and found her crying in a fit of despair.

"I couldn't get anywhere with her," she reported. "I don't know. I'm wondering whether Vicky can do anything."

"Why? Does Vicky know what's happened?"

"She does," Joel said grimly. "The mother of one of those little girls is a friend of Gertrude's. You'll be interested in hearing Gertrude's opinion. Vicky told me that her lovely pseudo-mother always suspected that things weren't all 'on the up and up' with us. Vicky, to her credit, was disgusted."

"Nevertheless," said Caroline, "we don't want Vicky talking to Eve."

Lore defended Vicky. "Why not? She's

good at heart and knows how to get along in the world. I like her."

"I don't dislike her, Lore. But I just don't think she's the right person to understand this situation."

"You underestimate her. She's never had the right chances in life."

"Lore, dear, you make excuses for everyone."

"I think we should call Al Schulman," Joel suggested. "The child can't be allowed to cry all night. Perhaps he'll have something to calm her. I don't know. Anyway, I'm going to call him."

Dr. Schulman came at once. The summons had not surprised him, for Emmy had already heard the story from someone who had stopped at the Main Street Orangerie and overheard a conversation about it. Therefore, needing little explanation, he went directly to Eve and stayed almost two hours, while the others waited below in a high state of tension.

"She's calmer now," he said when he returned. "We had a serious talk. I think, though, she has become a few years older overnight. But that's no cause for despair. It's astonishing what a child who is loved can manage to overcome. The Holocaust, for instance." For a second, his voice faded. "Eve is loved," he resumed. "And now that I've spoken to her, I must think about you two parents also. In your different ways, you have suffered a great blow. I'd like to talk to you about it if you will."

When he had finished, it crossed Caroline's mind that once she had declined to confide in this doctor because he had seemed too shallow. How wrong one can be in one's judgment of another human being!

"Talk to Eve candidly," he concluded. "Don't be deceived by her age or by some childish remark she may make. She is capable of understanding more than you think. Tell her frankly how everything happened and how you feel about it."

Everything? thought Caroline later, lying restlessly awake against Joel's comforting shoulder. He slept, but all night long her eyes watched the shadows on the ceiling, heard every creak as the old house rustled and even the tiny jingle of the tags on Peter's collar when he thumped and stirred in his sleep.

Everything. Tell her everything.

"I need to know about him," Eve said. "What did he do? What did he look like?"

They were walking along the lakeshore down at the solitary end of the drive beyond the row of houses.

"Get off by yourselves," Dr. Schulman had advised. "Just mother and daughter. I think the first emotional blowup is past, although there will surely be many others from time to time. But they'll be smaller once the first shock and rage have been absorbed. And give her a few days, maybe till the end of the week, to stay away from school. The kids will have some other excitement to talk about by then."

"Do I look like him?" Eve asked for the tenth time or more.

"You know very well that you look like me. Everyone tells you."

"Exactly like you?"

"As exactly as any two people can re-semble each other."

And yet, now that the issue had become moot, Caroline was seeing things in Eve that she had not observed, or had not wanted to observe, before. Those horizontal lines across the forehead, so noticeable in a very young man, were already forming on Eve's forehead. Eve was left-handed; she had not allowed herself to recall that he had been left-handed, too. Eve was compulsively neat in ways that I never was, thought Caroline, and she saw now that she was being directed to see long fingers and long, narrow feet, and the way a head tips back in a roar of laughter. . . .

She stiffened her shoulders. He hadn't had much to laugh about, had he, when they all went down to defeat? Hold that thought, she said silently, for whatever small comfort is in it.

They were going before the wind, into its rush. Eve's long hair streamed as she walked, head down, kicking pebbles. It was already late in the afternoon, and the sun was pale. They had been talking intermittently all day—it was Saturday, and Eve was home—and Caroline was tired. For a person who was known to have energy, she was incredibly exhausted, waiting for Eve's next words.

"You said you hardly knew—knew each other when you got married."

"Do you mean when I married your daddy?" Caroline asked gently. "You still sometimes hesitate, I notice, to use the name. *Daddy.* Say it. He's your father, the only one you'll ever know."

"That other—he—will he ever come looking for me?" asked Eve in a voice so low and fearful that the wind almost carried it away.

"Darling, he doesn't know you exist. And if he did know, you'd be the last person that he'd want to see. Anyway, it was a long war, and he may well be dead."

As they walked, the pebbles flew, scuffing the tips of Eve's shoes. Suddenly she looked up at Caroline, demanding, "How could he have left you like that after he—"

After we had "made love" she meant, and was too embarrassed to say it. Caroline, trying to remember what images of her own parents' bed she might have harbored when she was twelve, found that she was unable to. Such images were forbidden, and had therefore been hidden away in the remotest chink of the brain.

"After we 'made love'? Because he realized that he didn't want me. He had made a mistake. It had been an aberration, which means a really crazy mistake. People think for a short time that they want a thing and then wonder whatever can have made them want it." Expressively, Caroline threw her hands up. "Why, that's all wrong! It's not for me at all!"

"It was very wrong, all the same," Eve said.

Caroline thought gratefully, she's beginning to see that I am not the complete, sole villain.

"So then you quickly fell in love with Daddy, right?"

"Yes, that's the way it was."

Al Schulman might say, "Tell her everything," but there had to be limits.

"And you're still in love with him now?"

The enormous, questioning eyes were looking straight into Caroline's face. "In love"—the stuff of movie magazines, words that came without meaning, as far from the actual tangle of human emotions as if they had been written for an English-speaking reader in Bulgarian or some other unknown language.

"I love him," she replied.

There are so many, many ways. . . .

"He loves you, too. He always tells me so."

"I know. Shall we go back home?"

"Not yet."

"The afternoons are getting shorter. It will soon be time for dinner."

"I'm not hungry."

"But maybe other people are."

"I don't care. I have too much on my mind."

Caroline had to stifle her sigh. It wasn't over yet, not by a long way. These questions and answers would have to be repeated over and over. These ghosts would rise and reappear.

Now Eve's defiance sparked. "Jill said

her mother said you had to get married so I would have a name."

Did people have nothing else to talk about but someone else's pain? True, most people had, like Emmy Schulman, been behaving with maturity and tact, but many had not. How quickly all this information had leaked out and spread! If only that fool of an Annie had kept still! They had written a nice thank-you letter from California without making mention of anything else. Maybe they hadn't realized the damage she had caused. Joel said they must realize it and that the letter was to be ignored. But Caroline contradicted him. "If it weren't for those wonderful, good souls we wouldn't be here. Put this behind you, Joel. And besides, when will we see them again? They're at the other end of the country."

As for herself, she must keep her temper and her patience. "I did not have to do anything I didn't want to do," she told Eve. "I wanted you to have a father, a good one. And that's what you have. What we both have, a man to love and trust. That's what matters, Eve. Goodness matters."

"Do you hate him?"

"Who?"

Temper flared again. "Him. That Walter. That Nazi you gave me for a father."

"I thought we'd gone over all that, Eve."

Why does anybody ask that question? Joel has never asked it, and he's the one who's entitled to if anybody is. But Lore asks it now and then, and it bothers me, though I don't tell her so. There are so many feelings mixed in that single word and mixed in me: sadness, fury, astonishment, and contempt. What difference does it make now, anyway, whether I hate him or not? It was a long time ago.

"Susan says her parents think maybe you were a Nazi, too."

"Eve, you positively stop me in my tracks! I ask you, have you ever heard anything more ridiculous than that?"

The two stood still. And suddenly, as Eve said no, they both burst out laughing.

The days, the weeks and the months passed. Gradually the conversation at home turned to natural subjects: school, Lore's hospital, and business in the Orangeries. Very, very gradually it became possible to put an arm around Eve, to kiss her and receive a kiss in return.

"We're getting back to normal," Joel said. "I think it's going to be all right, don't you?"

Without him, and without Lore, too, it would have been very different. They were a pair of sturdy people. Better not to think about how it would be if she had to cope with Eve alone, thought Caroline.

"Yes," she replied, "I think so."

Yet there remained in Eve an anguished curiosity that at odd times, in the midst of buying a pair of shoes, setting the table, or feeding the cat and dog, would surge to hurtful words that had to be spoken before they could subside.

You might, Caroline told Joel once, compare Eve's anguish to a bleed that has to seep until it stops. It will take a long while until only the scar remains.

NINE

These were the Eisenhower years, when tourists began to fly across the Atlantic to Europe, and when television was no longer the novelty that had brought the neighbors in to see the first set on the block.

Nevertheless, most people still traveled by train or car, and that was how Joel and Caroline would have taken Eve out West if other things had not intervened.

They stood before the latest Orangerie, now nearing completion in a town some fifteen miles down the highway from Ivy. Most of the familiar orange awnings were already up, the lavish shrubbery was in place, and men were laying flagstones on the rear terrace where in summer, under cool shade, the tables would almost surely be crowded.

"I'm still not used to it," Joel said. "Number six! Can you believe it? How could we have dreamed when we started in Ricci's little place that we'd see anything like this?"

Caroline smiled at him. "Nothing succeeds like success. That's what they say, isn't it? This all began with your good bread, you know."

"And your imagination."

"Aren't we a mutual admiration society this morning? Come on, we need to start back. I've that appointment with Al Schulman."

"Didn't you just have your annual checkup?"

"Last week. But I always go back to get the report."

"And thank God, it's always good. Strong as a horse, you are. Just let me remind the masons to curve the corners of the terrace.

If somebody should trip, at least he won't strike a sharp point."

She watched him walk away. At forty, he was still trim, just beginning to acquire the slightly round-shouldered look of the deskbound, as well as the equally slight swagger of the man who was casually conscious of his good, hand-tailored suit and his real-estate investments. But Joel was one who must be forgiven for his pride, and it wasn't much pride, at that. From the hot bake oven to all this! And she had to smile to herself, remembering the first little room at Ricci's that she had decorated with some chintz and an orange tree ordered from a catalog.

"Why didn't I think of it first?" he always said. "I was supposed to be the businessman."

Like too many men, he took pride in saying that he had never had a vacation. It worried her, especially because of his diabetes. He was careless about what he ate, and he worked too hard. It was a triumph for her that he had finally agreed to the trip West. Most likely he had agreed because of Eve.

"I want Eve to love this country as I do," she had explained. "The best way to love it is to know it. You should, too, Joel. All we've had are a few hasty glances at Chicago and New York, those and the local towns with their Elm and Maple streets."

"How about seeing Europe?" he had asked.

"Maybe someday when we can afford it."

"No problem about that right now." His grin showed pleasure in his ability to be generous; often she found herself checking his tendency to spend too much on everything and everybody.

He had pursued the question. "Don't you want it now?"

"Not particularly. I went all over a good part of Europe when I was a child, from Norway to Greece, from one fancy hotel to another."

"That's not the reason. You don't want to go for the same reason I don't."

"So you were just testing me?"

"I was. It's far too soon after what's happened there. We'll need a lot more time before we'll feel comfortable."

LEGACY OF SILENCE

So they were buying a station wagon and heading west. There were to be four of them, including Lore.

"It's such a beautiful thing to see, the way Joel includes Lore," remarked Emmy Schulman. "You don't see many men being as thoughtful to their wives' families. But then, he is special."

"Goodness, he'd even take Vicky if he could find somebody to fill her place in the office. He's had special sympathy for her since she was a young girl being brow-beaten by Gertrude. Now, after all these years, she almost seems like some sort of third cousin to us."

"I never liked her, to tell you the truth," Emmy said, which was an odd remark coming from one who was usually forgiving.

Vicky did have a reputation of sorts. Nearing thirty, but looking younger, she had not married, but was always seen with a presentable man. Her smart clothes were just on this side of vulgarity, and so were her manners, alert yet jovial, and quick with a retort that was almost, but not quite, rude.

In the office she was irreplaceable, an ab-

315

solute whiz with numbers. "She could run that office single-handed," Joel declared.

Nevertheless, Caroline, who liked her well enough, was pleased that she was not going along; in a subtle way, she would destroy the atmosphere.

"I'll drop you off at Al's office," he said now, "then go check on the station wagon."

"If you think of it, will you get a new dog bed for the trip? The shop is across the street from the car place."

Peter Number Three was a stray, a terrier mix that the dogcatcher had found abandoned on the highway. Pure white—when he was fresh out of the bath—and floppy-eared, he bore no resemblance to Peter the Second other than his expression, which was sad. Joel could never resist a forlorn face.

"Do we have to bring him?" he asked now. "He'll be a big responsibility."

"Eve won't put him in a kennel. And she'll take all the responsibility."

"Okay, then. I'll take her word. Her word's her bond."

"That's true."

"She's come a long way in the last four years, don't you think? She seems so much older than sixteen. I wonder whether that bad time, that shock is the reason, or part of it, at least."

"I don't know, but she's much more mature than I was at sixteen, and for some time after that, too."

"She never mentions it to me, hasn't asked since that first year. Does she ever talk to you about anything?"

"Anything" meant "him," Caroline understood. Not half a dozen times had Eve made any reference to what must have been her most salient discovery about herself. Yet, painfully, Caroline recalled each one. There had been the time, for instance, when Eve had remarked, "I suppose, if a person grew up in a terrible family like *his*, maybe he couldn't help being like the rest of them." And, as if he had been standing there in front of her, Caroline had seen again the bullheaded, crop-haired monster with the Fascist regalia on his lapel, crossing the sidewalk in front of his house. Eve's grandfather! She scarcely remembered how she had answered.

"No," she said now, "we don't talk about it."

Joel did not answer. The conversation was heading into deep waters, and she changed it abruptly.

"Lore is so excited about this vacation. It's a pleasure to hear her."

"What does she get out of life? Work, work, and a concert in the city now and then."

"She loves her work, you know that."

"True, but I'd hate to think that work was all I had."

They were on the lake drive passing the Schulmans' house. He slowed the car to look at the neat front walk between low juniper hedges and the side lawn, on which jonquils in scattered clusters were coming into bloom.

"You know," he said, "we ought to buy a house here. You've always dreamed about living by the lake. What are we waiting for? We're not kids anymore."

"They're much too expensive, Joel."

"We've got enough in the bank to buy two of them, my dear."

She let her eyes rove up and down the street. There was no ostentation about these quiet houses set among the comfort of large, old trees; just so had stood the white stone house of her childhood; solid, made to last, to keep and hand down in a family. How well she remembered it! And then she remembered herself only a few years ago, a scared and penniless outsider invited by kind women to a ladies' luncheon on that street. . . .

"No," she said, "leave it in the bank. We're fine where we are."

"Think about it," Joel replied. "Should I come back for you at the doctor's, or will you walk?"

"I'm going to stop at our Main Street place, anyway, before I go home. I'll walk."

The woman who went up the steps at the doctor's office was not the woman who came down them half an hour later.

Dr. Schulman took both her hands and laughed at her bewilderment. "Well," he said. "Well. Have I got a surprise for you!"

"Don't tell me you won the lottery."

"Much, much better than that. Caroline, you're going to have a baby."

"Al, you must be out of your mind."

"Not today, at any rate. It showed up in your routine specimen. Somebody at the lab mistakenly added a pregnancy check, and there it was. Are you dazed? Yes, of course you are. But happy, too, I hope."

"Al, are you absolutely sure of it?"

"Yes, I asked for a second check. There's no question. You look dumbstruck. Sit down."

"I am dumbstruck. Good Lord, I'm thirty-six."

"So? Women have babies at thirty-six."

"But after all these years! It seems ridiculous."

"It seems quite wonderful, Caroline. Here's Eve soon to leave for college, and here's a newcomer to liven the household."

All kinds of doubts went scurrying through her mind. "I wonder how Eve will take another shock, when she's barely out of the first—if you can say she'll ever really be out of it. And you can't."

"Eve will be fine. She's had much more than this to take, and she took it."

"I hope so."

"For that matter," Dr. Schulman said, "so did you, when your turns came."

"I wonder what Joel will do."

Here Schulman laughed again. "Joel? He will want to announce it on national television. He will burst his buttons. Go on home, my dear, and make an appointment with Arnold Baker. He's the best obstetrician in the area."

Weak in the knees from sudden panic, she walked out into the spring sunshine. The day was now completely altered; where before there had been a lazy quality to the air—spring fever—there was now a quality of urgent hurry, as if time were pressing; a thousand changes to be made, words to be spoken and things to be done, all at once. Questions, exclamations, words. Only until she almost tripped and fell over a curb did she realize that she had been running.

Al Schulman calls it "wonderful," she thought. Of course, every birth is a natural wonder, whether it's wanted or not. I certainly can't say that this one was wanted, though. Still, I can't even say it wasn't wanted, because the fact is I haven't thought about it for years. I simply assumed, and eventually I suppose Joel assumed, too, that it wasn't going to be. But here we are. It will take getting used to.

It's amazing how quickly you forget what to do with a baby. When I see that new one next door asleep in his carriage, I'm ashamed to say that I can barely remember Eve at that age. Lore says it's because of the circumstances. I was still holding on by the skin of my teeth.

This time, though, it will be different. This one, at least, has a sure place in which to lay its little head. This one's father is a *man.* What would it look like, he or she, like Eve again, or will it have Joel's face, round and pink? What an adventure it is to wait through these slow months for your surprise!

Then she began to feel foolish. She would be so conspicuous pushing a baby carriage. And yet, an incredible new life! All these emotions were pulsing in her body.

And, too, knife-sharp, was the recollection of that other day, of the doctor on the ship who had known at once that she was pregnant and told her not to speak of it. "Moral turpitude," he'd said. Moral turpitude! Her Eve, her graceful, tender, thoughtful Eve. Her chest was filled with hot indignation.

Ah, but now the required ring was on her finger. The title was attached to her name. Not even Vicky's carping Gertrude could have anything to say except, perhaps, that thirty-six is too old.

Me! At that she had to laugh. And she walked fast now, laughing her way homeward.

JOEL, as Al Schulman had predicted, was really bursting his buttons. Unfastening his vest—he always wore a proper vest under his jacket—he helped himself to another piece of the whipped-cream masterpiece that Lore had baked for the celebration.

"Two portions, Joel. You know you shouldn't," warned Caroline.

"To hell with diabetes. Pour me another glass of wine."

This was the first time any of them had seen him even slightly tipsy. His face was one big, crinkling smile.

"When did you say? When?" he demanded again.

"I've told you a hundred times. December. Late December."

"I'd better get started on the cradle. We should have kept the one I made for you, Eve, but we gave it away. If I say so myself, it was a beauty."

"Well, you've got eight months to make another, Daddy."

Eve was curious about the proceedings, as if it were somehow quaint at this point to introduce a baby into the family. Her latest boyfriend's mother had just had what the boyfriend called an "accident," a baby at age forty. In her case, though, it was the fifth, so it couldn't possibly be as interesting as Caroline's was.

"Not really. There'll be a lot to do before January. We're going to move." And Joel looked expectantly around the table.

"Move! What are you talking about?" cried Caroline.

"You, Mrs. Caroline, are going to have your lake-view house. Yes," he said, beaming his triumph. "Yes, that house on the corner piece, the double lot, the house with the blue spruce that you always admire. It's going up for sale. I heard about it at the bank this morning, and I made an offer right away, no dickering. I'll pay the asking price and we can move in by September."

"Oh, Joel, I told you not to take our savings and—"

"I'm not taking our savings. There's a syndicate that wants to put up a garden apartment on this street. We're right in the middle of the row, which puts us in the position of wrecking their plan if we should refuse to sell. I met with them last week right after you gave me the great news, and I told them they could have what they wanted if they'd pay enough to buy a house overlooking the lake."

The three women were stunned. As if they were having the same thought, all turned to the window and looked out over what they still called "Angela's vegetable garden," where the dark earth was newly harrowed in preparation for seeding.

"It'll seem so strange to move," Eve said. "I've never lived anywhere else."

"A move is very expensive," Caroline said. "People tell me you always find a lot of unexpected things to be done after you move in." A house near the lake had been a glamorous fantasy to enjoy, but the actuality, added to the surprise pregnancy, was suddenly daunting. "What do you think, Lore?"

"I think this house is good enough," she replied. "It's comfortable here, isn't it? Do we need grandeur?"

Joel laughed. "It won't be comfortable here with a fifth person in the house and all its—his or her—paraphernalia."

"It takes a lot of maintenance, a lot of money, to keep those big lawns," Lore argued. "And you don't have time to do it yourself, tearing around to six places every day as you do."

"Let me worry about that. You know what?" Joel teased. "You're worried that there won't be a room for you in the new place, that's what it is, Lore. Listen. If you won't come, we'll drag you there by the hair. You're going to have a room in the front of the house with a view of the lake whether you like it or not."

"Oh, you," said Lore.

She was pleased at being wanted. And Caroline, noting how, although Lore was not yet fifty, she had aged, how her sparse hair was graying and her bad teeth were being, one by one, replaced, felt, as so often, a soft pity. I am so rich, she told herself, not meaning the new house or the business or anything but human wealth; the goodness of Joel, the loveliness of Eve, the faithfulness of Lore, and the startling joy of the new life on the way.

THERE was too much to be done for them to spare a month on the western vacation. That would have to come some other summer. Papers for a sale and a purchase would take the usual amount of time, and the house with the blue spruce trees would have to be furnished before Caroline grew too uncomfortably large to go running about.

It was a lovely house, old and a bit neglected; the kitchen, for example, was dilapidated beyond what even a thorough cleaning could repair. The banister was dangerously rickety, and the front steps sagged. With pad and pencil in hand, Caroline went around making notes.

"Look at yourself," Joel said with some delight. "And you were the woman who didn't want to move."

"Well, since you forced me, what else am I to do? Let's see. Would it cost too much to change the window in the library? I always like a bow window with a wide ledge, where you can sit and read on a dark, rainy day. And when it's light outside, the whole room is bright with it. The bow window could be extended to our bedroom above it, too. It would be lovely to wake up and watch the seasons move across the lake."

"Why not? It's no big job."

"Also, the same carpenters could build a

nice fence around the property, so Peter won't get out."

"Peter? Not the baby?"

"Joel, do you really think the baby, when it walks, will be allowed out alone?"

"Just kidding. We really should stop calling it 'it.' Anyway, it might really be a 'they' —twins."

He was enjoying every minute of life these days. He must have been wanting and wanting a child without ever saying so.

"Do you think a rose plot in the center would look right? Roses need a lot of sun. Or perhaps over on the left against the fence would be better?"

"Of course, you know you're trying to copy Father and Mama's house," observed Lore one day.

Caroline was, for the moment, shocked. Truly, she had not been aware of it, and she said so.

"The subconscious does strange things. Well, maybe not so strange. And surely you think of all your past with your conscious mind. It's only natural."

Lore could rarely enough, but sometimes,

be a real gloom. "I try not to," Caroline said dryly. "That's only natural, too."

"Let's buy Lore a phonograph for her room," suggested Joel. "Then she can enjoy her music in peace and quiet when she wants to."

Perhaps, Caroline thought, although he had never said so, she reminds Joel of someone he had known in that town, which also for obvious reasons, he rarely mentions. Or possibly it was simply his nature to empathize with people, whether with Vicky and her defects or the waitress in Number Three Orangerie, whose child was deaf.

As the weeks passed, Caroline became aware of her own euphoria, and other people noticed it, too. This was not uncommon in pregnant women, her doctor said. And so, far from shrinking from any reminder of her childhood's home, she went on joyfully to duplicate a few things that she had especially loved about it.

There was the wallpaper in Mama's sitting room, pale gray-green, with trailing crimson peonies in a Chinese effect. There was the pair of cloudy Venetian mirrors in the hall, and an old clock with a moon face over a mantel. Now that there was space enough for the books she wanted to own, she bought in secondhand shops complete sets of the Western world's classics to read again and hope that her children would read. *Children.* The very sound of the word was pleasant to her ears.

On the walls of Joel's small home office, she put photographs of famous buildings from around the world, he having lately revealed a new interest in architecture. Whereas Father had had photographs of Roman ruins, to Joel she gave an eclectic grouping: Angkor Wat, the Empire State Building, the Paris Opera, and the glass geometry of Mies van der Rohe. As she hung them, all in their uniform, narrow frames, she had a sudden recollection of the day in New York when he had described with awe his first and only visit to a museum. And touched by the recollection, she thought, we shall have to take time now for things like that. He has been hungry without realizing it.

All that summer and fall, the house was a

family venture. Joel duplicated the perfect cradle. Lore sniffed with scorn of "bought, machine-made junk", and sewed all the ruffled curtains by hand. Eve and her friends worked on a project, a combination flower and vegetable garden like the one being left behind in the old place.

"We're in a race here," Joel said as fall deepened and Caroline grew larger, "between you and the house."

"The house will win," she assured him. "We'll be in it before the first."

Through the streets of Ivy she walked now, carrying the sweet fragrances of respectability and prosperity. Funny, I'm the same person, she often thought as she was met and greeted, who arrived here from New York carrying all I owned in a trunk. Some who, like Gertrude, had scorned, now fawned. And I want neither.

Meanwhile, the smoky fall air turned raw, the north wind churned the lake, and she was barely able to bend and fasten her boots.

Joel did it for her. He *wanted* to do things for her; it was as if he could not do enough.

It surprised him that she had no cravings for strawberries at midnight, or pickles, or anything; or that she had no aches or pains and was seldom tired.

"How can you look so delicate, when you're not?" he marveled, with head to the side as if he were making a sketch or a study of her. "It must be your bones, so light and slender, that and your skin. It's like cream. You look like a girl. And after all these years, you've having my child."

They had their final Thanksgiving dinner in the old house. Lore and Eve did the cooking: the turkey, the pumpkin pie, and as always, Lore's chocolate cake. Joel shoveled the first heavy snow from the walk, put an awkward bunch of flowers on the table, brought champagne for toasts, and scarcely permitted Caroline to move.

Like a reluctant queen, she let him have his way. And from her place at the well-used table, she looked around her at the simple room in which more than a few thousand meals had been eaten. Their real start had been made here in this house; here they had woven themselves into a family and endured and come through. Now tomorrow was moving day, and as on every momentous occasion, one's thoughts could not help but be complex.

So ends, thought Caroline, so ends our time in the little brown house.

On a snowy day shortly before the New Year, Jane Hirsch, wrapped in a hand-embroidered pink blanket made by Lore, came home to the new white house and was placed in the cradle made by her father, alongside the bed where her mother rested.

"God, she's beautiful," Joel said.

Caroline smiled. The baby was healthy and chubby, with Joel's round face. Perhaps she would grow up to be beautiful, but right now she was too young to be either beautiful or homely. Only let her not suffer too much, thought Caroline.

It was dark outside, the lake was glowing like mother-of-pearl, and Caroline, gazing, felt a deep peace.

"So now you have your view of the lake," Joel said, following her gaze.

"I have everything," she answered.

They both bent over the cradle to examine again this fascinating stranger.

"Look at the size of her fingers. Amazing, aren't they?" His voice was roughened by emotion. "My mother would love her. My father would, too. He was a big man, Caroline, almost six feet and a half, not like me. But he had very fine hands, like an artist's or a musician's. He was a person who understood people. Strangers recognized that in the first minute. I wish our Jane could know this grandfather of hers."

She was silent. And he said quickly, "Her other grandfather too, of course. Lore has told me so many things about him."

But she was not thinking of Father. She was thinking of Eve's other inheritance, of the brutes. In her mind, when she was forced to remember their existence, that was the name she gave them: *brutes.* Those who slaughter and tear.

"Are you thinking of our Eve?" Joel asked softly.

"Yes. How did you know?"

"I don't how I did, but I did. Sometimes that happens to me when you are silent."

"You are extraordinary," she said, meaning it.

"I know I should not ask, but—do you feel different now that we have this baby?" He knelt down on the rug so that his face was on a level with hers. "What I am trying to say is—do you still ever think of—of *him*?"

"Of him? Why would any thinking, intelligent woman want to waste a second of time on a Nazi monster?"

"Feelings aren't guided by intelligence."

"I know that. But my answer, anyway, is no, I don't."

"I can't think where I heard a saying, something about how with every couple there is one who loves and one who is loved."

"Some French author wrote it. But it's not necessarily true. I hope you don't believe it."

She reached over and stroked his hair. He trembled, and she kept stroking. When at last he raised his head, he put something in her hand.

"Open it."

It was a velvet box, ring-size, and it made her want to cry. He was too good to her. . . .

"Open it," he said again.

The lamplight flashed upon a ruby within a narrow circle of diamonds.

"Mama's ring," she said, and then did cry.

"I tried to remember the size. I wanted to duplicate it. Of course, it's not her ring, but you can pretend it is."

"Oh, my dear, I don't deserve it," she said.

"What are you talking about? Don't deserve it? That's crazy. My beloved wife!"

Where had he heard such old-fashioned expressions? People in this flippant age didn't talk that way anymore. And maybe people didn't kiss people's hands anymore, either, yet on sudden impulse she took his hands and kissed them, one and then the other.

There was such an ache inside her, the

familiar ache of tenderness and pity. And suddenly she remembered a wistful remark, a request really, that he had made a long time ago about having another child; she had denied him so long, and she was sorry. If only she could have felt for him then and could feel now the passion and the longing that he had for her!

The baby stirred and whimpered. When the whimper ran to a wail, Joel picked her up.

"Jane's wet, I think, or can she be hungry?"

"Both, probably. Give her to me."

Then, while her hands fussed over the infant, her thoughts took another turn, and she rebuked herself. What is this drive for perfection in all things? she asked. It makes no sense. After all you have seen of life and do see now whenever you look around at the world, you ought to know better. A few minutes ago, until Joel asked you a certain question, you were filled with peace. And well you should be filled with peace. Look again at this baby and this man. Raise your eyes and look around at the calm, safe night that surrounds your home. . . .

"What are you seeing again out there?" asked Joel.

"The starlight on the lake. It will be a bright day tomorrow."

He smiled. "Every day is bright," he said.

TEN

In the North, the year moves to the dance of the thermometer. Snow falls, deepens, piles high on the below-zero nights, and thaws in late winter above thirty-two, after which it can blast a blizzard in early spring. Caroline was impatient to see the ice gone from the sidewalks so that Jane might be exhibited abroad. Eve wanted to get seeds into the garden plot that she and her friends had dug. Joel was impatient to get a sandbox readied for Jane.

Lore was amused. "The baby's not even

sitting up yet, and you're talking about a sandbox. Anybody'd think, the way you carry on, that this is the first baby the world's ever seen."

Joel spoke quickly. "Not the first. The second."

He was always careful to refer to Eve along with Jane, and Eve understood why. She was, after all, not the average sixteen-year-old high school sophomore, who would hardly be jealous of a new baby in the family. She had a *past,* and she could almost be envious of the baby who had none. But she was not.

No, Eve often told herself, it is not so much my past as it is two other people's, Mom's and *his.* Occasionally, prompted by some event or remark, she would ask herself honestly: How much thought do I really ever give to *him*? She certainly tried to give no thought at all, for what could not be changed must be accepted and buried. Yet that was impossible. For one thing, too many people in Ivy knew. She could tell who knew by the sudden change of subject that sometimes occurred. It was kindly meant, in order not to embarrass her. Yet she felt discomfort. Sometimes she wondered what it would be like to meet *him*; then, at the very thought of it, she would shudder. He was nothing to her. She had a father, a real one, and his name was Joel.

As to Mom, all anger was gone. Only sympathy was left of that first raging grief, sympathy and a vow never to repeat Mom's foolish mistake. Eve could not imagine herself being so naive, so impractical, as to allow any man to trick her like that. Poor, childish Mom! Eighteen, she had been, and Eve, at sixteen, knew better.

It's good to see Mom so happy now with this baby, she thought. You can tell how happy she is because she stays home to take care of her. Jane's a cute thing, already able to smile. I didn't know babies that young knew enough to smile back when you smile at them. It's so cute to look at her fat, crinkly cheeks and her pink mouth with no teeth. I think she's going to look like Daddy, which is all right, because although you wouldn't call him terribly handsome, he has such a nice face, and people like him right away. My friends all like him. They like to come to our house, and that makes me feel sort of proud because lots of parents don't make you feel welcome. They're afraid you'll break things, I guess. Anyway, they come here. They like to look at Jane, out for an airing in the yard. And they like Lore's cookies. She makes them when she gets home from the hospital. You'd think she'd be too tired, but she never is.

"Tired?" said Lore. "I'm as strong as I ever was, and I go back a long time. I rocked your mother in her carriage and you in your cradle. Now I'm rocking Jane. And if I'm alive, Eve, I'll rock your babies, too."

By June, when Jane was six months old, she napped in the garden, where roses were already flourishing in a circular bed with a sundial in the center. When he came home, Joel liked to find Caroline reading there beside the carriage and the sleeping dog.

"It's good to see you resting," he told her. "As long as I've known you, I think I can count the times I ever saw you not busy."

"Well, you do know I'm going back to work, don't you? I'm staying home until Jane goes to nursery school. Are things doing all right in the office without me? Not that I'm indispensable, I know, but still, I worry."

"No need. You've trained Vicky very well. And I've had the accountant come in regularly, which of course we didn't have to do when you were there. But he can supervise her, and we'll manage fine until you go back. Jane needs her mother now."

Summer days were long and wonderfully slow. In the evening when it was still light enough at half past eight to take coffee under the trees, you could wish that time would stop right there and save that hour: the silence before the nighttime insect choir started, the fragrances of flowers and pine, the interruption of cheerful, teenage voices, Eve and her friends going down the street, Lore's music coming faintly from her open window, then silence again.

And Joel exclaimed, "How young you

are! You could pass for twenty. There's not a mark on your skin.''

"Darling, it's almost dark, and you can't see my skin. But did I see you putting sugar in your coffee?''

"A quarter—an eighth—of a teaspoon," he said guiltily.

"You know better than that. I'm ashamed of you.''

"You're right. I hardly ever do it. I won't do it again.''

"Well, don't. You simply can't get sick. You have Jane to think of now.''

"And all the rest of you. I plan to reach one hundred. I'm strong as a horse, and you are, too. A strong, gentle mare.''

"Thanks a lot.''

They were bantering, affectionate and united. All through those summer evenings they sat there, until in September it got too cold, and they moved themselves inside with their plans. They had so many plans to make: college for Eve, and the postponed western trip that they really should take before she left. Surely they could take Jane, too, couldn't they? She would be walking well by then and they could make the trip in easier stages, more relaxed and perhaps a little shorter.

"Lore, Eve, and I can take turns staying with her sometimes while the others are seeing the sights," Caroline said.

"It's hard to believe she'll be one year old in a few months. By the looks of it, she'll start to walk before then. A lot of kids do."

"We'll have a party and a little cake with one candle on it for her alone, the way we did for Eve."

This, however, would be a real party. At Eve's first birthday, they had still been strangers in Ivy. The Riccis had come, Vicky had walked upstairs to join them, and that was all. The Schulmans had been out of town. It would be different this time.

FALL'S colors brightened and deepened. The maple outside Joel's office in Orangerie Number Three was clear yellow. Glancing up from his desk, he observed that by tomorrow the wind would have stripped it bare. Then the telephone rang. He was to remember it all distinctly: leaves, the *Wall Street Journal* not yet unwrapped, a cup, and a half-eaten roll.

"Hello," Al Schulman said. "Are you busy right now?"

"Never too busy for you, Al."

"I meant, have you got time to come over to the office?"

"Well, I can, but—right now?"

"Sometime this afternoon, then. I'd like to talk to you, and the telephone's no good."

There was a twinge, a slight lurch in Joel's stomach. "Why? Is anything wrong?"

"Joel, don't sound upset. Let's meet, and I'll explain."

"What's it about? Don't keep me in the dark."

Schulman's sigh was audible. "It's a problem with Caroline, an unexpected problem. But please don't get upset until we talk. I know how you are."

"What kind of a problem? For God's sake, Al, tell me now. When you say 'problem,' it's so upsetting that I'd probably wreck the car on the way over to you. What is it? Come out with it."

"She has melanoma."

"Oh, Jesus."

Silence.

"Are you sure?"

"Take it easy, Joel. It doesn't have to mean disaster."

Don't baby me. Don't you think I know what melanoma is? Caroline. When everything is going so well for us, and we're living in paradise.

"I'll be right over," Joel said, shivering in the sunshine that was pouring on his shoulders.

There were several people in the waiting room, yet he was admitted ahead of them. He strode rapidly, closed the door behind him, and said at once, "Tell me. Tell me everything."

"When she was here for the annual checkup, I saw the raised spot on her back. Medium-sized, dark, irregular. I didn't like the look of it. So I took a specimen and sent it to the lab. The report came back a week later, and it was bad." Schulman paused. "I didn't want to say anything until I was sure. But I was sure, only I didn't want to be. So I tried a second lab, and it was the same. Sit down, Joel. Listen, we're going to do everything for her. This isn't a hopeless situation. Listen to me, Joel."

"I'm listening." His mouth was dry. His hands quivered, and he knotted them to keep them still.

"Then I did a blood test. It confirmed everything."

"Have you told her?"

"No."

"She must wonder what you're looking for."

"She knows."

Schulman was playing with a pencil, tapping a notebook with the point, then tipping it to tap with the other end. Joel wished he would stop. It was enough to drive a man crazy to watch him.

"What makes you say she knows?"

"She is a highly intelligent woman."

"You say it's not hopeless. So what comes next?"

"We have to hope it doesn't metastasize.

We did a chest X ray, and it was clear, so that's a very good sign."

"We have to hope it won't spread? Just hope? That's all?"

There was no answer beyond a nod. From the street came some whoops and shouts; schoolchildren were going home to lunch. Jane, he thought. And her mother . . .

"I've heard that sometimes pregnancy can hasten the growth of cancer that's just beginning. Is that true?"

"You hear all kinds of things. But what difference would it make if it were true?"

"Why didn't I see the spot on her back? Maybe I did and didn't think anything of it."

"What difference does that make, either? We'd do just what we're doing now."

"Which is?"

"Another chest X ray. Keep checking on her periodically. And I want to talk to you both together."

"Why now? Why have you waited so long?" He was angry, and he needed to howl his rage. "Why didn't you tell me right away?"

"It hasn't been long, only two weeks, Joel. I wanted to wait until there could be no doubt. And I wanted to prepare you first, so that you can be strong for her. No offense, Joel, because I think the world of you, but there aren't many people with the stamina that Caroline has, and you're not one of them. Neither am I. Would you like me to walk over this evening?"

When the two men stood up, the doctor put his hand on Joel's shoulder and gave encouragement. "I had to tell you the possibilities, but they're only that, nothing more. If the thing doesn't spread, and it very, very often doesn't, we'll be in the clear. If it does—well, we'll cross that bridge when we come to it."

"LISTEN to this." Eve looked up from her book toward Joel and Lore. " 'It was the season of Light, it was the season of Darkness, it was the spring of hope, it was the winter of despair.' That's from Dickens. That's us."

There was nothing to say, and no one

did. Lore was mending. Joel was holding an unread paper, and Caroline was in the hospital. Hope, he was thinking, is a cruel fraud and trickster.

All through the fall, she had been totally herself. In December she had given a first-year birthday party for Jane and a dozen neighborhood babies, with presents, smeared ice cream, and Polaroid pictures of the event. In January, she caught a cold that did not go away but kept her coughing for a month, so that her ribs hurt. In February it turned into pneumonia in the lower lobe of the lung, and she was put into the hospital with a high fever. By the first of March, an X ray showed lymph nodes above the heart. A surgeon-oncologist did a biopsy, and they had their answer. So fast. So fast.

He knotted his hands and held them on his knees. The posture, and the dull disbelief had become by now a habit of which he was occasionally aware. The clock ticked. It was an old, tall clock that Caroline had found and repaired. He remembered the day it had been set up in the hall. She had been so delighted with it.

"It's a treasure. Look at the date. Don't you love the sound? Bong!"

"My God, my God," he murmured.

Eve rose and put her arms around him. He felt her wet lashes on his cheek.

"I think I hear Jane," said Lore, putting the mending away. "She still wants a late bottle sometimes, but I'm not going to give it to her. She had enough at suppertime."

She moved and spoke briskly. It was her way of telling them that life has to go on.

By late spring, Caroline knew that she was waiting at home to die. In a great soft chair, she sat by the window, watching a storm pass over the lake. Far out, a boat—what was it doing there in this weather?—made an iron-gray blur on the pale surface. Trees here on the lawn were stirring under the force of the rain.

"I am thirty-seven," she whispered to herself, and thought how extraordinary it was to be dying so young. And she remembered how only a short time ago, she had considered herself very old to be having a baby at thirty-six.

Now the baby was walking, taking her wobbly steps all over the house. She was a funny little thing, with Joel's curly brown hair and stubborn ways that were unlike anyone else's in the family. You wouldn't think that she and Eve were related, much less that they belonged to the same mother.

I suppose, she thought, that Eve and Lore will bring her up. Or Lore will most of the time, since Eve will be away in college. I want her to have the education that I would have had if things had been different. Thank God there will be money enough for them both.

How is it that I can look toward their future without me and not weep over the cruelty of it? All my perceptions are dulled; even music has lost its power. Perhaps this is a kindness of nature, to ease the way for those who would otherwise keep hoping when there is no hope.

In the matching chair, Lore was knitting a sweater-and-skirt set for Jane. The tiny white skirt was not much larger than a table napkin. There was, as there had always been, great comfort in Lore's presence; now, though, there was also a feeling of guilt because Lore had taken an indefinite leave from the hospital to stay at home.

"You should be at work," Caroline said.

"I like being home. The change is refreshing."

"You don't fool me."

"Who's fooling you?"

"Remember, Lore, how we thought you had cancer? You had all those symptoms, all that pain, while I had no symptoms, and here I am."

"Yes, here you are, and you'll be fine if you'll just eat something. I made split pea soup for dinner and roasted a duck. The body needs good rich food to recover, and I'm going to be very hurt if you don't eat."

Oh, Lore, when will you and Joel stop pretending? Still, if that's the way you want it, I'll go along. Only Eve is able to stare straight into the face of the truth.

"Will you take care of Jane when I'm gone?" she had asked Eve.

"Mom, you know I will. I take her in the stroller every day when school is out, don't I?"

Along the lakefront they had walked years ago, when she had gone with Eve, first in the stroller, and later walking with Peter, holding his leash in her hand. The wind had blown her little summer dress and her long black hair. Sometimes people had paused to admire and smile. . . .

Oh, I remember so much and still so little, thought Caroline. You wish you could recall everything, every hour of precious life, but all you can ever retrieve are moments, some so beautiful that they bring tears, and others so dreadful that you must strain to stop your tears. You stare at your anxious, pink-rimmed eyes and blot your cheeks with powder to hide them.

"Don't be ashamed to cry," Eve said one time. "At night I cry in my room. Maybe Lore and Daddy do, too, when they're alone."

There she had stood, a tall young woman, calm and serious, with her great eyes so sad. She was beautiful. And suddenly Caroline had seen her again standing in the kitchen on that awful night, defiant, with her clenched fists hanging at the sides of her skinny little skirt, her skinny little body just beginning to bud.

Often Caroline thought about the difference between her feelings for her two girls. Jane had no hovering cloud above her. Jane was Joel's daughter, while Eve was—

"Marry a man like your father," she told Eve abruptly.

"Like—Daddy?"

"Of course. Who else but Daddy? A good man whom you can trust. But first go to college. If you want to go to California, do it."

"I don't know why, but California's been on my mind forever. There's a magic about the Pacific Ocean."

"I understand. I always planned to go out west to the mountains. Eve, you'll be all right. You will."

"Mom, darling, I know. I'll have to be."

ALWAYS the seasons moved across the lake. Now, in summer, the surface looked hot; the sun blazed upon it so that it glistened like a sheet of metal that would scorch one's hand. August was a dreary month. The tired leaves hung listlessly, and the grass was as dry as straw.

Caroline lay on a wicker chair under the shade, watching Jane in the sandbox. Soon she would be two years old, and she hardly knew her mother. Other women, Eve and Lore, had to care for her.

Now they had all ceased to pretend. It was not what was said, but rather what was not said, that told how Lore and Joel had finally come to acknowledge the nearness of death. No longer did either of them put Jane, so strong and vigorous, upon Caroline's lap to twist and bounce and pull her hair. There was no more mention of the western trip. Talk was cheerful, but neutral.

Lore was sewing, taking in one of the dresses that now hung loose on Caroline. She had so many visitors, and Lore understood that she wanted still to be "presentable." That had been Mama's word, her proper mama's "presentable."

And suddenly, without having planned to speak, Caroline said, "Will you take care of my children, Lore?"

She had asked her the question before. Always the answer had come: "Don't talk like that. You're not going to die." But this time, Lore said only, "Yes," put down the sewing, and looked away.

After a long moment, Lore spoke again. "Your hair's all sweaty on your neck. Eve's bringing cologne. Let's go in. It's a little cooler in the house."

Joel wanted to get an air conditioner for the bedroom, but it wasn't necessary. A fan would do.

"One day every house will be entirely air-conditioned," he said. "In the meantime, we can do one room, can't we?"

But she did not want to block the window. She wanted to see the lake. "I need to," she said. "I see people walking there. I see the clouds move."

He said nothing, and bought a powerful

fan that whirred and soothed them as they lay together.

The nights passed slowly. Their sleep was uneven. One or the other drowsed, and waking, spoke whatever had come to mind.

"I wish my parents could have known you," she said once. "They would have been so happy for me."

And he: "You have been everything to me. Everything, my kind and loving wife."

Her dreams, flickering, shattered into vivid, colored fragments and were gone: Mama's gleaming black piano, orange awnings, Dr. Schmidt's gray mustache—"You're strong, you'll be all right," he had said—and the pink linen dress of a summer long ago. . . .

"What is it?" asked Joel.

"Nothing. Nothing."

"I thought you cried out."

"Did I? I don't know why."

By the end of the summer, she stopped going downstairs. It was too hard to climb back up. And she felt her own fragility in her tired arms and legs. After a while, she left the chair at the window and stayed in bed all day. They moved the bed so that she could see the blaze of autumn light outside. She heard crows call, going south. She heard a bee buzz against the window, and drowsed again. She gazed and drowsed.

One day she heard Joel's voice talking to Eve, or Lore, or both. She thought he was weeping.

"Dear God, let the time of her suffering go quickly. Or else let time stop so I may keep her."

There were other voices, too, a whispered hum, as if there were many people there. She did not know, and it did not matter. The voices faded, as if they were very far away.

Death seems so wasteful, she thought, when I have so much left to do. . . .

PART TWO

1959

EVE

ELEVEN

"**Y**our mother wanted you to," Joel said, "and you've been talking for years about going to college in California."

They were walking on the lakeshore drive, with Jane in the stroller and Peter, who was clearly Jane's favorite in the household, trotting, as usual, alongside. Eve looked back at the house and its landmark blue spruce. Her feelings during these last months had been painfully ambivalent; on the one hand, the house was home and shelter, with known faces and all Mom's familiar possessions in place; on the other hand, it echoed with the silence of Mom's stilled voice. The cheer in the house was forced and false.

Lore, too, had been pressing her to leave. "Go on and get your education. Look at me. What have I ever done? All right, I'm a nurse, and that's important work, but all the other things that I could also have learned —the arts, and literature, and history—that I didn't learn. Don't be a fool, Eve. Go."

"I'll tell you what," Joel said now. "We'll take the station wagon and we'll all drive to California. I'll sell the car out there, since we've no more use for a second car, and the rest of us will fly home."

He was quite right. Of course she must go. Hadn't Mom always said "forward"?

"Do you want to take the northern route through the mountains, the one Mom told about when those two men—what were their names?"

"Lewis and Clark."

Suddenly, Eve's spirits brightened with a vivid image of Indians and Spaniards; she heard strange music and saw brown faces, striped cloth, turquoise and silver. "No, let's go south, through Santa Fe."

"That's a good idea. Your mother would have liked that, too. She always wanted to know more about Indian life. We'll see it through her eyes."

He will always see everything through her eyes, thought Eve.

FROM her window in the women's dormitory, she watched the station wagon turn and follow the driveway between the umbrella palms. There was a last, quick glimpse of Lore in the backseat with Jane, whose curly head was barely visible at Lore's shoulder. Peter would still be in his basket at their feet; having slept his way contentedly across the continent, he was probably asleep again. Vicky was in the front seat next to Dad.

It had been Lore's idea to take Vicky along.

"I don't think she would enjoy it," Eve had told her.

"She would be a help. She could stay

with Jane while the rest of us go to the Santa Fe opera, for example. They're having a marvelous season this summer."

As Eve had made no answer, Lore had continued, "You never used to dislike her so much."

"I didn't say I disliked her."

"But it's obvious that you do."

"You're wrong, Lore."

But Lore had not been wrong. Quite simply, Eve had feared to sound foolish if she were to reveal her reason for resenting Vicky: that she flirted with Dad. Dad, being Dad, was almost certainly not aware of it, but Eve, being a woman, recognized all the signs: the gaiety, the flouncing walk, the hovering concern.

On the westward journey, whenever Dad drove, Vicky sat in front. When Lore drove, then Eve sat in front, while Dad and Vicky sat in back with Jane and the dog. Thinking about it now, Eve's anger rose. What did she think she was doing? And besides, she was coarse, from her foundation cream, thick as pink plaster, to her mascaraed owl eyes and her yawning boredom. At the splendid Sangre de Cristo Mountains, she had cast a cool, exasperated glance, as if to say, "Well, they'll do, but I don't see what the fuss is all about."

The station wagon disappeared around the curb. Eve was alone. All the daily concerns of home were beyond her now. Never before had she been in a place where she knew no one and no one knew her. And she sat there gazing out at the palms, alien, green, and foreign to eyes that expected red and yellow leaves in autumn.

She had the room to herself. Dad had wanted her to have the pleasure of privacy for study and sleep because she was an early riser who went early to bed. He had given her every luxury, far more than was necessary according to Lore, who in her Spartan way had strongly disapproved. She sat now surrounded by these luxuries, still unpacked. Her luggage was of the finest leather, ordered from a first-class shop in New York. There were skis—in case she might want to spend a winter weekend in New Mexico—and a surfboard—in case she might want to try surfing, which she was certain she did not want to try—and a tennis racket; there was a coffeemaker, a fan, a radio, a flowered silk quilt, a type-writer, a superb camera, and on her wrist a gold watch. The closet was not large enough to hold all her clothes without cramming. Mom would never have let Dad provide all this stuff.

She got up and unpacked Mom's photo-graph in its beautiful frame. On the well-used dresser she placed it beside a family grouping of Mom, Dad, Lore, and Jane, whose baby face smiled, showing her new, tiny teeth. The memories, crowding, came back: neighbors at the door, bringing flow-ers, food, and pity for the baby; letters of condolence spread out on the dining room table; Lore's worn face and Dad just sitting there, staring at nothing.

Loneliness overwhelmed her. And yet she was surrounded by people here. Every room was occupied. Voices passed in the corridor. But who were they all? Where had they come from, and where were they go-ing?

And she examined again the particular

photograph that she already knew to the smallest detail: the curve of the eyebrow, the fold of the skirt—taffeta, she remembered, and silver-gray—the ruby on the finger. She remembered her rage at her mother, not all that many years ago. *Now I am the age that Caroline Hartzinger was when she fell in love with the monster who fathered me . . .*

Such moods do not last unless the possessor of them is prepared to wither away, and Eve was not about to let herself wither. After a while, she felt able to summon what she called "old-fashioned common sense," to set her room in order, and go to see who was living next door and down the hall. It was time to become attached. Here she had been planted, and here she must take root.

At Christmas, it pleased Eve to bring home a prideful account of her first semester, with grades as high as they had always been. Joel nodded with satisfaction.

"Your mother would be so happy, Eve,

and I am, too. Tell me, are you having any fun?"

"Oh, yes, I'm taking a dance class, I've made good friends and went with a group of them to Mexico one weekend. It was wonderful, and I want to go back. What really fascinates me is archaeology. We went to see some Mayan ruins in the Yucatan and they were marvelous. So I've signed up for some courses."

"What about your languages?"

"Well, I'm going on with both French and German advanced literature. Of course, they're no effort at all for me, which may seem lazy and probably is, but it's also practical, because in a pinch I can always teach either language. Or I could do translations, I think."

"That's practical planning."

It also pleased Eve to find at home that the deepest gloom had been lifted. It is likely, she reflected, that Jane is the explanation. Little more than a toddler and slightly small for her age, she had become a personage, very bright, persistent, and eager to know absolutely everything.

"What's in your book? Is that Humpty Dumpty?" she demanded while Eve was reading a biology assignment.

"Why has that man got a bombella?"

"Why can't Daddy eat candy?"

"She's not what you were, Eve," Joel said more than once. "You were energetic, but nowhere nearly as determined. Lore says I spoil her. Well, maybe I do, but I don't mind if I do. She'll be all right. And in the meantime, she's adorable."

"You certainly spoil me, Dad. I can't think of anybody who came to college as well supplied as I did."

"As long as you appreciate it, and you do, you're not spoiled." Joel leaned back in the lounger, savoring his cigar. "Tell me, how's the man situation?"

"Very good. Good for tennis and Saturday parties, but no lover, since that's probably what you mean. Lightning hasn't struck me yet."

"I don't mean. You're much too young. For God's sake, Eve, don't make any mistakes."

For an instant, the atmosphere was

clouded; but only for an instant, as Joel changed the subject. "What do you really think of our Jane? Quite a change since you saw her last, isn't there?"

"Frankly, I give her credit for lifting some of the despair in the house." Eve had to laugh. "We went for a walk yesterday, she, I, and that big pull toy that keeps turning over. I wanted to walk by the lake, but she insisted on going the other way. I found out why—she led me straight to the candy store on Main Street."

"And I suppose you bought her some."

"I'm ashamed to say I did. Only two chocolate kisses, though."

"I know, she's not the easiest little kid to handle. I was a little worried about how we were going to manage after you left. But it's all worked out quite well. Naturally, Lore is back at work, but I've been able to get more people in the office so that Vicky can pick up Jane from nursery school and stay here in the afternoons until either Lore or I get home. I feel safe having her with Vicky instead of with some total stranger. Don't you agree?"

"I guess so," Eve said, although she very definitely did not agree.

"There's something untrue about Vicky," she complained later in a discussion with Lore.

"Untrue? I don't know what you mean."

"Well, I always feel somehow that she's pretending. Her laugh seems faked. It comes out like a snarl, and I hate the way she makes sure you see her perfect teeth."

"Well, they are perfect, even as a row of kernels on an ear of corn. If I had them instead of my miserable teeth, you can believe I would display them."

"You don't understand. I meant that the laughter itself isn't real."

"Who knows? Real or not real, Jane enjoys her. When she stays over for supper with us sometimes, she livens the place up, and it does the poor man good. So she annoys you, but what difference does it make? You're hardly ever here anymore. You have your own life to think about, Eve."

That was true. Lore had seen right through to the truth. Going away, and preparing for an independent future must mean a loosening of ties. That was an elementary psychological dictum. *Grow up!* Jane is not your responsibility, she's Dad's. Besides, Vicky isn't doing Jane any harm. Besides that, Dad isn't going to marry her, for heaven's sake.

And it really was a lovely Christmas. Carrying a sweet memory of it along with her, she returned to California.

TWELVE

Eve met Tom Tappan during her sophomore year on one of her rare bad days. She had come, visibly shaken, out of a class in modern European history, where during a discussion one of the students, a bare acquaintance of hers, had related some Jewish family history. Her parents had escaped to America, but her grandparents had perished in the concentration camps. When the instructor asked whether anyone else had personal contact with those events, Eve, to her regret, had spoken up. And then after class, this girl, quite understandably, had sought her out to compare their stories.

"And the other grandparents?" she had asked. "They, too?"

What else was there to do but lie? "Yes," Eve had answered. And then the trembling had begun.

She was hungry, but wanting neither conversation nor companionship she went outdoors, carrying her books as if she intended to study in the shade, and sat down with her head resting against a tree trunk. She was so tired of having to be reminded, so bitter and tired! Really, really, she ought to get over it or put it out of her mind once and for all. But how realistic was that expectation? How could you forget who your father was? And if he was, in addition, a man who filled you with horror and shame? There had been long intervals during which she did not think about him, but then, inevitably, there had come an hour like this one. And she tried to imagine what her mother must have kept hidden behind her normal, everyday face.

"Are you feeling all right?"

When she opened her eyes, she saw a young man looking down at her.

"I'm all right, thanks. Just drowsy."

"You didn't look drowsy. I thought you might be in pain."

"I'm fine, truly. But thank you, anyway."

He kept looking at her with such candid curiosity that she was embarrassed. When he put his books on the grass and sat down, though at a suitable distance, she was annoyed.

"I'm Tom Tappan," he said, and paused so that she was obliged to give him her name in return.

He said next, "You are absolutely beautiful."

"Thanks, but I think you're crazy."

He laughed. "A trifle eccentric, perhaps. But not crazy. You should respect me. I'm getting a Ph.D. in archaeology. I teach part-time, and I'm older than you. So what's funny?"

"I guessed that you weren't an undergraduate. Your hair is neat and your pants are pressed."

"Observant and humorous, too, as well

as beautiful? Because you are, you know. You must know it. And I'm not being a smart aleck. I paint. I'm not an artist, I paint as a hobby, but only landscapes or seascapes, so I'm not going to ask you to pose. You do have a perfect oval face, though. I'm sorry if I've scared you into thinking I'm some sort of dangerous nut. If I'm bothering you and you want me to disappear, I'll go right now."

At some other time, she would very likely have been much more than annoyed by this odd intrusion, and in her best cool manner, would have let him see that she was more than annoyed. But into this moment's desolate mood, his frank warmth had brought a kind of cheer.

"You're not bothering me," she said.

Actually, she was thinking that in a vague way he reminded her of Dad. But no, it was only the sandy, curly hair and friendly eyes that were the same. This was a big man. Moreover, Dad would never, never go up to a strange woman and talk to her.

"Eve, I've got a class to teach. The professor's away. He's lucky to have a handyman like me, don't you agree? When he comes back next Monday, you can ask him about me if you care to. I hope you'll care to. Professor Mills in Room 309. He'll tell you I'm respectable."

SHE never had a chance to inquire about Tom Tappan—not that she would have done it, anyway—because before the next Monday came, something else happened. A letter arrived from Dad.

"Dear Eve," she read, "I'm writing this instead of telephoning with my news because, frankly, I'm afraid that you may take it badly. If you do take it badly, then the letter will give you more time to think it over, and maybe then you will begin to feel better.

"Vicky and I were married yesterday. It was a sudden decision, so there was no celebration, just a businesslike ceremony in front of a judge at the town hall. Even Lore wasn't there. The two witnesses were a young lawyer, one of Vicky's friends, and to my surprise, Gertrude. I never thought Vicky would have wanted her there, although they do seem to be getting along better lately.

"Eve, dear, please understand that this has nothing to do with, that it is not remotely like and can't possibly ever be remotely like, what I felt for your mother. There is no one on earth who can take her place. I will never love again. This is only a matter of companionship, for me and for Jane, because these two years since we lost our Caroline have been a hell of loneliness. I tried to hide it when you came home, but it was always there.

"Vicky has left the office and will stay home to run the house. She is a decent, hardworking, warmhearted woman, and a good-natured mother to Jane. Lore, after all, has her own life at the hospital, although she will continue to live with us. She and Vicky are fond of each other, as you know, and they both adore Jane. But Lore is over fifty, which isn't all that old, yet she seems much older, and although she would never complain, I feel she is too old to run after an extra-lively four-year-old.

"As for me, I'm feeling some age, I think.

It's my loss, of course. And it's also my diabetes, which seems to be getting worse. I don't always have the energy that I'd like to have for Jane.

"I hope you will understand all this. I will telephone you after you have had a day or two to digest it. Or you can call me right away if you want to. All my love, Dad."

Eve flung the letter onto the floor. Vicky! Of all the women in Ivy, if he had to have someone, why her? The thought of her living in Mom's house, touching Mom's things, was sickening. *A good mother to Jane.* Vicky a mother to Mom's baby? He must have lost his mind! How could he? How dare he?

First locking her door lest someone should come in and behold her rage, she went to the telephone and called Lore's private number.

"You have the letter," Lore said at once. "I can tell by your voice."

"Yes, I have it. I had to read it three times to make sure I wasn't hallucinating."

"Listen, dear, it's not as bad as you think.

The man was lonely, and loneliness is a disease. It comes down to that."

"But why that awful woman?" Eve wailed.

"To him, she obviously isn't that awful."

"But after Mom?"

"Look, Eve, she was here, under his nose. He wasn't about to go out searching. She was here, she's lively, and she cheers him up. He's been miserable, a tragic sight."

"Lore! You sound as if you approve. You amaze me. And Mom dead only two years."

"God knows, I understand. But what's the sense of making yourself sick over it? I'm not thrilled, either, but it's a fact and there's nothing we can do about it."

"And she's to be a mother to Jane."

"No, no. That's an exaggeration. Jane is already in nursery school. She'll spend most of her life in school from now on. Don't worry about Jane."

"Mom would die all over again if she knew."

"Let me tell you, your mother understood how to make the best of a thing that can't be changed. Listen to me. It's not as if Vicky were evil. She's not the kind of person that Caroline was or that you are, it's true. But she isn't evil. Accept her for your dad's sake and for your own peace. Go do your work, dear, and live." Lore laughed. "And be glad you're three thousand miles away."

Yes, Lore made sense. She always did. You weren't apt to go wrong when you listened to her. Yet it was more easily said than done. Why hadn't Dad at least told her beforehand what he was going to do? If I had known he was that lonesome, I would have gone home to study. But this—

In great agitation, she went downstairs and started toward the library, there to recover without interruption from friends or telephone. The evening sun was low and blinding as it flickered through the trees, so that, walking head down, she almost collided with a man walking fast, and also head down.

"Oh!" said Tom Tappan. "I was on the way to you. I tried phoning, but there was no answer."

She only wanted to be let alone. . . .

"What's the trouble?" he asked. "And don't say there isn't any because it's written on your face."

Eve shook her head.

For a moment, he considered the situation. "I'm sorry." Then he said, "It's rude of me to question you. But you looked so troubled a few days ago, and since now you still do, I forgot myself. I have a tendency to interfere where I shouldn't."

His tone was so rueful that she had to respond. And she said what a moment before she would not have said to anyone. "Today's trouble is different. This isn't my week, it seems."

"I've had some weeks like that myself. By the way, you didn't inquire about me. Is it because you didn't want to?"

"No, because I didn't think it was necessary."

"One could take that two ways. Can I take it to mean that if you aren't going to any better place, you'll go down the street for a drink?"

"What kind of a drink?"

Tom ran his eyes from her saddle shoes

up to her yellow sweater and strand of small pearls. He smiled. "I would guess that a Coke might be your idea of a drink. Am I right?"

She nodded, and for the second time in his presence, felt how much better it is, after all, when your head is heavy with thoughts, not to hide away alone.

She had no intention of spilling these thoughts, however, to a stranger who would only be bored by them. Yet before an hour had gone by, Tom knew about Joel's letter and what had led to it.

"I feel so lost," she finished. "I feel untied, unattached. I don't know what I'm supposed to do, or feel, or say."

"Do? Nothing. Or rather, one thing. When you go back to your room, go to the telephone and tell your father that you hope he will be happy. And tell him that you love him."

"But I'm still so terribly angry."

"You can be angry at people you love. You do love him, don't you? It seems to me that love has run all through everything you've been saying."

When her eyes teared, he looked away until she had finished wiping them. "You're very soft," he said. "If you say anything to hurt him, you'll feel terrible afterward. You'll go to bed sorry about what you said and wishing you could take it back."

She was silent. They went out to the street and walked a long way aimlessly before they turned around. By the time they got back to the campus, the sun had gone from sight.

"We haven't had any dinner," Tom said.

"I don't mind. I'm not hungry. But you go ahead."

"I'm not hungry, either."

Now they were both silent. On the campus, lights were already going out, and Eve reminded herself of the time.

"I have to be in by midnight."

"I'll watch the clock. I don't want you to be in any trouble," Tom said.

They sat down beneath the palm where he had first seen her. Neither of them apparently wanted to leave.

Abruptly, Eve broke the stillness. "You're right. I would be sorry if I were to tell Dad what I think about his marrying Vicky. You reminded me of how much I owe to him. He was my support in my worst time. He was always, for all of us—'' She stopped. "I'm suddenly realizing that all evening we have been talking about me. That's awful. Boring you with my problems, when you haven't said a word about yourself."

"We'll get to me. But you've wanted to talk about yourself. You've needed to. That's true, isn't it?"

Yes, it was true. Never in all these years had she completely revealed herself to anyone. Psychologists called it "suppression." And she had been satisfied to suppress, had felt no need to speak, until this had come up. And so there in the soft night, she spoke.

She told Tom Tappan the story of Caroline and Walter. She gave him descriptions of everyone and everything, from the little brown house to the house on the lake, and the Orangerie, and Lore, and baby Jane, and Peter the dog.

Then he spoke. He told her about his family's home in the Midwest and his small beach bungalow from which he commuted daily, and what he called his "dabbling" in art. Most of all, he talked about his fascination with Central America.

"So you were there," he said. "You saw Uxmal and Chichén Itzá, the carvings, the snakes, eagles, and the great, sacred jaguar. So you know what I'm talking about. I have to go back. I need another year or two of studying here, and then I'm going to join a group dig in Guatemala. There's more, much more, in Guatemala. There are things deep in the jungle where I'm sure no explorer has yet been. There's a whole civilization, people who had ballgames and dances, religion, art, and human sacrifice. I have to know more. I'm driven. It's what I want to do with my life."

"You make me feel as if I've known you a long time," Eve said, surprised at herself as she spoke.

He looked at his watch. "Not counting our first, very short, short meeting, you've known me for exactly four hours and ten minutes. Now back to you. What about your life from now on?"

"I don't know yet. There's so much to learn, and I'm only beginning. I'm taking a course in archaeology, a beginner's course, but sometimes I think about earning my degree in European literature. Or maybe when I'm through with college, I might like to have a marvelous bookstore, the kind with all sorts of odd, rare books that you don't find in most places. Or—well, I've grown up watching my mother, and maybe I'd like to work at the business she began. She had visions of making it grow from coast to coast. All I know right now is that I'm going to do something important. Important to me, at least," she added, to amend what had perhaps sounded childish.

In the very faint light she could barely discern his smile, but her ears could detect it in his voice.

"You'll come with me to Guatemala," he said. "That's what you'll do."

A year later Tom's prediction about going away with him no longer seemed extravagant. It seemed natural. It was visible to anyone who had eyes to see that they were a couple. They were seen as such on the campus, but not seen at all at Tom's beach bungalow.

He called it his "shack." And perhaps it was one, bleached gray, veiled by beach grapes, and except for sparse, essential furniture, bare. It was clean and sunny, with a far view of Eve's romantic ocean.

To its wide deck she often brought her work, spreading out textbooks and papers on half of the table, where on the other half Tom spread his paints. There was always a painting in progress on the easel. There were ships on the horizon. Gulls called and sailed in the sky.

At night, when the gulls were still, they lay warmly in bed, listening to the breeze, or the squall, or the gale. Often after he fell asleep, for he slept more quickly and soundly than she did, Eve lay awake, or half awake, sliding in and out of memory. And it came to her that for the first time, she truly understood her mother. Ignorant, priggish little child that I was, she thought, when I blamed her for what happened with—*him*.

She had felt for *him* what I feel for Tom when he puts his arms around me, and when I do not see him for a few days that feel like a year. Yes, now I know how it is. He is everything to me. Everything. I can't take my eyes away from him. And it happened so quickly to us both! A few hours only . . . And for my mother, it must have been the same. Only, *he* betrayed her. How did she live through it? If Tom ever does that to me, I will die.

At home she had told Lore and Dad, but not Vicky, about Tom. She could never speak intimately to Vicky. It was enough that the surface between them was smooth; for the sake of peace in the house, it would always be smooth. Let Dad be content. She was glad that he seemed to be so, and she was relieved, too, that she need not worry about him. Indeed, the longer she was away from Ivy, the more it receded from her and no longer seemed like "home." Automatically now, "home" meant here on the rim of the Pacific, or more exactly, it meant wherever Tom was.

In another year she would graduate and

go to Guatemala with him. His direction had now become hers. She was studying archaeology with total seriousness, and eventually would also earn a graduate degree. Who knew where they might yet go together to study and work? The world was large, a great blue ball swimming around the sun. She was filled with the joy of it.

THIRTEEN

Shortly before examination week in her senior year, Eve was called home. Lore came straight to the point.

"Joel had a stroke last night. But please, please don't be too frightened. It's a mild one."

Visions of horror shot before Eve's eyes. "Is he paralyzed?"

"No, no, except for a slight weakness on one side. His speech hasn't been affected, and he can walk."

"I'll be right home. I'll take a night flight."

"Eve, don't panic. You don't have to rush tonight. It's not bad. You'll see."

Tom drove her to the airport, first having packed a few textbooks into her carry-on bag. "You may have time sitting around, and you might just as well use it," he advised. "Give Joel all my good wishes and tell him I feel related to him already."

He looks like a husband, Eve thought, as he stood watching her at the airport until they were out of each other's sight.

By the time she had gotten through all the connections and waits and reached Ivy, it was after noon. The taxi crawled to the door; it seemed as if even the transcontinental plane had crawled. Tremulous and hoping, she sped up the front steps, stumbling once, and lightly touched the bell.

Vicky opened the door. "You're here?" she exclaimed with her owl eyes widened. "My goodness, you needn't have come all this way."

The old, stifled anger was prepared to flash in Eve. "For Dad I needn't have come?"

"You're certainly welcome, but he's doing fine. He's upstairs taking a nap, so that's why I'm going out for an hour."

You don't have to explain yourself. And you don't have to tell me I'm "welcome" to my father's home. It's my home, too, remember?

She said quietly, "I'm going upstairs to wash and change these clothes that I slept in."

"Don't wake him."

"Of course not."

When did we begin to hate each other? Or is hate too strong a word? To think she was my baby-sitter when Mom and Lore were at work!

Walking in rubber-soled shoes, she peeked into the bedroom. Her first thought was that Mom wouldn't recognize the room. Understandably, the bride, Vicky, had immediately bought a new bed, a thing of white and gold and shining, coral-colored silk, but in addition, everything had more recently been changed to coral or pink. A mirror covered one wall. And she wondered what Dad could be thinking of it all as he lay there in Caroline's room.

He opened his eyes. "I'm not asleep," he said.

"I was so quiet."

"But I've been expecting you. When I heard the doorbell, I felt it was you."

When she bent to kiss him, she saw that he had tears in his eyes. His familiar, round cheeks were sunken. It seemed extraordinary that in the few months since she had last seen him, this change could happen, extraordinary in the first place that he, the strong one who had always been there to care for other people's aches and ailments, was lying weakly in the bed.

His voice was barely above a murmur. "I knew you would come. Still, you shouldn't have come all this way."

"But I wanted to see you, Dad."

"How's Tom? When are you going to bring him with you?"

"He'll come the next time, I promise. He wants to come. But this is exam—" She stopped. It was careless of her to let him know that she had felt it necessary to hurry home in this crucial week.

But he had not noticed, asking instead whether she had seen Jane.

"I haven't seen anyone but Vicky."

"Lore must have taken her for a walk. She comes here almost every day after work. Lore doesn't live here anymore, you know; she's taken an apartment."

Eve knew. Lore had long been complaining about the noisy evenings when Vicky's friends occupied the house. Lore didn't know how Joel stood it.

"Jane's adorable," Eve said now, wanting to change the subject.

Joel smiled. "She's very different from what you were at that age. She's feisty. I think maybe she takes after some of my brothers."

"Maybe so. She looks like you, though."

"God help her. I hope not."

"Dad! What's bad about looking like you? She's darling, curls and all."

"I've made a new will, Eve. I want you to know."

"It's much too soon to be thinking about wills."

"That's foolish talk. People die, even young people."

Both heads turned to Caroline in the fine dark frame on Joel's chest of drawers. At least Vicky hadn't changed that.

"It was time to update. I hadn't realized how far the business has spread upward and outward since the previous will. It seems some kind of a little miracle when I think about it. There'll be plenty and more than plenty for everybody—for you two girls and Vicky and Lore, when I go."

"Dad! You're not going anyplace except to California to see Tom and me. You're going to approve of him. He's smart, and funny, and good."

"Well, he'd better be good. When I see him, I'll tell him so. Then we'll celebrate. I'm going to be all right, you know."

"Of course you are."

A tender, prescient sorrow brought a lump to Eve's throat. And drawing a chair close to the bed, she held his hand while, both knowing well what they were doing, they talked deliberately of trivial and pleasant things. After a while, when Vicky came in to bring loud, manufactured cheer, Eve went downstairs.

"I think," she told Lore, "I'll call Dr. Al and find out exactly what's happening to Dad."

"He's not on the case anymore. She's brought all her own people in. Schulman's too old, she says."

"Too old? I wouldn't care if he was two hundred. Everybody knows he's the best internist on the hospital staff. You yourself always say so."

"Of course I do. But you try telling her anything she doesn't want to hear. You might as well reason with the refrigerator or the stove." And Lore threw up her hands.

"Who's a wefwidguwator? Vicky?" demanded Jane, coming in from the yard.

"That's grown-up talk, honey. Don't you see who's here?"

Milk and a cookie, one of Lore's huge chocolate chip specialties, were waiting on the kitchen table. But Jane, giving a cry at sight of Eve, ran past them, jolted the table, upset the milk, and rushed to her.

"What have you got for me, Eve?"

At Christmas, the last time she had been home, Eve had brought a splendid doll and a box of puzzles. Now, in her haste, she had brought nothing.

"Darling," she said, hugging Jane, "I didn't have time yesterday. I'm sorry."

"You don't love me."

"You see what I say about spoiling?" Lore scolded.

"It's deeper than that," Eve said.

But that sort of pop psychology was ridiculous. As if some sudden wisdom could have revealed itself only to her! Yet, must the child not have been affected by all the changes in the house?

And hugging her close, she promised, "Tomorrow you and I will go to buy something nice for you. Where's Peter?"

"Outside. He likes it there. I'm going out with him, too."

"You can take your milk and cookie and sit on the step," Lore said. "Here, I'll help you. Take a biscuit for Peter so he won't grab your cookie."

"A handful, as they say," she remarked when she came back. "Extremely smart.

She sees everything. She told me the other day that Vicky doesn't like her."

"Is that true?"

"I haven't seen anything really wrong. I've only sensed that the child's in her way, and if I sense it, you can be sure Jane does."

"Does Dad see it?"

"Who can say? He's too reserved, too much of a gentleman to complain to me about his wife, if he has any complaints."

"Well, do you think he has?"

"I'll tell you what I think. I think he has regrets. I think he knows he made a foolish mistake on impulse, and now he feels guilty, poor man."

"I could say 'I told you so,' but I won't."

"No, it wouldn't do any good, would it?" Lore agreed.

Eve, sighing, wondered aloud, "What's going to happen to Dad?"

"If I had a crystal ball I could tell you."

"But you see so much in the hospital."

"Each case is different."

"You didn't make too much of it on the telephone."

"I didn't want to scare you to death. The

fact is, though, it is a mild stroke, and although he's bound to have another one, it may be years away. Let's hope."

"First Mom, and now this. I'm going over to the Schulmans' tonight and get Dr. Al's opinion."

"You don't have to. He's coming over here. He visits Joel every evening, just as a friend. Vicky may not like it, but he comes anyway."

Eve sat with Dr. Al—Dad always said that respect demanded that a young woman of her age use the title—in the sunroom, now refurbished in feverish pink. From above came intermittent spurts of earsplitting talk and laughter.

Dr. Schulman frowned slightly. "The young crowd," he said. "Well, maybe they entertain him, I don't know. I don't suppose it does him any harm, and they mean well."

"Not his style, Dr. Al."

"A new era, Eve."

She would have liked to go up and throw them all out of Dad's room with their racket. Then, if he wanted her to, she would play the soft music he liked, or would read aloud, for he had always enjoyed that. And now especially—

"Lore told me his sight is affected."

"It's blurred. He can't see equally in every direction. Diabetic retinopathy, it's called."

"Explain it, please."

"Okay. Diabetes is associated with vascular problems, which can cause bleeding into the retina, or lead to amputation of a leg, for that matter. Fortunately, Joel doesn't have that problem. But vascular trouble can lead to heart attack or stroke, and Joel does have that."

"Oh, I wish you were taking care of him. It's outrageous that you aren't."

"Don't make an issue of it, Eve. As things are, I know pretty well what's happening."

"And what's going to happen?"

"He may either be up and about in a couple of weeks, or—he may not."

"You're telling me—"

"I'm not telling you anything, Eve, except to pray with all your heart."

The week rolled on. Each day that passed was like the one before it; Joel was neither better nor worse. And Eve did pray that this was not to be her second time waiting for death in this house. Dad was too young to die.

Sometimes, though, it seemed to her that he was fading away. He slept too much, and as if he was too weary to raise his voice, spoke so softly that it was an effort to catch his words. Then she would tell herself that he was not "fading," and that she was only, out of her dread, imagining it.

Tom telephoned often to suggest that perhaps she ought to come back and take make-up examinations. She could always go back if things should take a worse turn at home. And when Joel at last got out of bed one day and walked around, the Schulmans agreed. Vicky, too, urged her to leave, but of course, Eve thought, Vicky would.

Nevertheless, one morning when she had begun to pack her bag and arrange for a taxi to take her to the airport, Lore knocked on her door. Her face was drawn.

"Joel's gone," she said. "Vicky called the doctor just after midnight. There was no need to wake you up. It was a heart attack, over in minutes."

IN the quiet space of Joel's den, under the row of photographs that Caroline had chosen for him, Eve sat with Lore and the Schulmans. There had been a crowd at the services, followed by a crowd afterward here at home. But except for Vicky's visitors, who had gathered with her in the sunroom, the house was now empty. Even Jane had been taken to play with the Schulmans' grandchildren.

"So many friends," Emmy Schulman said, and sighed. "They were a remarkable pair, Caroline and Joel. With all they went through—" She sighed again. "I remember the little flat above Gertrude's, and your young mother acting brave, but obviously as bewildered as if she had landed on Mars. Now half of Ivy comes to pay its respects. I suppose you'll be going back in a day or two. You have exams to make up."

Dr. Al corrected her. "She has to wait for

the will to be probated. That should be early next week."

"I don't want to do that," Eve protested. "It seems—it seems ghoulish, waiting to count poor Dad's money. I hate it."

"But that's life. And death is part of it, Eve."

"I didn't do it when Mom died."

"That was different. Your father was here then. You're older now, anyway, an adult with responsibilities."

"I still feel horrible. What do I have to do?"

"Just go to the lawyer's office and listen."

"What about lawyers?" asked Lore, overhearing as she passed.

"An awful business with Dad's will. I hope you'll go along with me to O'Malley and Fried."

"Oh, they're not the lawyers anymore. She's got rid of them, too. The new one's some young fellow who came here a few months ago when Joel felt too weak one day to go downtown. I forget his name."

From the sun parlor, where Vicky's

friends were gathered, came a burst of laughter at which Eve and Lore looked toward each other.

Sadly Eve said, "Everything's changed, hasn't it?"

"Yes, everything's changed."

THE stiff new paper crackled in the young man's hands. His reading had already taken too long, and there were still some unread pages left. Eve's mind wandered along with the monotonous voice through convoluted clauses, "whereats," and "notwithstandings." Her gaze moved from the dreary brown law books on the shelves, then surreptitiously to Vicky, who was dressed in widow's black from head to toe; her little black pillbox, in imitation of Jackie, the First Lady, sat on a beehive of stiff hair that no gust of wind could ever stir.

Finally, her gaze came to rest on her own hands, folded on the lap of her best navy-blue suit. Dad had bought it for her when she had left for college four years ago; it was still her best suit, and she would never part with it. Never.

Nor was she ready to part with the ruby ring on her finger. Lore had brought it to her the day after the funeral.

"Joel told me to keep it safe. Here's the insurance policy. Be careful to pay the premium. I'd advise you to keep it with the ring in a safe-deposit box. It's too valuable to wear every day."

"Mom wore it every day. It's not flashy or anything."

"It's very refined, that's true."

She was going to wear it because Mom had worn it. She would wear it if it were worth a million dollars or ten cents. It was hers until it was time to give it to Jane, because it was Jane's father who had given it to Mom. She sat there examining the ring, the way light flashed upon it and was scattered into sparks, when the droning voice broke off.

"You both have a right to read the will. I have a copy here for each of you."

Eve was still only halfway through when Vicky finished, folded her copy, and put it into her alligator handbag. Eve's glance traveled down to the matching shoes. She had learned fast, Vicky had. But that was Vicky's business, not hers. She must read the thing carefully. You could almost say that it had been written to complicate, to confuse, rather than make clear.

She went back to the start, fixing her mind tenaciously upon each phrase, not allowing any impatient cough or creak of chair to hasten her. When she had finished, her blood was racing.

"I'm not sure I understand this," she said. "The way I read it, all that Jane and I are to receive is twenty-five thousand dollars apiece, plus an education trust large enough to send Jane through college. And Lore is to get twenty-five thousand dollars. Correct me if I'm wrong, please."

"Why, no," the young man, bland in his proper suit and matching tie, bland with his neat brown hair and matching eyes, replied. "That's plainly stated."

"But I still don't understand. What about all the rest?" Quite suddenly came a surge of anger. "You don't mean that the business, the properties—"

"That, too, is plainly stated. Turn to pages two and three, where it says, 'The balance to my wife, Victorine, to have and to hold—' etcetera."

"The balance means everything except twenty-five thousand each to Jane and me and Lore, plus Jane's education? Why ever would Dad do that? The house, the business that Mom created—Dad always gave her full credit for it—it goes to—"

And she looked toward Vicky, who while caressing the new handbag did not return the look.

"Why ever would my father do such a thing?" she repeated.

The bland young man replied with another question. "Nobody else can very well answer that, can they?"

"But he said, he told me only days ago, that Jane and I would be 'okay.' That's what he said."

"Well, twenty-five thousand dollars is a fairly fine sum. Most people would think so."

A stealthy animosity had crept into the room. This dialogue was like fencing: thrust and evasion. And Eve thought, thought fast. The other night when the Schulmans had invited her to dinner, Dr. Al, as he often did, had gone reminiscing about past times, about the Orangerie, its beginning and its immense expansion.

"Incredible what they accomplished together. She had the imagination and the drive. He had the business sense and the drive."

Now Eve pressed forward. "This is the final will? There are no other papers?"

"No. This is the most recent will. It supersedes all previous ones."

"I see."

She was stunned. She was filled with rage, not at Dad, because this was not the work of the Dad she knew, but at the two in this room who, having all the power here, were silently waiting for her to leave it. She stood up, and without a word, left.

That evening she reported, "I went right over to O'Malley and Fried. I had no appointment, but they saw me right away, both of them, and were very nice. They'll certainly take the case, but have you any idea what it can cost to contest a will? It could go on for years. Vicky will be able to afford to go through all the courts, but how can I?"

The Schulmans, aware of the tension in what was now Vicky's house, were visiting Eve and Lore in Joel's den.

"Nevertheless, I would try," said Doctor Al.

"It was horrible. You were smart not to go, Lore. You would have felt like punching her."

"I admit I have sometimes felt like doing it, anyway."

"Still, you almost always made excuses for her."

"That, too, I'll admit. She had a bad start, and I felt sorry for her. Besides, it's only fair to say she can be very likable. I'll correct myself. She used to be."

The doctor objected. "We're digressing. Never mind Vicky's personality. Let's stick to the point. The point is that there has been fraud and robbery here."

"But Dad signed the will!"

"The poor man couldn't see well enough to read what he was signing. And even if he had had proper eyesight, he wouldn't have had enough energy to concentrate. No, it's a dirty business, that's all it is, and they mustn't be allowed to get away with it."

"This I never expected from her," Lore said. "She had her ways, God knows, and she's done things I surely don't approve of, but I never expected this."

"I'm thinking," the doctor said, "about those properties. The bare land out on the highway where Orangerie Number Six stands is worth a fortune. That one piece alone."

Emmy's round eyes were wide with amazement. "And it all belongs to Vicky?"

"It seems that way," Eve said.

"Joel never knew what was being put over on him. I'll vouch for that," Schulman said, as if at that instant, he had read Eve's thoughts.

The dog came in, stood for a moment in the doorway to contemplate them all, then turned and trotted away.

BELVA PLAIN

"He's been looking all over for Joel," Lore explained. "Poor thing, he keeps returning to the bedroom as if he's asking himself why Joel isn't there."

"I suppose," Eve said bitterly, "he goes with the house. Doesn't he, too, belong to Vicky now?" She looked around at all Mom's books, in three languages, and at Lore's needlepoint chair seats, and out at the lake view that Mom had so loved.

"What do you think you'll do?" asked Emmy.

Lore answered for her. "She's going to get married. You don't mind if I tell, Eve? These are our old friends. Why should you keep it a secret?"

"Really, Eve? How wonderful!" exclaimed Emmy.

"Joel already told me your secret," Dr. Schulman said. "He was so glad you were happy. He told me it sounded as if the young man was just right for you. A scholarly type, he said."

"But not a starving scholar, thank goodness," observed Lore. "A little financial security never hurts. And now that this will's

416

been read, a lot of financial security will be better yet."

"I don't care," Eve protested, "whether Tom has a dime or not. I only wish he were here."

"Of course you don't care," Schulman agreed, "and that's as it should be. But let's get back to the will. You absolutely must try to upset it, Eve. If I were that young lawyer, I'd be shaking in my shoes. He should be, and could be, disbarred."

"How so?" asked Lore.

"How can you ask? It's obvious. The will is shot full of holes. Where's any provision for Jane's care? A minor child left without a guardian?"

"I'm sure Dad must have provided for that. As I remember," Eve said, "when I turned eighteen, he made me her guardian."

"But this is a new will. You need to fight," the doctor reiterated. "That's my advice. Don't you agree, Emmy? And Lore?"

"Of course you're right," Lore said. "But I think it will be hard to prove anything crooked was done. Joel's mind was sound to the end."

Emmy mourned, "To think they were upstairs in this house, planning and plotting to take it away from Eve and Jane!"

"Happens all the time," Schulman said. "Sometimes they get away with such stuff, and sometimes not. But you need to fight, Eve."

"What about exams, my degree, everything?" There was such a whirling in Eve's head. . . . "How am I going to come back here for courts and appeals and stuff? How am I going to pay for it all? And I have no heart, anyway, for a fight that may go on for years."

Emmy asked suddenly, "What's going to happen to Jane?"

"I don't know," Eve cried. "I can't leave her here. I won't leave her with that woman."

"You may have to fight that, too, in court," Schulman said. "Vicky's the legal wife, and she has the home for the child. What have you got? I'm playing devil's advocate, of course."

"I'm the sister. If she makes any fuss, I'll steal my own sister. I'll take my money and go to Australia with her, or—or—"

"Don't worry about that," Lore said. "She won't make any fuss about Jane. If you ask me, she'll be glad to get rid of her. A child that age can consume a lot of one's time."

"She sat there in that office today with such a look on her face—like a cat licking cream. And ever since the funeral, she's been walking around the house as if she resented my coming into a room when she was in it."

"Oh, the lady of the house," Lore said sarcastically.

Eve stood up. "I'm going to talk to her. I'm going to say it all, flat out. First thing in the morning, I will."

The doctor shook a warning finger. "Let your lawyer do the talking. Don't you say a word."

"Dr. Al, I know you make sense. I've been robbed, and I should fight. But I just don't know . . . Let me ask you again. What do you say, Lore?"

"Well, I tend to agree with you, Eve. But I hesitate to take a stand because I'm not a lawyer, and I may be all wrong. Still, personally I think you never can tell what will happen in a courtroom. You could just as easily lose. In this case, you probably would lose. So, with apologies to you, Dr. Al, I think, in the last analysis, I would put the mess away and advise Eve just to go on and live."

THE rhythmical throbbing of bass drums came up through the ceiling. A raucous racket had kept Eve awake for what seemed like many hours, but this was the worst. Not, she thought now, that I would have slept well anyway. Dr. Al is right. It's common sense, plain as day, plain as the nose on your face. You read these things in the newspapers all the time. Young nurses trick senile patients. Doctors are in cahoots with relatives. Vicky's lawyer might be her lover, or maybe merely a financial partner in the deal. It's a scandal, and I should attack them, should tear them both apart.

And yet, it would take up my life. It's an enormous, dangerous mountain that I'd have to climb with the hope of finding justice and peace on top. But there may well be no peace or justice on top. If I lose the case, I'll be a thousand times worse off than I am now.

Lore said I should put it all behind me, and live. Tom's out there waiting for me—

The bedroom door opened. Light fell upon the bed and the hands of the clock, standing at midnight. Light fell upon Jane in her elephant-printed nightgown.

"Where's my daddy?" she demanded. "I'm looking for my daddy."

"Darling, we told you he's gone away. And you," Eve said very gently and no doubt ineffectually, "should be asleep."

"Where did he go? I want to go there, too."

"You can't. He went far away, and you can't. I can't, either."

"Why?"

Oh, dear! What advice would a child psychologist give right now? Eve had no idea, and having none, had to improvise.

"Because—you see, you have to be older to go there. You're too young, and I am, too."

The canny, small person in the doorway came close to the bed. Her cheeks were wet, her nose was running, and her stare was suspicious.

"You know where he is, and you won't tell me," she said. "Vicky says he's in heaven, but that's not true."

"Yes, yes, it is true," Eve cried. "People have to wait their turn, you see, and it's very, very far, so that's why—come into bed with me," she urged as the wet face began to crinkle into tears. "Here's a tissue for your nose. Get under the covers and—no, let's go to your bed. You should be asleep. It's late."

From the bottom of Jane's lungs, there burst a howl. "I want my daddy. I don't want my bed, or yours either, and I don't want Vicky's. I don't like Vicky. I went down to the music looking for my daddy, and she was mean to me. I'm not going to her bed, I said!"

"No, no, you don't have to."

"I want Lore."

"Lore went home to her house right after your supper. You need to go to bed. Come, I'll take you."

"I don't want to, Eve, I don't," Jane screamed.

You definitely never bribe a child. That was elementary. Still, in an emergency . . .

"If I give you a cookie, will you go like a good girl?"

Jane considered. "Two cookies. Chocolate chip. I don't like the other kind."

"All right. Climb into your bed while I go to the kitchen and get them."

Quieted by chocolate, the tight little compact body relaxed against the pillow.

"Where's Peter?" Jane asked.

"In his basket in the kitchen."

"I want him to sleep with me. Will you let him? Vicky won't let him."

"Of course I will if you want him. Now turn the light out and you'll go to sleep. Right? Promise?"

Vaguely, she remembered that you weren't supposed to bargain with children, either, and she waited.

"All right. I promise."

Eve went to fetch Peter. She was about to emerge from the kitchen in her bathrobe with the dog in her arms, when abruptly the music ceased and Vicky's guests trooped into the front hall with loud good-byes. When the front door slammed, Eve came out and started upstairs, hoping to avoid Vicky. Midnight was too late for the inevitable confrontation, but she was not quick enough.

"Where are you taking that dog?" Vicky called.

"To Jane's room. She's upset, and she wants him."

"That's nonsense. Joel started it and it ought to be stopped. He sheds all over the rugs. Anyway, what is she doing awake at this hour?"

"The noise kept her awake," Eve said quietly, "as it did me."

"Nonsense. Healthy people should be able to sleep through a little music."

All the turmoil in Eve boiled up and swamped her resolve to control herself until morning.

"Music? Nobody's ears," she said, "could withstand that racket. It shook the house."

"I'm awfully sorry that my taste in music doesn't suit you, Eve. But what can you expect? I haven't had your high-class opportunities."

"A remark like that is disgusting, and you know it."

"Don't you tell me I'm disgusting. Who do you think you are, anyway, walking around here as if you were smelling something bad? From the day Joel died, you've been looking like that."

"I am smelling something bad. Very bad. The dirty deal you put over with that phony will you had my poor father sign."

"Phony will? You're out of your mind. What did you think, that he was going to leave everything to you? I was his wife, and you'd better believe it."

"Oh, I believe it. You've made it obvious enough." Eve's anger was red now, a red blur in front of her eyes. "But now you're a widow, and somebody ought to tell you, in case you don't know, that a proper widow

425

doesn't give rowdy parties until at least one year has gone by."

"Rowdy party! Because a few friends dropped in to cheer me up? What do you want me to do, sit around and cry?"

"I don't want you to do anything. I don't give a damn what you do. You can burn the house down for all I care as long as I'm not in it."

"Burn the house down!" Vicky laughed. "Fat chance. If I stay here, I'm going to build an addition. It needs more space for entertaining."

The two women, Eve halfway up the stairs and Vicky at its foot, were glaring at each other. And suddenly, in the midst of Eve's rage, there came a striking memory of the little brown house and the yard with the grape arbor, where Vicky had been her part-time baby-sitter, playing in the sand-box with her to earn some pocket money.

How had they come to this enmity?

"So this house is not large enough for you, Vicky?"

"The bigger, the better. Now will you take that dog back where he belongs?"

"No, Jane wants him."

"You're forgetting that I am the owner here now, and you are a guest."

"Not for long. As soon as I can pack and get a seat on the plane, I'm leaving."

From the bedroom now came Jane's cry. "Where are you, Eve?"

No, there was no way she could ever leave this child behind.

"You've won, Vicky. You've played dirty, and you've won. Except for one thing. You can't have Jane. I'm taking her with me, and you'd better not fight me."

Vicky laughed again. "Fight you? Good God, that kid is the last thing I'd fight for. She's a pain in the neck. You're welcome to her."

Suddenly, Eve felt curiosity. "Don't you care about anybody at all? Anybody but yourself? No pity, no feeling for this little baby?"

"Of course I have. I'm no monster. But I know you'll be good to her, and anyway, Joel would probably want you to have her. He never said so, but—I suppose Lore told you we weren't hitting it off too well, Joel and I. Not that anybody but Lore would have noticed."

"Well then, that's settled," Eve said.

She slept the rest of the night on a lounge chair in Jane's room, while Jane slept peacefully with the dog.

Emmy Schulman and Lore came the next day. Emmy worried and wept.

"I don't know how you're going to manage. Now you say you have to take two make-up courses for eight weeks. For goodness' sake, whatever are you going to do with a child? Oh, honey, I just don't see how you're going to do it. This whole thing is abominable. If Caroline knew! Her lovely house and all her labor gone up in smoke."

Having made up her mind, Eve went briskly about the packing. A carton of toys and a carton holding photographs and some of Caroline's favorite books were to go by express. She had bought a large new suitcase for all of Jane's clothes. They were leaving nothing behind. She wondered aloud whether Peter was small enough to fit in a container under the seat, or whether he ought to go in a crate.

"He'll probably be more comfortable in a good-sized crate," Lore suggested. "The vet can give him a tranquilizer beforehand."

"You're not taking the dog!" cried Emmy. "Lore, I don't think she knows what she's getting herself into."

"You worry about Eve more than I do," Lore said, lightly scolding. "Eve's a practical person. She's like her mother. Besides, she has a rich boyfriend. He'll be a big help."

"Not because he's rich," Eve said. "I suppose his family is, but he doesn't take anything from them. He works hard and lives a very plain life."

Tom, after the first telephoned appeal, had arranged everything. Eve was to move off campus into the top floor of a private house owned by a pleasant old couple. Since the arrangement was only to last over the summer, they would be willing to take care of Jane, and the dog, too, while Eve was in class. On weekends, Eve and Jane would go to Tom's beach house.

"Does he know these people?" asked Emmy.

"Friends of his know them well. Tom
checked, and everything is okay."

"What about after the eight or nine
weeks?"

"I'll cross that bridge when I get to it,"
Eve replied.

Emmy admonished her gently. "A little
before then, I hope."

"Yes, of course."

"She's well meaning," Lore remarked
when Emmy had left, "but sometimes she
really can be a wet blanket."

Eve wanted only to get out of the house.
It was just a container, after all. It had contained Caroline and Joel, but they were
gone, and with them the soul of the house
had fled, leaving behind some dead possessions that would acquire new meanings
as through the years they might pass, by
gift or auction sale, from one owner to another.

This, she thought, cramming Jane's
stuffed Kanga and Roo into the carton, is
no time for sentimentality, no time for
weeping.

But along with this stifled grief was a

great stir of excitement. It mounted as the departure neared. Positive visions floated before her eyes: Tom, waiting at the airport with that spectacular smile spread from his twinkle to his teeth; friends, and their amazement to find her returning with a child; the shack, and the beach, and the ocean winds at night.

Jane was thrilled about it all. She had found a spot with no trees to obscure the view, where, for long minutes, she stood watching the sky and keeping count of passing planes. On learning that Lore was not coming with them, she was temporarily stricken, but with Lore's promise to visit, she was comforted. The atmosphere was clearing.

And Vicky, now that affairs were settled, was even trying to make some civilized amends. "It's foolish to fly tourist class with Jane and all your carry-ons. Why be cramped and miserable? Let me treat you to some first-class tickets, my parting gift."

"We won't be miserable," Eve told her, "but thank you for the offer."

So that was that. One could only wonder

what was in Vicky's mind, whether she had any conscience at all, or whether she truly thought that she had merely protected her rights as a wife.

Lore shrugged. "You'll break your head if you wonder too long about human motives. Your own family's history should teach you that. The Hartzingers, and your mother— well, no need to draw pictures for you."

No need. Think, rather, of the blue Pacific.

"I wonder whether I'll ever see Ivy again," she said.

"What? You're abandoning me?"

But Lore knew better. And Eve, torn between a need to get away and pain at the sight of Lore's last-minute grief, hugged her close, saying, "You'll come for long, long visits. You'll fall in love with the climate, and you won't want to leave."

Early on the last day, the rented station wagon arrived to take them on their long ride to the airport. Eve, Jane, their heaps of luggage, and their dog were loaded in, while Lore, containing her tears, waved from the doorstep. The car took the road to the highway, and Ivy fell behind them.

The sun was just appearing at the bottom of the sky. Then, as they rode along, it made a stupendous leap; upward it soared, streaked the dark dome with its flame, and scattered its diamond spangles through the still-dark trees.

"Look, Jane!" Eve cried, and pointed. "Look! You've never seen it before. It's the sunrise."

FOURTEEN

The room had been carved out of an open attic. There were windows on both sides with the breeze coming through them, and when you looked out, a garden below. Twin beds with fresh white coverlets stood against one wall. There were shelves convenient for Eve's few textbooks, and in one corner, a large, red-roofed dollhouse.

"This was our daughter's room," Mrs. Dodge explained. "We rent it out to students now. It's taken from mid-September on, but that fits right in with your schedule, doesn't it? I hope you'll like it."

"It's lovely. I'm delighted," Eve assured her.

"It's a long time since we've had a little girl in the house. But Jane and I will get along fine while you're working. Our son lives on the next block, and his boys are Jane's age. They're nice, Jane, twins, and you'll have fun with them. I understand you and Jane are sisters? Your friend, Mr. Tappan, told us and was quite concerned that everything should be in perfect order for you."

"Yes, he's a good friend."

The woman was curious. Obviously, she would like to hear more. Nevertheless, you could tell that she was kindly. And after the events of the last week, her welcome was a warm bath.

"Oh, my, I just remembered what time it is. We're three hours behind you. You must be starved."

Jane promptly announced, "I want a hamburger."

"Tom's taking us to dinner. Wash your

hands," Eve said. "We'll unpack and bathe later. She's a good child," she explained while Jane was in the bathroom. "She's had a bad time since our father died, but I don't think you'll have any trouble with her. Or with the dog, either," she added, remembering Peter, whom Tom was now taking for a much-needed walk.

"Mr. Tappan bought a basket for him. I forgot to bring it upstairs for you."

Tom had thought of everything: flowers, candy, and a basket for Peter. From the first moment when they had trooped off the plane, he had wrapped them with love.

In the evening, after a quick supper and Jane's quick removal to bed, they sat together at the back of the Dodges' garden.

"Let me look at you," he said. "I've hardly had a quiet chance between the airport and the hamburger joint."

"It's dark."

"I've got a pocket flashlight. Look up." And when she obeyed, he pronounced that she was as beautiful as he remembered. "But you do look a bit worn. It must have been a hellish time."

"It was awful. I'll miss Dad terribly. Three thousand miles apart, but I always knew he was there for me. The rest of the nastiness that went on after he died, all the stuff I've told you about, is nothing, really. Not in the sum total of life."

"Not all that money?"

Eve shook her head. "It would have cost years, and disrupted you and me. People never retrieve the years they throw away."

Tom took her two hands and leaned forward on the bench to kiss her. When the long kiss ended, he whispered, "I don't want to waste minutes, let alone years. I wish there were two rooms with one bed up there instead of one room with two beds."

"Don't be silly. The Dodges wouldn't allow you to stay all night, or even to go upstairs in the first place."

"So what are we going to do? Go to my place every night?"

"Impossible. She'll only take care of Jane while I'm in school. There's no nighttime child care in the arrangement."

Tom groaned. "My fault. What a dunce! I should have thought of that."

"We'll have to wait for weekends."

"The week will be very, very long."

"But the end will be worth waiting for."

And of course, it was. As a host, Tom had outdone himself; he had bought a sandbox with pails and shovels, beach balls and water wings so that Jane might swim in the shallow cove around the bend. On their first day they ate a picnic lunch on the sand. The dog went swimming with Jane, and Tom took their picture to send to Lore.

"I feel like a father," Tom said, and laughed, "sending a picture of my child to my third cousins."

"I miss Lore," Jane said.

"But you're having a good time here," Eve protested.

"But I love Lore. I love Tom, too."

"You do? Why?" Tom asked.

"Because you bought me the sandbox and the candy."

"Little devil," he said. "You're cute, do you know it?"

They lay in the shade of the beach grapes, watching the child and the dog. There was no other life in their cove except for the eternal gulls, swerving over the water. Eve was suffused with a sense of freedom, an odd, new, happy sense that she had never before experienced in just that way.

She tried to describe it, although it was not easy. "It's many things, being with you, being here in all this peace. There's a freshness in the air here, as if the future will be all different and unencumbered. Do you understand what I mean? And there's something else. In Ivy, everybody I ever knew had heard the family story." She hesitated. "You see how I still hesitate? And people who didn't know the story soon learned about it from those who did know it. It was always a monkey on my back. Perhaps here I can throw it off for good. Do you think I can?"

"Darling Eve," Tom said, "I don't know."

That night after Jane had been put to sleep, they closed their door. They had been starving for each other. It was as if years instead of weeks had passed. When they were satisfied, they lay still, slept, awoke, and turned to each other again.

Tom's arms were around Eve when the door banged against the wall.

"What's that noise outside?" Jane cried. "I want my daddy. Somebody took my daddy away, and I need him."

Eve got out of bed and opened her arms. "Come here, honey. The noise is only a little thunder. Don't be sad now. Daddy wouldn't want you to be sad or scared."

"I don't care. I want Daddy."

"Good Lord," Tom groaned, as Peter, in a running jump, landed on his stomach. "Midnight visitors."

"I'll stay in the other room with her for a while. Come, Jane, back to bed. I'll cover you up and we'll talk a little. Then we'll all go to sleep."

"I want to sleep in here with Peter."

"You can't. This is Tom's bed."

"But you were in it."

"Oh, dear," Eve sighed.

" 'Oh, dear' is right. Jane," Tom said, "go back to bed. You're too old to behave like this."

"No. I don't want to. I'm not too old."

"Good Lord," he groaned again. "A little pampered, wouldn't you say?"

"No, I wouldn't. 'Troubled' is a better description right now."

"Okay, okay, you handle it."

"Come, Jane. Peter, come, too."

On top of the covers, Eve lay alongside Jane with Peter on the other side.

"Daddy is thinking of you," she whispered. "He knows you're with me and Peter. Lore's thinking of you, too. We'll call Lore up tomorrow, and you'll tell her about Mrs. Dodge, and the twins, and the beach, and everything. Listen to the waves. Isn't that a pretty sound? Like whispers, like music. The thunder's gone away. Listen . . ."

Tom was awake when, shivering in the night breeze, Eve returned. She saw that he was cross.

"Remind me tomorrow to get a latch for our door. It would have been awful if she had come in a few minutes earlier than she did."

Lying back on the pillow, Eve began to feel a vague anxiety. Then she scolded herself: I do tend to be a worrier. Lore always reminds me that, after every exam, I'm sure I did poorly; when I get a bad spot on a dress, I'm sure that the dress is ruined. Still . . . . it was a lovely day, no doubt about it. But we spent it taking care of Jane. Of course, being so close to the water, we had to be vigilant. But back in town, we'd be careful, too, about other things. There was no end to child care.

"SHE'S a nice little girl," Mrs. Dodge reported, "feisty and sweet."

Feisty. That had been Dad's very word for Jane.

"When the boys get rough with her, she holds her own. A lot of girls don't, but she wades right in and protects herself. She never starts a fight, though. My daughter-in-law says the same when they play over at her house. The only time Jane got upset about anything was when my son came home and the boys all ran to him calling for Daddy. So they brought her back here, and I had to quiet her down."

"Jane's had a hard time," Eve said, remembering Vicky's harsh voice. "I'm very grateful to you, Mrs. Dodge. I stay away all day with an easy mind because of you."

"How's the work going?"

"Fine. It's just make-up work, really, to fulfill the requirements so I can get my diploma."

"And after that, the real world. What kind of a job are you looking for?"

The real world. Where was it to be? The jungles of Guatemala? With Jane? Jane, with Joel's curly hair and a timid core beneath the bold smile; surely there is much of our mother in her, too, much that is yet to unfold, still hidden now like the tight bud in the sheath. But what am I to do with her?

She had not answered the other woman's natural question, and she said quickly, "I'm not quite sure yet. It's a big decision."

"Oh, yes, that it is."

"I was wondering, Mrs. Dodge, whether you would be willing to watch her some nights? They have concerts on the campus, you know, and there was a movie—" She faltered. Actually, Tom had complained very mildly, it was true, that they were missing some worthwhile events, and surely people needed to get out together now and then.

"I'm afraid not, dear. We're not young people, and I'm pretty tired by nightfall. Mr. Dodge likes me to sit with him while we watch TV."

The next day, on her way to the library, Eve saw Tom approaching from the opposite direction. The campus was so huge that a chance encounter was rare. How haphazard was the world! Things—leaves, birds, people—all whirl and collide at random. So it had happened that on a day, in a moment, he had seen her sitting under a tree. If he had been walking on the other side of the lawn, what then?

But here he came; he had a calm, easy stride, and his face was tilted upward, as if to feel the sunshine. His mouth had its familiar touch of humor.

"Well, well," he said. "A good thing I took that picture of you, or I might forget what you look like. It's been a long time since Sunday."

"I haven't changed. It's only Wednesday."

BELVA PLAIN

"Only? Have you asked Mrs. Dodge?"

"She can't do it."

"Damn."

"I'm sorry, too, very, but what can I do?"
He threw his palms up.

"Look, Tom. You go by yourself. Jazz
concerts like this one don't come here every day. You go. I don't mind."

"Great fun, going alone."

"No, but even married couples have to
do it sometimes. I remember my mother going to things without Dad, and him without
her."

"Speaking of married couples, I'll bet you
can't guess what I just heard. There's a ru-
mor about us. Some bright guy said Jane is
our kid that we've kept hidden."

"Is that ever stupid! But I suppose wherever we go with her, there'll always be
some idiot who'll think something."

Did she imagine that the flicker of humor
on Tom's mouth had died away?

"I want you to hear that music tomorrow
night," she said brightly. "Honestly. It's no
big deal. Go and tell me about it. If there's a
record, buy one."

446

"All right. All right, I will."

They stood looking at each other. There were unspoken words between them.

"I can't even phone you," he said.

"I know."

"It's absurd that there's no phone in your room." Tom looked at his watch. "I'm due in Room 309 in five minutes."

She nodded. "See you Friday. My last class is out at four."

"I'll pick you up here, and then we'll get Jane."

He walked away. She watched him reach the corner of the building, stop, and come back.

"I can't imagine living without you," he said almost roughly, turned around, and this time did not come back.

In the library, Eve sat with an unopened text before her. *Wherever we go with her,* she had said. The careless phrase, repeated, was suddenly not so careless. For where, indeed, were they going? And, clearly, she saw that to have traveled across the continent without any definite plan had been foolish and irresponsible.

She had simply assumed that because Tom was here, everything would be simple. And now it was not.

Distraught, she had fled her home, and in bliss she had arrived here into his arms. They had made love, but no decisions. Tom had, as yet, said nothing about any plans. It worried her that they were not yet married. Admit, Eve, that you would never have done, without marriage, what you are doing if you had been nearer to home. Imagine if Dad had known! Imagine if Lore were to know! She is like her mother, they would say, making the same mistake.

Yes, she must speak seriously. On Saturday night at the beach house while Jane slept, she would ask Tom what they were going to do. There were only a few weeks left of the summer session. It was time.

But shouldn't it be the man who does the asking? Logical or not, a woman wanted to be sought.

ON Saturday they went out on a fishing boat. Tom owned quality gear; deep sea fishing was one of his enthusiasms, and Eve had made trips with him before. She took no pleasure from dragging out of the water a pathetic, live creature struggling for its life, but she was no pious overseer of other people's tastes, and she went along. Her eyes were always turned away toward the outer rim, where the sky met the ocean. Tom knew her feeling. They understood each other's feelings.

Today, however, he had not quite understood. "You'll be out for hours," she had explained, "and I don't see how Jane can fit in. I've never seen anyone bring a child along."

"Well, maybe other people have a place to leave the child."

Had she imagined again that his answer had been unnecessarily short? Anyway, here they were, Eve and Jane, alone in the cabin.

At first Jane had been fascinated by the embarcation, the ropes, the engine room, and the people climbing onboard with their cameras, slickers, and baskets of lunch. The men and the women—very few women

—had spoken the usual pleasantries to her, no doubt wondering why she had been brought on this outing.

"Look at her, isn't she adorable in the poke bonnet?"

"It's the only thing I could find to keep the sun off her face," Eve explained.

"Cute. Looks like my granddaughter," one man said.

"I'll bet you'll catch the biggest fish in the ocean today, little lady."

The pleasantries over, the boat had sputtered into motion and lurched its way out to sea, gathering speed and climbing the waves, dropping like a plunger elevator and climbing again. Now the windows were washed with spray, so there was nothing at all to see.

"I want to go outside," Jane said.

On deck, the wind was powerful enough to carry a light person overboard and to stop a heavy person's breath. Eve clutched Jane's hand.

"Great, isn't it?" Tom called from an eagle's eyrie above them.

She did not think it was great. She

thought that a storm was coming up. "Too rough," she called back, but the wind must have carried her words away, for he did not reply.

"I want to go in," Jane said. "It's too cold."

No doubt it was far too cold for her. Eve should have let Tom go alone. But he had already gone alone to the concert this week.

Tom called again. "What? Going inside?"

"It's cold."

"You're losing all the benefit of the day."

"Can't help it. Anyway, the wind's so high I can hardly hear you."

"I'd like to bottle this pure air and take it home."

Didn't he know that she would happily have faced the weather on top with him, but that she had Jane to consider? Smiling, she waved to him, calling, "See you below," and went below.

"Let's read," she said. "I've brought three Babar books. Which one shall we start with?"

They were charming books; even in

translation, the writing was original and vivid. There was a cozy pleasure in reading aloud with Jane's head resting so comfortably against her, and a surprising pleasure in the child's bright attention.

"I think Babar is very nice to the old lady."

"Why do you think so?"

"Because he's an elephant, and he could squash her if he sat on her, but he doesn't."

She is so little, so alone, and too innocent to know how alone she is, except for me and for Lore. But really, for me.

The boat rocked and pitched. From side to side it flung a package, probably a lunch that someone had left under a seat. Up and down it seesawed, flashing now and then a forward glimpse of the tilting horizon.

"I'm hot," Jane said.

"But you were too cold just a little while ago, and it's not even warm in here."

"I need to take off my jacket."

She was sweating. When she began to cry, "My tummy hurts, my tummy hurts," Eve knew.

"Lie down on the bench," she commanded, "and close your eyes."

Once, years ago, on a sailboat on the lake at home, she had been miserably sick. Afterward, the family joked about seasickness and the death wish. But it wasn't laughable when you were having it.

The copilot, hearing the cries, stepped down from the front to offer advice. "A chicken sandwich is a big help. I keep a few handy. How about it, kid? A nice chicken sandwich?"

"No!" roared Jane.

"Really, a chicken sandwich will taste good. Better eat."

An instant later, Jane's stomach emptied itself, as the contents of the morning's breakfast erupted onto her jacket, Eve's sweater, and the well-scrubbed floor.

"Oh, dear," Eve wailed, concerned about Jane and embarrassed about the floor. "Leave it, please. If you'll get me a pail or something, I'll clean it up in a minute. I'm so sorry."

"Don't worry about it. The kid can't help

it. Just take care of her and never mind the floor."

Now Jane wailed, "I'm sick. I want my daddy. I want Lore."

"I'm here. Don't cry, honey. I know you feel awful, but you'll be better if you lie down and stay quiet."

"I hate this boat. I want to get off."

"How much farther are we going?" Eve asked.

"Just up and down along the shore, north and south. Rambling around, looking for fish. A couple of folks upstairs have been hauling in some good ones."

"What I really meant was, how much longer do we stay out?"

"Supposed to dock around two. That's the time you paid for."

It was only half-past ten and she supposed, or rather hoped, that there would be no more vomiting. There was nothing to do but endure.

Half an hour later, after Jane had finally lain down to sleep, Tom came upon Eve curled over her knees and trembling with cold. Having nothing to do but read, she had been occupying herself with a mental translation of Babar, first into German and then back into its original French.

"What's going on here?" he cried. And after she told him, "We shouldn't have brought her."

"I know that," Eve said simply, as the boat climbed a dark green mountain and slid like a terrifying avalanche down the other side.

Jane woke up, mumbling, "I want Lore. I do. I do."

"I thought she was so attached to you," Tom said.

"She is. But I've only been with her during vacations. She's been with Lore every day of her life."

"I want to go home. I hate this boat," Jane shrieked.

Tom shook his head. "She hates too many things," he said.

"Tom, you can't expect her to be sunny all the time. Nobody else is. And she's been under a lot of stress. And—" Eve stopped. They were talking about Jane as if she weren't there hearing, and possibly under-standing, what they were saying.

"It's a raw day, starting to rain." And shaking himself as he spoke, Tom scattered drops from his jacket.

"Does that mean we go back?"

"Not unless everybody wants to, or a real storm comes up."

"What if we ask them to let us go back?" Eve asked.

"Eve, these people have paid for five ex-pensive hours. I can't ask them."

"I would pay for the lost time."

"That's ridiculous. Let Jane go to sleep again. Put on my jacket and come up with me."

"Now you're being ridiculous. You can't stand outside in this weather without a jacket. Take it."

"No, you take it."

Why were they having this absurd argu-ment? But she knew quite well why . . .

Tom left a troubled stillness behind him. His jacket lay where he had flung it. Jane had stopped her plaints to stare up at Eve as though she were making a study of her face.

"Tom's angry," Jane said.

She did not answer, thinking: Well, if he isn't angry exactly, he's certainly stubborn. But then, so am I. Her arms were almost blue with cold, yet she refused to wear his jacket. If he wanted to prove something—prove what?—she did, too.

She got up, went forward, and handing the jacket to the obliging copilot, asked him whether he would please go up and give it to Tom. "He forgot it," she said.

After that she lay down, holding Jane close for warmth. They were still lying there, Jane asleep and Eve too cold and agitated for sleep, when people came stamping down into the cabin, lamenting the storm. A heavy rain was falling, and the boat was turning homeward.

"Well, it wasn't much of a day," Tom said, "especially for you."

"I haven't said so," she answered stiffly.

"You don't need to, with that glum expression. I see you can be as stubborn as I can."

"Every bit as much."

So they went home, took hot showers, and still barely speaking, ate the sandwiches that were to have been their jolly lunch on the boat. In midafternoon when the rain stopped, Eve and Jane went to the beach on a hunt for shells, while Tom got out his easel.

He had been working for the last two weekends on a seascape. The subject was a difficult one: Surf advanced in strong, level parallels toward a rocky promontory and broke up into a dazzle of spray; it all happened in twilight. He chooses difficulties, Eve thought now. That's something I'm just learning about him. This morning's weather, the Guatemala jungle, and now this that it would take a Turner to do well, are each a challenge. What is he trying to prove? she wondered with some impatience.

He was still working at the easel when she returned with Jane. And knowing that he wanted to be undisturbed, surely a reasonable request, she went inside to let Jane help her make some cupcakes for their dinner.

"We'll have a party," Jane said. "Cupcakes are for a party, and I'll wear my party dress."

The dress had been brought along for the weekend because Eve had thought they might go out to dinner. Tom had mentioned "the best seafood restaurant within fifty miles," but then he had said nothing more about going. Well, why not wear her party dress?

Eve's thoughts were making her heart beat faster. They must speak. This chilly sulk could not be allowed to go on.

She was waiting for him when, after Jane had gone to bed, he brought his painting indoors. "We need to talk," she said. "What have we been doing since ten o'clock this morning? We've wasted almost twelve hours of our lives being nasty."

She had not meant to give way, and did keep her voice firm, but her eyes teared.

"I could cry myself," he said unexpectedly, "cry with shame. All afternoon while I was working at this thing, I've been wanting to say something to you, but I saw how you were, and I didn't know how to start. A paltry excuse, I know." He put his arms around her. "I apologize. Okay? Let's forget the whole stupid business."

They would forget it, of course. It was their first fight, if you could even call it a fight. And she was about to say, "We need to straighten out our plans and be definite," when he spoke first.

"I guess I've been cranky because I'm not used to having a child around. I know it's nobody's fault, and I'm sorry."

"I wasn't in the best humor, either," Eve admitted.

"She's a cute little kid when she behaves herself."

"I think she's starting to feel secure. She's been much better lately."

"Okay. Shall we call it a day?"

This was probably not the best moment, after all, in which to get down to business. "A day," she said.

"I was really talking about bed."

She laughed. "At this hour?"

"Why not? At any hour. You and I, at any hour, Eve."

THE body, the two bodies, so marvelously fitting, blended, becoming one, soared, returned into the soft night, and floated away to rest. Only much later as she fell toward sleep did Eve recall that somewhere there had been a worry, a lurking, vague thing, dark in a corner. But she could not think of what it was . . .

She was jolted awake into daylight. From the outer room came voices, a man's rumble and a child's frenzy. She jumped out of bed, caught a robe, and ran.

They were standing in front of Tom's painting, Tom towering over the crying child. Then she saw what had happened. In the forefront of the picture where he had labored to create an iridescent spray, a large red blob had been superimposed. The paint was still wet.

"It's a boat," Jane cried. "I only wanted to make it pretty."

Tom looked at Eve, at the ruin, and back

at Eve. Apparently, he had run out of words. There are times when you have suffered such a beastly assault that you do run out of words. Yet for some implausible reason, Eve felt an impulse to laugh.

Still, she spoke severely. "Jane, you've spoiled Tom's picture."

"I didn't spoil it, Eve! I fixed it. There was no boat, and it needed a boat." The foot stamped, and the tears poured.

Oh, damn. Bright Sunday morning, and here we are again.

"The picture doesn't belong to you, Jane. How would you like it if somebody marked up your new Babar book?"

"That's different, Eve!"

"No, it isn't. People's things belong to them, and we don't touch other people's things. You do know that."

"Words, words," Tom said. "You're wasting your breath."

"What else would you have me do?"

"I know what I'd do."

"I can imagine. And what would that sort of thing accomplish? Come here, Jane. Let me wipe your nose. Then tell Tom you're very, very sorry, and you'll never do anything like that anymore."

"No. He's mean. He's very, very mean."

"Tom's never mean. His feelings are hurt because you spoiled his work. Please say you're sorry, and he'll feel better."

"Not necessarily," Tom muttered. "A nuisance, that's what."

"I'm not a nuisance," Jane roared.

"I know you didn't bargain for this," Eve said, "but what can I do?"

"You can make some other arrangements for her."

Now Jane was scrutinizing first one, then the other, as she had done at the table last night. You wouldn't think that a child's eyes could reveal such canny appraisal. She is figuring out, Eve thought, what is going on between Tom and me.

And Jane said, "Tom doesn't like me."

"Of course he likes you."

"He doesn't, Eve."

"Well, let's not argue about it this minute. You're still in your pajamas. Go on and dress yourself. I'll come in if you need help."

"May I wear my party dress again?"

"Yes, if you want to."

Tom was slashing red paint all over his twilit ocean. She followed him outdoors to the trash can, where he tossed the picture away. The lid clanged shut.

"I'm sorry," she said desperately, "I really am, Tom."

"She's some little treasure. A joy to have around."

"She really is, Tom. She's fundamentally very good. You should hear Mrs. Dodge talk about her. She just has her moments and this was a bad one."

"Eve, what are you going to do with her? You've got to get rid of her."

"Get rid of her? You can't mean that."

"I most certainly can, and for your own good."

"*My* good? What about hers? She never knew her mother and has lost her father. She can't understand death, she feels that Daddy has simply abandoned her, and now you want me to abandon her, too?"

"I said you have to think of your own good sometimes."

"I don't know you when you talk like this, Tom."

How was it possible after last night that they could be standing here face-to-face like adversaries? Or like two dogs, she thought roughly, preparing to fight.

"You'd think," Tom said, "that I was telling you to leave her on somebody's doorstep. What I meant is, find a top-notch boarding school for her. I know they're expensive, but I can pay. I'll be glad to. And you and I will go off to our dig as we planned."

"Tom, let's get this straight. I'm not going to go out of the country and leave a six-year-old among strangers, even if there is such a thing as a boarding school for children her age, which I doubt."

"So that's it. You weren't intending to go with me at all. After two years' worth of plans, you were simply going to walk away."

"I intended to be with you here, to get a job. I never intended to 'walk away'!"

"That's not how I understood it."

"The trouble is that neither of us thought

to question the other. We're both at fault. We just assumed." She was protesting, pleading and trembling. Then she threw pride away. "You never said a word about marrying me, and being a family."

"I thought you took it for granted." He picked up a handful of pebbles from a potted cactus and threw them, one by one, over the fence. "The truth is, Eve, this baby business has thrown us all off course. She's taken up all your time, or almost all of it."

That was true. Or almost true. Yet she had to defend herself. "What would you have had me do? Thousands of mothers have to fit their jobs into child care or the other way around."

Tom answered quietly, "But you are not her mother."

"I am aware of that," Eve said, tasting her own bitterness on her tongue.

When he stooped for another handful of pebbles, her patience broke. "Will you please stop doing that?" she cried. "You're driving me crazy."

"I'm not the one who's driving you crazy,

Eve. It's this responsibility, for which you are entirely unprepared."

That, too, was true. And she thought for the first time how different it would be now if she had inherited her fair share of the estate: Jane would stay on in their home with a first-class nurse, and Lore there after work every day to oversee things. Then she herself would go with Tom, and they would make long, frequent visits to Ivy. How different it would be. . . .

"Where are we?" Tom asked, shattering all the "if's."

"Eve," Jane called, "the button came off my party shoe."

"Where are we?" Tom repeated.

"I know where I am. I'm in a state of exhaustion. Maybe you should drive us home. Then you can have the rest of Sunday in peace."

LIFE had been turned inside out, and she knew no way to right it. She felt completely alone. Women of her age, here on this campus, did not have enough experience to advise her; each one's opinion would be based only upon her particular temperament. Several times she went to the telephone, thinking that Lore might be able to give counsel, but each time she withdrew her hand. For Lore knew nothing about loving a man. She was virginal. Confide in Mrs. Dodge, maybe? You could tell that she was a sensible woman. But no, in the last analysis, you had to make your own decisions.

Haven't you already made it? she asked herself then. The rest is now up to Tom. She stood above the bed where, in the nightlight's pale glow, Jane slept with Peter at her feet. The whole of Jane, body, cheeks, and small, plump hands, was round, soft, and so very, very small. Inside the curly-haired head dug deeply into the pillow, a *person* was forming, a person sensitive, vigorous, and smart. This was Caroline's child. . . .

A week passed without word from Tom. She had one more examination to take. In two weeks after that, the Dodges would reclaim their room. Then what?

Late one afternoon when she returned to

the house, Mrs. Dodge had a message for her. "Your friend Tom phoned."

Curious, as she had been from the start, she was waiting for a reaction. When it did not come, she gave the message. "He wants to meet you at five on the campus today. Under the tree. He said you'll know where."

Five minutes before the hour, Eve sat down under the tree. The walls and lawns, in the hiatus between the end of the summer session and the start of the next, were almost deserted. This stillness created a sense of departure. Her diploma was in the mail. The college years were finished, their finality emphasized by the realization that she had no address for the delivery of the diploma. It was to be mailed to Lore's apartment.

A breeze came up, clattering through the palms. The afternoon was cool and blue. Blue. Memories take such funny turns and have such funny quirks! At the beach one day they had argued over the blues in sky and water, he naming one and she another: cerulean, or turquoise, or lapis lazuli, down the long list. How could those days, that laughter, ever come to an end?

She closed her eyes. When I open them, I will see him striding down the path around the back of the library. "We'll postpone Guatemala," he will say. "We will work here together, and when Jane is of a proper age, we will find a plan that is good for us all. Don't cry, Eve," he will say, because there is no doubt that I will cry. They will be my thankful tears.

"Eve," he said. No familiar humor touched his lips or his eyes. "What are we going to do?"

"I was waiting for you to tell me."

"Well, I do have an idea, although I suppose you won't like it. We can take her to Guatemala."

He knew very well that she "wouldn't like it." He hadn't even spoken Jane's name.

He was standing there looking down. Their positions rendered them unequal, making Eve a supplicant. She got up to stand straight and almost as tall as he.

"A little child on a dig in the jungle, Tom? Is that the best you can do?"

"I took a chance with the idea. I couldn't think of anything else."

"Not of postponement?"

"I've already waited around here for an extra year until your graduation."

There was a physical pain in her chest. Broken heart, she thought, is an accurate description. And she did not reply, but looked at him.

He was bracing himself by a hand on the tree trunk. "I told you that first day, it's been a dream of my life. People unearthing ancient civilizations, building from clues, a shard, a scrap of carving, a piece of a calendar, a reading of the stars—I told you."

"I wanted to do it with you, Tom."

"Your family!" he cried out. "You've been strangled by them. The monstrous father who haunts you, and compassion for your mother, and now this obligation you feel for her child—an obligation that isn't yours—"

Now, suddenly, her anguish turned to wrath. "If it isn't mine," she said passionately, "then tell me whose it is."

"Oh, Eve, I don't know. We've come to an impasse."

"An irresistible force meeting an immovable object. I always thought love was the irresistible force."

"I love you, Eve, you know I do, but—"

"But not enough," she said.

"Don't say that, Eve."

"I suppose I should understand your need and admire it. And I do admire it. You have a scholar's mind, and you have to go where it leads you."

The chapel clock chimed the half hour. Time, as usual, flowed while two human beings wrestled with future time and how to spend it. Eve felt that she could not endure another minute here, looking at the so-beloved face. And yet, the wrath was still inside her, that and the pity.

"Pity," she said. "I pity us both."

He put out his arms, but she moved away. Get it over with. Do what has to be done. And she ran. And he did not follow.

FIFTEEN

The plane swerved over the Pacific, followed the coast for a while, and turned eastward. A California idyll was over. There was no place else to go but home to Ivy.

"Come back," Lore had said. "We'll work out a solution. There's always a solution."

So here they were, Jane in the window seat craning her head to see everything, to exclaim, and as always, to ask questions.

"Who lives down there? Where is that boat going? Have they got candy on this

473

plane?" She worried about Peter. "Are you sure they won't lose him?"

"No, no, he's safe in his crate, probably asleep. We'll get him back when we land."

She worried about Vicky. "Are we going to see Vicky again? I don't want to."

No, they were not going to see Vicky again. I was a fool, Eve thought. I should have fought for what was mine. I depended instead upon Tom, not on his money, but on him, which is very different. And she thought of her mother, who had also depended on someone, a man who failed her by a desertion far more terrible than Tom's. But when you catch your fingers in a closing door, it doesn't help to be reminded of another person's cancer.

For the long flight, she had equipped both Jane and herself with a coloring book and crayons, a doll to be dressed and undressed, the Babar books, a newspaper, and a paperback novel. Between these, lunch, and perhaps a few naps, the time would pass. She craved a nap. Occasionally as her spirits ebbed, she wished she might sleep forever.

"If I close my eyes, will you let me sleep, Jane? Not talk and wake me up?"

"Yes, because I think you're sad," Jane said.

"I'm not sad," Eve protested. "What makes you say I am?"

"I saw you cry yesterday."

"I told you I had a cold."

Jane shook her head. "No," she said solemnly, "I saw you cry."

The plane rose through clouds that darkened as it flew toward the declining day. Dirty gray, like watered milk, they measured off the miles from California. She wondered what Tom was doing, whether he was already packing for his departure to the jungle, whether he felt the bewildered anger toward her that she felt toward him. Or was as maimed as she.

She slept a little, and watched Jane sleep with the new doll clasped to her breast. They landed, checked Peter's whereabouts, and waited for the connecting flight. They landed again and found a taxicab to take them to Ivy. The ride seemed to last as long as the flight from California. Over the highways, the underpasses and overpasses, the old cab rattled. Past shopping centers and bowling alleys it sped; past red neon signs and billboards with depressing exhortations to eat, or smoke, or wear, all for your welfare, it sped on.

At last came Ivy. Here was the high school where she had sat, here was the war memorial, noble and stately, and here was Lore's apartment.

"Come, darling, Lore is waiting for us. Hold Peter's leash while I pay for the ride."

Beaten, she thought. I'm not going to let myself feel beaten if I can help it, but the fact is, I am.

LORE had always done things with style. The cloth that covered the card table had a border of her typical hand embroidery. The pottery dishes were a copy of a famous French bone china. A little pot of supermarket daisies stood at the center of the table.

"Why not?" was Lore's cheerful response to Eve's compliment. "Why not dine as nicely as any millionaire?"

She had prepared a chicken and baked a cake, thus filling her little rooms with the savors of roasting, mingled with a trace of chocolate.

"I'm thinking of making a move," she said. "This place is so cramped that I had to put a lot of my things in storage, my bedroom furniture that your mother gave me and all my books, a lot of stuff."

Eve understood that to avoid the painful fact of this unexpected return, Lore was making conversation.

"You remember the Wilmott estate? They're breaking it up for garden apartments, good-sized rooms and not too expensive, I hear. So I'm looking into it."

Mechanically, Eve responded, "That will be lovely."

"Oh, there've been changes in this town since you went away to school. It seems as if they couldn't have happened in only four years, but everything's moving so fast these days. Ivy's almost become a bedroom town. Commuters and plenty of money. Take a walk, and you'll see what I mean. Boutiques, fancy foods, fancy clothes. Yes, a big change."

"Why are we eating in your house, Lore?" asked Jane. "Why don't we go home to our house?"

The two women looked at each other as if doubtful about how to answer.

"We can't. It isn't our house now," Eve replied gently.

"Why not?"

"Well, because—because we went to California."

For a moment Jane considered that, and then made a demand. "I want to see the lake, Eve. I do. Remember, we took Peter, and sometimes Lore, but not Vicky." Emphatically she shook her head and frowned. "Never Vicky. And afterward we had a treat."

Eve remembered, but did not say that as a little girl, she, too, had walked along the lake. She was terribly tired, with the tiredness of a bruised heart and a bewildered brain. She was walking through a wilderness without a map.

She had thought: *If he ever leaves me, I'll want to die.* But dying is not so easy.

Jane, with a mouth full of icing, announced, "I know my ABC's. I'll say them for you if you want to hear, Lore."

You've got to get rid of her, he had said.

Lore had a loving smile. "I certainly do want to hear. But first, will you feed Peter? I forgot to buy dog biscuits, so you can give him the chicken scraps. Careful, no bones. He'll choke on bones. And after that, you can turn on the television by my bed."

"So how are you?" she asked when Jane had left them.

"As you see. I kept nothing out when I telephoned you. The call cost thirty dollars. I was a wreck."

"Men," Lore said contemptuously. "Men."

"Not all of them. Think of Dad."

"Yes, Joel was a good man. He was different. But even he—"

Having talked all around the core subject, they had now reached it. "Things have happened here overnight. As I told you, Vicky sold the house before a week was out.

Would you believe I heard she made a fortune on it? Almost double what Joel and Caroline paid. The new people are painting it mustard yellow, and the Schulmans are having a fit because they have to look at it."

"Mom's pretty house. She was so happy there. I remember when Jane was born and they had the party on the lawn. And my party on my sixteenth birthday."

"Well, what can you do? It's life, Eve. You win and you lose."

"We made a mistake, both of us. We gave in too easily."

"You could have lost just as easily. But that's neither here nor there, now. The big news is that the McMulligan chain has bought the Orangeries, all six of them. And Vicky has moved to Arizona with Gertrude. It's amazing how those two get along. But of course, since Vicky has all the money, she has the upper hand, and Gertrude is as meek as a lamb. People are not always what they seem to be, are they?"

The question required no answer. Tonight she and Jane were to sleep in a motel, where Lore had made a reservation. The

Schulmans, kind as always, had offered their guest room, but Eve had told Lore to refuse. As a homeless guest, she would have felt poignant defeat; in the motel she would still feel independent.

"Just please keep the dog for a while, Lore," she said now. "Jane can go along while I start my job hunt. I'll take anything that pays enough to feed us in a couple of rooms someplace."

"Where do you plan to start?"

"I thought I'd go first to an agency and find out what my possibilities are. I have no skills, after all. A college degree with a string of good marks doesn't prepare you to do anything."

"What about teaching languages? You're as fluent in French and German as any French or German native."

"I have no teacher training, no license, and no time now to get one."

"You don't need one in a private school. Now, I'll tell you something." Lore's face crinkled into a sly smile. "I think I may have something for you. I had a patient last week, emergency appendix, a teacher at the Dale Forest School, out in Dale. We got talking for a couple of minutes, and I suddenly got the idea of finding how the land lies in private schools. They don't have any language program there yet. The place is so new that they're still organizing and expanding. A school like that is bound to do well. A lot of these new people in town have ideas about education."

"Snobbish?"

"Not necessarily. Would you be interested?"

"Lore, you mean well, but I don't stand a chance."

"Don't say that. I asked this teacher what she thought, and she advised you to apply. They've got a new head, a master this time. Headmaster. Go try. What have you got to lose?"

THE Dale Forest School had been a steel magnate's redbrick Georgian mansion. Austere and dignified, it reposed in a grove of ancient shrubbery surrounded by lawns, which were in turn surrounded by open woods and meadows. Outbuildings and playing fields now occupied the meadows.

Across from all this space the outskirts of the village had spread some years before. These streets were filled by dowdy, comfortable, late-Victorian houses complete with turret and wraparound porch.

Eve parked the car, borrowed from Lore, and went up the walk holding Jane by the hand. It was absurd to be applying for a position with a child in tow. But there had been no place to put Jane this morning.

"I brought your new coloring book," she said. "Now, sit right here at the door and don't move. Don't move, do you understand? I won't be long."

"I want to go with you. I want to."

"Please, Jane. You know how to be a very good girl. Please promise me not to move."

Jane studied her. "You're sad, Eve," she said solemnly, as she sometimes did.

For the first time, Eve admitted it. "I am, a little."

"Don't be sad. I promise I won't move. I'll be a very good girl, Eve."

She had a lump in her throat as she walked down the great hall. For God's sake, don't let me sprout any tears, she prayed, then straightened her back and addressed the receptionist with firm assurance.

"I have an appointment with Mr. Will Bright."

The headmaster had serious eyes that forced her to look at him when she was so nervous that she wanted to look at the floor, or the book on his desk, or out of the window, where the crimson oak flamed. He had a slow, patient manner and a short, fair beard that called attention to his mouth. Did he wear the beard to look older?

"So you speak French and German equally well?"

"I speak them both fluently, as well as I speak English."

"There is not nearly as much demand for German as for French. Still, it would be excellent for us to offer both."

He kept looking at her. Apparently, it was her turn to speak.

"I will take tests right now if you have any," she offered.

"Yes, of course, for the record, but not now. I assume, if you say you are fluent, that you are. What do you know about teaching?"

"I've been thinking that if you know the subject, can it be so hard to teach it? I don't mean to be presumptuous, but isn't it better, more important, to know the subject than to have a lot of courses in teaching method without knowing the subject that well? I keep reading that that's part of the trouble in the schools these days."

Mr. Bright smiled. "Let's get back to method for a minute. It's your first day in, let us say, French class. What will you do?"

"Why, I will turn to page one, the first lesson in the textbook, and proceed from there. Read it together, explain it, take questions, and test them on it the next day."

"Not bad. Now it's your turn. Don't you want to ask me something?"

What do you ask? Would it be too crass to ask about money before inquiring about the philosophy of education, progressivism versus traditionalism, etcetera, etcetera?

But money was what she had come for. The time in California, the rent, the airfare, the dentist, and all the other expenses had already eaten deeply into what Dad had left, and was eating into it this very minute at the motel. She felt a surge of panic.

"I suppose," she said, "I should really not begin like this, but what I have to know before we talk any more is the salary." Her voice fell. "I'm in great need," she finished, as if to apologize.

His glance went to her wrist, where the heavy gold bracelet watch gleamed. Clearly, her appearance did not indicate great need. The fine navy suit that had gone with her to college did not look four years old, nor did her handbag and linen blouse. Dad always had said that well-made clothes are cheap in the end. Dad could not possibly have imagined this scene, this room where she was, in effect, making a plea.

Will Bright was frankly curious. "Do you want to tell me about it?" he asked.

So she told, not everything, just the skeleton of the story concerning the death of her parents and the fiasco of the will.

He nodded with recognition. "I've had plenty of good meals at the Orangerie in these past two years. Ever since I graduated ten years ago, I'd been wanting as far back as I can remember, to live on a farm. But I also wanted to go on teaching. The two never seemed compatible, though. Then a second cousin of mine died and left me his run-down place a couple of miles from here, just around the time when this school was looking for somebody. I had the credentials, and—" He broke off. "Let me get it straight. The child is your little sister, and you are her guardian?"

"Yes, that's how it is. I need a position that will make allowance for that so I can care for her properly."

She saw that he was moved and that he spoke with regret. "We're too new to have much of an endowment yet. We can't offer much."

Into the stillness through the open window came the chiming voices of passing children. The autumn air was warm, seeming to smell of apples. She felt a homelike peace in the atmosphere; it touched the piled papers and the marigolds on the desk; it was friendly.

When she looked up, she met the questioning eyes again, and they, too, were friendly. The wall clock read eleven. She had been here almost an hour.

"I don't need a lot," she said.

"How's that?"

"Well, I do need, but not an awful lot," she said hopefully. Saying so, she felt a touch of pride.

"Suppose I let you know definitely by the end of the week what we can possibly do. You can decide then whether it will be enough for you."

Eve was astonished. "Are you saying that if I'm satisfied, you'll hire me?"

"Provided that you pass the language tests. Yes, I'll take a chance on you. Where do we reach you?"

Giving him Lore's address, she explained, "She's my aunt. There's no room for us in her apartment, so Jane and I are staying at a motel." She stood abruptly. "I left Jane in the hall. I'm sure she's all right, but I'd better hurry."

"You left her in the hall?" He stood up at once and followed her.

Jane was on the last page of a coloring book. "You took so long!" she cried.

"I'm sorry. Mr. Bright, this is Jane."

"That's a funny name," Jane said, giving her hand as she had been taught to do. "What's your other name?"

"Will," said Mr. Bright. "Is that funny, too?"

Jane thought about that. "No, it's nice, but not as nice as Peter for a boy. My dog's name is Peter."

"My dogs' names are Pat and Barney."

"Where are they?"

"At my home. It's in the country, not far from here. Do you go to school, Jane?"

Hurriedly, Eve explained that this was her next immediate project. "Naturally, school depends on where we'll be living."

"If you should come to us here, I have a suggestion. One of our teachers owns a house down that street. The whole top floor is for rent. Four good-sized rooms. Then Jane could go to school here. Tuition is free for faculty children."

Eve looked at him. Heaven keep me from having tears again, even tears of gratitude.

"Oh, I hope it works out," she said, sounding prayerful.

"I hope so, too," said Mr. Bright.

Although she had never done it before, she telephoned Lore at the hospital. "It sounds wonderful," Eve said. "Only it's happened too fast."

"Don't say that."

"No, it's too wonderful to be true."

"Oh, my," said Lore, ignoring her. "You'll be so near that we can be a family again. What kind of a man is he?"

"Goodness, I don't know. Young, nice-enough-looking. Kindly."

"So you're feeling a little better?"

"Well, I mustn't let my hopes rise too high, but for the moment I'll admit that I am."

"You know, this seems almost like a repeat of my life with Caroline. Down at the bottom, and ready to start right up again. Yes, just like your mother. God bless you, Eve."

PART THREE
1993
JANE

SIXTEEN

"Of course you know that he married her," Jane said.

"That's the one? Will?"

"The same and only Will Bright. He must have fallen in love with her that first morning; in fact, he admits he did, and they've just had their twenty-eighth anniversary. Wait till you see her, David. She's absolutely beautiful. You would never think she was fifty-three years old. When you meet her, you'll see that she looks as young as I do, and I'm thirty-six."

"Do you look alike?"

"Heavens, no. She's a copy of our mother."

Both heads turned toward the corner of Jane's living room, where, as if enshrined, a small bouquet of roses stood next to the photograph of a young woman wearing a graceful dark dress and a strand of pearls.

"Eve is tall, like her. All Eve's children are tall. I'm the shrimp."

"Hardly. And don't belittle yourself, no pun intended. You're a remarkable woman, and I love you. You know you're remarkable, don't you?"

Jane shook her head. "No, I know I'm fairly smart, I've always worked hard, and I've been very lucky. Another pancake?"

"No, thanks. I'll just fill my coffee cup and that will do. We ought to have a new coffeemaker. I'll get one downtown."

It pleased her that he enjoyed domestic things, and she smiled at him. He returned the smile, and they sat together in the warm, Sunday-morning light.

Directly in view, across the street and one floor below them, was somebody's lavish garden terrace, and below that, an oblique glimpse of the avenue, seventeen floors below. Behind David's shoulder in the opposite direction was the bedroom, where the metal four-poster bed was draped in white net. Often Jane amused herself by buying incongruous objects, a fussy, comfortable, Victorian love seat to be placed near a pair of stainless steel cabinets, or a black-and-white photo montage of New York's skyscrapers near a bold red flower print in frank imitation of Georgia O'Keeffe. Somehow, the effect was charming. Most people who walked into the apartment for the first time exclaimed it: "Charming!"

The apartment was small. You had to pay fortunes in New York if you wanted what most people would call comfortable space. As it was, she was probably paying more than she could sensibly afford, but she was having such pleasure in it! To be still young, to have a doctorate in psychology, a busy practice, and a marvelous lover like David, who wanted to marry her—what else could she ask for?

"Yes," she repeated slowly, "I've been

very lucky. I had a wonderful childhood with Will and Eve. They gave me a beautiful life in their little farmhouse. It's not been easy for them, either. Even with two salaries, teaching's no road to riches, I needn't tell you, especially with four kids in college and graduate school. Four, one right after the other, and all very, very special people." She laughed. "Some people, Eve told me, thought that I was their illegitimate child, born a few years too soon. The same thing happened on the campus in California. I barely remember the place or the man with whom she was then so in love that it nearly crushed her when they broke up. Yes," she said in reminiscent mood, "you can bet that that one didn't like being mistaken for my father. He wasn't fond of children, to say the least."

"That's the man who wanted to come back to her?"

"Yes, he wrote a contrite, pleading letter after one year in Guatemala. He'd made a terrible mistake, he had discovered that archaeology was after all not what he wanted to pursue for the rest of his life, he missed

Eve dreadfully, and he was ashamed of himself."

"Quite a confession."

"But by then she was already rather taken with Will. Yes, and I was, too. He was marvelous with children, a kind of Pied Piper. His school was so free; we often had classes under the trees and we heard grand music and had a lot of nature study, hikes through the woods, and—David, are you really interested in hearing all this? You're not asking me about it just because you have a good heart?"

"Certainly not. If I'm going to be a son-in-law—no, brother-in-law—to these people, I should want to learn about them, shouldn't I?"

"Well, then. Let me tell you for starters why I know a few things about birds. Will is a birder. On Saturdays he used to take any of the older kids who cared to go along on his excursions. Eve was the teacher's aide. I never found out whether she had volunteered, or he had asked her to help. Probably it was a little of both. I imagine from hints she's dropped that they were both very shy at first. Anyway, she had to drag me along on those hikes, and that's why I can tell you when ducks stop off on their migration to Canada, and that when you think you are hearing ducks quacking in a pond in the spring, you're really hearing wood frogs.

"So that's the atmosphere in which I grew up. When Eve married Will and we moved into his house, I thought nothing of it. It simply seemed natural. I loved it. I loved the wedding. I was not yet eight years old, and I wore a lovely, long dress, pale green, that Lore made for me."

"Speaking of weddings," David interrupted, "it's time. Lawyers like things to be legal, you know. And since I've become a partner—"

"I've no objection. None at all," she said.

"What about a really nice diamond? I feel temporarily affluent."

Jane put out her hand. "Let's get a very nice wedding band instead because I already have the ruby, and I have to wear it every day."

"It means that much to you?"

She thought of the day that Eve had removed the ring from her own finger and given it to her. She had been eighteen, old enough to wear and understand this gift that her father had made to her mother: a gift of love for a woman so soon to die.

"It is a symbol," she said now. "Does that make sense to you?"

"Dear Jane, it makes sense." And David reached across the coffee cups to press her hand. "But tell me. What's made you keep me waiting so long?"

"I don't know. Family history, I guess. My mother's mistake, deep in the subconscious. It affected Eve, and indirectly I'm sure, it's affected me."

"You've all carried a lot of very heavy baggage."

"Not I, not really. It's Eve who still carries it. She's a strong woman. She may have been born as long ago as 1940, but she was a modern woman long before anyone ever talked about 'modern women.' She hardly ever speaks about what she went through. It's other people who told me things, people like Emmy Schulman, who helped my parents when they were bewildered refugees. And then, of course, there was Lore, who knew everything about the family, who was part of it, all the way back to our grandparents. My God." Jane sighed. "I can't believe she's dead."

"How old was she?"

"Eighty-four or eighty-five. Well, at least she had a quick, easy death. They found her after her heart attack yesterday morning with the 'Prelude' and 'Liebestod' still on her record player. Eve's taking it very hard, Will said. It's harder for her than for me. I associate Lore with dinner at our house every Sunday, being at all my school plays and games, and having long, grown-up talks together when I was a teenager. But Eve has other memories. They must hurt like hell."

"About her father—"

"I never think of him as her father. Joel was her father," Jane said stoutly.

"Still, facts are facts. It must have been a blow between the eyes for her."

"Yes, I remember being stunned myself when I learned about it. I think Eve didn't want me to know, but Will insisted. I was about twelve when I overheard them talking about me. Will said, 'If you don't tell her, somebody else will. Think of how you found out.' Eve thought the truth would mar my opinion of her mother."

"You always say 'her mother,' " David remarked.

"I suppose I do. Eve says, 'Mom,' but the name doesn't come naturally to me. Sometimes I stare at that photograph, and still she doesn't seem like my own mother, only a lovely woman whom I never knew. And Dad is a loving man whom I remember in fits and starts. He smoked cigars all the time and gave me a Raggedy Ann."

What odd things you remember, she thought. There was that day when one of Eve's pupils invited us to her house, and it turned out to be our old house. I can still see the wallpaper. *Peonies,* Eve said, my mother's favorite. And when I told Lore, Lore said something about how far the family has fallen. Eve didn't like to hear her talk like that. . . .

She finished abruptly. "I'm making too much of all this, and I don't know why."

"Because I asked you to. You've said yourself, Miss Psychology, that it's bad for people to suppress things."

"All right, Mr. Curious, what else do you want to know?"

"Nothing specific, although I do admit to being curious. It is an interesting family."

"Everybody alive is interesting."

"Of course. But what I mean is, you've had such astonishing ups and downs. There's your grandparents' awful story, naturally. Then came all the success, and then that business with your father's will. To lose all that hard-earned wealth, and the beautiful house! It's mighty hard to go downhill when you've been at the top. I still don't see why Eve didn't fight for it."

"I've told you why. I think she was simply too tired to assume another burden. Ever since childhood, she's been carrying the horrible burden of her father. How would you like to be the son of a rotten Nazi and live with that all your life?"

David grimaced. "I wouldn't like it at all."

They were both silent. A woman across the street came out to water the asters and dahlias in her terrace garden, while they watched as the sun broke through the clouds, gilding the day.

David broke the silence. "We have good flying weather, anyway."

"Hadn't we better get ready? What time is our flight again?"

"Twelve forty-five. Let's get started. We can't miss the connection to Ivy."

THEY buried Lore in a little churchyard not too many miles away from Ivy. It was still rural there, and Eve hoped it would remain that way.

"Mom always said Lore had a love affair with old trees," she said.

Her only love affair, Jane thought, in a life of labor and small, lonely pleasures. Nothing more.

It was surprising to see the numbers of people who came to the cemetery. There were nurses and doctors at the hospital from which Lore had long since retired, neighbors in her apartment house, and family friends of the last half century. Emmy Schulman came in a wheelchair to tell everybody how her husband had met Lore at the train back in the fall of 1939.

After the cemetery, there was lunch at Eve and Will's house. To David, Jane remarked how odd it was that people who seldom ate more than a quick sandwich at noon would eat enormous quantities after a funeral.

"Some wit once wrote that it's because they are rejoicing over not being dead," he replied.

"Maybe. I prefer to think it's because good friends provide food that you can't resist."

"Do you know what's missing?" Eve asked. "Lore's chocolate cake. I don't suppose we'll ever taste anything like it again. What do you think, Jane?"

"I'm afraid you're right. No matter how I try, mine never tastes like hers, not that I try very often."

"It will seem so strange not to know that she's somewhere available when you need advice, or just need to talk." Eve's black eyes could shine with tears that she always managed to blink away before they fell. "Whenever there was a crisis, she was there. She was so—so *necessary*. I only hope she knew how much we appreciated and loved her."

"I'm sure she did. She must have," Will said.

Jane was thinking what a nice man he was and what an unusually appealing group Eve's family made in their friendly, simple house with their books, and dogs, and Halloween pumpkins on the doorstep. It was too bad that David's introduction to them should have come on this day when there was no humor in them, for the young ones were each noted for possessing a wide comic streak. And the fair-bearded father with the scholarly face and outdoor vigor had a delightful wit.

"So you two are off to Europe?" Will asked.

"Yes. The firm has a case that involves some lawyers in Zurich, so we'll be going there after our pleasure trip. When we come back, you'll be invited to our little wedding. We're having a honeymoon in reverse."

They were all standing in the uncertain silence of people who are weary and who do not know what else to say. The day had worn them down. And David, sensing this, reminded them that, "Unfortunately, it's never quite over with a funeral. Somebody should go to the apartment and make sure that it's secure until you're all ready to clear it out."

Eve nodded. "I know. Papers and knick-knacks. All that's left of a human being."

"Jane and I will only be away for ten days. Leave everything to us," David said kindly. And then he laughed. "Now that you're about to have a lawyer in the family, you might as well get a little special treatment. We'll do it all."

LORE's rooms were impeccably neat, as might have been expected. The only disorder was the pile of records strewn on the shelf.

"She had been arranging an evening

concert for herself," Jane said. "She always did that. Look, all Wagner. She certainly never expected to die within the next hour or two. I really think she expected to be one of the rarities who live till a hundred and four."

Lore's housewifery was superb. Her green plants were well tended, and her books were in alphabetical order by author. The only costly articles were Caroline's bedroom furniture from the lake house, the sound system, and the heavy silver frame, a gift from Jane, in which was the photograph of last year's Thanksgiving dinner.

"It's eerie," she said now, regarding Lore's homely, sagging face. "This is my first close experience with death. I was a tiny kid when Dad died, and all I have, as I told you, is my memory of cigars."

"Hey, look at all this, all these notebooks in the closet. Handwritten, too."

"Oh, that must be her daily diary from year one. Here. I'll put it back. Even our grandfather used to tease her about it, Eve said. He claimed that it would end up being longer than the Bible. David, I know I keep saying it, but I can't believe she's gone."

"Well darling, she is, and we had better be going, too. We have to be at the airport again by seven thirty in the morning."

SEVENTEEN

As the little rented Fiat struggled out of Italy up through the Alps, they hoped that the engine would not fail; then, as it inched down deep slides, they hoped that the brakes would not fail. But it was grand adventure. They were moving through a jumble of clouds and slanted shafts of light, of somber evergreens and flamboyant autumn.

" 'Ridi, Pagliaccio,' " David sang. "Oh, these heights make me feel operatic."

"You were operatic all through Italy. I

thought I knew you, but I never knew you had a good voice."

"Flattery will get you a seat in the park."

"No, it's true."

They had laughed their way through Italy. They had hiked its hills, eaten out of a basket on its country roadsides, and been enchanted by its music. It was the morning of their world.

"I won't need too long in Zurich," David said. "We've done all the preliminaries on the case by phone and fax. You'll be on your own for two days at the most."

"Don't worry about me. I'm a walker. I'm not a shopper, but this time will be an exception. There are a few things I want."

"A cuckoo clock, I'll bet."

"Yes, and lederhosen and a hat with a feather for you. I'll make you wear them, too."

"As long as I don't have to wear them at my meetings."

"Okay, a loud hat and a loud clock with a loud cuckoo. We'll have fun."

"We always do."

It was only when the little car rattled

across the border into Switzerland that Jane felt the small shock, the swift return of a hidden, vague unease. Under the peace and sweetness of these days, it had been waiting.

ON the second morning in Geneva she remarked, "I was wondering whether you'd like to do a little exploring into the past with me. You remember that my mother spent some time near here before she left for America? She stayed near Geneva with a doctor who'd been in medical school with my grandfather. No one's ever heard from them since, and I was thinking that I might like to visit them."

"That's ancient history. They're probably dead by now."

"It's not so ancient. They'd be old, but not necessarily dead. In fact, Mrs. Schmidt is very much alive, although the doctor isn't."

"How do you know that?"

"I looked them up. While you were working, I found a medical society and inquired.

They were very nice. They even telephoned her for me."

"It's not the best idea," David said seriously. "I should think, given the circumstances then, the peril and the final agony, that the very sight of the place would be insufferable for you."

She did not answer at once. She was trying to analyze her feelings, which were fearful, sorrowful, and yet resistant to sorrow.

Below the window lay the great lake, flat as a blue platter between a curve of hills. Lore had described everything in detail. The house was old with a timbered overhang, Swiss style. It stood at the end of a long, narrow lawn that ran almost to the edge of the water. There was a narrow walk along the lake. So does a family's legend stay alive . . .

"It's not far from here," she said. "Will you go?"

"Jane, I really don't think it's wise. It seems like morbid curiosity. It will be bad for you."

"Perhaps it will be bad," she said. "Still, it seems to me that if I don't go, I will regret it once we are home. I will feel that I should have gone.''

It's a dreadful story, she thought, and I dread hearing it again. I've heard it often enough from Lore, who witnessed it. Yet I need to hear it.

She looked at David. "Will you go?" she repeated.

"All right," he said gently. "I'll go. When shall we do it?"

"Tomorrow afternoon? We'll browse through the Old Town and have lunch first."

They sped, the next day, over a small road parallel to the lake. On the left lay pastures dotted with grazing cows.

"Cliché," said Jane. "It's like a picture book. All clean and tidy."

"You don't have to make conversation, Janie. I know how nervous you're feeling."

"Yes, I am, awfully. But it would be so much harder for Eve. He was her father, after all, not mine, thank God."

"Are we almost there?"

"We should be. They told me to watch for a church on the right, about two miles after the village we just went through. It's a stone church, I think they said. Fifteenth century or older."

"The more I see of Europe, the more I wish I knew about architecture."

"I wish I knew more about everything. Oops, we almost went by it. That's got to be the one. The house is opposite."

The house, too, was stone. They stepped out of the car into perfect silence, went up a path bordered in yellow and bronze chrysanthemums, rang the bell, and waited. Around them, the afternoon slept.

After a minute or two the door was opened. A white-haired woman, who might have been ninety or might have been seventy, stood before them. She wore dark blue and a gold locket. Words ran through Jane's head: Old World. Refined.

She gave their names. "I believe you're expecting us, Mrs. Schmidt."

"Yes, I am. Come in, come in."

They entered a large room that must have faced the lake, for an immediate gleam met their eyes. Here was old, carved furniture, interrupted knitting on a chair, and a row of ruby glass objects on a shelf. Even the swiftest glance around a stranger's house told fundamental things. Here were tradition and dependability, or so Jane hoped.

And she began, "It's very kind of you to see us, Mrs. Schmidt."

"Oh, I'm happy to help if I can. But I have to say I'm puzzled. Some people from the medical society said you want to ask about your relatives. And please excuse my English. I seldom use it and I'm out of practice."

"I can already hear that it's a great deal better than my German."

Who of us is the more tense? Jane wondered. The poor lady is probably expecting to be interrogated about some criminal.

"Come, before we go any further, please sit down. Here, at the window. You are American, I think?"

"Yes, but my mother wasn't. Did the Zurich people give you any names?"

"To tell you the truth. I forgot to write it down. I didn't understand anyway what it was all about. I don't know anybody in America."

"This was a long time ago, just before the

war it was when my mother stayed here with you. Her name was Caroline Hartzinger."

Jane's mouth was dry, and in her ears her own voice sounded like the quaver of a child who, not having done her homework, is being called upon in class.

Mrs. Schmidt removed her glasses, stared at Jane, and replaced the glasses. She was trembling.

"I know this must seem very strange to you," Jane said gently, "I was hoping you might remember her."

"But you—excuse me, but you are—thirty, maybe?"

"More than thirty. Why do you—"

"Ask? I ask because she went to America, we took her to the train in August 1939, and she died soon after they got to America. How can you be her daughter?"

"Died?" cried Jane. "Yes, she did die, but not until years later when I was a child."

Her shaking voice stopped while the two women kept staring at each other. David came to the rescue.

"We're assuming that you're talking

about Caroline Hartzinger, the daughter of a physician who was a friend of your late husband. She was traveling with an older woman, a sister, an adopted sister, Lore, who was a nurse and—"

"Yes, yes, of course we're talking about the same person. A lovely, darling girl. It was Lore who wrote us about her death. Very sudden, she said, and then we never heard any more. We were stunned."

Jane spoke into the sudden silence. "This is unbelievable."

David spoke again. "Let me start from the beginning. Here, very briefly, is what happened, Mrs. Schmidt. Caroline was pregnant when she left for America. She did not know it while she was still in your house. In New York she met a young man who, knowing she was pregnant, was so much in love with her that he married her, nevertheless. The baby was a girl. They named her Eve, and she grew up as his daughter. She is Jane's much older half-sister."

"Pregnant? Oh, yes!" Amalia Schmidt smiled a little knowingly and a little sadly.

"We wondered about that sometimes when she and the young man wandered off together. They were so very much in love. You must remember that it was 1939, very different from today. Of course, it was wartime, too, or almost, and who knew what might happen to either of them?"

Energy and strength all went streaming out of Jane as water leaves a leaking container. And lying back in the chair, she repeated, "unbelievable."

Mrs. Schmidt was alarmed. "Are you feeling all right? Can I get you anything?"

"No, nothing, thank you. It's your news. It's an awful shock. Awful."

David rose, paced to the window and stood there frowning in thought. Then he said slowly, "Obviously, we need to get back to Lore. Why ever would she have said such a thing? We shall have to work backward. Jane, you start."

It took every effort for Jane to speak. "I only know," she said simply, addressing Mrs. Schmidt, "that Lore has been the faithful heart of our family since the time she lived with my grandparents in Berlin.

520

She was with my mother when she married, when my sister Eve was born, and when I was born." Unable to say more, she stopped. "You go on, David."

"I think Jane's told you all that she can, and I myself know nothing more. Can you think of anything, Mrs. Schmidt?"

"Oh, I suppose I could search my memory and come up with many, many little things that I think I have forgotten. But I haven't really forgotten. It's all there hidden in the brain cells, you know," she said, tapping her forehead. "Nothing is ever really lost, nothing at all. Yet for now, this minute, nothing comes to me."

They waited. The old lady was so visibly disturbed, that she might be totally unreliable. Now, in her agitation, she made hostess gestures, intended perhaps to calm or delay; she offered coffee or tea; when these were declined, she brought a pitcher of water, placed it on the small table between Jane and David, and took on her lap a cat that had followed her from the kitchen. The cat's bell tinkled in the stillness.

"I'm trying to think," she said.

And David answered gently, "Don't try too hard. Take your time."

"Well, first there were the parents, Caroline's father and mother. She was so worried about them. She was terrified. Did she ever find out what happened to them, how they died?"

Jane was looking down at the rug, a very old Oriental, worn where a chair's feet had stood. Pink faded flowers lay between dark-green octagons, and a vine crept among them. In the grandparents' house, Lore said, all the floors had been covered with Oriental rugs.

"Yes," she said. "After the war, my mother found out how they died."

"And Walter? What did she know about him?"

The name, as neutral and common as any Thomas or William, would always have the power to shock; even I, thought Jane, who have no connection with the owner of the name, still have my store of pictures, imagined from what I have been told, and remembered from what I have seen in Eve's eyes.

"Only," she said bitterly, "that she loved him and thought he loved her, and that he deserted her."

Another sad smile, mingled this time with irony, passed across the old face. "Deserted her? He couldn't very well help it, could he?"

"What do you mean?"

"Don't you know that he died?"

"How would we know?"

"We wrote to Lore. He was killed, you see, and it would have been too shocking for Caroline to open such a letter."

"Killed in the war?"

"No, no. Just before the war. The Nazis caught him."

"But he was one of them!"

"A Nazi! He was never a Nazi." The old lady gasped. "Is that what you all think? My God, what a pity. Poor young Caroline! How awful, how very awful, that she never learned the truth. Terrible as it is, it would have made all the difference in the world. No, Walter was never a Nazi. Never at all. Quite the opposite. He was arrested with a group of students who had plans to assassinate Hitler."

Jane's heart, which had quieted, awoke to beat in her very ears. "Mrs. Schmidt!" she cried. "This is mad! It's mad! Are you sure of it? Why, Lore said—"

"Lore was mistaken. The entire episode was in the German papers, and of course we learned of it here. It got particular attention because Walter's father was such an important industrialist and Party man, that the whole affair was all the more shocking. In fact, the father was in serious trouble over it and only managed by the skin of his teeth to survive."

"But Lore," Jane insisted, "but Lore said—"

"It doesn't matter what Lore said, my dear. These are the facts."

"But, Mrs. Schmidt—" Jane stopped to put into some sequence a torrent of questions.

Now David interrupted. "Let Mrs. Schmidt finish. How did all this happen? What else do you know?" he asked.

Amalia Schmidt sighed. Making a little

steeple with her fingers, she began to speak with such fluent ease now that surely she must have told the story many times before.

"You must be aware that during those shameful years, the Nazi program was very popular in the universities. Educated people who should never have been infected— well, no matter. That's how it was. At the same time, though, there were some young people, not enough of them, but some, who were decent and courageous enough to go against the tide. The particular group to which Walter belonged, or so I construct the event from the accounts, was caught when one of the students was picked up with pamphlets in his possession. The rest I suppose you can imagine."

"Oh, I can imagine. Nazi justice. No trial," David said. "Quick justice, shall we say? Quick and over with."

"Quick? A bullet in the head? No, unfortunately not. Prolonged torture as only they knew how to do it. Then death by hanging in a most grisly—well, never mind," Amalia said after glancing toward Jane.

"My poor sister," Jane whispered. "All her life she has been tormented by this. She never says much, but she doesn't need to. Please, can you tell me something about Walter as a person, something I can bring back to her? Anything you can think of will be precious."

"I haven't very much more than some impressions. He wasn't here long. And when he was here, he was out of the house with Caroline. My impressions? He was a cultured person, perhaps even an intellectual. Mannerly and refined. And very deeply in love with Caroline, very tender with her. I remember that sometimes he called her 'Rebecca' in fun because she looked like those old engravings of Rebecca with the long black hair."

Jane was thinking: My mother was here with him in this house. She might even have sat in this chair.

"History," she murmured. "So long ago."

Amalia corrected her. "Not so long. It is very real to me, and there are still many others who remember those years. You only feel like that because you're young."

"I feel like that because I am here in this house with someone who knew my mother when she was not yet nineteen. What can you tell me about her? Any little thing at all?"

"Ah, my memory is funny. One minute it's so clear, and then the next minute it isn't. Well, let me see. I can't tell you much, but I can say that she was charming. She had a delicacy, an innocence that you don't often see these days. She was very young for her age. Obviously she had been sheltered. Very likely she was more sheltered than she would have been if the times had been different. But they were violent, and the German streets were full of rowdies. She had needed protection. Oh yes, there was 'law and order,' too, under that government, plenty of order—depending upon who you were.

"My husband saw something in Caroline that I admit I did not see. I worried about her when that blow struck and she learned that he wasn't coming back to her. And there she was, setting forth across the ocean without her parents, for I had little confidence in their survival, even though it was before we knew as much about death camps as we later learned. But my husband was a discerning judge of people, and he always said that Caroline was strong. Resilient, he said. Good stock."

"Jane," David suggested, "tell Mrs. Schmidt about the business that this very sheltered young girl built up—with your father, of course."

"I can't," Jane said. "I'm sorry, but I think I'd like to go outside for a few minutes."

When Amalia Schmidt stood up to follow, David stopped her. "I know her ways. She needs to be alone when she's troubled."

"One has to wonder whether traits like that are inherited. Caroline, in her worst despair, used to shut herself in her room upstairs or else go out alone and walk for hours."

The scene was as Lore had so often described it: a long, sloping lawn, a walk along the rim of the lake, and even a group of rustic chairs beneath the linden tree, which must have been much smaller then. And

Jane stood quite still with no constructive thought in her smitten brain, only a sum of maddening questions.

Why had Lore told them that Caroline was dead? It made no sense. In fact, it was so senseless that it was not to be believed. Caroline, weighed down by grief and helplessness, must have been in a wretched state. So Lore might simply have written that she feared for Caroline's health and had been misunderstood by the Schmidts. Mrs. Schmidt was now admittedly forgetful; perhaps she was even entirely confused.

Looking outward as now toward the calm gleam of water and sky, Jane was struck by its contrast to the muddy turmoil of human affairs.

When she returned to the house, Mrs. Schmidt had spread photographs out on the dining room table. "I haven't taken anything out of that closet in years," she was saying. "But I suddenly thought that there might be some pictures in there. Look at these. Our neighbor took one of my husband and me with Caroline and Walter. Now that I see it again, I remember the day.

Here's Caroline. She had on a pink dress. I think it was her favorite. And Walter—you see how tall he was? A distinguished young man. Too bad it's faded, but you can still see—"

Jane took the picture to the light. So often and so carefully had Eve tried to describe their mother, yet even she could not describe Caroline at the age of nineteen. So here is Caroline; does she seem happy? I can't tell. She is close to him. Almost touching each other, they stand apart from the older couple. The photo can be enlarged. I can have a copy for my own. What is she seeing behind her quiet gaze? Her shoes have two straps, back in style now. They were probably white. And so that's the pink dress. She has a ribbon band, Roman-striped, tying her hair back. This is her brief, sweet summer. No, it's not even a whole summer, only a few days. She has no idea what is going to happen to her life. But then, none of us ever has. Eve says she got over him when she married my father. I wonder. I doubt it. No woman could ever forget such loss.

Mrs. Schmidt's memory, reviving, flowed like a stream. "They each had a trunkful of beautiful clothes, no difference between the two of them in quality. Lore said she was one of the family. They were wonderful to her. You could see that she appreciated everything, the good clothes, everything. She told us that once the doctor reached America, they would be 'back on top.' She was a very intelligent woman, very clever. The doctor had entrusted Caroline to her, and she felt the responsibility. Yes, you could see that."

After a long while, as the afternoon drew in, signals began to pass between David and Jane. It was time to leave; they made the usual motions and spoke their words of gratitude.

"Why not stay awhile?" Mrs. Schmidt was not ready to end the day. "Stay and have a little supper."

But neither wanted to, so with more thanks they accepted the photo, promised to write, and departed.

In the car they were stunned and quiet, their mutual disturbance palpable in that silence. The wave of dread that Jane had managed to fight down while at the Schmidt house now threatened again to swallow her.

David started to think aloud. "I can't seem to make up my mind whether the stuff is true or not! In some ways the old lady seemed very sharp, and then in the next moment she was unsure of herself. She could have gotten Walter's name wrong, and that business about Caroline's death did seem very far-fetched. Didn't you have the feeling that she was sometimes wandering a bit?"

"I don't know. I'm not sure. But I think maybe not."

David gave her a sharp look. "You know something you're not telling me, Jane, such as why you wanted to go there in the first place."

"If I ever wanted to hide anything from you," she replied ruefully, "you'd catch me, wouldn't you? Yes, I did have a reason, but it seemed so cockeyed that I hesitated to tell you about it."

"Well, tell me now."

"I almost don't know where to begin."

"At the beginning."

"Remember when you and I went to Lore's apartment and you remarked on the rows of notebooks in a closet? You opened one and I put it back on the shelf, but not before I had glimpsed something that I thought very, very odd. It went something like this. 'I feel so much guilt because they've been so good to me all my life. When I feel this way, I'm always so sorry. I can't bear to remember all the things I have done to them.' That's all I read, but it's haunted me ever since. What do you make of it?"

"Are you thinking she meant your family?"

"Who else?"

"I would think, perhaps, the people at her job in the hospital."

"All her life?"

David looked sober. "Well, perhaps not. Are you connecting what you just quoted with what we heard today at Mrs. Schmidt's?"

"I'm not sure. Of course, I can tell myself,

as I have been trying to do, that the Schmidts misunderstood the whole business. Someone did, and it was either Lore or Mrs. Schmidt."

David, still looking very sober, asked, "What about her saying that Caroline was dead?"

"To spare her from learning from the Schmidts how Walter died?"

"If indeed he did die."

"David, my head's splitting. And what about Eve? Shall we tell her?"

"No, wait. There's no point upsetting her until we know what we're talking about. I suggest that we fly back tomorrow, go out to Ivy, and read that diary."

EIGHTEEN

"**I**t feels so strange to be here among her things," Jane lamented. "It seems wrong to be snooping in her diary."

In his orderly, decisive way, David, now in the fourth hour of their search, had taken charge. "It's funny how, after the first few of these fat tomes had been written in German, she suddenly switches to English."

"She was a perfectionist. As soon as she became fluent enough to speak English well, she thought it was inappropriate to

535

use a foreign language in one's new country."

"Born before the First World War! She saw a lot of history in her time. These early ones are especially fascinating."

Far from being fascinating, Jane thought, most of them were very dull. She had already gone through fifty-five pages, and all they seemed to do was record every penny Lore had ever spent: so much to have shoes resoled, so much at the pharmacy . . . It was touching.

"Make believe you're panning for gold," David advised. "You have to pick through tons of rock and dust before you find a nugget. Somewhere in all this stuff there are nuggets, I'm convinced."

Filled with discomfort, Jane gazed toward the rainy twilight out the window. A life, a long, humble life, lay revealed in these shabby notebooks, and they were exposing it as if they were stripping a person's clothes off on a public street.

David advised again, "Incidentally, it doesn't matter that we're not reading chronologically as long as we mark the dates on the record sheets and make a few short notes. The books are so jumbled up, and it's not worth taking time to put them in order."

"Records? Notes?" asked Jane. "You talk like a lawyer."

"You always say that." David laughed. "Don't worry, I know I'm a lawyer."

The atmosphere, in spite of his effort to lighten it, was heavy. There was Lore in the photograph, staring at them behind her thick glasses, as if to accuse them of trespass. And there was the sibilance of turned pages as Jane flipped through them.

"Dr. D. was furious this morning. That stupid R. forgot his patient's medication." Continuing, she found that the price of lemons was outrageous and that the new coat was not warm enough for this climate. Drowsiness had begun to set in when David startled her.

"And now this. 'How astonishing it is,'" he read, "'that all their calamities come out well in the end. Except, of course, for the poor parents, but that was a worldwide calamity that very few escaped.'"

"What's the date?"

"June, 1955."

"There's nothing special then that I can think of, unless maybe my father's buying the lake house."

"Wait. There's more on the next page. Listen. 'Who would have thought she could change like that, a girl who never did anything but look pretty, that she could work day and night and build up such a business? I wouldn't have believed it if I hadn't seen the way she pulled herself together after Eve was born. She used to ask my advice on every little thing, and now she actually gives me advice.' "

"There's nothing wrong with that," Jane said. "It's admiration for my mother, that's all. It's praise."

"Perhaps a little envy mixed in?" David suggested.

She did not reply. The rustle of pages resumed for so long that Jane, who had started another notebook, was growing weary with impatience, when suddenly David spoke again.

"Oh, oh. Here's something. 'Who would

have thought that out of such a marriage she would have gotten so much? Look at the house they live in and now, a new baby besides. Some good fairy must have waved a wand over her just as some other fairy frowned on me.' Nineteen fifty-seven. That's when you were born, Jane. You're the baby."

They stared at each other, Jane thinking, who could have guessed that Lore was so bitter?

"I made a note back here," David said, "something about another baby. It's way back, 1940. Here it is."

"What? That's when Eve was born."

" 'Well, life will be very different for this poor baby. No rose garden, no velvet dresses, and no governesses. No father, either, poor little thing. Just struggle, struggle. However will Caroline manage? What tricks life plays!' "

"The baby Caroline managed rather well, didn't she? And the baby Eve didn't do too badly either."

"Good lord, listen to this. 'It's more clear than ever that she had to marry Joel. That's why I made up the cancer scare, so that she would accept him.' "

"She made up the cancer? Actually made it up?"

"So she says. 'He wanted her, and I am just not able to cope with everything by myself, the strange country, her moods, and an infant, too. But I promised to take care of her and I'm doing the best I can. It's a matter of honor.' "

"She talks of honor!" Jane cried. "Oh my God!"

"Wait, here's more. 'Joel is a moral man, an innocent with a strict conscience, and he will see her through. He will be good to her. But when her parents, if they survive, meet this son-in-law, it will be a shock, I'm afraid. The daughter of that house, married to an uneducated working man! They will find out how the poor have to live. But I could tell them. I have memories enough. I could—"

Jane interrupted. "What a mean thing to say about my father! Mean and snobbish and stupid. On top of everything else."

"Yes and no," David spoke judiciously. "There's some truth in it. His background actually was very different from your parents'! And think of the other good things she did say about him."

"You're not excusing her, I hope! A person who tricks a woman into marriage, who lies—"

"I'm excusing nothing. I'm investigating."

"How much more can there be to investigate? A woman who could do what she did to Caroline and Joel can do anything. I'll tell you: Amalia Schmidt was right, she knew what she was saying."

"It was hearsay, Jane. You can't depend on hearsay."

"Stop talking like a lawyer."

"Well, I am a lawyer. Come on. We've that whole pile to work through."

"All right. I'll close my eyes and grab. Here, 1961."

Page after page was still cluttered with mundane affairs: endless hours on duty in the hospital, an occasional concert, a birthday party for "little Jane" and visits to the dentist to bewail her "awful teeth." There was an appalling sameness in the record of these days.

Then, finally, as she started another volume she came across some lines that should have been marked in red ink. And she read them aloud.

" 'Now that it's happened, I know that it went too far. I had my suspicions when Vicky brought in the new, young lawyer. I had no idea she would grab almost everything, but I should have guessed. She has changed from being the poor girl, the outsider that I was when I went to live with the Hartzingers. She's turned into a greedy, vulgar shrew. Eve said Joel told her there would be plenty for everyone, including me. Why didn't I speak up and protect Eve? Because it was too late. Vicky knew that I had my suspicions and I would have been in the middle. I am sick. I am so ashamed of myself.' " Jane broke off. "David, I think I must be hallucinating."

"As to your father's will, you've known all along it was a fraud."

"Yes, but never could I have known that Lore knew it beforehand."

"Go on," he said grimly.

Her hands, supporting the notebook on

542

her knees, were cold and trembling. " 'Poor Joel,' " she read, " 'I really liked him. I'm glad he's past knowing what was done. I would never have wanted to hurt him. He, too, came up the hard, hard way.' "

David raised his hand. "May I interrupt? Here's a note I made this morning. See how important it is to keep notes? Listen. '. . . telling me he's marrying Vicky partly to have a mother for Jane! She, a *mother*? When I'm the only one who loves Jane. And Jane loves me. If that's what he wanted, what about me? I would have been a better wife to him, too.' "

"My God. Did she really think my father could have wanted her for a wife?"

"Apparently she did. Come on, let's finish. We've only got another half dozen to read through."

Baffled and sickened, Jane skimmed further. After a long interval, another terrifying revelation leaped out.

" 'While Eve was packing to take Jane to California, I could hardly keep myself from screaming, "Stop! I think I may know something about all this. Stay and I'll help you fight. Don't go." Instead, I just watched them leave for the airport and I went home and I cried.' What to make of that? Or this, later. 'It's good to have them back in Ivy, like having a family again, going out to visit them at the school, or making dinner for them here. I've been so lonely. My loneliness is sometimes more than I can bear.' "

And then there was this. " 'So she's marrying a schoolmaster instead of the California millionaire. It's all theater, this life is, a theater. Caroline herself used to say her own life had been a drama. Sometimes one has to feel sorry for all the little actors with their pride and sense of independent power. And I do feel sorry for us all.' "

The notebooks lay between them in a jumble on the floor. Jane sat there in disbelief. Like coiled, poisonous snakes ready to rear and strike, they lay.

"David, I don't want to read all this about Lore. It's distorted. It's terrible. Let's throw these things away."

"You know we can't do that. Somewhere here we'll find the truth about Walter."

Three notebooks remained. Jane's arms

were almost too limp to hold a notebook on her lap. Her eyelids wanted to close. And the clock ticked on through the awful, interminable day.

"Here, I made notes from an earlier book," David said. "1927. 'Graduation,' she writes, 'I have my cap. I passed third in my class. They gave me a little party at home. Some of Father's colleagues came. They are all so good to me.'" He stopped. "The other side of the coin, isn't it? Love and gratitude." He read on. "'They will get me a job in the hospital. Even Mama, who is not too bright except at the piano, treats me like a daughter. I am a daughter of the house. Father is so proud of me. Oh, how I hate calling him "Father"! He has everything a girl could want. Handsome and tender and wise. I love him so. If only he were younger and I were older.'"

"My God, in love with my grandfather!"

"Here's more. 'There's so much loving in this house. I remember when I came here how they fussed over Caroline . . . Where I lived before, there was a new baby every year and people hardly paid attention to it except to feed it. In most ways I admire all this loving and yet—it's funny, but sometimes it annoys me. I almost feel angry. Watching them together. Is that queer of me?' "

"Yes," Jane said. "Queer and very, very sad. David, I really don't want any more of this. I'm too confused, too angry."

"I'll do the rest. You can stop."

"No, I take that back. This is my family's problem and I should have the guts to deal with it. I'll finish."

After a long, quiet hour David made a sound that came out midway between an outcry and a groan.

"Jane, Jane, listen to this. 'Caroline is slowly dying. It is terrible to watch her suffer. I think of all the times she has been so dear to me, sometimes like a mother, and sometimes like a daughter. I think of the things I should never have done.' "

"Now I really can't stand any more," Jane said. "David, I can't."

He looked at her. "You're played out. Lie down on the sofa while I finish the rest myself."

The eyelids that had been trying to close now did close; yet no sleep came. Wide awake, as the noisy clock kept on, her thoughts struggled to find order in a tumbling sea of tragedy and killing rage. How Caroline had suffered! And Lore the comforter, the wise adviser who had done so much good, was at the same time the stranger, seen through a fog, glimmering for an instant and fading again into the dark.

The only thing that was clear, she thought at last, is that Lore had been miserable. She called herself an "outsider." But why, considering how we loved her? Perhaps she was not capable of unconditional love? Dreadful things seem to have happened to her before she came to live with the family, things that no one knew about.

And slowly, as she had been trained to do, Jane tried to form in her own mind a picture of Lore's mind. She despised her body. Among handsome people, she must have felt stigmatized. She had said so often enough. She wanted a man to love her body, and no man ever had. Our grandfather is supposed to have foreseen a hard life for her. Perhaps as a doctor, he had seen something that other people couldn't.

She woke to find David standing over her with an extraordinary look of anxiety and tenderness upon his face.

"You finally fell asleep. You needed it. I've finished them all."

She sat up, questioning. "And what?"

"Amalia Schmidt was right. Lore did tell him that Caroline was dead. She didn't want any 'further contact' with the Schmidts, didn't want Caroline ever to know anything. So she sent one letter saying that she, Lore, was moving out West and giving them no forwarding address."

"That's it?"

"No, there's more," David said solemnly, and paused.

"The story about Walter? True or not?"

"True."

For a moment neither spoke. The last gray-blue light, as the shortening day gave place to night, lay on the windowpanes. And grief wrote itself on David's bowed back as he stood there.

"My God, Jane. She says that she never

went to that house in Berlin. Never spoke to the servants about Walter. Never went anywhere to look for him except for a minute to the university address, where some students told her he had gone to the country. So all the Nazi business, the entire story that she took back to Switzerland, was a fabrication. Let me read: 'I wasn't able to find out anything at the university. He must have gone off with another woman and jilted Caroline. Found somebody else with big eyes, marvelous hair, fine teeth, and none of the complications that go along with Caroline. What else can it be? Lucky girl, whoever she is. It's all luck, anyway. If I had half a chance I could make him so happy! Those few times we were alone together, when he gave me a lift in his car and once when he took me to the theater, we had such marvelous, intelligent conversations. We were exactly right for each other. Why couldn't he see that we were?' "

"I don't recognize Lore at all," Jane whispered. And memories flashed: Lore walks fast, she bustles from one task to the next; she is busy, she is so cheerful—

"What else?"

"She was glad they were going to America together. Then the parents might come, and the family would be reestablished. If they should fail to come, at least she would have Caroline and would not be alone in the world. Walter would have taken her away. So she made up a story that would remove him forever. She turned him into a Nazi."

"She simply made it up. She simply broke a girl's heart, just like that. My mother's heart."

"The shocking twist is that forever afterward, according to the diary, her conscience tormented her. She felt she had ruined Caroline's life. But of course it was impossible then, if it had ever been possible, to make any atonement. She had caught herself in a tangle of lies. Oh," David cried, "do you realize how Lore manipulated your lives, all your lives?" Then he broke off. "Stupid question. Of course you realize. But can you explain? Can it be explained?"

Jane was barely able to speak. "A love-hate syndrome," she said at last. "Needing people—us—to assuage her loneliness. Resenting us because she was obliged to us; being proud and hating herself for being dependent."

"Psychology!" David said, half scoffing.

"Well, I am a psychologist."

"Go on, then."

"I guess you have to say that she was taking her revenge on life because of what she missed and felt entitled to. I'm certainly not sure of any of this, David."

"Psychobabble. She was pathetic, but she was a witch, too. As simple as that."

Jane shook her head. "It's never as simple as that."

"It is. It's pure evil."

"Is there such a thing?"

"From what I've seen in my profession alone, I'd say yes, there is."

"I suppose in the last analysis each of us has a valid argument. They argue it out enough in the courts, I know."

"Well, we look at it differently, and there's no use arguing about it." As always, David was practical. "The question is now: What do we do with this junk on the floor? There's enough of it to paper a house."

"Burn it."

"Or shred it. I'm wondering why anyone would keep such incriminating stuff. Surely she knew she would die some day and people would find it."

"I thought of that. You know, it's possible that in a perverse way she wanted us to know the truth about her."

"Then she was really crazy."

"To a degree, yes. But what degree? There are hundreds of them. Whatever it was, we must have pity for her."

For a moment they stood there, clinging together as people do in the face of disaster or the force of a storm. They had passed this whole day in disaster and storm.

"What to do about your sister now that we know Mrs. Schmidt was not mistaken?"

"We'll have to think hard. It's pretty clear that Walter's dead, but we still don't know whether he ever intended to go back to Caroline."

"And we'll never know."

"Perhaps we should just let it stay as it is,

leaving out the gory details of his death. He was shot, that's all. That's enough, and bad enough."

"I'm assuming you don't want to say anything about Lore and the diary."

"No, I know Eve can bear it, but why should she if she doesn't have to? She's borne enough in her time. And why should we spread the story of poor, troubled Lore? Let her rest with her reputation intact. Let everyone keep a good memory of her."

"Okay, let's gather up the evidence and dispose of it."

He was bending down to begin when he straightened again and inquired curiously, "What happened to your anger? You were furious before and now suddenly you aren't."

"You're wrong, I'm still terribly angry and always will be. But I'm also pitying and sad and willing to put the tragedy away. I told you before, there is nothing simple about any of this."

For a moment David regarded her with an expression of wonder and a small, tender smile.

"How do I love thee? Shall I count the ways? Well, because I love your curly hair and your pretty laugh and your brains. Also, you are a wonderful lover. But mostly I'm thinking right now, that I love you farthest down in my heart for all the goodness that's in you."

And he put his arms around her.

SOME weeks later a letter from Amalia Schmidt arrived in New York.

"I do want to thank you for the lovely roses you sent. I have been thinking much about the afternoon we spent together. It was very moving for me and I can only try to imagine how it must have been for you.

"Something has just occurred to me. Perhaps if you agree that it makes some sense, you might want to investigate at the banks here. Walter could very well have gotten some money out of Germany—I wouldn't be surprised. It seems worth a try."

"Looking for a needle in a haystack," Jane said.

"Probably, but not necessarily."

"David, the sooner we put this entire horror behind us, the better."

"Yes, but have you any objection if I call those lawyers in Zurich and ask them to take a look? They owe me a small favor."

"It seems absolutely ridiculous, but I suppose there's no harm."

NINETEEN

The day being very warm for early spring, Will had opened the doors to the porch, so that Jane now looked out directly upon a row of pear trees in white bloom that she had helped Will plant when they were saplings no taller than the child she had been then. She turned her eyes toward the other people in the circle, people of various bloods from various places, carrying their separate memories, like hers, of the pear-planting. At the moment they were all connected by the thin, strong thread of an event that had occurred on another continent half a century ago. It is a truism, she thought, that each one of us is the result of decisions made by those who came before us, and they in turn are the product of actions taken by others, and back and back. . . . It is a truism that we rarely think about. Yet here we are. Eve has been controlling her tears. Holding her hand in loving protectiveness, is Will. On my left hand is the symbolic ring that David put there, while my mother's ruby is relegated to my right. David's own hand rests on a sheaf of papers, from which, with care and thought, he has for the last hour been reading.

"Fifty thousand dollars in a joint account. That's like half a million today."

No one answered. A numbness had set in. There had been all too much to encompass.

Then Eve's voice came faintly, as if from another room. "Poor Lore. If only she could be here with us now! Those people told her he was a Nazi because it was well known in the neighborhood that she was not one. So they mocked her with their lie."

Poor Lore, indeed. But she must curb her angry tongue. "Poor mother," Jane said.

"It's a miracle that Mrs. Schmidt kept the picture all these years," Eve marveled, holding it up to the light with an expression of disbelief and awe.

And Jane, trying to imagine how you must feel on seeing for the first time the face of your father, was unable to imagine it. She had grown up among albums full of her own father's cheerful, beaming face, and among people in Ivy who had known Joel well.

"I wonder what he was really like," Eve mused. "Lore said he knew art and architecture and loved music. Still, that doesn't tell you very much, does it? I could have asked Mother for more, I guess, but it would have been too cruel. She was so in love with Joel that she had almost forgotten, or made herself forget, the past."

Do you really believe that? Jane thought. I don't.

"I apologize, Eve," David said, "for opening the letter that came with the documents. I hadn't realized that it was a personal one."

"I don't mind that you saw it, or who sees it. It isn't my letter, anyway. It belonged to our mother, and it's as much Jane's as mine. Here, Jane. You read it aloud. I already know it by heart."

"My German is too awful."

"Then I'll do it. The date is May, 1939," Eve read.

" 'Darling Caroline, when we are together again, I will be able to tell you what I am doing here. Then you will understand why I could not have told you sooner, and why I am writing this on the remote chance that my undertaking does not succeed.' " Eve raised her head. "It's so scrawled, he must have been in a tremendous hurry. 'This money is for our life in America, and I pray God, for the life of your dear parents when they join us there. I write this in great haste, as when one runs toward shelter in bad weather.

" 'The storm I see is a war so awful that it will change the world. I see Europe devastated once again, as it was the last time. It will be worse this time. I see the victims in the concentration camps, the bloodied dead and wounded, the bombarded, burning cities, and the refugees on the country roads. I see my own country in ruins. I see Americans coming across the ocean to die. It is a nightmare beyond description.

" 'Darling Caroline, understand that it is just five minutes before midnight on the clock. I want to stop the clock.

" 'Darling Caroline, I remember the day you wore your black silk hair in braids like a schoolgirl's, with red bows on the ends. And I remember your pink summer dress. Save it and wear it again for me. And I remember—' " Eve faltered and stopped. "That's enough for now."

"It's too much for you," Will said gently.

"And for Jane, too," added David.

They were all subdued. From outdoors came the fragrance of rain upon wet grass. The carriage clock tinkled on the mantelpiece. Lore had appropriated it from the house on the lake.

"Your mother was fond of it," she'd said.

"She would have wanted you girls to have it."

Eve's modest house contained some lovely things of Caroline's: her candelabra, and books, and Dresden figurines.

"I stole them all for you," Lore had said with a mischievous grin. "Vicky doesn't need things she doesn't know enough to appreciate."

It is like threads in a weaving, Jane thought. They start together, and separate, and come together again; sometimes they fray, and the pattern goes awry.

"To get back to the subject," David began, "the money is clearly yours, Eve. Half at least is in your mother's name, and Walter was your father. The rest is Jane's, I should think."

Jane said quickly, "Oh, no, I don't want it."

Eve followed. "Nor do I."

She rose and stood in the doorway with the green spring evening at her back. Tall as she was, she seemed even taller in her dignity.

"Are you quite sure?" David asked.

"Quite sure. Let it go to survivors in need. That's where it belongs. Will and I have everything."

Yes, it was plain when you looked at them together that they did have everything.

"It's your legacy," David said.

Eve smiled. Her face was illuminated. She is extraordinarily beautiful, Jane thought.

And Eve spoke. "I have my legacy. Now at last I know who I am. I know my father. He was a good man, and honorable, and very brave. He was a prince."